MEDICAL

Pulse-racing passion

Marrigae Reunion With The Island Doc
Sue MacKay

Single Mum's Alaskan Adventure
Louisa Heaton

MILLS & BOON

MARRIAGE REUNION WITH THE ISLAND DOC
© 2024 by Sue MacKay
Philippine Copyright 2024
Australian Copyright 2024
New Zealand Copyright 2024

First Published 2024
First Australian Paperback Edition 2024
ISBN 978 1 038 90552 9

SINGLE MOM'S ALASKAN ADVENTURE
© 2024 by Louisa Heaton
Philippine Copyright 2024
Australian Copyright 2024
New Zealand Copyright 2024

First Published 2024
First Australian Paperback Edition 2024
ISBN 978 1 038 90552 9

MIX
Paper | Supporting
responsible forestry
FSC® C001695
www.fsc.org

Published by
Harlequin Mills & Boon
An imprint of Harlequin Enterprises (Australia) Pty Limited
(ABN 47 001 180 918), a subsidiary of HarperCollins
Publishers Australia Pty Limited
(ABN 36 009 913 517)
Level 19, 201 Elizabeth Street
SYDNEY NSW 2000 AUSTRALIA

Cover art used by arrangement with Harlequin Books S.A.. All rights reserved.

Printed and bound in Australia by McPherson's Printing Group

Marriage Reunion With The Island Doc

Sue MacKay

MILLS & BOON

Sue MacKay lives with her husband in New Zealand's beautiful Marlborough Sounds, with the water on her doorstep and the birds and the trees at her back door. It is the perfect setting to indulge her passions of entertaining friends by cooking them sumptuous meals, drinking fabulous wine, going for hill walks or kayaking around the bay—and, of course, writing stories.

Visit the Author Profile page
at millsandboon.com.au for more titles.

Dear Reader,

There is something very special about Rarotonga and many couples choose to marry there for that reason. So naturally when I wanted to bring Alyssa and Leighton back together, I couldn't think of a more romantic setting. Of course, it doesn't go as smoothly as they'd like.

With both of them attending Leighton's brother's wedding to Alyssa's close friend, it brings them together and reminds them of all they lost when they broke up, but can they overcome the trust issues Leighton holds? He is afraid to reveal his heart again, because if Alyssa walks away once more, he'll never recover. But can he live without her?

Alyssa wants to take a second chance, but she knows Leighton's not telling her everything, which suggests he's not ready to let her in and may never be. How will these two resolve their problems and get their happy-ever-after?

I hope you enjoy finding the answer to that.

Sue MacKay

DEDICATION

This story is dedicated to the Raro girls,
Vicki, Lenore, Joy and Kerry.

Great friends to spend holidays with in Rarotonga—
along with our husbands.

CHAPTER ONE

'WOULD ALYSSA COOK please come to the check-in counter?' came the request over the intercom at Nelson Airport.

Alyssa headed across the room. Hopefully this meant her flight to Rarotonga was sorted. Being delayed here meant she was going to miss the connecting flight from Auckland to the islands, but fingers crossed there was a seat going spare on the next one.

'Hi, I'm Alyssa.'

The woman behind the counter looked harried. The airline was dealing with a lot of annoyed passengers because one of the pilots for the Nelson to Auckland flight hadn't turned up for work and there'd been a hold-up getting a replacement.

'Good. You're probably aware you won't be catching your flight out of Auckland, but we have put you on the one later in the afternoon. You won't get to Raro until around ten tonight their time.'

'Which means a whole day hanging around the airport.' Not a lot she could do about it, and at least she would still fly out today, and wouldn't miss out on too much of the things the girls had planned. 'Thank you for sorting it out for me. I really appreciate it. Even nicer that you called me over and didn't just ping my phone.'

Seemed the personal touch wasn't completely out of fashion.

The woman's shoulders drooped and a small smile appeared. 'Thank *you* for not biting my head off.'

'It's hardly your fault this has happened.'

If only she could grab some shut-eye somewhere comfortable, but that was unlikely. She'd knocked off work on the cardiac ward after a double shift two and a half hours ago, rushed home for a shower and to grab her gear, thinking she'd sleep on the flight to Rarotonga. That might still happen, only a lot later than planned.

'You'll be boarding your flight out of here in a few minutes,' the woman told her.

'Then I'll send some texts now.'

Two other nurses from the Nelson hospital where she worked had overnighted in Auckland and would wonder what was going on when she didn't turn up for the flight they were catching to Rarotonga. Damn, she was going to miss the party tonight with some of the girls. Thank goodness the wedding they were going to was still days away.

In Auckland Alyssa walked from the domestic terminal to the international one to fill in some time and get fresh air. Once through Immigration she found a café and had breakfast before doing the rounds of the duty-free shops. Time dragged and when she finally looked down at the well-lit runway at Rarotonga airport she'd lost count of the hours since leaving Nelson. A sigh slid over her lips. At last. She'd made it. Now the fun could really start.

Though what she wanted most was a hot shower followed by a cold drink beside the pool at the resort she was staying at along with the others from work. Despite being exhausted, she wouldn't be ready for sleep for a little while. It felt good to be going on holiday for the first time in what seemed like for ever, and falling into bed wasn't the way to kick-start the break from the pressures of the job as Head Nurse of the cardiac ward. A doctor and a nurse who was a close friend, from the same ward, were getting married on the beach, which promised to be stunning and a whole lot of fun. Even better, she was here for a whole fortnight. Fourteen days with nothing more to do than relax and enjoy herself. Unheard of lately.

The queue inside the terminal wound up and down the small space, roped-off lines keeping everyone crammed together, but no one seemed to be in a hurry to get through Immigration. Like her, they were already in holiday mode. She grinned as she watched an elderly man sitting on a raised platform in the corner playing a banjo and welcoming everyone to the Cook Islands in a low, crusty singing voice.

Perfect, Alyssa thought. Checking her phone, she found a photo of the happy couple, Collette and Jamie, on the beach outside the resort, laughing their heads off as one of them took the shot.

Alyssa had a momentary pang of envy. When she'd married after a whirlwind romance, it had been in a register office with two other couples and the parents of her husband-to-be witnessing the ceremony followed by a meal at a local restaurant. She'd been unbelievably happy despite the glares from her in-laws. These two had family and friends joining them for the celebrations in an idyllic location. She wished them all the best and a happier, longer-lasting marriage than she'd experienced. Jamie and Collette hadn't rushed to get married, and had taken time to really know each other, unlike her. Wham bam, married. Then separated a year later after some acrimony at the end.

'Next,' called the officer behind the immigration counter.

Alyssa stepped up.

'Welcome to Rarotonga,' said the woman as she stamped Alyssa's passport.

'Thank you.' Now that she was through the barriers she couldn't wait to get started. Her back tweaked when she lifted her case off the carousel. Too much sitting around airports and on planes. A long walk would help, but not happening tonight when she knew nothing about the area.

A woman wearing a blue and white floral dress was welcoming passengers as they made their way out into the open-air arrivals area. 'Where's the rental car office?' Alyssa asked. Preferring to be independent, she'd booked a car for her and her friends to get around in even though buses ran every thirty minutes and took only about an hour to circle the island.

'Depends which company you're using. One's open, the other closed after the last flight left.'

When Alyssa named the company the woman grimaced. 'Sorry, that's the one that's shut. You'll have to come back in the morning. Do you want me to get you a taxi?'

'You're kidding, right?'

'Unfortunately I'm not. When your flight was delayed in Auckland the girl who should be working had to go home to look after her child as the father had to go out on his fishing boat.' The woman's face crinkled into a smile. 'That's how it is here.'

Alyssa drew a deep breath and counted to ten. No point in losing her temper. Nothing she could do about it. 'It's all right. Where're the taxis?'

'Come with me. Keep the receipt from the driver and you'll be reimbursed when you pick up your rental.'

Within minutes she was ensconced in the back seat of a well-used car heading to the resort, the driver talking non-stop about the sights she'd see more clearly in the daylight. Thankfully she'd soon be in her room and pouring a glass of champagne from the bottle that was part of the accommodation package.

'Miss Cook, welcome to Seaview Resort. I am Pepe.' The young man behind the desk smiled. 'You are very late.'

'Yes, my flight was delayed from Nelson so I missed my connection in Auckland and had to wait ten hours for the next flight. So, I'm looking forward to getting to my room. I did send an email advising you.'

'Yes, we got that, thank you, but I have to tell you there's been a problem with your booking.'

No, don't do this. Not today.

Alyssa snatched her phone from her bag and tapped the screen. 'There can't be. I have a copy of the confirmation right here.' She pushed the phone across the counter. 'See?'

'I know you have a booking but you were late arriving and the couple who were previously in your room have to stay another night because their flight to Australia has cancelled due to bad weather in Brisbane.'

Of course it had been. She'd have been surprised if there'd been any other outcome. 'So I don't have a room? Is that what you're saying?' No car, now no room. What next?

'Please, we have made arrangements for you.'

Her patience was running out. 'They'd better be good.' What were the chances?

A huge smile lit up the man's face. 'They are very good, Miss Cook. We have bungalows next to the main building and you are to have one of them. You will be close to the pool without everyone being able to see into your room. All your breakfasts are free and you're to stay there for the first week you are with us.'

From the research she'd done, Alyssa knew the bungalows were wonderful, and she'd have loved one except she couldn't justify the expense when she was saving every dollar she could to buy her own house. The only downside to the bungalow was she wouldn't be on the first floor with the rest of the gang, but hardly a problem. A bungalow was a no-brainer. 'Thank you very much.' It did sound too good to be true, but tonight she wasn't asking. She'd take what was on offer and sort things out in the morning if necessary.

'I'm glad you are happy. The cleaners are still preparing the bungalow as the last occupants only checked out two hours ago. The concierge will take your bag across now but you'll have to wait in the bar for a little while longer.'

How long did it take to clean a room? But this was Rarotonga and she'd heard the place ran on island time. Right now she'd be happy with a shower and a single bed in a wardrobe so she could begin unwinding from weeks of extra shifts and difficult cases. 'Do you sell champagne by the glass?' she asked, because if she'd wanted one before, she was desperate now.

'They do in the bar. I'll ask them to pour you one. On the house.' Pepe grinned.

Suddenly she laughed. She was here, in the islands, on holiday. Everything could start going right. Looking around, she realised the bar was barely twenty steps away. She headed across.

A sound from long ago reached her as she leaned against the counter waiting for her drink to be poured. Whipping around, she stared at the apparition sitting on a lounger beside Jamie, the groom. Got that wrong, didn't she? Lots more had just gone wrong. Really wrong.

Leighton?

Couldn't be. She must have brain fade from almost no sleep in more than thirty-five hours. Leighton could not be here. Not after all this time. She was not prepared to see her ex-husband. Didn't want to. They were over and done with.

Turning her back on whoever that lookalike was, she reached for the glass being placed on the counter and took a big gulp before pointing at the glass and saying to the young man, 'Another, please.'

Don't wait until I've emptied this one.

She took another mouthful and the glass was nearly empty. She was on holiday, remember?

A shiver tripped over her. She had to know. Had to make sure she was wrong and that it wasn't Leighton sitting only metres away. She'd had a day full of let-downs. There weren't any more to come. There couldn't be.

'Hello, Lyssa. Long time, no see.'

Only one person had ever called her Lyssa. And that voice was so familiar it was lifting the hairs on her bare arms. Her head spun and she gripped the counter. Leighton was for real.

* * *

Leighton Harrison held his breath in an attempt to calm the pounding in his chest. Lyssa was on the island. After four years of not seeing her, or knowing anything about what she was up to, here she was, looking even more stunning than he recalled. So much for thinking he remembered everything about her, right down to the moment when she'd walked out on him. She'd be twenty-seven now, right? Naturally she looked more beautiful. Her face had matured and those eyes that had haunted him for a long time appeared greener and more intense. As for her mouth—still sensuous. More so. Proof of that was in the tingling in his hands where those lips often used to caress him.

'A very long time,' Alyssa said, staring as though caught in headlights. Then she blinked and took a step towards him.

Automatically he reached to give her a hug, and instantly regretted the move as the scent of citrus and exhaustion caught him. So damned familiar it hurt. It shouldn't. He was long over her. Well and truly done with them as a couple. So why hug her? Because he'd moved without any input from his brain. Some things hadn't changed. Dropping his arms without touching her, he stepped back. That was different. 'You here for something special or taking a break?'

Alyssa looked around the room before coming back to him. 'I'm here for Collette and Jamie's wedding. I see you're sitting with Jamie and some of the others I work with. Have you just met them or do you know one of the group from home?'

'Just Jamie.'

My half-brother you never knew about. A huge part of why I withdrew from you and became less than the man you married.

Seemed the truth had a way of coming through no matter what. He'd try to dodge that bullet for a little while longer. Jamie didn't know Lyssa was his ex, either, because he never talked about her. Losing her had hurt too much. He'd loved her deeply and then failed her big time by not being open and honest after what he'd learned about his family after they'd married.

Hey, Lyssa failed you too by packing her bags and leaving without trying to find out what was going on with you.

'If you're working with these people I presume you live in Nelson.' He hadn't tried to keep up to date with her life during the years since their marriage fell apart. No point. They'd rushed into marriage and fallen out just as fast. Cracks had formed in their relationship with him working long hours and Alyssa going out with her mates a lot, though nothing serious to raise concerns she mightn't be happy with him.

Soon after she'd gone he'd learned the truth about the other immoral thing his father had done. Make that what his father had tried to do, but, Alyssa being Alyssa, she'd thrown the offer of money if she refused to marry his son back in the old man's face. He'd been furious with his old man. So much for being close all his life, and being teased for being so alike in many ways. He hadn't had a clue who his father was. Learning what he did made him fear Alyssa would think he was capable of the same hideous things his father had done.

Lyssa had loved him. Yeah, and she'd left anyway without mentioning what his father had done before they married, breaking his heart along the way.

Add in the secret about his brother that his parents had kept from him, and his life had turned upside down and inside out, leaving him uncertain of who he was and what to do about the future. He felt as though he'd lived a lie all his life and needed Alyssa to love him unconditionally.

Except he'd been opening a Pandora's box of ugly truths and painful emotions he was struggling to cope with and did not want to share. He'd been the strong one in the relationship, supporting Lyssa with insecurities brought on by her past, and he hadn't wanted her thinking he wasn't as tough as she'd believed. So he'd hidden behind his work, using it as an excuse for not being at home with Lyssa as often as he should've been. If only he'd overcome that fear and kept the lines of communication open, things might've turned out differently. Crunch time had come when he'd forgotten her birthday and while she'd packed her bags she'd yelled at him that he was selfish and didn't care about her.

Which couldn't be further from the truth. He had loved her but apparently not enough. He'd lost focus on his wife and their marriage while spending too much time brooding about his stuffed-up family and what they'd done to him and Jamie. He hadn't deserved her. Or, more bluntly, she deserved a hell of a lot better. But it'd still hurt when they split. He'd needed her support even when he hadn't told her about his father's duplicity. She had been quick to leave when life hadn't been all fun and laughter. He sighed. Unfortunately there was no undoing the past.

'I'm the charge nurse of the main hospital's cardiac ward.' Pride spilled out of her. She'd always had ambitions to be the best at what she did, and now it seemed she'd achieved at least one of those. No surprise there. He looked closer.

She appeared so much more confident than the woman he'd married. The haunted look in her eyes had gone, those shapely shoulders were upright, not drooping, her spine was straight. Interesting.

'Here's your drink, Miss Cook.' Pepe held out a glass of champagne.

Leighton winced. Miss Cook. She'd dropped his surname. That shouldn't hurt, but for some unfathomable reason it did. He'd think about it later. Along with what he had to tell her about Jamie, because no way could he ask his brother to keep quiet when he had his own issues with their father. It would be impossible anyway. Some time in the next few days someone would mention them being brothers. It was time to put it out there without explaining why he hadn't told her four years ago. He wasn't going to give her all the details, just the basics.

'Thank you, Pepe.' Lyssa took the glass in a shaky hand. Turning back to Leighton, she frowned. 'So you're here for Jamie's wedding?'

'I'll be at the wedding, yes.' He wouldn't say he was the groomsman in case she already knew that was the role of Jamie's brother. A memory struck. Jamie saying, *'There's a nurse coming to the wedding on her own. You two will hit it off perfectly. She's just your type.'*

Great. He ground his teeth in frustration. That

nurse had to be this one, his ex. He just knew it. He needed to talk to Jamie fast, and then Lyssa first thing in the morning. He was putting off the inevitable, but it was late and she looked shattered. She didn't do empathetic when she was overtired. Or she didn't used to. Nor had she stood so straight before. Something to be aware of. She'd changed and he had no idea who she was any more. They'd both have grown up a bit, having been quite young when they married.

'Alyssa, you finally made it.' Jamie joined them.

'It's been the day from hell but I'm here and all's good.' She gave his brother a brief hug. 'Where're the girls?'

'Collette's hit the sack. Says she needs her beauty sleep to look good for the wedding, though why she thinks that when she's beautiful I don't know. Some of the others are on the party bus that goes to various bars in town every night. They can't be far away.' Jamie was looking at him with a grin.

Leighton shook his head. It was not happening. 'Got a minute before I head home?'

Jamie frowned. 'I guess. Alyssa, those of us in the bar are about to head to our rooms but if you want company while you down that drink I'll be with you after I've heard whatever Leighton's got on his mind.'

At least he hadn't said 'my brother', Leighton thought with relief.

'Home?' Alyssa asked. She was quick. Again, no surprise.

'I'll be over with the others.' Jamie stepped away.

Leighton wasn't sure whether to be pleased or not. 'I've been here for five months working as a locum at one of the general practices.' She wouldn't know he'd left the medical centre he'd joined when they were together, and opted to work as a locum in general practices up and down New Zealand. There were lots of things she wouldn't know, and no doubt wouldn't want to. For her, finished had meant exactly that. It had for him too, though there'd been plenty of days he'd struggled to believe it because she'd always wanted so much of him. When he hadn't been trying to deny it, he'd missed her so much it hurt. Now the past had come back to bite him on the backside and he had to talk to her sooner rather than later. Maybe he should dive into it tonight, get it out of the way.

Alyssa's eyes had widened. 'You didn't keep the partnership in Remuera Medical Centre?'

'No. I'm working all over the place and enjoying it.'

Her smile was disarming. 'Go you.'

A fraction of the tension eased. 'It was a good

decision.' He didn't have to get to know people too well and learn later he'd got them wrong.

A racket of laughter and music drowned out her reply.

'That's the party bus pulling in,' he said. The rest of the wedding party returning gave him the excuse he needed to escape. Now that his ex-wife had turned up he wasn't in the mood to sit around casually chatting. He'd be constantly on alert for anything Lyssa said. Alyssa, not Lyssa. That was in the past along with everything else.

Except technically they were still married as neither of them had filed for divorce. A kernel of hope for the future he'd deny if anyone asked kept him from finalising it. Why Lyssa hadn't done something the moment the two years required before a divorce could go through were up was beyond him. It had to be because she was busy and didn't need it, not because she was waiting around for a second shot at them getting together. Presumably she hadn't met someone else she wanted to marry. Hope rose, then disappeared. What was he thinking? They were finished. Over. But—she was beautiful and filled him with happy memories. There were plenty of those as well as the others.

'I was meant to be on that bus with the others,' she said. 'Never mind. We can party now.' Then she yawned and grimaced. 'Maybe not so much. It's been quite the day. With a double shift beforehand.'

The urge to wrap her in his arms was so strong he spun around and charged back to where he'd left his beer at the table Jamie was sitting at. He was not touching her. No hugs. No idle chit-chat. Nothing. They were long done for. She hadn't stayed around to support him when he needed it. Now he wanted to hug her? Get real, man. She should've known him well enough to understand something was wrong and that he needed her. He'd loved her, but had he really *known* her? Do it again and he'd lose his mind. She'd only let him down again and there was no way he'd manage the pain of that.

His gut cramped. So much for being over her. Of course he was. It was the shock at seeing her walk in catching up. Strange how he still felt that instant attraction to her after all that had gone down between them when they broke up. She'd stolen his heart the moment he'd set eyes on her five and a half years ago, sitting on a stool in the cafeteria, talking and laughing with other trainee nurses as though she hadn't a worry in the world. Which was untrue, as he'd come to find out over the next few months as they'd got to know each other. She had a lot of insecurities after losing her mother while still at school. There'd never been much money to go round and

Lyssa had struggled financially. Naturally he'd helped out when they'd got together and she'd been studying to become a nurse.

Aren't you forgetting something?

Forgetting how at first she had tried to find out what his problem was and support him, but he wouldn't tell her what was going on, wouldn't share his pain and refused to let her in, no doubt making her feel worthless. He'd grappled with what he'd learned about his father and that had devastated him further. He'd told her he couldn't take any more. What he should've said was that he'd learned his parents weren't the people he'd believed them to be. But he was still trying to come to terms with that. The man he'd done so much with as a child and enjoyed fishing and hiking with in his teens was an out and out bastard.

Alyssa had never asked for a share of their matrimonial property when he'd sold it, or any of the possessions, all of which he'd bought because she hadn't had a dollar to her name. His family were wealthy, and he earned a good income that he'd happily shared with her. When he'd tried to deposit her share of the property finance into her bank account he'd learned she'd closed it. He mightn't love Alyssa now, but he certainly admired her for her fairness.

The beer suddenly tasted sour. Of course he

hadn't forgotten any of what went down back then. Nor had he forgotten how much it had hurt when she left. He'd loved her with all he had, and still kept her at arm's length.

'So you already know Alyssa?' Jamie asked when he joined him.

'She's my ex-wife.'

Jamie stared at him. 'Hell. I knew you were married when we met but as I returned to the UK shortly after I never met your wife. Nor have you ever talked about her.' Now he was looking thoughtful. 'Wish I'd known.'

'What does it matter?' They still struggled talking to one another about anything that had gone on in their lives before they'd learned the other existed. Opening up about his family life when Jamie had missed out on knowing his father was difficult because *he* had been so happy growing up. It was just as difficult to talk about Alyssa.

Jamie crossed his legs, uncrossed them again, picked up his empty glass. 'Unfortunately there'll be no avoiding each other at the various evening events leading up to the wedding. We haven't got such a huge crowd of guests for you to hide amongst,' he added.

'Don't worry, we'll cope. We're adults.'

'What were the odds?' Jamie shook his head.

'I did think you two would get on great, but I'm a few years too late.'

'Ironic, huh?' Sadness filled him. He had loved Alyssa so much. Just seeing her brought back a load of memories and until those final months they were all good ones. Better than good. Wonderful. Sexy and caring. Sharing and fun. 'I'll see you tomorrow,' he said. 'I need to hit the sack.' He needed fresh air and quiet time to think about what Lyssa's appearance meant. 'I've got an early start tomorrow.'

Early in the Cook Islands meant any time after a late breakfast, though he was usually at the medical centre by eight. Mainly because there was nowhere else he had to be, or anyone to be with. Now he sounded sorry for himself. Better keep a straight face though. He couldn't have Alyssa seeing he wasn't totally engaged in the life he'd worked so hard to achieve. Bet she was wondering why he'd sold out of the medical practice he'd busted his gut to get into.

'We're meeting at the wharf at eleven,' Jamie reminded him.

Not that he needed it. The guys' fishing trip would be fun. He'd been out fishing once since arriving here and thoroughly enjoyed the experience. It was great how most of this week one of the other doctors was covering for him so he could spend time with Jamie. It *had* been perfect and then Lyssa had walked through the door. Now he was hurting when he had no reason to. So much for being over her. But he was. Wasn't he? Better be. He wasn't going through that pain again.

'See you at the wedding,' Lyssa said as he walked past her.

His head spun. She had no idea. 'I guess so.' There'd be no getting away from her over the coming days. Tomorrow the women were going out to the reef in a glass-bottomed boat while the men were fishing, but there was a barbecue arranged for everyone here at the resort, hopefully with the chef cooking any fish the guys caught.

'Leighton.' She had followed him.

He paused, needing to know what she might say, yet wishing she weren't here. After all this time the fear of rejection still nagged.

'You're looking good. I'm glad you're happy with your work choice.' Then she walked away, leaving him startled and with too much to think about. Which he didn't need right now, or ever.

Yet he couldn't take his eyes off her as she strode out of the bar, head high, shoulders tight, and that sassy ass as curvy as ever, and making his body tight. Then she was gone, and he could inhale some air. Alyssa had come back into his world. However temporarily, it was going to be awkward. Might be interesting. No doubt about it. She'd changed. The new confidence suited her and made him want to learn more about who she'd become.

A man appeared in front of him. 'Dr Leighton, can you come? A lady fell off the bus and is bleeding.'

'Sure, Amiri.' Nothing like a bit of medicine to distract the mind. 'Is this woman a guest at the resort?' Hopefully not one of the wedding party. Thankfully Collette had opted to stay in for the night.

'No, she's not,' Amiri said as they headed outside. 'Here's the doctor. Let him through.'

Leighton reached the woman sprawled over the tarmac and winced. Alyssa was ahead of him, already dropping to her knees and taking a wad of tissues from someone to press onto what must be a head wound causing the bleeding. 'How bad?'

Alyssa's eyes widened, but all she said was, 'The bone's exposed.'

Crouching down, he tapped the woman's shoulder. 'Hello, I'm Leighton, a doctor. Can you tell me what happened?'

'I was pushed off the step by someone trying to get back on the bus after realising he was at the wrong hotel.'

'What's your name?' Alyssa asked.

'Michelle.' The woman blinked, looking confused.

A man crouched down beside them. 'She's Michelle Hopkins. We're staying at the family resort near the airport. She's my sister,' he added softly. 'I'm Andrew.'

Concussion was top of the list for injuries given she'd slammed her head onto something hard resulting in the injury. 'I'm going to do a quick look over her before driving her to the medical centre where I can fix her up.'

Alyssa shot him a startled look. 'No ambulance? She's not going to the hospital?'

'Things are done a little differently here.' He wasn't explaining the health system in front of the crowd of onlookers, but sometimes seeing a patient who was a visitor to the island in the medical centre saved hassles with insurance and the airline if the patient needed to return home in a hurry. Unless they were in a serious way, that was.

'I need some more tissues or paper towels.' Alyssa looked around and her eyes lit up. 'Pepe, can you get me some?'

'I'll be right back.'

'Is she going to be all right?' the brother asked. 'Wouldn't she be better going to the hospital?'

'I work at the local medical centre and we

have all the equipment necessary to look after her.' As up to date as any in the hospital anyway. 'Your ankle's twisted, Michelle.'

'Leighton,' Alyssa said quietly. 'Her ear?'

It was torn away from the side of Michelle's face where more bleeding was going on. 'Are you on any medications?'

'Blood thinners,' Andrew answered for his sister.

That made perfect sense. It was going to take more than tissues to slow the bleeding. 'You'll need to stop taking them for the next two days so that the wound can start healing.'

'Is it safe to do that?' Michelle asked. Her thinking seemed to be getting clearer.

'Yes. It's no different than if you were to have surgery. The doctors would get you to stop taking the thinners to prevent haemorrhaging. Right, let's get moving. Alyssa, are you okay here while I get my car?' At least he'd called her *A*lyssa. Surprising when one look at her evoked so many Lyssa memories.

'Of course.'

Silly question, but he was being practical, not denigrating her medical abilities. 'I'll be right back.'

Their patient pushed up onto her elbows. 'Let me go. I want to get back on the bus.'

Alyssa gently pressed her down. 'I wouldn't

recommend it. You've got a serious cut on your head that needs stitching.'

'You can't stop me going on the bus.'

Andrew leaned in. 'Sis, calm down. The bus is leaving and the driver doesn't want you on board like this.'

'I'll only be a minute,' Leighton said to anyone who was listening. His car was parked on the road outside the main entrance.

'I'm coming to the centre with you,' the brother called after him.

'No problem.' It'd be good having another pair of strong hands to lift the woman if she struggled to walk to the car.

It was also handy having Alyssa around. She was competent and unflappable, which always made things easier with difficult patients.

Fifteen minutes later they were at the medical centre and Michelle had become very subdued.

'Are you all right?' Alyssa asked her.

'Yes.' She nodded. 'Feeling stupid though. I've had a bit to drink.'

'That's the nature of a party bus.' Alyssa smiled. 'Now we have to get you fixed up. Leighton's got some sewing to do.'

He nodded. 'Take her through that door on your left while I get the equipment I need.'

'I'll wait out here,' Andrew told them. 'You

don't want another patient on your hands if I faint.'

'You've done all right so far.'

'I wasn't looking.'

Lyssa laughed, sending inappropriate ripples of longing down Leighton's spine. He headed to the equipment room, glad of some space for a moment. Being around Lyssa wasn't easy, though he couldn't think of a better nurse to have at his side in this situation.

You have no idea what she's like when it comes to nursing.

He'd never worked with her, but she'd handled Michelle calmly.

Thirty minutes later the taxi he called drove away with Michelle and Andrew and his phone number, along with a list of instructions about taking care of the wound and ankle and signs of concussion to look out for, and Leighton sighed.

'I'll give you a ride back to Seaview, Lyssa.'

Alyssa, not Lyssa, he reminded himself. Old habits.

'Thanks. I've got a rental car booked but the office was closed when I arrived. I'll deal with it in the morning.' She headed outside without waiting for him.

'Big day?' he asked once they were on the road.

'Very. At least I'll be able to sleep in.' She

tipped her head back and closed her eyes. Conversation over.

He'd go along with that. There wasn't anything to talk about anyway. Other than his brother. But he wasn't doing that when she was half asleep. He needed to be sitting down looking at Alyssa with his wits about him when he told her about Jamie. Right now he was more in need of sleep than an argument or trying to explain himself. As if sleep would be possible. His body was firing up on all cylinders with Alyssa this close.

Of course, sleep wasn't an option when he got home. Alyssa's sudden reappearance in his world wound him up tighter than a coil so he took a mug of tea out onto his deck and sat staring into the distance, hearing the waves crashing on the reef as he fought the picture of his wife now front and foremost in his mind. Thinking about making love to her. How she'd cry out his name as she came. One touch from her light fingers and he'd be gone. Yeah, his body could remember those touches. Her heat. Her body accepting his.

Jamie had hoped they'd naturally gravitate towards each other because he was into matchmaking and thought everyone should be as happy as he and Collette, but to believe Alyssa would be right for him made Leighton shiver.

He'd laugh, only it was painful even thinking about her.

Because unfortunately his brother was right. He and Alyssa had been made for each other, until reality had got in the way.

Reality as in learning that he had a brother he'd never known about. More reality had come to the fore as he'd found out how his father had paid Jamie's mother to keep quiet about his role in bringing Jamie into the world. His father had had an affair with his wife's best friend and Jamie was the result. He'd become the financial provider for Jamie as long as the boy never learned his identity. Jamie's mother had gone along with the deal because she'd wanted Jamie to have every opportunity possible in life, but she'd left a letter to be given to him on her death that named his father and why she'd sworn to keep his name a secret.

When he'd found all that out Leighton had been stunned, and hurt. He had a brother he hadn't known existed. It had explained the state of his parents' marriage and the sometimes awkward atmosphere between them.

But it was no excuse for not being open with Alyssa so that she could've had the opportunity to support him. He hadn't made it easy for her to stay. He'd been hoping she'd understand he needed her without being told, which was ridiculous really. By not talking he'd done what he'd most wanted to avoid—become secretive like his parents.

It was that more than the hurtful things she'd said that had kept him from asking her for a second chance. She hadn't known his true family. If she'd found out about Jamie and his father's affair, would she have believed him to be like his father in every respect? He couldn't face finding out. After she'd gone, the first bombshell about Jamie had been followed by another when he'd learned his father had also treated Alyssa appallingly and he'd been ashamed to be the son of a man who hurt women. Worse, by refusing to talk to her he'd done much the same. He could still see the anguish in her face when she'd packed her belongings and left, accusing him of shutting her out of his life. What cut deep was that she'd been right.

Now she appeared to have moved on with her career and made new friends along the way. From what he'd observed while helping Michelle she was different: stronger, self-assured, focused. It could be a front to keep him at arm's length, but he doubted it.

He'd left the medical centre to take on locum jobs, moving all over the country, unable to settle anywhere for long. His own ambitions had gone down the drain along with his belief in his family. Not only his father's appalling behaviour but his mother's acceptance of it had riled him.

Where had Alyssa been over the past four years? In the beginning he'd heard she moved to Perth, Australia, but after that her whereabouts were unknown to him. There was nothing he could have done for her, other than tell her the truth and he hadn't been prepared to do that for fear she'd despise him by association with his father.

But the time had arrived when there was no avoiding the truth, which just made it clear he should've got it out of the way right back when it mattered the most, because once Lyssa heard what he had to say she'd be even more glad she'd left him.

CHAPTER TWO

ALYSSA OPENED HER eyes and rolled over to look around the bungalow. Sun streamed in around the edges of the blinds and the temperature was toasty. She'd been so exhausted she couldn't remember getting into bed last night and had no memory of taking a shower but the damp-looking towel on the rail indicated she had. Not even Leighton running around in her head had kept her awake. Unbelievable because his presence last night had shocked her to pieces.

Loud knocking on the door grabbed her attention. Was that what woke her?

Go away. I'm on holiday.

But she scrambled out of bed and snatched the resort bathrobe off the back of the door because it had to be one of her friends. She tripped. Or Leighton. She so wasn't ready to see him. Anyway, why would he be here?

'About time.' Collette laughed when she opened the door. 'We gave up waiting for you to join us for breakfast by the pool, but you can't sleep the whole day away. We've got a boat trip starting in under two hours.'

'What's the time?'

'Ten fifteen.' Collette stepped around her to gaze at the accommodation. 'I heard you got an upgrade. Well done.'

'Is coffee supplied? Or do I need to ring for some?' Coffee was the only thing that would get her moving. Her body felt like concrete.

'It should be here any second.' Collette's smile slipped. 'I'm here before the others gatecrash your peace and quiet because I've got a confession to make.'

A chill touched her warm skin. She had no idea what Collette was talking about but something about her stance suggested she wasn't going to be happy. 'Let's sit on the deck in the sun.'

'Here's the coffee.' Collette took the mugs Pepe held out. Did he work everywhere, every hour? 'Thank you.'

'Did you sleep well, Alyssa?' Pepe asked.

'I was unconscious all night.'

'That's got to be good in the circumstances,' Collette murmured as she headed for the deck and Pepe left them alone.

The first two mouthfuls of coffee went down fast and Alyssa started to come alive. 'Come on, spill. You look like you've swallowed a lemon.'

'You're not going to be pleased with us.'

Us? 'You and Jamie?' The picture was becoming clearer. 'This is to do with Leighton, isn't it?'

'The thing is we didn't know you used to be married to him.'

So Leighton had told Jamie. No surprise. It had to come out some time. 'Why would you? I didn't know Leighton and Jamie knew each other, and even if I had I wouldn't have mentioned him. We're finished, been separated for years.' The second man to abandon her, even if she had been the one who'd left.

She'd never known her father. He did a runner before she was born and apparently died in a boating accident when she was about eight. She'd clung to her mother even more after that. Despite the lack of money everything had been fun if her mother was involved. Except cancer stole her mum away when Alyssa was seventeen, leaving her with a burning desire to become a nurse after caring for her mother over the last months of her life.

Words poured out of Collette. 'Jamie's been up to his old matchmaking tricks. We arranged for you two to sit together at the wedding dinner. He really thought you'd hit it off.'

She'd have laughed, except it wasn't funny. 'He's a bit late for that.' More coffee went down her throat. Great. Her ex would be beside her at the wedding. They could be civil to each other. They'd managed with looking after Michelle last night without getting in each other's face. They'd do it again, and this time there would be lots of laughter and fun going on around them to make it easier. 'It's all right. Honestly.' She'd do her darnedest to make sure it was.

'Thanks.' Collette stared over the pool. 'You never talk about your past relationships.'

'What's there to say? We were happily married, then it went belly up and I'm running solo.'

'You don't think you'll try again?'

'With Leighton? No, I won't.' Once hurt was more than enough.

'There are other good men out there.'

'Alyssa?' Leighton stood with a woman beside the deck. 'Kara's from the car rental company. Can she come through?'

'Of course.' The coffee regurgitated in her stomach. What was he doing here?

'I brought coffee but I see Collette beat me to it.' Worry filled Leighton's eyes as he glanced at her friend. Wondering what Lyssa's reaction was to learning they had to share a table?

'Think I need to get dressed.' A shower would have to wait. 'I'll be quick.' Alyssa headed inside without waiting for anyone's comment. So much for a slow get-up on the first morning of her holiday. There was a crowd out there. One person in particular was very attractive and disconcerting.

Damn you, Leighton. We're long finished. I shouldn't feel anything for you.

When she returned outside, Kara held out a set of keys. 'Hello, Alyssa. I'm sorry we were closed when you arrived last night, but Dr Leighton told us you're staying here. Your car's now parked outside the resort.' The young woman looked uncomfortable. 'I just need to get you to sign some paperwork and show me your licence.'

Leighton organised this? Why? They weren't a couple, not even friends. 'That's kind of you to bring the car here. I could've gone in and got it. Please don't worry about last night. It was probably better I wasn't driving anyway. I was very tired.'

'Thank you.' Kara smiled softly.

Leighton looked relieved. Did he think she'd give Kara a telling off for not waiting for her to arrive? If so, he didn't know her very well. Then again, he'd probably forgotten more about her than he remembered. If only she could do the same, but it seemed there were a lot of things she was suddenly remembering. Like how a kiss could turn her into jelly. Or the way he'd generously make sure she always had enough money in her account not to have to go without anything, because sharing was his nature. The times he'd helped her with her study leading up to the nursing finals. His hands on her hips as he pulled her over him to make love.

Her body slumped. He had been perfect. Until it all went wrong. She reached for the paperwork. Time to stop thinking about the past. She no longer needed propping up on the difficult days. Having grown a backbone, she did that all by herself. Having to totally rely on herself for decisions about everyday things had strengthened her resilience big time.

Ten minutes later she'd signed the rental papers and was looking over the yellow sporty-looking car with its top down. Swinging the keys in her fingers, she grinned. 'Awesome. I'll take it for a spin shortly.' The air blowing through her messy hair and over her face would clear the cobwebs from her mind. And the heat brought on by Leighton from her body.

Collette appeared beside her. 'Don't go without me. I'll be by the pool with the others. They'll want to come too.'

'Let's go now.' So much for thinking they'd have a chinwag.

'Leighton's waiting to talk to you.' Collette looked everywhere but at her.

Dread filled her. 'What's going on?'

'Nothing. I'll see you later if we don't have time for a car ride. We're meeting out here at midday for the van that's picking us up to go along to Muri for the boat trip.' Her friend headed into the resort's main building at a fast clip.

The dread increased as she returned to the bungalow. 'Leighton, why are you here?' she demanded the moment she stepped onto the deck. 'I need a shower and then want to take the car for a spin before going out with the girls.' Being sidetracked by Leighton's good looks and gorgeous eyes wasn't an excuse for sitting around. 'I don't have time to chew things over with you.' They didn't have anything to talk about. They were history.

Then she recalled the look on Collette's face and knew she was wrong. 'What's going on?'

'Here's another coffee if you want it.' He handed her the paper cup he'd brought with him and went to stand by the railing, staring out over the beach beyond the pool area.

He was so still and quiet, she was puzzled. And worried. This was nothing like the man she'd known, who was always under control, taking charge. He looked uncertain. Definitely not her Leighton. Worry bells began ringing. What had happened? Did he need her support about something? Could she give it to him after what went down years ago? Yes, absolutely. There was no way she wouldn't. No matter what they'd said to each other back then, she still cared enough to want to be there for him if needed. He was the only man she'd ever loved. There'd always be a place in her heart for him, no matter how awful their break-up was. She sank onto a chair, not taking her eyes off him for a moment. 'Leighton?'

He turned to face her. 'Jamie's my brother.'

That wasn't a problem between her and Leighton that needed sorting. Phew. Then what he'd said hit her. 'Jamie and you are brothers? But—' She stopped before she said something inept and stupid. There hadn't been a brother in sight when she knew him. There had to be more to this. 'Go on.'

He drank some coffee and stared at the deck between them. Then he crossed to sit beside her. 'We're half-brothers. My father had an affair with my mother's best friend and Jamie's the result. I never knew until Jamie turned up on our doorstep.'

The coffee was warm on her tongue, but what Leighton said made her blood boil. She'd loathed John Harrison for how he'd treated her, he'd never felt she was good enough for Leighton or their family, but this was far worse. For Leighton *and* Jamie. 'What happened for Jamie to come and tell you?'

'His mother died. That's when he learned who his father was, and, after some research, found

me. He came from the UK where he was special-
ising to tell me the sordid details, even brought
DNA results as proof. All those years as kids
that we missed out on.' Leighton drained his
cup before turning to her with such despair in
his eyes that the urge to hug him swamped her.

She held her cup tight in both hands. She was
not hugging Leighton. She'd never let him go.
Not a good idea. 'Continue.'

Drawing a deep breath, he rushed on. 'You
were at work the day he turned up at home. It
was a deliberate move as he didn't want anyone
else to know until he'd talked to me. I think he
was afraid I'd send him packing, and if you were
there you might have stood up for me and undermined everything he had to say.'

Quite likely. She wouldn't have accepted the
news without digging into the proof first. 'You
never mentioned any of this.'

'No. I am so very sorry I didn't.'

The lights were starting to go on in her head.
'This happened around the time we stopped
communicating so well by any chance?'

'Yes.'

'If only I'd known.' What difference would it
have made? For one, she'd have helped Leighton
deal with the shock by being there with a shoulder to lean on and letting him talk it through
uninterrupted. It must've been hell, at the very

least. Then she'd left him—because he hadn't seemed to care for her or them any more. Maybe he hadn't. He had a brother he'd known nothing about and parents who'd betrayed him.

But, 'We were married, Leighton. In love and supposed to share everything, not just how the day had been or who we'd seen.' What else had he kept from her? She was getting angry. He'd had no right to hide this from her. She'd been his other half. Or so she'd believed. But when he'd withdrawn from her she'd been reminded how her father hadn't wanted her and she'd started protecting her heart too.

'Yes.'

'That's it? Yes.' When he said nothing, she continued. 'Our marriage fell apart because you withdrew from me. You'd spend hours at work studying or doing extra hours in the medical centre and not coming home to have a meal with me or go to bed to make love and curl up together. I felt redundant.'

'Really?'

'Yes, really.'

'I see.' He still wasn't really talking to her. He'd covered the basics and that was it.

Not good enough. She'd loved him, and would've done anything for him. The old her might've let him get away with this, but not any more. 'I need more, Leighton. Why didn't you tell me?' she snapped. Seriously? How could he not have talked to her? Enough so she'd understood why he was so withdrawn. They might've saved their marriage. 'I deserved better. So did you.'

He stretched his legs out in front of him and studied the view beyond as if it were about to disappear for ever. 'I was angry at Dad for never telling me I had a brother. Like, *really* angry. Jamie should've been a part of the family scene even with his mother being my mum's friend. I also felt hurt and bewildered. Dad wasn't who I'd believed.'

'That would've been very awkward for everyone.' Leighton's mother would've been hard on Jamie. She was an unforgiving woman at the best of times so to accept Jamie on the scene would've been impossible, and who could blame her? Alyssa was beginning to understand the woman a little better. Her husband and her friend had had an affair and produced a son along the way. Appalling. 'I do understand you missed out on so much with Jamie.'

'Mum has had nothing to do with her friend since she learned about the affair.'

'But she stayed with your father.' The woman did like the comfortable lifestyle, but that much?

'No comment.' The bitterness in his voice said more than any words could.

Alyssa dropped the subject of Leighton's mother. It was only rubbing in salt. 'You and Jamie seem to get along fine.' Funny that she'd never heard Leighton's name mentioned whenever she was with Collette and Jamie. Then again, Jamie was usually working when she and Collette did anything together outside the hospital. Besides, she never mentioned Leighton to anyone.

'Unbelievably well considering. I readily accepted Jamie. Once I saw the DNA proof there was no argument, and I was glad he'd sought me out. Having a brother is special.'

Again her blood heated.

I wasn't told any of this.

'You really didn't believe in us. In me.' Or surely he'd have talked to her about Jamie and the impact it had on him? They'd been married, loved each other. Didn't that mean they should have shared everything? So much for thinking he couldn't hurt her any more. He just had. Badly. Any trust she might've had when it came to sharing her heart had flown out of the window. Why did he marry her in the first place?

He gulped. 'I struggled to take it all in and accept I'd been lied to all my life. My emotions were all over the place. When I approached Dad with the news that I'd met Jamie he blustered, said he didn't know what I was talking about, then when I showed him the proof he went ballistic, accusing Jamie's mother of breaking the contract she'd signed where she'd accepted payments every month until Jamie turned twenty-one on the grounds she never told him or anyone else who his father was.'

John Harrison was a wealthy man and believed money was the answer to all life's problems. 'No surprise there.'

Leighton turned to her and touched her hand gently. 'He also said that you were stupid for turning down his offer of a payment to go away. I was stunned. You never told me that, Alyssa. Why?'

'It was between your father and me. To tell you would've put pressure on you. You adored John. I didn't want to make you feel you had to choose between us. Don't say you wouldn't have had to, because knowing he'd offered me money to leave you and how much I loved you would've raised barriers between all of us.'

She'd spent many hours considering the ramifications of telling Leighton, and it had always come back to the fact he thought his father could do no wrong and she didn't want to be the one to destroy that. It wasn't her fault John was rotten to the core but it wasn't her place to tell his son. She'd loved Leighton so much she hadn't wanted to hurt him, but she had to acknowledge what he'd be thinking. 'I accept you might be upset I didn't mention it. I'm more upset that you didn't talk to me about Jamie. Why didn't you?'

He swallowed. 'I know I should've approached it differently, but at the time it wasn't easy.'

'And now?'

'I accept I stuffed up, okay? But we weren't getting on great before Jamie turned up. You were spending more and more time with your friends.'

'Because you were never there,' she snapped.

'I was busy with work and studying, then had to grapple with my father's deceit on top of that. You obviously didn't notice anything was wrong. Or you didn't care.'

'What?' she gasped. Of course she'd cared. She'd loved him. This was unbelievable. She spun away, turned back to stare at him. Had she ever really known him?

'Alyssa, I'm sorry. That came out wrong. I know you loved me.'

'You just put it all back on me and then an apology is supposed to fix it?' She pointed at him. 'You could've sat down with me and got everything out in the open. I'd never have left you to cope alone. Never.'

He stared at her, raw pain in his eyes. 'We weren't getting on well,' he said defensively.

She shook her head. 'I don't believe you didn't

trust me enough.' Her chest ached and her head spun. This was too much to deal with.

His mouth flattened. 'I'd better go. We need to cool down before we say anything else to hurt each other.'

'Sure.' He was running away. But she did need space to absorb everything he'd said—and what he hadn't said. 'Just remember I'd never have left you to go through that alone.'

She might've left him in a fit of anger, but he hadn't talked to her much for weeks, even months prior. It'd been like living with a flatmate who worked opposite hours. Had she been fair? She'd had no idea what was going on and thought he'd fallen out of love with her. It had felt as if those who were meant to love her left her one way or another. What if she had insisted they talk? Would he have told her everything? Would they still be together? Her heart slowed. Was she just as much at fault?

'I mean it,' she snapped at his back as he left. She wanted to say more but let it go. Nothing to be gained by revisiting all the angst of those days.

Watching him walk away, she suddenly felt she was missing out on love. Leighton had been her love. Now he was here and winding her up in every way possible, and still her heart did a dance at the sight of him.

The coming week was going to be difficult with this anger sitting between them. She had to put it behind her fast. They were separated. Though not divorced. Why Leighton hadn't filed was beyond her. He usually kept on top of things, didn't like leaving anything hanging over him. She hadn't done anything about it either. She'd been busy with her career, but it would've only taken one visit to a lawyer to get the ball rolling. Hadn't she wanted to divorce him? Had she been hoping deep down that they might still love each other? Not likely. And less so now.

Her morning had gone belly up and now she needed to put aside her distress while out with the girls. They were not going to know about this.

'Lyssa.' Leighton was back at the gate. 'I know I should've talked to you about Jamie. I am truly sorry for not doing so.'

'My name's Alyssa, not Lyssa.' Not any more. *That was special between us and special has gone.*

Alyssa wouldn't forgive him easily, if at all. Leighton kicked a stone lying on the kerb and cursed the blue sky grey. Did it matter? They weren't together any more, weren't in love and thinking happy families in the future.

But it still mattered what she thought about him. No getting away from that.

He couldn't believe how much he wanted her understanding and acceptance for screwing up. It had been a difficult time and he'd blown it. Not everything had been his fault though. Once Lyssa, no, Alyssa—yes, he had heard her say that—qualified as a nurse she'd changed. She'd wanted to have the fun she'd never had as an adult, while he was still training as a GP, which had involved long, exhausting hours at the medical centre or in front of his computer. Truly, she had deserved to let her hair down after all the study, and the year spent nursing her mother. They couldn't get it right to be able to spend time together and strengthen their relationship. They'd crashed at the first hurdle, looking out for themselves instead of joining together and growing as a couple. If only he'd had the guts to tell her everything.

His father had put pressure on him to stay away from Jamie, saying it would only hurt his mother. As if it were his fault his mother had been hurt, and nothing to do with the result of his father's infidelity. She never talked about Jamie when he tried to find out more. Instead her stiff upper lip only got stiffer. He'd never felt unloved by her. They just had a different relationship from the close one he'd had with his father. Not that he blamed his mother, considering what her friend and husband had done, but he'd never understood why she stayed with his dad. Not even the fact she came from a poor background should've been enough to continue with their marriage. It wouldn't be for him. But then he wasn't an expert on making a marriage survive the pressures of everyday life. He and Alyssa hadn't made the grade, which had him wondering if he was cut out for love and commitment. Especially after learning how shallow his parents' relationship was and how the life they'd led had hidden a lot of ugly truths, and made him question how genuine their professed love for him was.

No wonder he moved around for work so much these days. He didn't feel he belonged anywhere with anyone. Now catching up with Lyssa had him wondering if deep down he'd been looking for her.

'You want a lift to the wharf?' Jamie called out.

Turning, he saw his brother and the other guys standing by the van taking them to the fishing boat. No, he didn't want to go along and act as if he were happy right now. There was a hole in his heart that needed plugging, put there by the shock and disappointment that had crossed Alyssa's face while he'd been talking about

Jamie. He still cared about her. More than he'd have thought when he'd got out of bed yesterday morning with no idea who was turning up that night. That he did have these feelings rattled him. They'd already argued, and there was more he should tell her. Until he did she'd turn her back on him if he showed he cared.

'Leighton?' Jamie stood in front of him. 'Get a grip. You're still in one piece. Alyssa now knows everything and you can put it behind you.'

'You're so practical,' he growled. Jamie was wrong. Alyssa didn't know everything. It wasn't that easy to tell her. She was such a huge part of his past dreams that seeing her again upset the deliberate calm he held over his emotions.

Laughter from the resort foyer had him turning. There she was, that gorgeous long blonde hair falling over her shoulders as she talked animatedly with her friends. He used to run his fingers through her hair, soft and silky against his skin, lighting him up and making him want her in an instant. Damn, how he'd loved her. His hands tingled with a yearning to touch her.

Spinning around, he headed towards the guys getting into the van. There was some fishing to do. Nothing like a big fish fighting the line to take his mind off annoying memories. That was all these thoughts were. Memories of a time when he'd been in love and happy and thinking he had nothing to worry about. Memories of a wonderful smile that could light up his bleakest moods, of being held tight after watching a patient bleed out on the table in front of him and not being able to save the person.

Memories being overtaken by a more mature and beautiful Alyssa who was getting to him as she did the first time they met. Her sweet smile had become confident and beguiling. Those green eyes that used to fill with caution in an instant now full of laughter and self-belief. She was so intriguing—and tempting, which was a worry as he was not following up on these feelings.

'Hey, Leighton, isn't this better than checking some patient's blood pressure and telling them they need to be more careful about what they eat?' asked Dan, a cardiologist who worked with Jamie. He looked as if he was trying to make Leighton forget whatever was bothering him.

'You bet.' These guys were a good lot, and he'd become a part of their group without any effort. He owed it to them to give the same back. 'Or it will be when I catch the biggest fish of the day.'

'Oh, right, here we go. Our local GP thinks he's going to show us up, guys.' Dan laughed. 'When was the last time you went fishing off the reef here?' Jamie asked with a grin, and with concern in his eyes.

Leighton squeezed into one of the back seats. 'A month ago. It was a bit of a fail, but I've heard a lot of success stories in the bar over a beer more often than I can remember.'

'Beer and a fishing story? Expect them to be truthful?' Dan rolled his eyes.

'Good point, but I'll give you a big story to take home with you,' Leighton retorted. Hopefully. 'Or I'll shout the first round when we get back.' He'd set himself up for a fall, but all in good fun. It was time to let Alyssa and the past go. Again. But hell, she was gorgeous. He got in a twist just looking at her. A very familiar twist he hadn't experienced in years—since she left him. There'd been the occasional fling to scratch an itch but not a woman to sidetrack him enough to think about a future relationship.

CHAPTER THREE

'I'M GOING FOR a spin. Anyone want to join me?' Alyssa asked her friends. There was a little time to spare and she needed to do something, anything, so she could stop thinking about Leighton and what he'd told her. Having Collette in the car with her wouldn't be a problem. Her friend knew when to keep quiet. She wasn't someone to talk for the sake of it, and she'd understand how Leighton's news would've rocked her. 'We've got an hour before we need to be ready to go to Muri for the boat trip.' She'd exaggerated the need to get ready when talking to Leighton to get him out of her space while she grappled with his news. A look around the island might help calm her down.

'Yes,' was the answer all round.

'We're going to look cool in your car.' Collette laughed. Moving closer she asked, 'You all right?'

'Yes.' Be honest. 'And no. There's a lot to take

in, but nothing's changed. Our marriage is over, and that's not going to be any different.'

'That's a pity. I reckon Jamie's right. You two are right for each other.'

Hearing that raised something like hope. Alyssa's head banged on the inside. She wanted to shove a sock in Collette's mouth. When she wasn't angry with him Leighton was still capable of heating her from top to toe with only a smile. Thankfully there hadn't been too many of those moments or she'd be a puddle by now. His honesty about Jamie had been too late, but there'd been pain as he'd talked and that opened her heart some, making her want to get closer to support him. She felt he had more to tell that could hurt her. A good reason to remain cautious.

'Cut it out, Collette. There isn't a hope in Hades we could get back together. Apparently I wasn't there for Leighton when he needed me, and he couldn't trust me enough to tell me what was going on.'

Not that she'd realised how bad he was feeling. Had she been too into her own need to get out and catch up on having the fun she'd missed out on growing up? During her final year at high school she'd looked after her mother through the last months of her life as cancer ate her away. She'd missed out on socialising with friends, instead spending what spare time there was working on school assignments to gain good marks. Her teachers had supported her, encouraging her to do her best. She'd done well enough to get into nursing school and had studied hard to make her mum proud of her even though she'd never know. It had been difficult, and then she'd met Leighton and fallen in love. Everything had been wonderful. Except there'd been holes in their relationship she hadn't seen.

Collette climbed into the front seat. 'I think Leighton's pleased to see you despite everything.'

'Sure.' As if Leighton had any reason to want to get back in her good books. He'd always been a good guy at heart, but it'd be going too far to think he might want to spend time with her. She'd believed he'd been glad to see the back of her four years ago. As far as she was aware nothing had happened since to make him think differently.

But then she wouldn't know, would she? They knew nothing about what the other had been up to in the intervening years, and she didn't need to know now. He might have a partner, for all she knew. She swallowed the spurt of jealousy. He was free to do as he liked. Damn it. Or he could be like her and focused mainly on his career by running solo. Wishful thinking?

'Where should we go?'

'The main road does a circuit of the island. Follow that and you'll get an idea of where everything is. It only takes about forty-five minutes, so we'll still be in time to meet up with Mum and my sister for the boat trip,' Collette answered. 'We're being picked up here so if we're a few minutes late they'll wait for us.'

'Let's do it,' Alyssa said with a grin, all feelings of exhaustion gone. To hell with her past. For now.

'Better warn you the speed limit is very low all over the island,' Collette said as they pulled out of the car park. 'But we're in Rarotonga and everything's great,' said the happy bride-to-be.

Again a feeling of longing struck Alyssa. Her wedding day had been quiet as it'd been a long weekend and most of their friends had already made plans to be away when they made the sudden decision to marry before Leighton's final exams six weeks later. They'd opted to get married by a celebrant in a restaurant where they had a superb lunch with their few guests before heading to an upmarket hotel that they didn't leave until Monday night.

She'd missed her mother more than ever that day. She'd have adored Leighton and been proud of her daughter. It didn't help Alyssa that she wasn't welcome in Leighton's family, but she'd known that from the beginning because John Harrison had told her she wasn't good enough for them, and Jean had kept reminding her she had no taste in clothes or anything else. When John had offered what was to her a small fortune to disappear out of Leighton's life she'd been shocked, then angry. She'd told him where to stick his money and received an even bigger offer, which had only made her more determined to see the man lose the battle. Though he'd won in the end without spending a dollar.

'Is that the medical centre you went to last night?' Andrea asked from the back seat. 'Looks like the one Leighton said he works at.'

'Yes, that's it.' It was modern and practical. She still couldn't see Leighton working here even if only for a few months. Being laid-back was one thing, but Leighton had to be kept busy or he got antsy. That was the man who'd always got her in a twist with a look. Not a lot had changed in that respect. She'd been in a twist when she first saw him last night, and again when he'd walked onto her deck with coffee in hand this morning. But it was possible he no longer had to keep busy every minute of his day. And night. That was one busy thing about him she'd loved. His hands were always touching, caressing, lighting her up in ways she'd never have dreamed of before she met him.

'Wonder if they need a nurse? I could handle working here.' Gina laughed.

Alyssa tuned out from the light banter going on amongst the others, instead concentrating on driving and noting places to return to over the coming days. There were cafés and bars everywhere. Plenty of beaches too. She wouldn't be short of things to do, though once this lot returned home it might be a little quiet. Unless she dropped in on Leighton. Great. That was not the best idea she'd had.

'The resort's around the next corner,' Collette warned her.

'That went fast,' she said. 'I'll have to do the loop again to really get my bearings.'

'There's the van for the boating trip.'

'I haven't got my gear together,' Alyssa said. 'I'll be a couple of minutes.'

'We should've changed into our bikinis before you took us for a drive. Would've looked the part in this car.'

She was more than glad she hadn't changed earlier when Leighton was still around. She might have given him something to choke over if he'd looked her way. There again, he probably wouldn't care one way or the other. The red bikini she'd bought last week left little to the imagination. Much the same as the other two she'd bought after being told by Collette she'd spend a lot of time in or beside a pool or snorkelling in the sea looking at the colourful fish and turtles.

'See you back here shortly.' She needed to throw on a little make-up and loads of sunblock, and she'd be ready.

'Bring your underwater camera,' Collette called.

'Will do.' Plus her phone, sun hat and towel, and a shirt for when she cooled off—if she ever did. Racing to the bungalow, she felt happier than she'd been in so long. Suddenly not even the idea of bumping into Leighton was hindering her fun. She was truly on holiday and going to enjoy every moment. Starting now. Really? Really.

'First we're having a barbecue lunch on the islet on the Muri lagoon,' the boat captain told them all as the boat left the beach at Muri. 'My men are already there setting up.'

Judging by the delicious smells wafting through the air when they all clambered ashore the men had been there for a while. 'That's making me hungry.' Collette laughed.

'So we're having two barbecues in one day?' Alyssa grinned. 'As long as the guys catch some fish, that is. Where were they going?'

'Out beyond the reef somewhere. Jamie wasn't too sure about the details as Leighton arranged it all. Like he did almost everything for the week, including this trip we're doing.'

Leighton… Leighton. There was no getting away from him. After so long apart it was strange how easily he came to life in her head. Tall, broad shoulders, slim hips and thick dark blond hair made him good-looking and interesting. The very first time she ever saw him she'd felt a moment of panic, as though her life had changed for ever. Turned out that was true, if not in the way she'd expected. They'd hit it off immediately and were hardly ever out of each other's lives from then on. Only work had kept them apart and the catch-up afterwards had been hot and heavy and wonderful. Six months later they'd married and her world had been a garden of roses. Sweet smelling, colourful and glorious.

'You okay?' Collette asked. 'It must've been a shock seeing him at the resort last night.' She knew where Alyssa's mind had gone.

'Can't say it wasn't. But I'm good.'

'I hope so.'

'This week's about you and Jamie, not me. I'm making the most of not having to prioritise patients and staff. I can't believe it's been more than two years since I had a proper holiday.'

'Let's celebrate with a cold drink.'

'I'm sticking to water until we're back at the resort. Call me boring but I prefer to be safe than sorry.' Champagne would've been great but there'd be plenty of time later for that. At the barbecue with the guys, and Leighton. See? Leighton was always there, whichever way she looked or thought.

'Lemonade for me,' Collette said.

The steaks and salads were as delicious as they'd smelt and then they were back on the glass-bottomed boat heading out to the reef where numerous colourful small fish soon came into view.

'Right, ladies, you can go overboard and swim with the fish. They won't be frightened away. Take lots of photos to show your families back home and then they'll come for a visit too.'

When it was her turn to slip into the water, Alyssa dropped off the edge of the boat fast and seemed to go down for ever.

Where's the bottom?

All around her the other women seemed to have paused, as though they'd reached the bottom while she kept going. Panicking, she began clawing at the sea, trying to get back to the top. Nothing happened, she was suspended in the water. Kicking hard, she gasped and swallowed a mouthful of salt water.

Don't cough. Kick again.

Finally she began rising to the surface. When her head burst out of the water she gasped mouthfuls of air while spitting out the salt water. Grabbing the side of the boat, she clung on tight.

'You all right?' a crew member called out.

'I want to get back on the boat,' she cried and took the hand reaching down to her. A moment later she was sprawled on the deck, coughing hard, bringing up salt water.

'What happened?' Andrea was beside her.

'I don't know. I kept going down and down and I swallowed a mouthful of water and started to panic.'

'Are you all right?'

Breathing in deep, she realised she was despite the knocking under her ribs. 'I'm fine.'

'Drink this.' The crewman held out a bottle of water. 'It's not very deep, but if you're not used to jumping into water above your head you can get a shock,' he said.

She hadn't jumped, she'd just let go and dropped down. 'Scary.'

'I'll stay with you for a bit,' Andrea said.

'No way. Go and see the fish.' She wasn't spoiling someone else's afternoon.

'Truth is I don't like being in the water,' Andrea told her. 'I nearly drowned as a kid and have hated swimming ever since.'

Coughing up more salt water, Alyssa nodded. 'I can understand that.' But she was all right, and there were fish to be seen. 'I'll go a lot slower next time.'

Everything was fine when she did, though she stayed close to the boat to be able to grab hold if she panicked again.

'Leighton, can you check on Alyssa? She swallowed a bucket load of salt water when she jumped off the boat.'

Thanks, Collette.

'I didn't jump in and I'm fine now.' They were back at the resort where the guys were celebrating a successful fishing trip with some beers. 'I'm going to have a shower and get changed into something more comfortable.' The bikini was fine out on the boat but not here in the bar with Leighton hanging around. It made *her* so aware of *him* when she was meant to be wary. All back to front. Go figure.

'I'll come with you.' Leighton was moving towards her.

'I am fine,' she reiterated.

'You probably are but I won't relax until I know for certain.'

Her stomach dropped. She did not want him in her bungalow. It was cosy but not when the second person was Leighton. 'I'm fine,' she repeated, getting nowhere because Leighton followed her inside anyway.

'What happened in the water? Did you gasp and take in a lungful?'

'I went over the side of the boat too fast and got a fright. When I returned to the top I spat out water a few times. That's all.'

I was scared silly but that's for me to know.

'Hold out your wrist.'

'My pulse is fine. Andrea checked it.'

'I want to be certain, Lyssa.' He swallowed hard. 'Sorry, Alyssa.'

Sorry? That hurt. Shouldn't, but it did. Holding out her wrist, she tried to ignore the warmth emanating from his fingers, heating her where she didn't need it.

He focused on his watch as he counted her pulse, almost as though he were practising on a dummy. Too focused, as in aware of her and not wanting to be?

Her pulse was probably going crazy. Not because she'd swallowed too much salt water but because of standing this close to Leighton. Too many memories came with those firm fingers. Memories she'd thought were long forgotten. Or was this new? Was she seeing him through new eyes? She shivered. Surely not?

'Your pulse is normal. Have you been coughing a lot since getting out of the water?'

'No. I told you, there's nothing wrong. I was surrounded by nurses who all had to check me out.' None of them had let her back on her feet before they did.

Leighton nodded, looking far too serious to be thinking about what she'd done. 'You're right. You're good to go.'

'Then I'll get ready for the barbecue.'

In other words, go back to your mates and leave me in peace. I need to get my head under control.

'Right.' He didn't move.

Her arm brushed his chest as she squeezed past him to head out to the deck in an attempt to make him leave, then she had to sit down because her legs were a little shaky. 'Did you catch any fish?' she finally asked to fill the void growing between them. Why was he still hanging around?

'We brought back two. Right now the cooks are preparing one for our dinner, and the other one is to be shared by the staff. Can I get you anything?' Definitely not in a hurry to leave. 'A drink perhaps?'

She should go in and have that shower, but she didn't know if she had the strength to stand. Not while Leighton was here, getting to her in ways she'd never have believed. So much for thinking they were done and dusted if he could rattle her this easily. She might as well have a drink and hopefully start to relax. He'd probably tell her she shouldn't but too bad. 'A glass of bubbles would be great. There's a bottle in the fridge.'

'Not a problem.'

She blinked. What? No argument from the doctor. Or had he moved on from the doctor role? To what? A friend? An ex wanting to keep an eye on her because he still cared a little? It made her head pound harder thinking about everything. 'Thanks.'

His laugh sounded hollow. 'There's nothing wrong with you and you're on holiday. Why shouldn't you have a drink?'

'Do you want to join me?' she asked, and instantly regretted it. She needed space between them, not Leighton sitting within a few feet of her.

'I'll take a rain check. I'm going home to get clean and put on some less fishy clothes for the barbecue.'

Relief warred with disappointment, which she couldn't explain other than he messed with her head. That was all. That was enough. 'I'll see you later.'

Did she want to? There was nothing to be gained by getting too friendly. They'd given marriage a shot, and failed. A second crack at it would only lead to more heartbreak. She would struggle to trust him to be open with her, and he'd probably always be looking for her to let him down. Her body needed to quieten down. They weren't hooking up.

Back at his place Leighton headed down to the beach instead of going inside. Anything to get away from the image of the despair in Alyssa's eyes that morning bringing back memories of them arguing. It wasn't there when he was checking her out after swallowing the salt water, but he knew she'd be thinking about it often. That was Alyssa. She always thought things through more than once before moving on. He should've told her about Jamie right from the get-go. Part of him had been well aware he was being selfish, but he'd wanted to absorb the news and look at it from all ways before putting it out there for someone to say he was stupid to think Jamie was there for anything but money and the family name.

Though Alyssa wouldn't have said that. Not in a million years, but he hadn't wanted to see compassion or sympathy in her eyes either. He was supposedly the strong one in their relationship. Though learning how she'd turned his father's offer down flat after she'd left him proved him wrong there.

Raking his hand through his hair, he swore. Alyssa had been everything he'd wanted in a woman. Warm, funny, kind, and generous. Especially loving. His heart had never stood a chance. There'd been some neediness about her too, but he could live with that. She'd lost her mother to cancer when she was seventeen, and there'd never been a father in the picture. Her mother had remained single and raised her daughter without any help, working two jobs to pay the bills. Alyssa always said she had the best upbringing, but she did want a family and to be loved again by someone special since her mother had gone. He'd had no problem with that. He'd loved her and could give her what she wanted with his parents at her side too. Got that wrong, hadn't he? Another blunder he was accountable for.

He couldn't have loved her enough or they'd still be together. He hadn't trusted her to support him when Jamie appeared on the scene, or to see he was different from his father. He'd been in a bad place, not getting to grips with who his father really was. Another mistake to overcome if they were to at least be friends. Yet when he'd told Alyssa about Jamie that morning she'd been accepting although angry because he hadn't explained years ago. He understood. He'd used his battered heart as an excuse.

He skimmed a small flat pebble across the water.

His father had disowned him the day he'd told

him how gutted he was not to have known about his brother. Apparently his loyalties should lie with his parents, and not Jamie. He wasn't supposed to share himself around. Was that why Dad tried to pay Lyssa off? Afraid she'd steal all his love?

Leighton stared over the water to the far horizon. No wonder he no longer called Auckland home. There was nothing there for him but sad and bitter memories. His wife had gone, his parents were distant, and Jamie had been living in England, though he was now back in Nelson, settled in permanently. Which was why Leighton was considering moving south. He owned a house in Auckland that he returned to between locum jobs but it did nothing for him. It was a house, not a home.

He was lonely. Keeping busy didn't fill all the gaps in the day. Until now he hadn't realised how much he'd missed Alyssa. He'd never have believed it, but then he'd been determined he wasn't going after her to beg for a second chance. She deserved better than being a part of the Harrison family, however remote that had become to him.

She still does.

He'd hurt her all over again explaining how he'd avoided talking about Jamie when he first found out he had a brother. Seemed hurting her came too easily. Something to remember over the coming days. She still distracted him far too quickly. That was his to deal with. He had to remain vigilant. She got under his skin far too easily so the barriers had to remain up.

Whatever he felt when around her, he did not want to get back together. This morning had shown there was too much hurt between them to forget the past. Both had made mistakes: Alyssa not sticking with him and him keeping quiet. They both deserved better.

His phone vibrated.

Jamie. 'Get your butt back here. The beer's getting warm.'

Turning back the way he'd come, he strode back to the house for a quick shower. Hopefully Alyssa had fallen asleep and wouldn't be at the barbecue for a long while, if at all.

He really didn't need to see her right now, or any time until the wedding. Even then he didn't *need* to spend time with her. No denying the heat that flared whenever she was near though. As soon as the wedding day was over he'd get back to his normal steady but quiet life as a GP. Jamie and Collette's family and friends would leave the island. All except Alyssa. Apparently she was staying on for another week. Their paths didn't have to cross then. She'd be a tourist, checking out the market and cafés, seeing the sights and visiting the bars. He'd be at the clinic or the house he called home for now.

Perfect. They had a history. They weren't getting a future.

Alyssa knotted her blouse beneath her breasts and sucked in her stomach. Her skin was too pale, since it was winter back home. Time by the pool every day she was here would go some way to fixing that.

Laughter reached her from the main deck where the barbecue was happening. Everyone was happy and enjoying the pre-wedding events. Tomorrow she and the girls were going to have massages and facials. Talk about dream living. She'd never pampered herself before. Cautious with money, doing something decadent seemed extravagant. Growing up, there'd never been spare dollars to have some fun, and she'd carried on much the same way as her mother had with her hard-earned money—which was why she was getting close to putting down a deposit on her own home.

Home. A place to feel safe and secure. Like she'd had as a kid with her mother supporting her in every way possible. Not quite how home had been with Leighton. They'd bought an apartment on Auckland's North Shore and they'd made it cosy, but as time had gone by they'd spent less and less time there together and it had begun to feel less like home and more like a house any-one might've owned, but not them.

'You joining us or what?' Jamie stood in her doorway, a sympathetic look on his face.

So he understood she was struggling with Leighton's presence. 'Just coming,' she lied. It would be easier to stay at the bungalow than face up to Leighton and the way he set her tingling all over, but these days in Raro were about her friends, not herself.

'I imagine it astounded you learning about Leighton and I being siblings. It came as a sur-prise to realise you two had been married too. Small world, eh?'

'It's okay, Jamie. I'm over the shock.' No harm in a little fib. 'Really, what does it matter? If anything, I'm glad you both have each other. Leighton often said he'd felt lonely growing up as an only child.' Whereas she'd been more than happy being her mother's one and only.

'I've told Collette we're having a brood of kids.' Jamie laughed.

'Nappies and bottles on their way,' she re-sponded. Kids. Hard to imagine what having one of her own would be like. She and Leigh-ton had talked about having a family one day and she'd been excited to think she could be a mother. But they'd agreed to wait until he'd qualified as a GP and by then their marriage was falling apart. Maybe a baby would've kept them together, except that wasn't a reason to stay in a failing relationship.

'Not this week,' Jamie warned.

'Here I was thinking I'd figured what to get for your wedding present,' she said as they made their way across to the group.

'Get this into you.' Collette handed her a cocktail. 'It's your favourite.'

'A margarita? You're a gem.' She really had the best of friends, and if Jamie knew she was struggling with Leighton's presence then Collette would be more than aware. But it was their special occasion and she wasn't going to spoil that for anything. Lifting her glass, she grinned. 'Here's to the happy couple and a fantastic wedding.' It really was wonderful being here, like the fun times she'd hoped for when she'd married and qualified.

'I'll drink to that,' Dan said and then everyone was raising their glasses and toasting their friends.

'Have I missed something?' Leighton asked from the edge of the deck.

A shiver went through her. She'd missed his arrival. Which had to mean she wasn't so caught up in his presence as she'd thought. Good.

'We're toasting Collette and Jamie.' She took

another sip. Without them she'd be back in Nelson still working her butt off and not enjoying the sunshine and that beautiful beach with the reef beyond where the waves pounded incessantly. She glanced that way and blinked. 'Hey, is that a whale leaping out of the water beyond the reef?'

'Quite likely,' Leighton answered. 'There are always some about.'

'I'll have to watch out for them.' Needing to put space between her and Leighton, she inched closer to Andrea. 'You got a bit sunburnt today.'

'Don't know how when I put plenty of sunblock on. How're you feeling? Not coughing up any more salt water?'

Leighton turned to look at her, obviously waiting for her reply.

'Not a drop.' She didn't need him looking out for her.

He's being caring, as he would for anyone.

She wasn't anyone special in his book. Though he had always been caring towards her until those last months. Had she acted in haste when she left? It was starting to feel like that. Not a good feeling. What if she had done a bunk too soon? Broken Leighton's heart along the way? She'd never forgive herself. He'd been her heart's desire and she'd believed he'd always be there for her. Sounded naïve now. Despite wanting to be there for him, she'd packed up and left when the going got tough. No one was perfect. She groaned. This was getting harder to take by the hour. But for everyone's sake, including theirs, they had to get along and not spoil the fun.

'At least you got back in the water,' Andrea said. 'I wish I had the courage to go in and see those fish. They looked so colourful and pretty through the glass.'

'I'll flick you some photos, though it's not quite the same as swimming with them.' The aroma of fish cooking on the barbecue reached her and her stomach sat up, reminding her she hadn't eaten much lunch. 'That smells delicious.' Then she laughed. 'Fish for dinner when we spent hours watching others swimming over the sand.'

'None of those would've been Mahimahi,' Leighton said.

'What he's not saying is I caught it.' Jamie laughed. 'He was certain he'd be the hero of the day and catch our dinner. He didn't even get a bite.'

'Had to let someone else have a chance,' Leighton quipped.

'I don't remember you being into fishing.' Alyssa instantly wished her words back. Talking about their past was irrelevant at the moment. Or at any time, come to think of it.

He looked surprised. 'It's something I'd like to do more often but never seem to get around to. I used to fish when I was younger. One of the doctors here at the hospital dragged me out once and I'm always hopeful we'll go again one day.'

'You'll be able to continue on the Hauraki Gulf when you return home. Snapper's yummy.'

'If I go back to Auckland.'

'Are you considering staying here permanently?' That didn't sound right. He liked to immerse himself in work and from what she understood it wasn't that busy here.

'No, not at all. I take locum positions up and down the country, only returning to Auckland in between jobs. But I think it's time to look elsewhere for somewhere to live. I'm well and truly over the big city.'

Really? He'd been an Aucklander through and through with no inclination to move anywhere else. 'What's made you change your mind?'

He shrugged as he studied the beer bottle in his hand. 'I'm ready for a change. I want to connect with people and feel at home somewhere. I haven't got that in Auckland.'

Hello? Is this Leighton? The guy who told you in no uncertain terms right from the get-go that Auckland was home and he was never moving?

'It doesn't sound like you're there much anyway.' A trickle of excitement warmed her. Leighton excited her? To be brutally honest, he did. He was different and talking about a different life from what he used to want. And more intriguing, with his matured looks and well-honed body. Give over. His body had always been a turn-on. Nothing new there. Just as the heat coursing through her now was nothing new.

'Perhaps that's why.'

Her hand shook as she sipped her margarita. How honest could he be? With her, at that? It wasn't like the Leighton she'd known. What was going on here? Had the fact he'd never talked to her about Jamie changed how he approached people? 'I know I'll never go back there.' She could do honest too.

'You like Nelson?' A tightness appeared at the edges of his mouth as if her answer was important.

'Love it. After Perth I travelled around Oz a bit, then returned home. I didn't even stop in Auckland. There was nothing there for me.'

Leighton winced. Not the answer he was hoping for? Or expecting?

Guilt sneaked in. All very well being blunt, but she didn't have to hurt the man who'd stolen her heart and then given it back. His shoulder felt muscular under her palm. 'That wasn't a dig at you, Leighton.' He had been a part of why she didn't return to Auckland, but not the whole picture. 'I still miss Mum but she's not about Auckland even though I grew up there. My closest friends have all moved away and the hospitals are so big there's nothing personal about working in them.'

You aren't a part of my life.

'You didn't used to speak your mind quite so clearly.' There was a wry smile on his face.

She probably hadn't known it so clearly. Guess they'd both changed. She'd grown up a lot, probably much the same with Leighton. That damned smile hadn't changed though. 'Maybe I should've. You might've had a clearer understanding of my needs.'

'There you go again. Saying what you think. I like it.'

'If you're not keen on returning to Auckland, where do you think you might go?'

Don't say Nelson.

It was her home town now.

'There's a certain appeal about Nelson.'

Her heart slumped.

No way, Leighton.

'Have you ever been there?'

'I've visited Jamie a couple of times since he returned from England. It's a lovely place with lots of outdoor attractions. Though for me the biggest attraction would be having family nearby.' He watched her intently. 'By that I mean Jamie and Collette. I have very little contact with my parents these days.'

'Since Jamie came into your life?'

He nodded slowly, as if wanting to steer the subject away from his parents. 'I'll see what's on offer workwise when I'm through here before making any major decisions.'

'You always knew exactly what you wanted and got on with achieving it.'

Her arms ached with the need to hug him, to take that sadness out of his eyes. If only she could do it without having to worry that he might see it as more than it was. He had always been a kind, caring man with a big heart. Leighton deserved to be loved. Just not by her. They'd tried and failed. It would be pointless to try again. As well as painful. She'd never fully trust him to be open with her about everything, and in hindsight she knew she'd let him down too.

'Guess you've got some decisions to make before you return home.' She was being glib, but this was getting too intense, which she did not want. Their time for that was long over.

He shrugged. 'I'm working on it.'

'Keep me posted. I'd like to know what you decide and where you end up living.'

'Really? Why?'

Because I've missed you.

Her drink sloshed over the side of the glass. She had? Surely not. They'd broken up because they weren't getting along, couldn't even hold a conversation without getting into an argument, and she'd missed him? Yes, she did, and probably had all along. Missed the funny, caring, kind man she'd fallen for. Not the withdrawn, 'don't share my feelings' guy who never came home for dinner or to make love.

'Now we've caught up again, I'd like to know how you're getting on.' Did that come out all wrong? Would he think she wanted to get close again? 'Sorry, I'll shut up now.'

'Nothing to apologise for, Lyssa.' He reached for her glass. 'I'll get you a top-up.'

'Thanks.' Lyssa. Seemed he still thought of her as Lyssa and not Alyssa.

'I call you Lyssa in my dreams.'

He'd told her that after he kissed her the very first time, and had never stopped using that version of her name all the time they were together. Lyssa. Her toes curled thinking about how 'Lyssa' sounded deep and sexy when he was making love to her and she was about to explode with desire. Her heart lifted recalling how 'Lyssa' was full of concern when he carried her to the couch after she tripped on the stairs of their apartment and sprained her ankle in the resulting fall.

Loud talk and laughter interrupted her thoughts. She looked around, suddenly remembering they were at a barbecue with friends. Everyone had moved to the long table, where they sat together as though there'd been a mutual agreement to leave her and Leighton in their own little space to get along. They probably meant well, but she wished they'd mind their own business and leave her and Leighton to decide if they wanted to spend time together or not.

Right now she felt bewildered. Listening to him open up about his home had her wondering what he actually wanted for his future. She'd always thought he knew exactly what he wanted, so either their break-up had affected him a lot more than she'd imagined, or something else had gone down in the intervening years. Jamie arriving in his life would probably have a lot to do with how he looked at things.

'Come on. We'd better get amongst it.' Leighton held out her refilled glass. 'Enough serious talk for one day.'

Enough for the rest of her time in Rarotonga, more like. It did her head in hearing him say he didn't know where he wanted to live. It underlined how much he'd changed. The idea of him even considering Nelson gave her goose bumps.

She was getting her own house there to settle down for good. It was her town, not his.

'Cheers.'

But it could prove interesting if he did move there and they were getting along.

CHAPTER FOUR

ALYSSA WALKED ALONG the beach, enjoying the sand pushing between her toes. At least it would wash off easily, whereas her hair was going to be a problem. The humid air was making it frizz around the edges despite the can of hairspray the hairdresser had used. Great. She was going to look like some toddler's stuffed toy after it had been left out in the rain. It didn't really matter. Today wasn't about her. Except she did like to look her best. She'd bought new clothes for every occasion planned for the days leading up to the wedding, going a little crazy with her overtime pay, but it was good to spoil herself for a change.

Then there was the gorgeous dress she'd got for the wedding hanging on the back of the door, ready to slip into when she returned to the bungalow. She was not thinking she'd like Leighton to see her all spruced up and looking hot in the dress with its narrow straps and long lines accentuating her breasts and hips. And her butt, one feature he'd always said was so damned sexy he could never resist her.

She wasn't.

Who gave a toss what Leighton thought?

Try again, Alyssa. This morning you spent hours preening yourself in front of the mirror because you're sitting next to him at the wedding dinner.

True. She had. The silly thing was, it seemed she'd never quite got over Leighton. She'd moved on from their marriage heavy-hearted but determined to be true to herself, and she'd done okay, but there'd never been another man to replace him. The few she'd known since just hadn't come up to his standards. That could be because she'd loved Leighton so much—and believed he'd felt the same—that when they broke up she didn't believe she was lovable.

Or because she hadn't stopped loving Leighton.

If he could walk out of her life so easily then he couldn't have loved her half as much as she'd thought.

You walked away too.

Yes, she had. Better that than stay and become even more disillusioned about their marriage and how it seemed so different from what she'd expected. Or so she'd believed. But she might've been too quick to give up. When he wouldn't talk, she'd got angry, not sympathetic, feeling as rejected as she had when she'd learned her father had wanted nothing to do with her.

The turmoil brought on by catching up with Leighton was too much at times, which was why she was out here and not sitting on the deck with the other girls counting down the final hour until everyone gathered together to witness Collette marry the man of her dreams. She was ready, apart from the sand on her feet and the dress to put on, but the agitation about the man who'd once been her dream grew with every minute she had nothing to keep her busy.

If someone had told her Leighton could get her in such a hot, flustered state as he used to she'd have laughed and told them to get a life. Except it seemed she was the one needing to do that. There was still some unfinished business to deal with about when Jamie turned up in his life that she was clueless about. Other than that there was no reason why he was messing with her head so much. She'd thought she was over him, and here she was getting hot and bothered over that sexy smile and lean body.

The sound of a racing motor scooter came from the road fifty metres beyond the beach, followed by a loud thump. Screams rent the air.

Almost relieved at the disruption to her walk,

Alyssa ran towards the noise. What happened? Had someone been hit by the scooter?

Shouts and more screams.

Scrambling up the low bank, she tore across the lawn to where others were aiming for. Running around the corner of a house, she gasped. 'What happened?' she asked aloud as she noted a woman sprawled on the ground with the scooter imbedded into the wall and the back wheel pressed into her stomach. The woman wasn't moving and blood was oozing from the back of her head.

'If it's anything like what Sarah did yesterday I'd say she used the accelerator instead of the brake by mistake,' another woman said. 'It's easy to do. The controls are on the handlebars. One to brake, one to accelerate. Sarah's mixed them up a couple of times. She's my friend,' she added.

Would've been better to have stayed off the scooter, Alyssa thought but kept it to herself. Dropping to her knees beside the woman, she said to anyone listening, 'I'm a nurse. Is anyone else a nurse or doctor?'

Apparently not, judging by the sudden silence.

'Can someone phone for the ambulance?'

'I'm doing that now,' a local man told her. 'They won't be long. Is there anything you need in the meantime?'

Alyssa looked at the scooter. 'We need to get

the wheel off her. Is there any way to move the scooter without causing any more problems?'

Two men carefully checked to see if the scooter was moveable. 'I think we can do it,' one said.

'Let me check Sarah's abdomen first,' Alyssa said. 'We don't want to cause further bleeding.' If the wheel was pressing on an internal injury it might still be haemorrhaging. But first, 'Sarah, I'm a nurse. Can you hear me?'

No reply. The pulse in her throat was rapid, but at least there was one.

She tried again. 'I'm Alyssa. I'm checking you over for injuries. Does it hurt where I'm touching your head?'

Silence.

'Hey, there's Doc Harrison,' someone said. 'Over here, Doc.'

Relief filled Alyssa. Having a doctor helping with this was going to make everything easier. He'd make the call on what was happening and what needed to be done. Only difficulty she had was it was obviously Leighton. Even better, he was calm under stress. That much hadn't changed.

He was already kneeling beside her. 'Where did you spring from?' he asked.

'I was walking on the beach when I heard the scooter slam into the house.' She shuddered at the memory. 'It sounded terrible.'

'I bet it did. What've we got?'

We. She liked that. 'I can feel a softness in her abdomen where the wheel is pressing. There's a head injury and she's not responding to my questions. Her name's Sarah.'

'The ambulance just left the hospital, Doc.'

'Good. I wonder if she hit the wall with her head or shoulder,' Leighton said as he began working his hands over Sarah's skull. 'The left shoulder looks dislocated.'

'Impact to the shoulder would be better than her head,' Alyssa said. 'These two men are prepared to remove the scooter when we give the go-ahead.'

'We're going to need to do that sooner rather than later.' Leighton's hand moved around Alyssa's as he felt for any injuries. 'That's where you felt a softness?' he asked.

'Yes. Shall I put pressure on it as the wheel is lifted?'

'Yes, but be prepared to have to shift the pressure as the wheel might be hiding the true extent of the damage.' Leighton looked around. 'Hey, Manu, Jacko, glad you're here. I'll give you a hand to lift the scooter away. What we have to do is lift it directly upwards, not drag it sideways at all.'

'Onto it. You tell us when, Doc.'

'On the count of three. One, two, three.'

The wheel was gone, the bike lifted over Alyssa's head and put aside.

She was instantly pressing down with one hand while checking for further injuries. 'Can't find any further problems,' she told Leighton. This was intense. They'd done a lot of things together in the past, but never worked on a patient until the other night, and this was far more serious than Michelle's injuries. He was calm, focussed, doing what was required without making a fuss. Leighton to a tee. He was often too calm for her liking, contained, not relaxing and doing nothing over a beer or a book type of calm, but right now he was perfect.

The friend moved closer. 'We're due to fly back to New Zealand tomorrow. What's going to happen to her? Is she seriously hurt?'

'She'll be taken to the hospital, where a doctor will attend her. Depending how serious her injuries are, she might be flown back to Auckland tonight.' Leighton was lifting Sarah's right arm. 'Shoulder's definitely dislocated. I'll try to put that back before she goes in the ambulance, otherwise she'll require surgery once she's back home.' He glanced at Alyssa. 'We don't have an orthopaedic surgeon, but there's a general surgeon I'll phone to let him know what's going on.' He pulled his phone from his pocket. 'Keep that pressure on, Alyssa.'

An ambulance pulled up, and she felt happier. Sarah needed to be in hospital fast. Then it dawned on her. 'Leighton, you've got to get ready for the wedding.' He was wearing denim shorts and a tee shirt, not wedding attire. Not for the best man.

He nodded abruptly and turned away to talk on his phone, presumably to the surgeon he'd mentioned.

The surgeon had better be available. Leighton couldn't miss his brother's wedding. He had to be there. It was important to both men. They'd gained so much when Jamie came into Leighton's life. Her heart squeezed. And she'd lost Leighton, though she couldn't blame all that on Jamie's appearance. If their marriage had been strong they'd have got through the difficulties and still been happy and in love.

'That's sorted. Phil will meet us at the hospital.'

'Us? You can't go. You've got to get ready for the ceremony.' Blood had splattered across his arms. He needed a shower.

Glancing down, she realised she did too. So much for having one earlier.

'I'm going in the ambulance with Sarah. The ambulance crew aren't paramedics,' he said quietly. 'Once at the hospital Phil will take over and I can come back to the resort for a shower.

Would you mind following in my car so I've got a lift back?'

'Sure.' She took the keys he was holding out in her free hand. 'Who's going to take over from me here?'

'Annie will do that. Annie, this is Alyssa, a nurse here on holiday. She'll show you where we need to apply pressure and you can take her place.'

It was busy for a few minutes while Annie replaced her, and Sarah was put on a stretcher before being lifted into the ambulance. The door was closing when Alyssa suddenly called to Leighton. 'You'd better call Jamie and tell him what's happened in case you're late getting to the wedding. Or do you want me to do it?'

'I'll do it once Sarah's at the hospital. My suit's in the car. I'll need a bathroom.'

'Use mine.'

Good thinking, Alyssa. You need a shower too.

The unit wasn't large when it came to two people using the bathroom and getting dressed for a wedding at the same time. She shrugged. They'd manage. She didn't have to worry about doing her make-up as she and the other girls had been to the spa earlier in the day before getting their hair done by a hairdresser who'd moved over from Wellington to set up a wedding business.

Leighton nodded and disappeared into the back of the ambulance.

Alyssa crossed over to his car. They just couldn't avoid bumping into each other. When she'd first found out he was part of the wedding proceedings she'd assumed she'd only see him whenever everyone got together for a meal or to go somewhere. Showed how wrong she could be. Leighton had a knack of turning up everywhere she went. She enjoyed his company, but mostly she wanted to keep her distance because her heart did feel vulnerable. This was supposed to be a holiday where she relaxed and had fun with her friends, and yet she was starting to look out for Leighton wherever she went.

'I *have* missed him,' she said as she swung the car around to follow the ambulance. 'More than I knew.' Was it because she'd been so busy with work she hadn't had much time to get to know a man, or give one more than a passing glance, and Leighton was here and she knew him and didn't need to go through the basics of finding out more about him?

Don't forget he let you down in the end.

They'd let each other down, but that didn't give him a 'get out of jail free' card. He'd hurt her with his endless hours of work and study. Now she knew there'd been far more behind it, it was still hard to accept that was reason enough to keep her at arm's length. Then there was the way his father had behaved, as though he'd done nothing wrong and it was everyone else's fault. Typical John.

How that must've devastated Leighton. He believed in his family, and had loved them wholeheartedly. As he'd claimed to love her. But with the revelation about Jamie and what his parents had done to keep that a secret, he'd hidden his feelings and hurt from her. He hadn't put the facts out there for her to be able to reassure him he'd still mattered to her, that she'd still loved him as much as ever.

While she was wondering why he didn't come home for meals or want to spend time with her, or go out with their friends, he was avoiding her because of his problems. They'd both thought they weren't what the other wanted any more. She'd been playing catch-up after spending years studying and had wanted Leighton to be a part of that. She hadn't liked it when he was always too busy to be with her, yet she should've understood. He was only working hard as she'd done. What would've happened if they'd just sat down and talked through their concerns? Would they still be together? Or would they have decided it was too tough and still broken up? Lesson for the future—always talk about problems.

Following the ambulance up the tree-lined,

narrow, windy road to the hospital, she shook her head. It was still hard to imagine Leighton living in Rarotonga, even if only temporarily. It was a wonderful place and she knew she'd be back again in the not too distant future for another holiday, but, for a man who liked to be non-stop busy, the laid-back lifestyle of the islands didn't fit him. But she was thinking about the man she'd known four years ago. Leighton today seemed more relaxed and accommodating of others. As though it wouldn't matter which side of the bed he slept on, only that he had a side. She sighed. 'Oh, Leighton, who are you?'

Pulling into a parking space outside the emergency department, she got out of the car to cross over to the ambulance where medical staff were crowding around to offload Sarah. Leighton stepped down and began talking to a man in scrubs, most likely the surgeon he'd spoken to on the phone. Lucky for Sarah he was available as there weren't many specialists in any field working here.

Another car pulled into the parking area and Sarah's friend leapt out. 'How is she? Is she going to be all right? Where are the doctors?'

Alyssa answered. 'They'll take her in the emergency room. I think that man talking to Leighton is the general surgeon and he'll see to Sarah.'

'This is awful. I told Sarah to be careful. She should've handed the scooter back when she made the mistake of accelerating rather than braking the first time, but she's so stubborn.'

'Take it easy. These things happen, and now you need to focus on being strong for her. Go inside and I'm sure the nurses will keep you posted on what's happening.' She walked beside the distraught woman until she veered off to head for the entrance to the department.

'All the best,' she said but doubted she was heard. It was hard for anyone to see their loved one in serious trouble as Sarah was, and knowing the local hospital wasn't set up with all the modern equipment for every scenario only made it more difficult to deal with.

'Thanks, Phil. If you're sure you don't need me, I'd better get cracking. Time's speeding by.' Leighton turned to her, looking relieved. 'I'm not needed.' He wouldn't want to miss the wedding, but if there hadn't been a doctor to take over with Sarah he wouldn't have hesitated to step up. Being the best doctor possible was always a big part of his make-up, one she'd admired and was glad hadn't changed.

'Here.' She passed him the car key. 'You're going to have to rush getting ready. Time's running away on you.'

'On you, too. I know you want to be there for Collette as much as I do for Jamie.'

Yes, she did, but it wasn't quite the same being Collette's friend as Leighton being Jamie's brother and groomsman. 'Let's go.'

The main road circling the island was busy with locals and tourists in cars, on scooters, walking along the roadside. The speed was slow and Leighton's frustration was rising.

'Did you call Jamie?' she asked.

'Yes. He said don't panic. They'll hold off until we get there. As long as we aren't going to be hours.'

'I'll send him a text to let him know you're on your way and that you need a thirty-second shower and you'll be ready.' Her fingers flew over the keys.

'That long?' He flicked her a quick smile. 'How long are you allowing yourself?'

'I don't have to be there as soon as you, so I'll take a minute.'

Leighton slowed for a turning car, accelerated away again. 'I'm not going without you. Collette will murder me if I leave you behind.'

'The bungalow's only a hundred metres from the wedding site on the beach. I'll be right behind you.'

'You'll be beside me, no argument.'

She shook her head. This was more like the

old Leighton. He was going out of his way to make sure she understood she was turning up with him. She wasn't asking why. She mightn't be able to cope with the answer, though it was probably because he felt guilty for dragging her to the hospital so he'd have a car to get back here. It wasn't as though he'd want her on his arm whenever he wasn't with Jamie. Which was a shame. It would be fun, and exciting.

Stop it.

They were turning into the resort car park as her phone pinged.

'Jamie says not to panic. Everyone's relaxed and having a glass of bubbles while they wait. Sounds idyllic. Bring it on.'

'You're relaxed about this,' he said with a smile that touched her heart.

He was right. She did feel comfortable with him and the urgency to get ready for the wedding wasn't bothering her.

'Whatever.' She shrugged and headed to her room to get ready with Leighton right behind her. There went the relaxed feeling. Her muscles were tightening. He was going to share her minuscule bathroom, her bedroom and the very air she'd be breathing. Things were looking up.

Leighton was buttoning up the white shirt that was the same as Jamie's for the wedding as he walked out of the bathroom after a fast shower. He stumbled at the sight before him.

Lyssa was stepping into her dress, her lace-covered breasts standing proud and reminding him how he used to cup them in his hands as his fingers caressed her nipples.

He gasped.

She spun around to face him full on, her face reddening instantly. 'Leighton, I thought you were still in the shower.' Then she blinked, and turned away.

Her back was satiny, her skin another memory long buried with all the pain of the past. Only these memories were firing him up fast. One step and he'd be close enough to bring them to life. And get walloped in the process. Along with looking crass. 'Sorry, I didn't mean to burst in on you.' He'd insisted she go first in the shower and now she was out here still getting ready. Turning away, he stepped back into the steamy bathroom. He was hardening fast. Hell, he needed another shower—a cold one. There wasn't time. But he couldn't walk back out there. She'd know he was hot for her. Bet that'd shock her.

'Leighton, I need the bathroom mirror as soon as you're done,' she called loudly. Too loud, as if she was embarrassed and trying to hide it.

'Sure. I'm finished in here.' He combed his hair with his fingers and headed back out to the lounge where his shoes were. Hopefully he looked all right. He wasn't hanging around in the cupboard-sized bathroom with Lyssa standing before the mirror fixing her hair or make-up or whatever it was she thought needed sorting. He couldn't fault a thing about her. She looked beyond beautiful. Her eyes were bright green and her face was open and happy. His heart went into overdrive.

'You've missed a button,' she said, looking anywhere but at him, but she had to have taken a look to know that.

So she wasn't entirely immune to him. He shouldn't give a damn, but unfortunately he did. She got to him far too easily, upsetting his equilibrium with a glance or a smile when he was determined to get through these few days without falling for her all over again. How was that going? Not so well if his erection was any indication. That had better back off, if nothing else. He had a wedding to attend. Time to get cracking. His brother needed him fully focused on the wedding and not taking an interest in one particular guest.

He cursed. He'd been adamant Alyssa would walk across to the venue with him. Going ahead without her now wasn't happening. Sitting down, he finished tying his laces.

'Let's go.' She headed to the door, her back

ramrod straight and her head high. Not Alyssa as he remembered fondly, though her long thick blonde hair falling over her shoulders and down her back more than made up for that. He liked this tougher version a lot.

Swallowing hard, he followed and waited while she locked the door. Then, taking her elbow, he escorted her to the wedding venue, where he led her to a seat before joining his brother for his important day. 'Hey, man, you look very dapper.'

'Dapper? I was hoping for sexy.' Jamie shot him a nervous grin.

'If I'd said that you'd have been worried.' Leighton laughed. Though it sounded a little hollow, because his eyes were on Lyssa as she talked to Andrea. The years since they'd gone their separate ways had been good to her. She'd matured into a confident and strong woman and her beauty reflected the changes from the pretty girl he'd married. He'd loved her so much back then. What was to say he couldn't again? Or was that still?

Jamie nudged him none too gently. 'Glad you're with me, Leighton.'

Which brought him back to why he was here. This was his brother's wedding day, and he shouldn't be thinking about his, no matter how hard it was to ignore. 'I wouldn't be anywhere else.'

The marriage celebrant, Clara, joined them. 'Collette's on her way. Time to get your special occasion under way.'

Collette was walking towards Jamie, holding her father's arm and beaming as though she couldn't be any happier.

Which he presumed she couldn't. Leighton felt a twang of longing in his heart and his eyes searched Alyssa's face as she watched her friend walk up the hibiscus-strewn aisle set between the guests' chairs. She brushed at her eyes and glanced his way, quickly looked back to Collette as colour stained her cheeks. Remembering their day too? Or was he making it up to suit his own feeling of missing out on love? Love that was all about Alyssa.

'Welcome to Rarotonga and this special occasion, everyone.' Clara smiled around at the group of friends and family. 'I am honoured to be marrying Jamie and Collette today.'

It seemed only minutes before Clara asked, 'Collette Brown, do you take Jamie Campbell to be your lawfully wedded husband?'

'I do.'

'Jamie Campbell, do you take Collette Brown to be your lawfully wedded wife?'

'I do.'

Clara nodded at Leighton and he dug in his pocket for the tiny box with the two rings. Opening it, he held it between the happy couple, and was stunned to see his hand shaking. From happiness for his brother, or because of the longing filling him, he didn't know. One thing he *was* sure of was one day he wanted to be standing in Jamie's place, telling the woman he loved how much he cared for her.

As he'd done once before. Look where that ended up. Not good. He'd been so sure he'd found his lifelong partner. His for ever love. Possibly he had and then thrown it away without thinking through the consequences of what he was doing. Leighton stared sightlessly at the ground. Was that true? Really? He had withdrawn from Alyssa when there had been more going on than just his reaction to Jamie turning up in his life. He'd found he had insecurities about trusting anyone with his heart after his parents showed their true colours. If only he'd realised back then, things might've been different now. Happier for one.

Loud clapping and cheers cut through his maudlin thoughts. Quite rightly too. He shouldn't be thinking about himself, today of all days. 'Congratulations, Collette, Jamie. I wish you every happiness.' He hugged Collette. 'Now I have a sister.' Then he slapped Jamie on the back. 'Well done.' He stepped away so others could move in and bumped into Alyssa. 'Sorry.'

She smiled crookedly. 'No problem. That was very moving.' Moisture sparkled at the corners of her eyes.

He nodded, afraid to speak in case he sounded too emotional. All very well feeling like this, but showing Alyssa would only make her see how much he cared and he needed her to think he was still an aloof man or else she might think there was more to his time spent with her than he intended.

'Leighton.' Her hand wrapped around his, warm and caring. 'You're allowed to be emotional. This is your brother's day, and you two are close.' She'd remember he didn't do showing emotion very well. Sometimes she'd complained that he was too aloof, and that protecting his feelings was unnecessary, especially with her. Even on their wedding day, he'd kept his feelings under control until they were alone in their hotel suite. Could be that deep down he'd always known something wasn't quite right between his parents no matter how hard they tried to hide it.

Right now, when he didn't need it, warmth spread through him from her touch and her understanding. 'You're right.' If only that were all this was about. But she'd only guessed the half of it.

'It's awesome you've got a sibling. I've always wondered what it would be like, though I never felt hard done by being an only child.'

'It's special.' He was having no trouble saying what he felt about Jamie, which was a worry. She'd better not ask how he felt about her, because she was still in his heart and there was nothing but trouble to be gained if he told her.

Her head dipped in acknowledgement. 'I imagine it is.'

'Here, you've smudged your mascara.' He dug in his pocket for a clean tissue and gently wiped the black stain from her cheeks. It would be too easy to drown in those beautiful emerald eyes. Stepping back, he pocketed the tissue. 'There you go.'

'Thanks.' She blinked twice, but not before he saw another tear appearing.

His heart expanded. How could they have broken up?

Then she looked to her friend. 'Hey, Collette, congrats. You look stunning. That dress is perfect for you.' Lyssa wrapped her arms around the bride and hugged her tight. 'You made me cry when you read your vows.'

Collette laughed. 'Nearly bawled myself. I am so lucky.'

'So's Jamie,' Lyssa returned. 'Be happy.'

'Where's the champagne? I could do with a

cold drink now my nerves have calmed down.'
Collette laughed some more.

'I'll get the waiter to bring some over,' Leighton said, needing to put space between him and
Alyssa after touching her cheeks. That reminded
him of the happiness and love that had filled him
when Lyssa had said 'I do' to him. It had been
the most wonderful moment of his life. Now *his*
eyes were moist. If only he could find that love
again, but it was unlikely.

With a heavy heart Alyssa watched Leighton
stride away. On their wedding day she'd truly
believed nothing could come between them, and
she'd thought Leighton felt the same. He did. She
was sure of it. Which only went to show even
the strongest love could go sour.

'He looks gorgeous in that white shirt and
black pants.' Collette stood beside her.

He certainly did. Especially that firm butt.
'Hey, concentrate on your man. He's pretty
hot too.' Not a patch on Leighton though. She
grinned. She felt good. The way he'd touched
her face to remove the mascara was so soft she'd
nearly cried.

Come on. You did cry.

'Yeah, I know.' Collette chuckled. 'Bring on
the night games.'

'You're supposed to enjoy the wedding feast and all the speeches first.'

'Of course, but the anticipation will grow with each passing hour. Ah, just what I need.' Her friend took a glass from the tray a waiter was holding in front of them. 'Thank you.'

Lifting one for herself, Alyssa tapped it against her friend's. 'Congratulations again. You deserve to be so happy.'

'So do you.' Collette tapped back.

They sipped their drinks.

'Go mingle,' Alyssa said. 'Everyone wants to hug and congratulate you.' She turned away and wandered to the end of the deck to lean on the railing and stare across at the reef. It would be perfect if a whale leapt up high right now. Like an acknowledgement of the words the bride and groom had shared—life was wonderful if you trusted it.

Rarotonga was perfect for a wedding. Turning around, she leaned back and watched the happy couple being swamped by family and friends, and felt happy. Truly happy. Those two deserved this. Everyone did. Including herself. One day she'd try again.

Would she though? Did she want to take that gamble and risk being hurt again?

Her eyes sought out Leighton. He was with Dan and the other two doctors with their partners from Nelson. Yes, she did. Leighton was gorgeous. Hot as hot could get. Her breasts rose on a deep inhale. Nothing had changed there. He'd always turned her on in an instant without even trying. She'd never known a man like him for making her come alive, before or since. Definitely a hard act to follow.

He looked around, locked eyes with her and waved her over. 'Come and join us.'

Good idea. Standing here on her own wasn't the way to celebrate. Not when she had friends to enjoy the occasion with. Did that include Leighton? Were they friends? Or had too much water gone under the bridge for them to come back to friendship at least? 'I was taking a breather,' she said as she stepped up to his side. 'All those emotions are hard to shove aside.'

'Embrace them. It's all part of celebrating these two and their marriage.' He was watching Collette and Jamie make their way along the deck, stopping to talk to every person on the way. 'Glad it's not a huge wedding party or we'd be here all night.'

Laughter bubbled up. 'The sun is nowhere near the horizon, Late.'

'Late?' An emotion she couldn't recognise slipped through his eyes, and disappeared.

Oops. Damn. Her pet name for him when they were making out had come from nowhere, just spilled free, feeling natural. She stepped sideways, putting space between them. 'Sorry,' she whispered.

'Don't be.' He was watching her too intently for comfort. 'You're being natural. I like it,' he added with a twist of those delightful lips. 'I used to like how you'd say whatever popped into your head.'

Especially when they made love. Her face flamed. He remembered? Was he deliberately winding her up? Whichever, the temperature had just risen a lot of degrees higher than normal for this island. 'I need water,' she muttered and headed over to the table where Pepe was handing out glasses of champagne and sparkling water.

'You want more champagne?' Pepe asked, nodding at the glass she was carrying.

'Ah, no. Water please.' She hadn't even noticed she was still holding the glass. Leighton was getting to her too damned much. That was the problem because she was not getting together with him. She wouldn't even share a kiss with him. As much as she'd like to when she wasn't thinking about the consequences. Awkward when he lit up every nerve ending in her body just by breathing. But she could not be vulnerable again. She would not go through the pain of another break-up from him. Yes, it would be a break-up if they kissed and then turned their backs on each other.

'Looks like you're thirsty.' Andrea laughed as she waited for Pepe to pour her a champagne.

Alyssa shrugged away the problem of Leighton and laughed with her friend. 'I haven't had my H2O quota for the day.'

Andrea gave her the 'You're not fooling me' look. 'Let's go take a seat in the shade while those two get their wedding photos done.'

'Isn't it the perfect setting? I love how everyone's so relaxed and the sound of the waves crashing on the reef is a perfect backdrop.'

Talking too much, girl. Andrea's not stupid. She knows you're in a pickle and probably also knows it's all over Leighton.

'The photos will be awesome,' Andrea agreed.

Photos. Leighton would be in a lot of them. She looked around and sure enough, there he was, standing beside Jamie as the photographer made the wedding party smile and laugh. Her heart stuttered. He looked good enough to eat. Her mouth watered as she pictured herself touching his chest with her tongue, tasting and feeling that firm skin. How had she managed to walk away from all they'd had? It seemed impossible now. 'The people in the photo look pretty damned awesome, never mind the setting.'

'You think?' Andrea laughed and downed a large mouthful of her drink.

'I do,' she admitted. Hopefully Collette would give her a photo of Leighton to keep under her pillow. The water she gulped went down the wrong way. Everyone turned her way. Embarrassing, and made worse when Andrea slapped her back.

'You all right, Lyssa?' Leighton was there in an instant.

'I'm fine,' she managed through another cough. 'Carry on with the photo session. They're waiting for you,' she added gruffly, not needing his attention. Not when he'd been the cause in a roundabout way of her nearly choking.

'I'm done. It's time for Jamie and Collette to have some taken of them alone. Pepe, can I have a glass of champagne, please.'

Lifting both her glasses, she looked from one to the other, and shrugged. What the hell. It was her friend's wedding and she was going to have fun. She drained the water and put the glass on the table, then finished what was left of the champagne and held that glass out to Pepe. To heck with Leighton and the way her skin heated and her heart pounded when he was near. To heck with being careful. This was a day of celebration, not one to waste being serious.

'Alyssa, Leighton, over here,' Collette called. 'I want a photo of the four of us.'

Alyssa laughed. 'Yeah, sure.' Collette was deliberately causing trouble. For once she didn't care. She wanted a photo of her and Leighton together. Tucking her arm through his, she said, 'Come on.'

He didn't hesitate. 'Let's show her who's in charge.'

'Really?' Cool. He stayed at her side when they reached the happy couple and didn't go to stand by his brother. Then he put his arm around her waist and drew her closer. The photographer didn't need to tell her to smile.

CHAPTER FIVE

ALYSSA'S HANDS LAY on Leighton's chest as they swayed in time with the music coming from a guitarist and piano player. They'd stepped onto the dance floor with everyone else and initially kept apart, but the music had drawn them close and soon Leighton was holding her as she danced, and she hadn't been able to resist him any longer. His hands were on her waist, holding her ever so gently. Their movements were in sync as though they'd never been apart. This was bliss. She hadn't felt so happy in for ever.

Every breath she took filled her senses with Leighton: a new outdoorsy smell of the sea and sun, the feel of his muscles under her palms, the sound of his heart beating, the suntanned skin where the top buttons on his shirt were undone. This was Leighton. Familiar but different.

Brushing her lips on his neck, she inhaled deeply and closed her eyes and drank in the wonderful sensations rolling through her as his hold tightened.

'Hey,' he whispered by her ear.

'Hey, yourself.' They'd often said that when they were hugging one another. Nice to think some things hadn't changed.

The music ceased.

Their feet stopped moving, though their bodies still swayed to a beat of their own. Alyssa continued leaning against Leighton, reluctant to move away.

'Okay, folks, the bride and groom are leaving.' Pepe stood by the musicians. 'Let's give them a big send-off.'

Clapping and catcalls filled the night air as Collette and Jamie walked hand in hand towards the exit. They were laughing and looking so happy.

Alyssa's heart lifted and she ran after them. 'Collette.' Throwing her arms around her friend, she hugged her hard. 'Have an awesome honeymoon. Love ya.'

Collette hugged her back just as tight. 'Love you back. Make the most of the rest of your time here.' Her wink was glaringly cheeky.

'Yeah, right.' She turned away and bumped into Leighton, who placed a hand on her waist before reaching out to his brother.

'Enjoy yourselves. See you on your way home.'

Jamie nudged Alyssa aside to hug his brother. 'Thanks, man.'

Then they were gone.

'Feel like a stroll along the beach?' Leighton asked the beautiful woman beside him as Jamie and Collette disappeared from sight.

'Best offer I've had all night.' Alyssa chuckled.

He could think of a few more offers to suggest, but even he knew when to shut up. Sometimes. 'I thought they'd never leave.' It was nearly midnight and the bride and groom had finally left for the upmarket resort where they'd booked a room for the night before heading to Aitutaki in the morning.

'I reckon they were making the most of the occasion.' Lyssa kicked off her shoes. 'Am I glad to take these off. My feet are killing me.'

They did look red in places. He'd love to rub them. 'Let's go.' He could still feel the heat of her body as she'd danced with him. 'How long have you got the bungalow for?' he asked as their shoulders touched, sending a thrill of heat throughout him. This was Alyssa and he was happy.

'Until I go home next weekend. Management upgraded me until tomorrow, but I decided to splash out and continue staying in it. They had to shuffle guests around but they've been so kind.' She looked embarrassed.

'Why shouldn't they look out for you? You're part of a larger group and helped with the woman who fell off the bus.'

'It's still very good of them.' The embarrassment hadn't faded. 'I could've kept the booking the way it was, but I couldn't resist staying on in the bungalow.'

'Go you. Why not have a bit of luxury?'

'Because I'm saving hard for a house and it's hard to justify spending money on this.' She glanced at him. 'But I haven't had a holiday in for ever, and it's magical waking up in the morning and seeing the pool right there with the beach only a few metres beyond the boundary.'

She'd never had fancy holidays growing up. All her mother's earnings had gone on the basics, yet not once had he heard Lyssa complain. She said she'd had a wonderful upbringing and wouldn't swap any of it for a more comfortable lifestyle. 'Knowing you, you'll get that deposit no matter what.'

'It hasn't helped with house prices skyrocketing over the last couple of years but, yes, I will get there.'

'I believe you. Believe *in* you,' he added.

She tripped, straightened and looked directly at him. 'Thank you. Sometimes I wonder if I'm asking too much of myself, but then I remember how hard Mum worked to give me what I needed because it was important to her and she loved me, and I know I've got a great role model.' She blinked, and turned to walk along the beach.

It had been a day full of emotions. His heart felt lighter than it had in years. 'You only ever said good things about her.'

'I didn't tell you how she used to growl if I wore odd socks? Or when I left my broken hair ties lying around?' She giggled like the kid she must've been.

His heart swelled with longing. Alyssa could be so much fun when she forgot to worry about getting everything right. 'She sounds like a perfectly normal mother.' His used to throw paddies when he didn't keep his shoes in a straight line in the wardrobe. 'She'd be proud of you buying your own home.'

If he ever got to share a home with her again, he'd make certain he didn't stuff it up. As if that would ever happen. His stance sagged. What if they could put the past behind them and try again? What if it went belly up again? He couldn't face the thought of watching Alyssa walking away once more. But neither was it possible to walk along the sand with her and not have some connection. Holding his breath, he reached for her hand.

When her fingers tightened around his, his lungs expelled the air they were holding.

'Mum would've liked you.'

Knock him down. That was new. Alyssa never said things like that. 'You think?'

'I do.'

I do. The saying of the day. Except this one was a long way different from when Jamie and Collette said it.

'I'd like to have known her. She's such an integral part of who you are.' Alyssa had talked about her a lot when they'd first met, though over time she hadn't so much. He'd wondered, when they'd first started talking about getting married, if she'd hoped his mother might be as loving towards her. Not a chance. His mother was very guarded about who she loved. He had come to understand his mother a lot better since Jamie turned up in his life, but he'd never get his head around her staying with the man who'd been unfaithful to her. It was beyond comprehension.

Alyssa looked around as they continued strolling along the beach. 'Mum worked so hard to raise me and make sure I never went without the basics.' Another pause.

He sensed she wanted to get something off her chest, so he kept quiet, giving her time to put into words whatever was making her hand tighten around his.

'I always felt I had to emulate her. Had to be as focused, as determined, so that having fun came way down the list of what I was allowed to do.'

Light-bulb moment. 'So when you qualified as a nurse and could toss the study notes aside you wanted to let your hair down for the first time.'

'You're onto it.' She sounded surprised. Then she laughed. 'Of course you are. You're smart.'

'I wasn't at the time. At the time I only saw it as you not happy being stuck at home while I was working all hours to get through my rosters and studies.' Something else he'd let her down over.

'Don't start blaming yourself, Leighton. I never explained how I felt. I don't think I really understood myself back then. I'd always been a good girl, trying to please Mum because she worked so hard, and after she died nothing changed. I owed her for all she'd done for me, and when she left me the wherewithal to go to polytechnic and become a nurse there was no way I was going to let her down.'

'Eventually the bubble had to burst.'

'So it seems. Not that I became outlandishly bad, just started to enjoy partying and time at a bar with friends.'

'And now?' He hadn't seen her being outrageous or over the top or getting drunk and making a fool of herself while here.

'Now I work a lot of hours and play up very little. More like the old Alyssa with a few exceptions.'

Turning to her, he smiled as he tried to ignore the way her beautiful eyes were focused on him as if there were nothing else to be seen, tightening him where he shouldn't be. 'I could never imagine you not working hard, but I also see a more confident and relaxed Alyssa.'

Her laughter was a tinkling sound causing heat to rush up his spine. 'I've grown up.'

'And some. You know who you are now, and what you want from life.' Had she had another relationship after they broke up? He didn't want to know if the answer was yes. Just the thought of her in another man's arms had goose bumps rising on his skin. Which was way out of line, considering they were no longer a couple. Obviously he hadn't let go of her as much as he'd believed.

Lyssa was gazing at him, a small smile lifting her lips and tipping his equilibrium further. That mouth. Damn but he'd missed her kisses.

He leaned closer, needing to share the air she was breathing. She wound him up while making him wonder what it would be like to kiss her again. Give over. He knew what her kisses were like. Had never forgotten the hot, tantalising sensations that her mouth provoked. But that was then. This was now, here on the beach under a zillion twinkling stars.

Her arms were reaching around him, pulling them together, their bodies touching breast to chest, thigh to thigh. Mouth to mouth. Tongue to tongue. Deep and touching, hot and exciting. Memories mixed with this new kiss. Hot, caring. Sharing.

Exciting.

Yes, her fingers were caressing his neck as they used to do, teasing, loving, hardening him. Lifting his mouth off hers, he whispered, 'Lyssa?'

'Yes, Leighton. Yes.'

Need mixed with relief and longing as he lifted her into his arms and carried her up the beach to the bank below an empty section. With every step he took Lyssa was kissing his neck. And he'd thought he was turned on. He was getting tighter by the second. 'Stop,' he growled. Or he'd never make it.

She laughed against his skin, hot breaths adding to his heat. 'Like that's going to happen.'

'No, seriously, I don't have any condoms with me.'

'It's okay. I'm on the pill to keep regular.'

He lowered her to stand in front of him by the

bank, his mouth covering hers, his hands sliding under the skirt of her dress, touching hot, silky skin. His groin pulsed hard, and heavy, and when he touched Lyssa's sex she was wet with need. He pulled his head back. 'You sure?' She had to be if she was that wet, but he needed to hear her say so.

'Absolutely.' Fingertips were tripping all over his chest, light as feathers, caressing, tightening him further as they headed south when he didn't believe it possible. 'Absolutely.'

He traced the outline of her breasts, first one, then the other, feeling her nipples harden under the light fabric of her dress. Sliding one strap down her shoulder, he followed it with his mouth, touching her there, everywhere. Feeling her skin heat and tiny bumps lift where he touched.

Lyssa worked at his trousers, undoing the front, shoving them down his thighs, over his knees to drop to his ankles. She sent his underwear in the same direction and he stepped out of it.

Hooking one leg over his hip, then the other, she wound her arms around his shoulders and opened herself to him.

He turned so he could lean against the bank, and breathed deep to absorb the scents that were Alyssa and the sea air. Magic.

'Make love to me, Leighton.'

Nothing could've stopped him from pushing into her warm, moist centre, and pulling back to push in again and again until he lost himself in her and felt her squeeze tight around his hard-on. When her heat increased and her body rocked, he waited for her to cry out as she always had. 'Leighton, now.'

Then he let go and joined her in forgetting everything but right now, this wonder that filled him with love. And then he forgot everything but being with her, and making love in this special place. It felt unbelievably good to be here. This was Lyssa, his woman, he was making love to and he couldn't be happier.

His chest rose and fell on harsh gasps for air. His head spun. Lyssa in his arms was special and wonderful, and he felt as though all his dreams had come together at once. Again.

'Let's go to my room.' Without waiting for his answer, Alyssa took his arm and headed back to the resort. Just as well they hadn't got far along the beach before they'd got caught up in each other and made love like something out of a dream because she could barely place one foot in front of the other. Her legs were weaker than wet bread. Thank goodness Leighton had his arm around her waist or she'd be a heap on the sand. Which wouldn't be too bad, given how warm it was out here. 'Why don't we go into the water and cool off?'

'Because we won't be able to see the rocks and coral in the dark and they can be seriously sharp if you kick them with your toes.'

'Sensible to the last.' She chuckled, not at all worried her idea had hit a wall. The bungalow was more comfortable and there was her spa pool to get into and cuddle up to him. 'There's champagne in the fridge.'

'Now you're talking. Though I have had a few today.'

'So have I.' It wasn't every day she attended such a romantic wedding. Or let her hair down and had so much fun and made love with a very sexy man. Another glass of bubbles, and maybe making love again, sounded ideal. 'What time are you taking Jamie and Collette to the airport?' How long could they stay in bed in the morning?

'Ten o'clock. But I'm going to call them an hour before to make sure they're awake and up, not lounging in bed together forgetting the time.'

They reached the steps up to her accommodation. Leighton turned and took her in his arms, held her tight. 'Let's not think about them. This is our moment.'

They were on the same page. She sagged against him, more than happy not to be thinking about anything or anyone but them. Stretching up, her mouth found his and she kissed him with all she had to give. This was special. Leighton was special. That was all she could think about.

When he swung her up in his arms again, she shivered with anticipation, her body already tingling with desire at the idea they'd make love again. On her deck, he paused. 'Want to sit out here? I'll bring the champagne out.'

'The key card's under the pot plant by the door,' was her way of saying yes, let's do this.

His smile made her heart swell. He was good-looking, but when he smiled that sexy smile he went beyond that to movie-star looks.

'Do you need me to undo your dress? It's very fitting.'

She could manage, but why give up an opportunity to have his hands on her? Spinning around, she lifted her hair and waited with her breath hitched in her throat.

When his fingers slid the zip down, as though one tooth at a time, tension tightened in her centre. She wanted him again. Already. It had been a long time since she'd known these sensations. With a quick flick of her head, she shoved that thought out of her mind. Now was for enjoying each other with no consequences.

'There you go.' His whisper against her neck sent shivers of longing all over her skin.

She'd only just had him and she was so ready again she ached. 'Leighton, please take me.'

He looked around. Her tiny deck was in darkness, the little spa invisible to anyone not in her unit. No doubt a deliberate move by the resort designers. His answer was to shuck off his trousers and toss his shirt onto a chair. Then he lifted her up and slid into the water.

She gasped. It wasn't too hot, but still a shock to her overheated skin. Under her hands little goose bumps rose on Leighton's arms. Seeking lower, she found his hard reaction and wrapped her fingers around him. Moving up and down in a slow, steady action, she leaned back and watched his eyes widen and darken as his need grew and grew.

Leighton pulled back. 'Wait, Lyssa. Not so fast. We've got all night.'

Magic to her ears. All night with this wonderful man. Her hand kept moving, up, down, up, down. But now it was hard to concentrate as firm fingers touched her, pushed inside her and found her button. Her back arched, her mouth dried and she cried out as everything came together and sent waves of desire rolling through her. 'Leighton,' she whispered through clenched teeth. 'Leighton.'

* * *

The sun was streaming into her room when Alyssa hauled her eyes open. Rolling over, she reached out for Leighton and came up empty-handed.

'Leighton,' she called.

No answer.

Where was he? Sitting up, she looked around for his clothes but they weren't there. So he'd left. What was the time? He had to take Jamie and Collette to the airport but it couldn't be that late. She never slept in past seven-thirty, even on the weekends.

Nine forty-nine.

Okay, seemed she could sleep past her normal time after a heavy night between the sheets. Leighton must've moved quietly. Or had she been that exhausted nothing would've woken her? Leaning back against the pillows, she grinned. It was possible. They'd had a big workout.

Coffee would be good about now, she decided. Picking up the phone, she called the restaurant and ordered one. 'Bacon and eggs too, please.' She was starving.

Leaping out of bed, she dived under the shower and washed away the night's activities. Next she put on a bikini and covered it with T-shirt and shorts, then made her way out to the deck with a book and sunglasses.

Life couldn't get any better, she decided as she sank onto a lounger. It was going to be hard leaving this to return to winter in Nelson. Not only winter, but the lack of a certain sexy man. Shoving those thoughts aside, she opened her book, but the words didn't make a lot of sense as memories of Leighton's hands on her body, his mouth covering hers, his sex pushing into her came to the fore. It had been a wonderful night. So good she wanted to do it all over again tonight.

'Here's your breakfast.' Pepe appeared at the side of the deck. 'Where do you want me to put it?'

'I'll have it out here, thanks. Do you know if Jamie and Collette have left for the airport?'

'Yes, Dr Leighton left to take them in his car about fifteen minutes ago. They were excited yesterday about going to Aitutaki. It is very beautiful over there.'

'So I've heard.' She'd like to visit the island but not on her own, and definitely not while the happy couple were on their honeymoon. They wouldn't want to be bumping into friends over the coming days. From what Collette had said it was a small island compared to Rarotonga and catered mainly for couples. There was a day trip she could do, which meant flying in, going on a boat and swimming with the fish, eating a gourmet lunch, and flying back to the mainland at the end of the day. Perhaps one day she might go with someone special.

The coffee hit the spot and she sighed happily. Her body ached a little as muscles that hadn't had a workout in a long time complained. Last night it was as if everything had fallen into place and there was nothing to get in the way of having fun with Leighton. Who'd have thought? Not her when she was packing her bags to come here. Even if she had been aware he'd be in the same place, the idea they'd get together would never have entered her head.

Where did last night leave them? They'd been all over the place since meeting up the night she'd arrived. On edge, then relaxed and comfortable with each other, then wary again. Yet last night there'd been no hesitation when they'd kissed. They'd gone from a kiss to making love in a flash. Not just once either.

For her, the romance of the wedding had filled her with longing and hope for a brighter future. A future that included someone who loved her. But that hadn't been the reason she'd been intimate with Leighton. He wasn't the future. At least, she doubted he was, despite how often she'd thought she still had feelings for him. It had to be a two-way thing, and Leighton hadn't shown any signs of wanting her back in his life other than for a bit of fun between the sheets, and on the beach or in the spa. Whatever.

She wasn't convinced she was ready to try again either. Losing Leighton in the first place had been horrendous, knocking her low confidence further down and making her question what she wanted in the future. But she'd overcome everything to get back on track. To risk losing that would be a huge step sideways, and she wasn't sure she could take it, though she certainly was tougher nowadays.

Was today going to be one of the cautious times? It was a little weird to have slept with Leighton, considering how they'd broken up, hurt each other, and not spoken in four years. Did they have a future, or was this a final farewell? What did she want to happen?

As she munched on crunchy bacon, she pondered the question. She wanted happiness, and, if the few liaisons she'd had over the years since Leighton were anything to go by, it wasn't easy to come by. Happiness for her meant love and trust and commitment. The things she'd believed she once had with her husband, only to learn that wasn't true.

'Help.'

'We need a doctor.'

Shouts came from down the beach.

Jumping to her feet, she shoved her phone in

her back pocket, locked the door to the bungalow and raced to the edge of the resort lawn.
Looking along the beach, she saw three frantic-
looking people grouped around someone lying
on the sand under some palm trees. 'Coming,'
she called back and leapt over the low bank to
run along the beach. 'What happened?'

'A coconut fell out of the tree and hit Matilda
on the head.'

'Are you a doctor?'

'Is she going to be all right?'

'She's not saying anything or responding to
my touch.' A man looked up at Alyssa.

The woman's head was at an odd angle and
blood poured from a deep indent on the right
side. Alyssa dropped to her knees. 'I'm a nurse.
Can someone run to the resort and ask them
to phone for the ambulance and a doctor? Tell
them it's urgent and that Alyssa is here, and if
Dr Leighton turns up I need him.'

The woman's pulse was hard to find, and
when Alyssa finally felt it her heart sank. It was
slow and getting slower. The head injury was serious. The impact from a coconut falling directly
onto her head would've been immense. What
to do? There wasn't a lot she could do about the
head injury, except keep it as clean as possible.
Sand was a problem. Looking around, she said,

'I need a towel or scarf, something to cover her head injury.'

'I've got a packet of tissues.' A packet appeared in front of Alyssa.

'Thanks.' Better than nothing, though there was a likelihood the tissue would stick to the wound and need cleaning away before doctors could do anything else.

'Here, use my shirt.' A man handed her his top. 'It's clean.'

Better than tissues. 'Thank you.' She carefully placed the garment over the injury. Where was the ambulance when she needed it? Stop being impatient. The hospital was fifteen minutes away. Hard not to worry when the woman was in such a serious condition. Her pulse was not improving, though Alyssa would have been surprised if it did without any medical input. There was nothing she could do except keep monitoring the woman and be prepared to do CPR if the worst happened.

There were moments when being a nurse sucked. She hated feeling useless, and would feel worse if the woman didn't make it.

'Hey, give me the rundown.' Leighton had arrived.

'Phew.' Her heart thumped with relief and something more personal she didn't have time to think about. Though she was aware she was no longer dealing with a serious trauma on her own. 'Major head trauma, pulse weak and fading. Unconscious and no reaction when I touch her.'

'Straight to the point. I like that.' Leighton was down beside the woman, lifting the shirt to study the impact injury, already assessing everything thoroughly. As she'd expect of him. 'Pepe says the ambulance is less than five minutes away. The crew were on standby at the football field.'

'Thank goodness. This woman needs to be in hospital asap.'

Leighton's fingers were gently touching the woman's scalp everywhere. 'Agreed.' He met her gaze with a steady look that said he knew she'd understand. 'We can't do anything here, except be prepared.'

In other words that hopefully the onlookers didn't get, the woman was at risk of dying and needed a lot more help than was available. 'I'm ready to do CPR.'

His smile was tight as he nodded. 'I'll call the hospital, alert them to what's coming.' Standing up, he stepped away with the phone pressed to his ear.

'What's happening? Why isn't Matilda moving?' asked the woman who'd handed her the tissues.

'She's unconscious,' Alyssa explained. 'Her

body is coping by shutting down everything but her vital organs to keep functioning.' Fingers crossed that was the case and those organs weren't shutting down too.

'Is she going to be all right?'

The dreaded question Alyssa hated. 'We're doing what we can.' Which was very little. 'The ambulance isn't far away and once she's in hospital she'll get the best care.' She'd probably be flown to New Zealand as soon as it was possible to arrange the medical aircraft to fly up here.

'The ambulance's here.' Leighton was back and tapped her shoulder lightly. 'I want you to come with us to the hospital, Lyssa. Just in case,' he added quietly so only she heard.

'No problem.' Of course she'd be there for him and their patient. 'Can someone follow us to the hospital? We're going to need your friend's details.' She didn't have time to put them into her phone.

'I'll go there now,' the man who'd handed over his shirt answered. 'Just need to get to the house we're staying in and get my motorbike. Her name's Matilda Maguire.'

'See you there.' She moved to take a corner of the stretcher once the woman had been shifted onto it.

It wasn't easy walking over the sand with a heavy weight balanced between four people trying hard to keep the stretcher steady so as not to move the woman at all, but finally they were on the path and heading to the ambulance. The heat felt intense and Alyssa could feel the sweat popping out on her forehead, but nothing mattered more than getting Matilda into Theatre without any further injury.

Two minutes down the road Alyssa called out, 'No pulse.'

Leighton was onto it, grabbing the defibrillator he'd already primed to save time if needed. 'Stop the ambulance,' he told the driver. 'Stand back, Lyssa.'

Matilda's body jerked as the current hit. The flat line rose and fell, albeit slowly.

'Better than nothing,' she muttered to herself.

'Agreed,' Leighton said.

The ambulance driver pulled out and drove carefully. It seemed to take for ever before they were backing into the parking space outside the emergency room at the hospital, and Alyssa could feel her muscles tightening all the way. She heaved a sigh of relief when they finally stopped. Now Matilda would get the help she needed. Or more than she'd received so far.

As Leighton climbed out of the back of the ambulance he told her, 'If I ever need a nurse to save my butt, I want you.'

Warmth spread throughout her. The compliment meant so much coming from him.

'Let's go to town for brunch,' Leighton suggested when Matilda was in hospital and there was nothing more they could do. 'I never got to have breakfast. Slept in and had to race to get the happy couple to the airport in time.'

'My breakfast's sitting on the table on my deck. I'd barely started when I heard the shouts from the beach.' She shivered. 'It was awful seeing her lying there.'

Leighton wrapped an arm around her shoulders. 'It wasn't good. They've already arranged for the Life Flight to come up from NZ.' He'd felt so helpless not being able to do much for Matilda but at least she was in good hands.

'That's the best news. Who'd have thought a walk along the beach could go so horribly wrong?'

'I should've warned you. That's the second time I've attended a person hit by a falling coconut. The nuts are huge and hard as rock. There's nothing forgiving about their impact. Never lie on the beach beneath a palm tree.'

Another shiver rippled through her. 'Believe me, I won't. I heard it was wise to avoid going under the palms, but today was an eye-opener.

The chances for Matilda of making a full recovery are slight.'

His hand tightened on her shoulder. 'I hate these cases. Which is why we need to do something to take our minds off it. Let's go relax over coffee and food, and then check out the market.'

'Why not eat at a stall in the market? I've been told the food's wonderful.'

He was more than happy to oblige. 'Waffles for me.'

'Make that two and we've got a plan.' She moved sideways out of his arm and took his hand in hers. 'Luckily I stuffed my phone in my pocket when I heard the shouts. There's a bank card in the cover. I might buy a few knick-knacks to support the locals too.'

'Things you take home and put in a cupboard never to come out again?'

She laughed. 'You're onto it.'

His heart soared. That was a sound he loved to hear. He'd missed it over the years. Hell, he'd missed a whole heap of things about Alyssa. But they were rapidly making up for lost time. The lovemaking had been wonderful, and exhausting in a heart-shaking, head-softening kind of way. They'd gone from wary to fully involved in such a short time. He knew he should be cautious, but it'd been so long since he'd fully relaxed with a woman.

Since he'd last been with Alyssa in fact. The women he'd dated over the intervening years hadn't affected him in the way she did. Alyssa was no ordinary woman. She'd already stolen his heart once. Not that he'd let her get away with that again. He hadn't completely got over the feeling he might be pushed away once more if he made another faux pas. That didn't mean they couldn't have some fun while she was here. He might even feel comfortable enough to think about what he really wanted going forward.

'How do we get to town? I don't see a taxi anywhere.'

'Follow me.' He tugged her hand, and led her around the corner of the building where a guy sat in a van. He was a cleaner at the hospital, plus the on-hand driver for any of the staff caught out without a vehicle for whatever reason, and he also picked up freight from the airport and seaport whenever it came in. 'Hey, Tomo, can you give us a ride to the market?'

'Sure thing. Hop in.'

'Tomo, this is Alyssa. She's here for a wedding. She's also a nurse and was there for the woman hit by a coconut this morning.'

'Hi, Alyssa. I heard about that. Not good for lady, or Rarotonga. Are you all right?' he asked.

She nodded. 'Yes, but I don't like seeing anyone seriously injured. It's always hard to take in.'

'I could never be a nurse,' Tomo said. 'I cry when my dog gets hurt.'

'I totally understand.' Lyssa smiled and clambered into the back of the van. 'Sometimes I wish I was a florist or dug ditches for a living.'

'You been busy this morning?' Leighton asked Tomo.

'Nah. It's Saturday, man.' He laughed. 'Then again it doesn't really matter what day it is around here, they're all the same—quiet when they're not busy. It's not called Raro time for nothing.' He pulled onto the side of the road outside the market.

Leighton dug out his wallet and gave him some cash. 'Thanks, mate.'

Tomo shook his head. 'You don't have to pay me. I was bored.'

As if he'd take advantage of the guy. 'Sure thing, but take it anyway. I'll give you a call when we're ready to head back to the resort where my car is. If you're not available I'll grab a taxi.'

'I'll listen out for you.' Tomo waved and drove off.

Lyssa was looking around at the many tents and small buildings that made up the market. 'I can smell something delicious.'

'In other words, food. Come on. I know exactly which stall we're going to for our waffles.'

He took her hand as they walked into the melee that was the Saturday market.

'Do you come here often?' Lyssa asked with a frown. 'I never knew you to be into shopping, let alone mingling with large crowds.'

'I often come for breakfast. It's good sitting back watching the flow of happy tourists pouring through the area.' It was good to hear chatter and laughter and be able to talk to the people behind the counter when they had a moment to spare, as there were times when he got sick of his own company. The work in the medical centre didn't keep him half as busy as he'd thought he'd be so there were plenty of hours to fill in and not a lot to do.

'Are you enjoying working here?' Lyssa asked after they'd put in their orders at the waffle stall and grabbed an empty table.

'It's been an experience. The pace is way slower and everyone's friendly, but I miss having more to do at work and away from it.' He leaned back in his chair. 'I also miss the changing seasons. The temperature range is slight and when it rains it remains warm. Never thought I'd say I miss the cold.'

'What do you do when not at work?'

'Not a lot. I've done the sights, flown to some of the outer islands for a night or two, and climbed over the top of Rarotonga. That was fun. Very slippery and steep in places and when I was almost at the top I came across hens. Totally left field to me, but then this is Rarotonga.'

Lyssa looked pensive. 'I can see how you'd get antsy for some action. You never liked sitting around.'

'I'm not as obsessive about keeping busy as I used to be, but I don't like doing nothing either. I can't say I regret coming here though. It has been an experience I'll always remember fondly.'

'It might be a shock getting back into the rat race of home.' A smile broke out on her face. 'Here comes the food.'

It was only waffles, but they were damned good ones. Alyssa's company was the best part of the meal. Funny how relaxed they were together despite their past. Probably because last night had been magic. Making love with Alyssa made him feel whole again. But one night of magic did not make a lifetime plan. His trust issues remained. Trusting her not to reject him wasn't going to be easy. But he'd have to get there if he wanted to take this further. It would be a struggle not to wonder if she might up sticks and pack her bags if something went wrong between them.

And you're open to talking about anything and everything that touches your heart?

'Where have you gone?' the woman slowing his appetite asked.

'Not far.'

You're right opposite me.

But she didn't appear to have figured out he was thinking about her, and them. 'Want another coffee?'

She stared at him with an intensity that brought back other, not so pleasant memories. She knew he'd dodged her question, and in doing so had answered one of his own for himself. He was not ready to be completely up front with her. It would mean putting himself on the line. Even after such a short time in her company, if she said he was too like his father for her to stay around his heart would break.

He waited for her to pounce with whatever was bugging her, but in the end she merely said, 'Yes, another coffee would be great.'

Getting up, he went to order two, feeling daggers in his back. Great. Now where were they at with their day? She'd probably tell him to leave her to get on with checking out the stalls alone. And if she did? Leighton drew a long breath, and made a decision.

'I'm coming with you,' he told her when she said exactly that. 'I haven't really looked at what's on offer before.' Souvenirs didn't interest him, but keeping Alyssa company did. He wanted to spend as much time with her as work allowed over the coming days. Last night had been too wonderful to turn his back on. It wasn't because the sex had been out of this world, it was more about who he'd shared it with. Alyssa had him in her hand once again, and at the moment he was happy to see where that led them despite the glitch over what he hadn't told her. He wasn't ready for a full relationship and might never be, but to be back on good terms with his wife held a lot of appeal.

'I'm sure you'll be bored,' she retorted as she headed over to a small shop full of floral sarongs in every colour imaginable.

'I doubt it,' he replied in a lighter tone. 'I might end up with a couple of bright floral shirts.'

A twinkle appeared in those heart-stopping eyes. 'Bring it on.'

He relaxed. He was back in favour, albeit only a little bit. It was progress. 'That colour would suit you,' he said when she lifted a red and white sarong off the rack. 'Or that yellow one.'

'Shut up.' She grinned. 'I don't wear yellow ever.'

'How about green and black?'

'How about you look at some shirts in the tent next door?'

'Yes, mam.' He went outside and stood watching people wandering around with bags in their hands or on their backs. Everyone was casually dressed, making the most of the warmth. This was what he enjoyed most living here. The relaxed atmosphere backed up by wonderful nature.

But he'd be glad to get home too. The restlessness that had him taking the job in the first place seemed to have left him since Alyssa had reappeared in his life. She gave him hope for a more grounded future, though he still wasn't one hundred per cent certain where he was going to work once back home. Auckland didn't hold any appeal, and while Nelson did tempt him there was a problem with that now. Lyssa living there would mean he had to be prepared to be a small part of her life even if they went no further with what they'd started last night, because she was close to Collette and Jamie. There'd be no avoiding her all the time.

Did he want to? No. So was he prepared to open up and expose his fears? That was the big question. The question he had no definite answer for, and wasn't ready to consider yet. If he ever would be.

'Next I want to find a sun hat.' Lyssa was swinging a bag at her side. 'Then maybe one of those small carvings to put on my sideboard. Or in the cupboard you mentioned, never to be seen again until I move into my house.'

Her house. Lyssa had moved on with her life better than he had. But she didn't have the distrust issues he did these days. 'Seems you've settled in Nelson for the long haul.'

She flicked him a wary glance. 'I have.'

He was pleased for her, and a little envious. 'I'm glad you've found somewhere you want to be, and that you're putting down roots.'

'I was always ready for that, Leighton.' There was an edge to her voice.

'You made our apartment look so homely it was always warm and inviting.' She'd repainted rooms and bought second-hand furniture that suited the place perfectly. He'd objected, saying they could afford new, but she'd claimed that she couldn't so when *she* was shopping second-hand was it.

'I had a lot of fun doing it up.' She looked wistful.

'Have you done the same where you are now?' He didn't even know if she lived alone or shared a flat with others.

'Not really. I haven't had a lot of time and I'm happy with most of the décor. I only rent anyway. Look at those.' She'd stopped at a stall selling colourful ceramic pictures of Cook Islanders going about their daily lives.

'Some of those would look good on your walls.'

'I reckon.' Lyssa held two in her hands and

was looking at others. 'These are amazing. I love that one.' It was a picture of three women dressed in sarongs with hibiscus flowers in their hair sitting on a grassy bank while talking and laughing.

'It's one of our most popular tiles.' The woman behind the table smiled.

'I'll take it, and these two.' Lyssa was still looking around. 'Plus that one on the wall behind you with the fishermen. Oh, and the one with the whale leaping out of the sea.'

Leighton shook his head. 'You should've brought your backpack.' Turning to the saleswoman, he said, 'I'll get her a bag for whatever she buys.'

'You don't need to do that,' Lyssa said.

'No, I don't, but I'm going to. One of the hessian bags,' he told the other woman.

'I might not be allowed to take that back with me. They might not allow hessian into the country.'

'It's all right. Tourists buy these all the time,' they were told.

'Now what?' he asked Lyssa once she'd paid for her souvenirs. 'Want to wander through town or head back to your bungalow?' They could sit out on the deck and watch the world go by on the beach. Or go inside and make love again.

'How about both?' She grinned.

She'd read his mind? The beach and making

love? No, she wanted to go through town. 'Give me that bag.' He reached for the one containing the ceramics.

'I wonder how Matilda is,' Lyssa said as they strolled along the pavement.

He'd been trying not to think about it. 'I hope no news is good news.' But it was doubtful the woman would have a good outcome.

Two minutes later his phone rang. He recognised the hospital's number. It was almost as though talking about Matilda had made this happen. 'Hello?'

'Leighton, it's Phil. I thought you'd want to know about the woman who was hit by the coconut. She didn't make it, I'm afraid.'

His heart plummeted. 'The brain injury was severe.'

'Yes. So much so I doubt whether she'd have ever recovered full cognition.'

'I'm sorry, Phil.' The surgeon would be hurting too. They all did when cases went belly up.

'Me too. Talk later.' He was gone.

Lyssa was watching him. 'Matilda?'

He nodded. 'She died.'

Lyssa blinked, looked away, drew a breath and looked back at him. 'That sucks.'

'It does. Terrible for the family. Here for a good time and this happens. Not fair.'

His hand was gripped tight. 'Let's go. Shopping doesn't appeal any more,' Lyssa said.

'I agree.' He looked around for a taxi. Nothing in sight. 'I'll call Tomo.' He wouldn't normally bother the man but right now he wanted to be away from the cheerful crowds. 'He's on his way,' he told Lyssa moments later. 'He'll meet us where he dropped us off.'

They turned around and headed back the way they'd come, hearts heavy.

Alyssa's arm brushed his. 'The joys of working in the medical environment.'

CHAPTER SIX

'IT'S STRANGE BUT those palm trees don't look so romantic now. The views are amazing, only there's a catch,' Alyssa said as she stood on the deck outside her room, then fell silent. Matilda hadn't lived to see another day, or any more amazing views anywhere.

Leighton came to stand next to her. 'Hey, it's all right. It's very sad, I know, but we can't watch every word we say because of it.'

'It never gets any easier, does it?'

'If it did then it would be time to get out of the medical profession.'

'True.' Move on. 'So whereabouts are you living?' She'd hoped they might've gone there rather than come back to the resort, but Leighton hadn't mentioned where he lived. Typical. Something else he wasn't sharing.

'In a small house about three kilometres back towards the hospital. It belongs to the family of the doctor I'm filling in for. It's great living with the lagoon only a few steps away and I can hear the surf pounding on the reef at night.'

'I haven't been off the main road yet. Bet there are some stunning views from up on the hills.' Hint, hint.

'You haven't exactly had a lot of spare time since arriving, what with the pre-wedding activities. Your hot little car hasn't done much mileage either.'

She gave up. 'It will over the coming days.' Andrea and Gina were flying out tonight to start back at work on Monday and she'd be on her own so she'd make the most of driving such a cute car. 'Are you starting back at work on Monday?'

'I am. It's going to be busy as there's a mammogram clinic happening over the week. A radiologist is due to arrive from home tomorrow and she'll read all the scans while here. There's no permanent radiologist in the country, all X-rays are usually read online, but they've done this so women will be more willing to come forward and be checked. At the same time, the medical centre runs a full medical check-up clinic for the women, many of whom don't visit a doctor unless it's urgent.'

'So the medical service here is tied into that back home?' It made sense since the Cook Islands were part of the realm of New Zealand.

Leighton nodded. 'Yep. Mostly it works except for serious illnesses and then the patient is flown to Auckland for treatment and follow up.' He paused to gaze out to the sand and lagoon beyond. 'Feel like a drink?'

'You know what? I'd love one.' It might help her relax after that awful news. 'But I haven't got anything in my fridge at the moment.'

'Take a seat and put your feet up. I'll go over to the bar. Be right back.'

It wasn't hard to do as she was told. The view was as stunning as the first time she saw it, and the air warm, plus she was shattered. They hadn't had a lot of sleep during the night, then throw in the shock of losing their patient and she was struggling to stay upright.

'Here, get some of this into you.' Leighton held out a glass of beer minutes later. 'Unless you don't drink lager these days.'

'Sometimes, and now seems like one of those. Thanks.' She took a sip and savoured the cold liquid on her tongue. 'I'll probably fall asleep next.'

'I have a plan.' Leighton laid a board on the deck table and then a small box. 'Remember one of these?'

'A chess set? Of course I do. We used to have a match whenever one of us was in the doldrums after losing a patient.' They'd played hard, winner take all, and it had helped negate the pain either of them had been in. 'That's a long time ago. I'll be rusty.'

He laughed. 'Good. I've played online occasionally but it's not the same as a current game with the opponent right here. Online games can take weeks and don't have the same buzz.'

She rubbed her hands. She was already feeling a little better. 'Let's do this.' Now was not the moment to let him know she'd played a few times recently with a patient who was on the ward for nearly four weeks and got bored easily. With a bit of luck she might've learned enough to beat Leighton for once. It didn't pay to get too cocky around him. He was smart and until she actually had him in a no-win position she'd stay quiet.

He tossed a coin and covered it with his hand. 'Heads or tails?'

'Heads.' Always.

'You win. But that's all you're winning.' He grinned.

'We'll see.' She made her first move, and sat back to wait for Leighton to take his turn, enjoying the light breeze touching her hot skin. 'This is nice. We don't often get a breeze here.'

'It's not usually what the tourists want.' He made his first move. 'There you go.'

An hour passed before Alyssa finally sat back with a smug smile. 'Got you.'

Leighton studied the board then looked over. 'You're right. You win. Well done.'

'Go on. Admit it. You're peeved.'

'Of course I am. I hate losing, and I've never lost to you.' He shook his head. 'Guess I had it coming.'

'Dinner's on you.' She laughed, then stopped. 'Thanks, Leighton. That was just what I needed.'

'Me too.'

'Where did you get the board from? I don't imagine you had it in the car.'

'There's a cupboard with board games in Reception. I took a look on the off chance there might be a chess set and voila.' He looked pleased with himself. 'Feel like a dip in the sea?'

'Good idea.' She pushed up out of the chair. 'I'll change into a bikini.'

His eyes widened. 'Perfect. I'll stay as is.' He'd been wearing knee-length shorts all morning.

'You carry a change of clothes in the car?'

'I do have a change of clean clothes at the ready. Never know when I'm going to get messy while helping a patient.'

'It's happened three times since I arrived,' she admitted. 'Which seems a lot.'

'Tourists do get up to some mischief at times. I thought you were going to change.'

'Impatient, aren't we?' She headed inside. Which bikini? The red one was her favourite, but the white one looked pretty good on too. No, the red one was better against her still pale skin.

'Woo-hoo,' Leighton whistled when she joined him.

Obviously red was perfect if the sexy look on his face was anything to go by. 'You like?'

'Like? I'm struggling not to rush you back to bed.'

'What's stopping you?'

'The housemaid's in the next unit and I suspect yours is next to be tidied.'

Nothing like cold water poured on her hot skin. 'Glad you noticed.'

'So am I, considering how turned on you make me.'

Her chest swelled. 'Let's hit the beach.'

'Where's the sunscreen?'

'Right there on the table.'

'Have you put any on?' he asked, picking up the tube.

'I was going to after I'd eaten breakfast, but got interrupted.'

'Turn around.'

Firm hands rubbed cream over her back and shoulders, increasing the heat in her veins. It was as though she was making up for the lack of sex over the last four years in twenty-four hours.

She hadn't been interested in getting down and personal with any man since splitting up from Leighton, always aware how good it had been with him. Suddenly her body was waking up, all because of him.

Leighton stepped in front of her and began covering her chest, neck and arms.

She groaned. She could not help herself. 'Stop or I'll drag you inside, to hell with the maid.'

He just laughed. 'Nope, we're going for a swim.'

She glanced down and laughed too. 'You can walk normally with that?'

'Damn you, Alyssa Harrison. I'll look like a waddling duck and everyone within sight will know why.' He dropped the tube on the table and swung her up into his arms. 'That bikini should come with a warning label.'

Harrison. No way.

'I'm Alyssa Cook.'

Leighton froze to the spot, then his arms loosened and she slid slowly down until her feet touched the deck.

A chill crossed her as she locked her gaze on him.

He looked bewildered and furious all in one.

She stepped back. 'Hello? You thought I'd be using my married name after all this time?'

'No, I didn't. I knew you weren't.'

'Then what's your problem?'

'I don't have one.'

'Try again, Leighton. Your body language tells a different story.'

Here we go.

'You won't talk about anything important, will you?'

'I got a surprise, that's all. It's a bit of a wake-up to what we're doing, despite being separated and all.'

She gasped. He didn't used to give sucker punches. But he might have a point. They had got down and sexy fast last night, with no thought about where it might take them. None on her mind, anyway. But still.

'We're having some fun, that's all.' Was it though? She wasn't looking for more? For something deeper to follow up on? Not likely considering they hadn't cleared the air between them. Sure, she'd heard how Jamie came on the scene and how that had affected Leighton to the point where he'd let her go, but he'd given her only a bare outline of what happened. Nothing about how deeply it affected him or what he hoped for moving forward.

'You're right, we were.' He moved further away.

'Were?' Time to draw a line in the sand. Except she needed to know why he was afraid to tell her everything that happened when Jamie turned up in his life. She needed closure, and suspected Leighton did too. 'Like we're not even going to see each other over the coming days?'

'It isn't that straightforward.'

'Meaning?' She'd make him talk, if at all possible.

He stared at her. 'You know exactly what I mean, Alyssa.'

It was impossible to get him to say what was really on his mind.

'We have a past.'

He didn't say a word.

'A past that blew up in our faces. But we still seem to connect when we're relaxed and not overthinking everything.' Like when they'd been making out on the beach or in her bed.

'I don't want to go there, Alyssa, so I'll head away now.' He was already turning away.

'Nothing's really changed,' she said sadly. 'Not that there's any reason it should've, I suppose.'

Leighton still kept personal issues close to his chest. If she got too involved it would only come back to hurt her. She could not face that for a second time.

She was right. Nothing had changed. He still hated opening up. Leighton slammed the car door shut. Even more so since he didn't know if he could trust her with his heart. Or if he even wanted to. Their marriage had failed, so what was the point? They weren't getting back together despite a fantastic time overnight and at the market.

His chest ached at the thought of not spending more time with Lyssa despite having walked away from her. He'd needed to clear his head and get over the hurt that slammed him in the heart when she said 'I'm Alyssa Cook' so fiercely. It was as though she was holding onto who she was and that she'd lost that when she went by his surname. It had meant so much when she'd taken it as hers. He'd never denied anything about her, always encouraged her to be herself so that was special. Now she'd reminded him that, while they were having fun, they were not a couple.

His foot pressed the accelerator hard and the car spun out onto the road heading in the direction of his temporary home. He did owe her an apology for being so abrupt and walking away. He also owed her an explanation, but first he had to figure out what was driving this need to get close to her and whatever it was preventing him making the move. Spending time with Lyssa felt good, and making love to her had been beyond wonderful. It had brought back happy memories and reminded him life didn't have to be so solitary if he opened up his heart.

If. It should be easier now she knew about his brother, but he was still afraid to let her see his fears, and that had become even harder after they'd made love. He felt close to her again, which only increased his worry.

I need to return to Lyssa and apologise.

The sound of a bird tweeting interrupted his dreary thoughts.

The caller ID on the screen of his phone said Amalie. He pulled to the side of the road. 'Hey, what can I do for you?' he asked the midwife from the medical centre.

'Mere Aro has been in labour for ten hours and now baby's the wrong way round.'

'I'll come. Where are you?'

'At the hospital.' Amalie hung up.

Yay, something to take my mind off Lyssa. He was almost grateful to Mere. Almost, but the woman would be desperate to give birth and worried sick that baby was stuck so he couldn't feel too pleased. Instead he needed to be the calm, confident doctor and not the man with a woman doing his head in.

Finally he laughed at himself, albeit a little sharply. As Jamie had said the other night, nothing ever went to plan. Though when it came to Lyssa, there weren't any plans other than to be friendly and try not to get too involved. Bit late for that after last night. He was already well on the way.

The road leading to the hospital came up on his right. Slowing to allow two tourists on mopeds to go past, he made a turn and headed up the hill.

'Glad you're here,' Amalie said the moment he stepped inside the birthing room. 'I think baby's getting desperate to come out.'

'Right, let's do this.' The sooner baby was here, the sooner Mere would be comfortable and holding baby to her breast. 'Hello, Mere. I hear you need some help.'

'You bet, Doc. I've had enough of this.'

'I'm sure you have.' Ten hours wasn't a long labour, but, as he'd been told in the past by various female nurses, he didn't know what he was talking about. He did know he'd hate it if his woman had to go through too many hours' labour. 'Where can I scrub up?'

Two hours later Leighton was home and mowing the lawn to keep busy. Baby Tepi weighed in at four and a half kilos and was very noisy. He was also very cute, and tugged at Leighton's heart strings when Amalie placed him on Mere's breast. If only he and Lyssa had stayed together, they might have had children by now.

The lawn done, Leighton went for a dip in the lagoon to wash off the sweat and cool down. He swam out to the inside reef and floated on his back, staring up at the endless blue sky. What a magical place. He loved it, but it wasn't somewhere to live permanently. Not for him. He needed more going on than happened here. Except for the past week. Plenty had happened. Where was Alyssa at the moment? Sunbathing in one of those erotic bikinis by any chance? She'd got him thinking about the future and how awesome it would be to have a life partner and even children. One look at her in that tiny red bikini and he'd wanted her. Just like old times.

Back on shore he walked the beach for a while, trying to ignore any thoughts about Alyssa. Finally he returned to the house and jumped under the shower, where he punched his fist into his other hand. 'Damn it. I give in. I can't ignore her any longer.'

Pulling on a white shirt and dressy shorts, he snatched up his keys and headed out. There was only one way to deal with the warring emotions going on between his head and heart. He had to see Alyssa.

Alyssa lay down on the lounger and closed her eyes. She stank of sunscreen but there was no way she was getting burnt.

She'd just returned from dropping Andrea and Gina at the airport for their flight home. On the way in they'd stopped at a popular bar on the beach for one final drink together in paradise. She'd opted for a soda as she was driving. Now she would relax and read the book she'd started on the flight over. So much for being a tourist and getting out and about, but it was nice to do nothing for a change. If only that included not thinking about Leighton's reaction to her putting the name she went by out there. Why wouldn't she go back to her maiden name?

Did she regret being so abrupt with him? No. She'd said it how it was. He wouldn't thank her for being a simpering idiot in an attempt to get on side again. It had come as a shock though, after how well they'd got on at the wedding and throughout the night. She'd begun to believe they might be able to make inroads into a deep and meaningful friendship. Silly woman. What was to be gained by doing that? They wouldn't pick up their marriage and carry on. It wasn't feasible. Leighton had to let go of his need to remain closed off to her because that said he didn't trust her. Until he talked she didn't fully trust *him* with her heart.

The gate leading into her area creaked. 'Hey, Alyssa, get your glad rags on. I owe you dinner, remember?' Leighton stood tall and proud, not showing a hint of remorse for what he'd said earlier.

She jerked in surprise. 'Really? After you walked out on me this morning?'

'Especially because I did. I'm sorry for acting like a sulky brat, Alyssa.'

But not sorry for not explaining himself. Did she bury this for now and enjoy an evening out with him? Or did she let her disappointment win and demand answers? It was a no-brainer. Making certain her bikini was in place, she sat up. 'Park your butt while I get ready.' She headed inside, paused and returned. 'There's a beer in the fridge if you want one.' Getting dressed and made up for a date took time. No way was she going out looking second rate.

His posture relaxed with those beautiful broad shoulders loosening and his chin softening with relief. 'Sounds good. I'll get it. Do you want a wine?'

'I'll wait until we're out wherever you're taking me.' Where were they going? There were a lot of great-looking restaurants all along the main road circling the island. Many of them were on the edge of the beach.

Leaping under the shower to remove the sunscreen, she tried not to smile too much. Leighton was taking her out. He'd also called her Alyssa.

It had to be a good sign or he wouldn't have bothered to show up.

Which dress to wear? There was only one she hadn't used so far. Sky-blue and slinky, a perfect match for the cream high-heeled shoes she'd given into buying while she was filling in time at the international airport earlier in the week. They'd cost an arm and a leg but were worth it. Though she'd probably rue the decision when she returned home and checked her bank account, something she refused to do while on holiday.

At a restaurant on the beachside they were shown to a table under the trees on a lawn that met with the sand. Terns danced along the beach and over the lawn, no doubt hoping for some crumbs from the diners.

'This is lovely,' Alyssa said as she gazed around. It got dark quite early but there were lights strung throughout the trees casting long shadows. 'Have you been here before?'

Leighton shook his head. 'I've thought about it but it's not a place to come on my own. I prefer company when going to a restaurant. That's not asking for sympathy. I'm just saying how it is. The locals I've got to know don't dine out often.'

'Aren't there quite a lot of expats here?' From what she'd read many of the bars and restaurants were owned by Kiwis and Australians.

'There are, and I've met a few, but they're usually working when I'm not.'

'Here you go. One wine and one beer.' Their waitress placed the glasses on the table. 'Ready to order?'

'Sorry.' Alyssa picked up the thin folder. 'I haven't looked at the menu. Too busy enjoying the scenery.'

'No problem. I'll give you a bit more time.'

Leighton handed her the glass of wine, and then tapped it with his beer glass. 'To making amends.'

She was over avoiding the issue. 'You believe it's that easy?'

He looked guilty. 'No, I don't.'

'Why is it so hard to talk to me?'

His fingers tapped incessantly on the table. Fear blinked out of his eyes, quickly covered by stubbornness then withdrawal.

Her heart went out to the only man she'd ever loved. He was hurting. She wanted to help. But to push further when surrounded by other diners could lead to an embarrassing altercation there'd be no coming back from. Leighton hated being the centre of attention. She'd give him some space. *Again*. Coward that she was. But that look in his eyes said she wasn't going to win tonight so she'd go for showing how much she cared about him.

Taking his hand, she held tight and found a smile. 'What did you get up to after you left me this morning?'

'I mowed lawns after I helped deliver a breeched baby,' Leighton said. 'A cracker of a little guy.'

The last of the tension gripping her slipped away. No matter that there were issues between them, she liked being with him.

'Aww. He's all right? Mum okay?'

'Absolutely. Everything went well and was over quickly.' He sipped his beer, staring outward. 'Is it wrong to say that seeing a new life come into the world helps cope with losing one? I'm not saying the baby replaces Matilda, but I did feel a little bit better.'

'I believe it's a natural reaction, and I admit just hearing about it makes me feel all soft on the inside.' A pity she hadn't been there to help and see baby's arrival.

Leighton was still gazing towards the water. 'I think Jamie and Collette intend starting a family fairly soon.'

'Collette hasn't said anything but then she's not one for talking about personal things much.'

'I'll be an uncle.' Longing clouded his voice, but whether for nieces and nephews, or for children of his own, who knew? Not her. They'd occasionally talked about having a family in the future when he'd qualified and had more spare time.

'Uncle Leighton. Sounds good.' Had he been in a relationship since they'd broken up? If he had it must be over because he'd made love to her. He was a loyal man and would never be unfaithful. He was not his father. She changed direction. 'Are the golf clubs getting dusty back home?'

'A little. Everyone's busy with family commitments these days. Jackie and Cain have two kids, Jordan and Maggie one, with another on the way, and Chris and Vicki's children are teenagers needing lots of attention.'

'Teenagers? Already?' They used to babysit those two when Chris and Vicki went on a date night. 'Time flies.'

'Sure does.'

Her hand touched her stomach. Would she ever be lucky enough to have a family? Having a man at her side came first, and so far she hadn't done very well there. The chances she and Leighton could give it another go were slim, if at all possible. 'You mentioned settling in Nelson. Does me living there give you cause for concern?'

He winced. 'Would it bother you if I did?'

'Answer a question with another one, why

don't you? Why can't you just say what's on your mind?'

Another wince. 'Fair enough.' He paused.

She waited him out. He could fill in the blanks this time. And if he didn't she would get up and walk away.

'I don't want to be in the way if we're not getting on. Chances are we'd always be crossing paths since you're friends with Jamie and Collette.'

'Then we'll just have to get along, won't we?'

'Are you suggesting I continue looking into moving to Nelson?' His eyes had widened a little.

'Hey, it's not a village. It's a small city, and there's also Richmond and Stoke down the road. We wouldn't be bumping into each other every time we went out of our front doors.'

'Right.' Leighton set his glass aside. 'Want to go for a walk?'

This was going nowhere. 'No, thanks.'

'Then I'll take you back to the resort.' Standing up, he reached for her hand and tugged her up against him. 'Thanks for joining me.'

'No problem.' It was actually. She was fed up with going round in circles. And she was tired beyond belief. Leighton was sapping all her energy, physically and mentally. Sleep was next on her menu. Alone. She was not making love with Leighton tonight. She did not know what she wanted with him at this point so she would tread carefully. No one else was going to protect her as fiercely as she would.

Parking outside the resort, Leighton hopped out and went around to open Alyssa's door. His head was spinning. They hadn't caught up on much of what they'd done in the years since they'd last seen each other, but he was learning more about Alyssa all the time. She was stronger, fending for herself rather than looking to others for support. She also seemed focused on what was right for her. He couldn't fault that, whereas he still kept things close to his chest, afraid to be vulnerable. If anyone could hurt him, it was Lyssa. But he did want more time with her, and, yes, to explain himself. If only he knew how without seeming needy. Slipping his hand around hers, he started for the entrance.

'I'll see myself in,' she said as she pulled her hand free.

'I always see my date to her door.' Not that he'd had a lot of dates lately. Couldn't get enthused.

'Fine.'

When he reached for her elbow, she stepped sideways, increasing the distance between them in more ways than one, underscoring the fact he had to talk to her.

At the bungalow she swiped the key card and opened the door, then, instead of going inside, wandered over to the edge of the deck to gaze up at the star-studded sky. 'It's so clear.'

Tipping his head back, he could only agree. 'Magical.' As was the citrus scent wafting from Lyssa, stirring his blood. They could be so good together. And he wanted her so badly it hurt.

Slipping his arm around her waist, he drew her nearer. 'Alyssa, I am enjoying catching up and getting to know you again.' It was true. She was the same yet different. She seemed to have accepted who she was, and what she wanted. When he'd met her, she was still coping with the loss of her mother and wondering what was out there for her. Not any more. This was one determined woman.

'Have I changed that much you are starting at the beginning?' A wobbly smile appeared.

Don't stall now.

'Yes and no. You're still the same Alyssa with the quick smiles and wanting to follow your dreams. But I think you now know what those dreams are and have the strength and determination to follow through.'

She blinked. 'That's deep.'

Well, she had accused him of not opening up. 'I'm trying to answer your question.'

'Fair enough.' Her surprise remained. 'Honestly, you're probably right. I do know what I want for my future, and in some areas I'm working hard to make it happen.'

'What about the others?'

'I'll have to wait and see.' She tipped her head back to look up at the stars again. 'That's so beautiful.'

So are you.

'I couldn't agree more.' Wrapping her in both arms, he dropped his chin on her head and breathed deep. Her warm body fitted against his as if she belonged there and made him feel he was finally coming home. Her hair brushed his arm and he held her closer, before leaning down to brush her mouth with his. 'Lyssa.' Then he kissed her.

She kissed him back. A chaste kiss.

Lifting his head, he looked down into those big eyes. 'Alyssa?'

Stepping out of his arms, she shook her head. 'Not tonight, Leighton. I would prefer to be alone.'

His heart stumbled. She didn't want him? 'It's all right,' he fibbed. The last thing he wanted was to leave, but he wasn't saying. She'd got to him without him realising just how much. She was probably doing him a favour by withdrawing. Except he wasn't happy. He wanted to be with her all night and into the next day.

'I need my sleep.'

He didn't believe that to be completely true, but he'd run with it. Arguing wouldn't solve a thing. If she didn't want to sleep with him, he had to accept that. 'Fair enough.' He turned towards the gate, then turned back. He felt vulnerable but the need to spend more time together was greater. 'How about we do something together tomorrow morning before I go into work to prepare for the coming week? I'd like to show you some sights.'

She hesitated, then nodded softly. 'That might be fun. Any idea where we'd go?'

Relief flooded him. And yes, he already had an idea. 'Leave it to me. I'll give you a call later in the morning, give you time to sleep in.' She never used to do that, was always up with the sparrows, but who knew now? Not him, but he was working on learning more about this wonderful woman.

'Leighton, dinner was lovely.' She placed her hand on his arm, setting his skin alight with longing. 'I just need space.' Then she placed a light kiss on his cheek. 'Until tomorrow.'

Again his heart lurched as lemons tickled his senses. It took all his strength not to haul her into his arms and kiss her senseless. But he couldn't. She'd said she needed time to herself and he would not intrude. 'Goodnight, Lyssa.' Yes, he used that name deliberately because he cared so much for her. 'Sleep tight.'

CHAPTER SEVEN

DESPITE THINKING SHE wouldn't sleep a wink, let alone tight, Alyssa woke late the next morning not remembering anything from the moment she climbed into her bed and switched off the light.

Stretching luxuriously, she grinned. 'Heck, I feel good.' The holiday was obviously having a good effect on her sleep pattern. As for Leighton, she wasn't sure if he was good or bad for her. How she'd managed to pull away when his mouth was on hers she'd never know. It had taken every last drop of determination, but she'd had to. Last night had proved once more he wasn't about to open up and tell her what she needed to hear. Sick of trying to force the issue, she'd backed off. Could it be that the harder she tried, the deeper he dug in to avoid the questions? But if she left him alone nothing would change. There'd be no future for them and she wanted one more than just about anything else.

It was hard to face. Leighton had always been

quick to tell her he loved her, to show his pain whenever he lost a patient, talk about what made families special. She'd loved that about him. He had changed in that respect. And she'd changed by not being prepared to accept him keeping quiet about what was important to them as a pair. He couldn't keep doing this if they were to have a future. If he wanted one with her, that was.

After ordering coffee she leapt under the shower, humming to herself all the time. She opted for a sun frock over a bikini since she had no idea where Leighton intended taking her. He'd surprised her with suggesting they go somewhere today. She'd thought he might've stayed away after she pulled away from him.

Her heart softened. He was the only man she'd ever loved and now she wondered if she might not have stopped loving him. He made her feel so good without trying, just by being himself. Kind, funny, generous, gentle and tough. Yes, and afraid. He had the power to break her heart all over again.

So stand up and fight for him. Demand answers. Refuse to be ignored. Show him you care, that you won't hurt him.

Yeah, and get hurt in return.

Pepe knocked on the door, coffee in hand. 'Don't you ever stop working?'

He grinned. 'It's the family business and I'm the only son.'

'You've brought two coffees.'

'One for Doc Leighton.'

'He's not here.' Blimey, were the staff keeping tabs on them?

'He's on his way. He rang to order coffee for you and him.'

Alyssa scowled. Seemed Leighton was one step ahead of her. 'Typical.'

'So you're up.' The man messing with her emotions appeared on the deck. 'Sleep well?'

'Like a log. Everything's caught up.' Sipping her coffee, she shook away the thoughts plaguing her. 'What are we doing?'

'It's a surprise. You'll need your swimming gear, flippers and a snorkel. I've ordered a picnic brunch from here to have on the beach, that will be delivered once we've finished our excursion.' He looked pleased with himself, as though he'd done something out of the ordinary. Not a lot of dating been going on in his life? He'd always liked to spoil her whenever they went out, but that didn't explain why he looked so chipper this morning.

It wasn't until she saw the sign at a beach a few K's along from the resort pointing to Avaavaroa Passage that she knew what he had planned. 'Snorkelling with turtles.' She fist-pumped the air. 'Yes, that's on my list of things to do.' Doing it with Leighton added to the experience. 'This is amazing. Thank you so much.'

'Glad you're happy.'

'Are we doing it independently or with a group?'

'I've booked two places with the group as the organisers have lots of gear. Though the water's warm you may want the buoyancy of a wetsuit as it's quite deep in the passage.'

'No, I'll be fine.' She wouldn't be on her own if she panicked as she had the other day. Leighton would be keeping an eye on her. That was who he was. 'You're a gem,' she said with all her heart.

It was good to have someone with her instead of going it alone. Since she'd left Leighton, she'd never had someone at her side. She'd never met another man who understood her without having to be told every single thing. Throw in those sexy kisses and she'd been a goner from the get-go with Leighton. He was a hard act to follow, if it was even possible, which added to the feeling she still loved him.

'Let's do this.' He shoved his door wide and hopped out, swinging an underwater camera from his hand.

Her mind was so full of what to do next about Leighton she barely heard a word of the safety talk from the guides, nor the instructions on what to do when they reached the turtles. But once they made their way down to the water and slipped on their flippers and snorkel she began to focus on why she was here. As the water got deeper, Alyssa kept an eye out for Leighton, but she needn't have bothered. He was with her all the way.

Tapping her shoulder, he pointed. 'Look.'

A turtle swam beside them, totally unconcerned by all the humans flapping around nearby. 'Oh, my. That's beautiful,' she said around the mouthpiece. Not that anyone could hear her, but, hey, this was incredible. Rolling onto her side, she gazed around in awe. There were four turtles close to them. Big and cumbersome yet mesmerising as they moved along.

Leighton was taking photos of the turtles and her.

One of those might be the perfect photo of her dream holiday—if she accepted him back into her life. Something nudged her on the back and she turned to find a turtle merely inches away heading past. The creatures must be so used to people in their space it wasn't worrying them at all. How amazing. She rolled, and kicked and paddled, turning continuously to watch them. Every so often she bobbed to the surface and took a few deep breaths of air while checking on Leighton before dropping down again.

When the group leader called out that it was time to return to the beach she couldn't believe an hour had gone by. 'Surely not,' she said as she tore her mouthpiece off. 'We haven't been out here that long.'

'It's probably not an hour,' Leighton agreed. 'The time will include the talk and coming out here.'

Moving closer, she kissed his cheek. 'This has been the best.'

'You can come again during the week. I just wanted to be with you for the first time you got to see turtles close up.'

'Good. I thought I'd feel more comfortable in the deeper water knowing you were there but, to be honest, once I saw the turtles I didn't think about anything else.'

'I'm glad. Come on, brunch is waiting. I can see the resort's van by the tour site.'

She swam lazily towards the beach, happier than she'd been since they'd split up. The problems hadn't gone away though, would no doubt return before the day was over.

Idyllic didn't begin to describe the day. Leighton had got it perfect. She'd forgotten about the times he'd take her somewhere special and treat her like a princess. Careful. They might be having a wonderful reunion, but she was leaving in a week and then they'd be going their separate ways despite her new-found love for him. Did they have to though? They were older and wiser. Yet the problems were still the same.

'Where've you gone?' the man stirring her head—and heart, she admitted—asked.

'I'm right here with you.' That was how she wanted the rest of the day to go. Probably unrealistic but hope made her hide from her concerns. As they strolled up the beach, feeling so comfortable and at ease, she was tempted to take his hand, but it would only add to the confusion between them. She still wasn't ready to make love again. The past had to be resolved first.

'Those croissants look delicious,' she noted as Leighton unpacked the chilly bin containing their breakfast. Her mouth watered just looking at them with the raspberry jam and whipped cream oozing out of the sides.

'But wait, there's fruit first. Pawpaw, mangoes, bananas.'

'You're spoiling me.' He really had gone to a lot of effort today.

'I'm addicted to the fruit. Nothing like eating something that's straight off the tree. The bananas don't look wonderful but, believe me, they're tastier than most varieties we get back home.'

Leaning back in the beach chair, she sighed. 'I've never had a holiday like this. No wonder people rave about going to the islands to relax.' Would she do it again? On her own? Not likely. She'd spend the whole time thinking about Leighton, looking out for him while knowing he was back in New Zealand.

'Not bad, is it? I get to laze on the beach any day I like.'

'But do you?'

Tell me something about yourself.

'I prefer walking on the sand, not sprawling all over it.'

Alyssa watched two paddle boarders going past, their oars rising and falling in even strokes. 'Think they've done that before. I'm going to give it a go this afternoon. There are boards available at the resort.'

'Hope you've got good balance.'

'I'm sure I'll fall off lots, but it doesn't matter. Landing in the water isn't going to be painful as long as I stay clear of the rocky patches.'

'You're onto it.' Leighton sprawled out on the sand, hands behind his head. 'What else have you got planned for the week?'

'Not a lot. I'll go up to the Wigmore falls, browse the shops in town, swim and read, and just take it easy.' Nothing like what she'd ever done before, yet she was feeling chronically tired because of all the mental strain from thinking about Leighton and the future. 'I've been working long hours for what feels like for ever and it's hard to let go and do nothing.'

'Why the long hours?'

'Like every hospital up and down the country we're short-staffed. Being Charge Nurse, I feel responsible to take on the hours there's no one else to cover. I don't like patients not getting one hundred per cent care on my ward.'

Leighton looked at her. 'Yet it's not your problem to fix everything. You need to look after yourself too, Lyssa, or you'll end up not able to work at all because you'll be so exhausted physically and mentally.' The concern in his eyes nearly undid her resolve to remain cautious.

'I know, but it's not easy to turn my back on people.' She probably exaggerated the problems on the ward, but that was because she cared so much.

He didn't say anything more, so she closed her eyes, making the most of the warmth. 'I could get used to this.'

'The place or the lack of action?'

'Doing nothing.'

'Yeah, right. That'd last all of a couple of weeks and then you'd be beside yourself for something to do.' He sat up and stretched his arms over his head. 'I don't recall you ever not having more than one thing on the go at a time.'

'I still do. Work and more work.' She bit her lip. He looked good enough to eat. Or to make love with. Yes, definitely the better option and not happening until she knew her heart was safe. She clenched her hands at her sides to keep from reaching out for him. Making love after the wedding had been wonderful. She'd missed that so much, along with most other parts of their marriage. She'd had a few flings but not one man she'd met had flipped the switch the way Leighton always had.

He still does.

'You need some balance in your life. More holidays?' The cheeky smile he wore ramped up the desire filling her.

'I am enjoying this so much I might have to go on some more trips.'

Want to come with me?

Shuffling upright, she looked out towards the beach, but there was no ignoring Leighton. He took over the air she was breathing.

His hand closed over hers. 'I'm glad you're having a great time. It's wonderful catching up and getting to know you again.'

'You think?' She hadn't learnt much about him except how stubborn he was, and that he was as wonderful as ever.

'I do.' Leaning closer, Leighton kissed her. A slow, soft kiss, filling her with loving.

Leighton, you're making me feel whole again.

He pulled back, looked directly at her. 'Thanks for joining me today.'

'The turtles were amazing.'

So was the time with you.

'I'd better get to work.'

Standing up, she brushed sand off her legs. 'Fair enough.' Thank goodness one of them was being sensible.

Leighton turned on the fan in his room at the medical centre and sat down at the desk. Pulling the stack of patient files towards him, he sighed. It had been hard to leave Alyssa to come in here, but if he hadn't he might've given in and asked some personal questions about if she'd been in a relationship since they broke up and what that meant if she had.

Alyssa had turned his head and his heart the very first time he saw her, and he'd known right from the get-go she was the one. The women he'd spent time with over the last few years hadn't come up to speed. They didn't laugh like Lyssa. Making love hadn't held the awe and tenderness it did with her. The list went on. She wasn't easy to replace, and now they'd caught up again he doubted he ever would find another woman he'd love as he did her. He'd loved her with everything he had, and still did. She filled him with a calmness that was new, and a turn around on their old relationship.

He owned most of the blame for their separation by not trusting her with the truth about his father. Then when he'd learned she'd already dealt with his father's blatant disregard for others he had been ashamed. The shame remained. Though to move forward and try to reclaim the love of his life he had to come clean and accept the consequences, no matter what they were. Alyssa held his heart in her hands. He needed to know where their future lay.

There was a glaring problem with being in love with Alyssa. Needing to tell her everything didn't mean he could let go the fear that she'd find him lacking.

'Hey, man, what are you doing in here on a Sunday?' Henri, another doctor at the clinic, stood in the doorway. 'Nothing's that urgent it can't wait till the morning.'

Jerked out of his thoughts, he tossed the pen aside. 'You're right.'

'Good. Now get your butt off that chair and come around to my place for a feed. Got some tuna off the fishing boat this morning and

Mela's making salad and doing something with potatoes.'

'Sounds good,' he admitted. Some company would stop him wondering how to approach Alyssa. 'I'll pick up some beers on the way.'

'You don't have to.'

Maybe, but he wasn't going empty-handed. 'What does Mela like to drink?'

'Buy her a bottle of Chardonnay and she won't let you leave the island.'

'Why don't you ask your friend if she'd like to join us too? I saw her walking along the road by the resort as I came into town so I know she's still here,' Henri added with a cheeky grin.

How did Henri even know he'd been spending time with Alyssa? 'I'll give her a call, but she's probably already got something on the go.'

'You will phone her?'

He picked up his phone and pressed her number, only to go straight to voicemail. Was that good or bad?

Alyssa wobbled as she tried to stand up straight on the paddle board. 'Whoa. This isn't as easy as it looks.'

'No, it's not,' returned the woman on her right. They'd met when she went to get a paddle board. Karin's partner, Jarrod, was out here too.

Splash. Karin was in the water.

Laughing, Alyssa forgot to maintain her balance and joined her. 'Oh, well. I knew I'd be falling in heaps of times. That's the first one out of the way.'

'Come on, you two. Get up.' Jarrod paddled past them, laughing his head off.

'I'll tip him in if he comes close,' Alyssa said. She wanted to paddle along the edge of the lagoon, but so far hadn't gone more than a few metres. She hoisted herself onto the board. 'I'm going to do this no matter how long it takes.' She began standing up, inch by inch, straightening until at last she stood tall. Slipping the oar through the water, she moved forward, wobbled, held her breath and paddled again. 'Woo-hoo. This is awesome.' Splash. She'd hit the bottom. 'Okay, I've made progress.'

By the time she made it back to her room she had aches in muscles she hadn't known existed, but felt really great. She was going to meet up with Karin and Jarrod for a beer and some nibbles by the resort pool. When she checked her phone, her heart sank. Leighton had called and she'd missed him. She'd been glad of the break from dealing with her mixed emotions and yet here she was wishing she'd answered his call and heard his sexy voice. Heat spiralled down to her sex. Damn him. This really was love all over again.

Except this time it was frightening. It could all fall apart too easily. Her heart had to be protected at all costs.

Her phone rang shortly after she sat down with her friends at the pool. The man himself. It seemed he couldn't stay out of touch for long either. 'Hey, how's things?'

'All good. How often did you fall off the board?'

'Countless times. I eventually managed to go a little way towards the other end of the lagoon and back.'

'Go you. I'm at Henri's, one of the doctors from the centre, and wondered if you'd like to join us.'

She'd love to. Wasn't she meant to be holding back? 'I'm with another couple I was paddle boarding with and we've already got food on the way.'

'Fair enough. How about we meet up tomorrow night for a meal?'

Her heart lifted. 'I'm on.' Despite the concerns about what was happening between them, spending time together meant possibly dealing with those concerns. It was a long shot but a necessary one. 'Did you get much work done?' She didn't want to hang up.

'Not really. Henri dragged me out of the office.'

'I can't imagine anyone dragging you anywhere.'

He laughed. 'You reckon? Anyway, I'd better get back to Henri's family. See you.'

'See you.' Why was it hearing his voice made her hotter than the warm weather did? Putting the phone aside, she picked up her beer and sipped the cold liquid. As for his deep laugh, that always tightened her on the inside. The very first time she'd met him, he'd laughed at a joke one of the other nurses she was with had said, and her tummy had knotted, and she'd been halfway to falling in love on that laugh alone. Warm, hot, exciting, suggestive.

The food was great, the company just as good, and when Alyssa finally headed back to her deck with a mug of tea in hand she felt so relaxed. Leighton mightn't be with her, but they'd spoken and he'd suggested hooking up tomorrow night for a meal. She'd agreed because she was over avoiding things.

She stepped onto her deck.

'Hey, Lyssa.' Leighton stood up from the sunbed and crossed over to her. 'Thought I'd drop by to say goodnight.'

Tea splashed over her hand and her heart

thumped. She wasn't ready, hadn't worked out what to say. Yes, she was. She'd had more than long enough. 'You should've joined me in the bar.'

'It's you I've come to see. Not your friends.' He took the mug out of her hand and placed it on the table. Then he wrapped his arms around her to draw her close to that wonderful body she knew so well, even after all the empty years. 'I wanted to hold you for a moment. Is that all right?'

Yes. No. Not sure, but she couldn't resist him. 'It's perfect.' Snuggling closer, she laid her cheek against his chest and breathed in his outdoorsy scent. Salt water and sunshine. Male skin. How had she ever left him? Because he hadn't been honest.

His arms tightened around her. 'Lyssa?'

She looked up, ready to tell him to leave, but her breathing stalled as his mouth touched hers ever so lightly. A feather touch that wound her up tight. She hesitated, afraid to kiss him back for fear of getting in too deep. If it wasn't too late. His eyes were focused entirely on her, sucking her in second by second. Heartbeat by heartbeat. Damn him. Stretching onto her toes, she kissed him back, harder, and deeper.

Leighton returned her kiss, touch for touch, pressure against pressure, heat on heat.

This was Leighton. This was them.

Then he stepped back. 'Goodnight, Lyssa. See you tomorrow.' And he was gone.

Feeling her lips with her fingertips, she sank onto the sunbed, smiling from ear to ear. 'Wow.' Every part of her was awake and quivering with need, and warm with love as well. 'Wow.'

Just like their first date, he'd left her with a kiss to remember him by, and a hint of more to come. Was he dating her now? That would be the way to go, exciting, interesting and allowing time to learn more about each other after their time apart.

Lying back, she stared up at the star-studded sky and smiled. Maybe that time together would allow him to finally open up to her. Bring it on.

Walking away from that kiss had been the hardest thing he'd done in a long time. Lyssa's mouth against his was a match to a firelighter. A conflagration of explosive heat. He hadn't been able to resist kissing her and, still, he'd known to leave before they went any further.

Because he still wasn't ready to have the conversation she was trying to dig out of him. He wanted to enjoy whatever time he had left with her before it all blew apart.

They'd fallen into bed fast the night of the wedding. If they were to progress he had to go slowly and build up to making love so that it meant more and wasn't a quick coupling. Though those were always intense and satisfying with Alyssa. Mostly he needed to sit down and spill out how afraid he was that she'd say he was a replica of his father and she didn't want a bar of him.

Moments ago he'd been a hot mix of desire and love. The love was a worry with so much at risk. The desire, yes, he could feed that time and time again and he knew it wouldn't be enough. There was no such thing as having enough of Alyssa. Slowly was the only way to go to see if they were still compatible in every way.

The problem with that was time was running out. She was leaving on Saturday and he wasn't returning to NZ for another month, and then he had no idea where he was going. It was the first time he hadn't organised a position almost before he started the current one. He liked to know what lay ahead; needed to, if he was honest. That way life couldn't throw ugly surprises at him— at least that was what he always hoped.

Back home, he made a mug of tea and sat on the deck under the night sky and listened to the waves pounding on the reef. It wasn't a bad life. Could be better though. Let Alyssa right in and it could be perfect. How to approach this? Other than telling her how much she meant to him and still did? Even he understood that wasn't going to cut it. She wanted answers. Only revealing his fear that she'd believe he was too much like his father to be worth staying, and that she might think he hadn't believed in her love for him, would be enough. The worst scenario for him. But the only one.

Unfortunately now he knew how his father operated he half expected more trouble to arise. If Alyssa was back in his life he'd always be worried about her reaction. He knew the answer was being open and frank all the way, but it wouldn't be easy after having watched her walk away the first time. His lungs exhaled slowly. He could do this. He would do it. There was no other option.

But nothing was perfect. He and Alyssa had fallen in love, only to let each other down. They hadn't had what it took to work their way through the problems driving them apart. What was to say they were any different now? If they did get back together, how would they handle the next crisis? Because there would be one. That was a fact of life. Hopefully they would learn to be open with each other, especially him. He could not tumble back into his hole again.

His parents had undermined his ability to believe in people. If they'd lived a lie all his life, then how was he to know someone else wasn't doing the same thing?

He trusted Jamie, and still didn't talk about their father much with him.

Did he trust Alyssa? He wanted to. If he didn't, then what was the point?

He drained his mug and stood up.

Actually he did trust her, when he wasn't over-thinking what might go wrong.

Hold onto that and stop procrastinating.

What about the fear of rejection? It might be getting smaller, but it was what could decimate him. So, slowly does it. One kiss at a time. His spirits lifted. Thank goodness Lyssa had agreed to dinner with him tomorrow night. He'd start with small steps in the right direction, convincing her she had to believe in him. Bring it on.

CHAPTER EIGHT

'WHAT DID YOU get up to today?' Leighton asked as they sat at an outside table at a restaurant overlooking the town and harbour.

'Paddle boarding with the two from yesterday.' She sipped her wine. 'When are you going to give it a go?'

'Probably never.'

'Wimp,' she teased.

His hair flicked sideways when he shook his head. 'It doesn't hold any appeal. If I want to be on the water there are things called boats. No getting wet or falling in.'

'Sounds boring.'

'Each to their own.' Suddenly he grinned. 'Tell you what. I'll go paddle boarding if you go fishing with me.'

She shuddered. She hated the smell of fish, the thought of winding one in and having to remove the hook from its mouth. But a challenge was a challenge. He did have a busy week ahead though, so she could accept and hope like crazy he didn't find the time. 'Paddle boarding first.'

He was laughing as he shook his head. 'You haven't won. I can do the board thing after work, and I have Friday afternoon off so I could arrange a fishing charter for then.'

Damn. She'd probably smell of fish all the way home the next day.

'Smile. You don't look good when you lose,' he teased.

'I'm thinking up ways to tip you off the board once you think you've got the hang of it.' Really, she was thinking about being in the water with him, and reaching for that gorgeous body to run her hands over his wet skin.

She gulped down the last of her wine and leaned back to study her husband. Ex-husband. Not quite. There was still a marriage certificate binding them together. But it wasn't the paperwork that mattered. It was their hearts, and she couldn't deny hers was well and truly caught up with Leighton's.

Swallowing hard, she said, 'Remember when we went fishing with your father and he got cross with me because I freaked out when a stingray got caught up in the net?'

John was a selfish man who expected everyone to go along with what he wanted to do, and he'd known she wasn't keen on fishing.

'I do.' Leighton looked annoyed as he stood up and pulled his wallet from his pocket. 'Let's go back to your bungalow for a nightcap.'

End of conversation. She'd deliberately raised the subject of his father, and therefore put a dampener on things, but she wasn't finished. 'I only went to be with you.'

'I figured that.'

'Leighton, relax. I'm not having a poke. I'm trying to get through to you that I struggled understanding what was going on and you didn't help.'

Anguish filled his face, and pain was in his voice. 'I get that.'

Still nothing of note. How much more could she take? She tossed her napkin on the table and stood up. 'Let's go.'

When they walked outside she slipped her hand in his to walk up the long pathway to his car, partly to save herself from tripping in the dark and partly because she wanted to reassure him she was here for him. It might help. 'Dinner was lovely, thank you.'

'Any time.' He leaned down and brushed her lips with his. 'We could do it again tomorrow?'

'Yes, please.'

Leighton pulled her into him to hold her close. Instantly her body fired up. It hadn't got the message about going slow. 'Still want to come back to my room for a nightcap?'

'Yes, ma'am.' A sharp answer but vulnerability blinked out at her.

She half expected him to drop her off and head home like last night when he'd stopped kissing her and left. Instead he walked her through to the bar to order drinks, then took her elbow as they strolled to her bungalow. Though her attempt to stroll was tense, with her hormones in a tangle while relief warred with the fact she was meant to be resisting him until everything was clearer between them, but she couldn't. He was her man. She loved him. She wanted him so much it hurt. Whatever the future held she couldn't say stop now, broken heart or not.

Kicking off her shoes, she sank onto a chair on her deck, pulling the other one close.

Leighton sat beside her, holding her hand softly on his thigh.

They didn't talk as they sipped the nightcaps. Alyssa gazed up at the sky and smiled, despite the heaviness in her chest. Everything was beautiful, magical. Except them. It felt as if this might be the end, not the beginning of a stronger, deeper relationship, so she wanted to reach out and grab whatever was on offer. Make some new memories to keep in the days ahead.

Some time later, Leighton stood up and reached

down for her, enfolded her in his arms and kissed her. 'Goodnight, Lyssa.'

She sagged against him. She didn't want him to go. Though best he did if this wasn't going to end in tears. She whispered, 'Goodnight, Leighton.'

His mouth opened on hers, his tongue slipping inside.

Her knees softened as she clung to him, never wanting to let him go even when she had to for her own sake.

'Lyssa.' Her name was so sexy on his tongue. 'We need to stop.'

Or they didn't. 'Leighton, please take me inside and make love to me.' Probably for the last time.

He pulled back and stared down at her.

Her heart thumped with desire and fear he was going to walk away again.

Then she was being wrapped up into his arms and they went into the bungalow and over to her bed, sitting down together without letting the other go, Leighton leaning in to continue kissing her.

Leaning back on the bed, keeping her mouth firmly on his, she began undoing his shirt, one button, one caress, another button, another caress.

He began trailing kisses down over her neck, lower to her cleavage, heating her to simmering.

The next thing they were naked. Alyssa had no recollection of undressing, only aware of Leighton's firm body lying against her, his arousal pressing against her thigh as his fingers worked some magic on her hot spot. And then they were together in the only way possible to be really together, giving and taking the ultimate pleasure. When she climaxed it felt as though her world were imploding, her body quivering, her head light, and her heart racing. Arms around him, she held tight, knowing she had to let go, and the sooner the better.

'Lyssa, sweetheart, I've got to go.' Leighton leaned down to place a light kiss on her cheek. She was so beautiful it hurt sometimes. It was tempting to climb back in beside her but that'd lead to more lovemaking. He needed to get home and get some sleep before the sun rose over the horizon or he'd be a zombie at work.

Her eyes blinked open. 'Leighton?'

'I'm heading home.'

Another blink. 'Okay.' She sounded exhausted.

Resisting kissing her one more time, he headed for the door. 'Have a great day tomorrow.'

Hopefully they'd catch up later because, despite his determination to stay away, he'd come to understand that was impossible. Lyssa was a part of him. She'd never really left, had been there in his psyche all along. No wonder he'd never found another woman he wanted to get close to. His heart was already accounted for. Time to unlock it, take the risk that had crippled him, and hope Alyssa would give him a second chance.

'Night.' Sounded as though she was already back asleep.

Making sure the door locked behind him, he went quietly around the main building to his car and drove home. A week ago if someone had said he'd make love to his wife again he'd have told them they needed their head read, except it was him needing that.

Alyssa would be gone in less than a week, not a lot of time left to sort things out.

So get a move on, will you?

Alyssa stretched full length in her bed and yawned. Her body was tired and replete. Two nights in the sack with Leighton and she still hadn't had enough. She couldn't remember their lovemaking being quite so wonderful, which was why she kept giving in instead of insisting on talking.

Her head ached. The lovemaking wasn't resolving a single thing. Leighton still avoided talking about the past, and, to be fair, she let him get away with it because he distracted her so easily. One touch and she was gone. Also, she'd more or less given up on getting him to talk to her, so this was about making those memories to tide her through the coming months when she'd be on her own again, all her dreams destroyed.

Time to toughen up, Lyssa.

There was another choice.

Try again. Demand answers.

What, when she'd tried often already? What would change Leighton's mind about talking to her?

There were no answers, so she picked up her phone to check for messages, and gasped. Ten past nine. She was paddle boarding with the others at ten. She headed for the shower, then dressed in a bikini with shorts and T-shirt over the top and went to get some breakfast.

With boards under their arms Alyssa and Karin walked down to the beach. Alyssa dropped her clothes on a towel she'd collected with her board, and waded into the water. 'Where shall we go?'

'Let's head towards the turtles. Not into the trench where they swim but in that direction.'

'Sure.' She hopped on the board and stood up, oar in hand, pushing away from the beach. She'd got the hang of paddling on the board now and loved the sensation of bobbing over the surface while she looked around or down into the water at the fish swimming from coral crop to coral crop. She might get a board next summer. Lots of people used them at home but she'd never thought of giving it a try.

They reached the edge of the turtle area and paddled out towards the reef, where Jarrod joined them.

'Got tickets for dinner and the local show,' he told Karin. 'Hope you've got something fancy to wear.'

'For me to know.' His girlfriend grinned.

Alyssa's heart squeezed painfully. If only she could have love like that with Leighton, uninhibited and easy. When she'd first met Leighton she'd fallen for him hard without any hesitation. Not once had she questioned his love for her, or hers for him. It had been real and there had been no reason to doubt it. Her current feelings were similar but she'd learned her lesson. Falling in love didn't mean falling into a perfect world, but they could do their damnedest to come close.

A loud splash made her look around.

Karin was in the water, looking awkward.

'You all right?' Alyssa called out.

'No, I hit a rock,' Karin shouted back, holding onto the board with one hand. 'My arm hurts like stink. I'm bleeding too.'

Jarrod was paddling furiously to get back to

her. 'Hey, babe, take it easy. I'll hold the board while you get back on.'

'I don't know that I can get on it.'

Alyssa paddled as fast as she could to reach them, wary of falling off herself. 'Let me see if I can take a look at your arm before you try to get on the board. I'm a nurse,' she added, in case she hadn't told them before. Getting off her board, she was relieved to touch the bottom with the water only reaching her armpits.

'She has to get back on it or how else are we going to get her to shore?' Jarrod sounded panicked.

'Karin, it's not so deep you can't stand and that would make it easier to check out the damage.'

'Okay.' Karin drew in a breath before easing down slowly until her feet were on the bottom. She continued to grip the board with her hand on the good arm.

'Tell me where the pain is.' There was a deep gash in the biceps with blood oozing fast.

'My arm's cut and I think I've scraped my thigh too.'

Carefully feeling around the gash on her arm, Alyssa noted Karin wince when she touched the bone. 'You might've broken it.' Which was going to make getting back to the beach difficult, and very painful. 'Jarrod, do you think we can lift

Karin onto the board so she can sit while we tow her?'

'No way,' Karin cried. 'I'm not trying to climb onto the board. It'll hurt like hell. I'll hold one of the handle things and you two can paddle your boards while holding one side each and I'll kick as hard as I can.'

'You've got a cut above your eyebrow too,' Alyssa told her. 'Is your head throbbing?'

'A little but it's the arm that's really hurting.'

'Let's get ashore and then I'll drive you to the medical centre where Leighton works.'

'We don't have far to tow you, babe, before it's shallow enough to walk if you want.' Jarrod hugged Karin. 'Hang on tight. I'll get on my board first, then Alyssa can follow suit. We'll have to sit to paddle and hold your board.'

Once Jarrod was ready, Alyssa got onto hers. 'Let's go.' It felt like hours before they reached the beach. Collecting their clothes, she slipped into her shorts and shirt, then helped Karin into hers before walking up to the resort, where she grabbed her car keys and phone, and picked up a box of tissues to use to cover the bleeding. Looking around, she couldn't find anything that would be useful as a sling. 'I need something to hold your arm in place to prevent movement adding to your pain, Karin.'

'Here.' Jarrod unbuttoned his shirt and shrugged out of it. 'Use this.'

While Jarrod helped Karin into the car, Alyssa called Leighton and told him what had happened. 'Is it all right to come to the medical centre or should I take her to the hospital?' She was thinking of the night they helped the woman who fell out of the bus and how Leighton had said she was better off going to the centre.

'Bring her here for an assessment. Chances are she won't need to go to the hospital. We've got an X-ray machine and the gear to make a cast if needed.'

'See you shortly.'

At the medical centre the receptionist was waiting for them. 'Hi, I'm Charlotte. Leighton said to take you through to his room. He's grabbing a bite to eat in the lunch room but I'll tell him you're here.'

'This way, Karin, Jarrod.' Alyssa led them along the corridor to a room Leighton had used the other night and held out a chair. 'Take a pew, Karin.'

'Th-thanks.' She was shivering. The shock from the impact had caught up.

'Charlotte, can you get this lady something dry to wear?' Leighton had joined them. 'Whatever she finds won't be very becoming, I'm afraid, but I want you out of that wet swimsuit. I'm Leighton Harrison, by the way. I'm sure Alyssa has told you I'm a GP.'

'This is Karin and her partner, Jarrod,' Alyssa told him. 'As I told you on the phone, Karin hit coral when she came off the board.'

'Your left arm took the brunt of the fall?' he asked Karin as he carefully removed Jarrod's shirt from around her upper arm and neck.

'My thigh too.'

'Right, change of plan. Let's get you up on the bed.'

Alyssa took Karin's arm and led her over to the bed. 'I think the humerus is fractured. It doesn't feel even near the elbow,' she told Leighton.

He nodded. 'I'll take an X-ray shortly. But first let's check everything else.' His fingers moved over Karin's head.

She winced. 'Ouch.'

'Does it hurt when I press here?' Leighton asked.

'No.'

'Here?'

'Yes.'

'The bone doesn't appear to be fractured, but I'll X-ray that too to be certain. I'd say you've bruised it and because there's nothing between the skin and bone to absorb the impact you'll be sore there for a few days.'

'The bleeding stopped pretty much after we had her out of the water,' Alyssa told him. 'Same as with the thigh wound.' She removed the wad of tissues she'd placed there earlier. 'How are your sewing skills?'

'Excellent.' He smiled at her, making her uneasy about the confrontation she intended bringing about as soon as they were alone.

Keeping her face straight, she reached for the box of sterile wipes on the counter and began cleaning Karin's thigh. 'This is deeper than I first thought.'

'It's rough too, which is due to the coral. All those spikes cause quite a mess.'

'You'll have seen a few injuries like this, then?'

His smile faded. 'Yes, and, Karin, the biggest thing to be aware of with these abrasions is infection. Especially in the heat. When do you fly home?'

'Tomorrow,' Jarrod answered for his partner. 'We weren't looking forward to it, but it might be for the best now.'

Alyssa shuddered at the thought of sitting on a plane with someone in the seat beside that arm. It wasn't going to be a comfort trip home. 'Have you pre-booked your seats?'

'Yes. A window seat and the one beside it.

Karin will have to use the window seat to protect her arm.'

'I agree.' At least her arm wouldn't be knocked by passengers moving about or the trolleys being pushed down the aisle.

'Alyssa, can you come with me and Karin to the X-ray room? You can help with getting her arm in the right position.'

She was sure he could manage blindfolded, but she wasn't turning down an opportunity to work with him, however small it was. 'No problem.'

Once they had Karin on the bed under the X-ray machine, Leighton moved her arm into a position where he'd get the image he wanted. 'I'll check to see if that's clear enough. You might have to shift it a little to the right, Alyssa.' He went behind the safety window and looked at the screen. 'Karin, can you turn your arm slightly towards me? That's it. Alyssa, the shoulder needs to drop a little.'

She helped Karin move and stepped out of the room while Leighton took the X-ray.

'Now for the head. I need Karin to turn so that area where she landed is facing up to the camera.'

'Don't you have a radiology assistant in the centre?'

'No. We can call in the one from the hospital

but all the doctors have had a crash course in taking X-rays for minor injuries.'

'Interesting. Right, Karin, we need you to turn your head to the side so the injury is exposed to the camera.'

Soon they were back in Leighton's room and he was stitching Karin's thigh, Alyssa helping by handing him whatever he required.

'You two have done this together a lot?' Jarrod asked.

'Never,' she said. 'Apart from those accidents last week.'

'Amazing. You work well together.'

Warmth stole through her. Yes, they made a great team without any effort in lots of ways, instinctively knowing what the other required. 'It's all part of the service.'

Working alongside Leighton was good, sharing the experience of helping Karin. All the misadventures in her time here seemed a lot for a small place, even filled to the brim with tourists. 'Blimey, am I bringing bad luck to visitors?'

Leighton's head tipped sideways so he could look directly at her. 'You'd better stay locked up in your room for the rest of your visit just in case.' Was he saying he'd keep her company?

No way. She had another agenda and this time she was not putting it off.

'We can't have too many tourists getting

knocked about while enjoying their activities. It wouldn't be a good look for the island.'

Karin smiled for the first time since coming off her board. 'Believe me, this won't put me off getting back on a board.'

Leighton opened his mouth to answer.

'It's okay. I'm not paddle boarding while my arm's broken.'

Leighton relaxed.

'Might do the hike over the top instead.'

Alyssa said, 'I'll come with you.'

He shook his head at them. 'Next stop is the plaster room. Then you can go back to your resort. I'm going to prescribe strong painkillers and antibiotics. You'll need to start taking the painkillers straight away so there's a build-up for the trip home. It's painful now but the chances of getting a knock on the plane are high and will increase the pain.'

'Thanks, Doctor.' Karin's smile had disappeared. 'I appreciate all you've done.'

'I'll get one of the nurses to do the cast as I've got patients scheduled from ten minutes ago.'

Jarrod shook his hand. 'Thanks from me too. I'm glad Alyssa knew to bring us here. She saved us a lot of time and hassle.'

'That's Alyssa for you. Onto it.'

His smile lit her up on the inside, and on the outside. She turned away before making a fool of herself by ignoring the warning bells ringing in her head. Nothing more was happening between them until she knew what was really going on with Leighton.

'I can't believe how fast the week's going by. I'll be heading home before I know it,' Alyssa said as she and Leighton wandered along the beach back to the resort after dinner.

'It has been a bit of a whirlwind,' Leighton agreed.

'Will I see you when you return home?' There were a few ways he could answer.

'Do you want to?'

She spun around to stare at him. She hadn't expected that. 'Of course I do. Why would you ask?' Where had he been when they were together? Didn't he get that she was happy being with him? Or had her doubts come through and made him cautious?

'Because you know I haven't been upfront with you.'

That was honest. 'No time like the present.' A brick was forming in her stomach as tension rose.

Leighton stared back at her, his face grim. 'Lyssa, it's been wonderful spending time with you...' He paused.

Here it came. The but. Her breath stuck somewhere in the middle of her chest as she waited.

He took her hand in both his. 'I want to have more time with you.'

'But?'

'But nothing. That's the answer to your question about seeing you once we're both back on New Zealand soil. These past days have been wonderful. Being with you, getting close again, has made me want more. We're so good together.'

Her heart crashed. 'That's not the point. Why aren't we talking about the reason our marriage failed?'

Dragging his hand through his hair, Leighton stared out over the water. 'It's not that simple, Lyssa.'

'Try.'

He continued looking outward.

What was going through his mind? Coming up with excuses to avoid the truth? Touching his hand, she said softly, 'You can trust me, Leighton.'

A shudder ripped through him. 'I want to.'

Her head flew up and she stared at him. 'You want to? You have doubts?'

'Yes.'

'You can make love to me, kiss me blind, tell me you have a brother and that your father betrayed your love for him, and yet you can't trust me?' There must be something really bad going on if he didn't believe she'd be there for him if he asked.

Leighton pulled her against him and held tight. 'I'm sorry. I've thought about this from the moment I saw you in Reception the night you arrived and I still struggle with what needs to be said.'

Pulling back, she looked into the face she adored. 'Start with telling me more about what went down between you and your father when you learned about Jamie.'

Stepping back, he swallowed hard. 'No. I'm not going there. I've told you enough already.'

Trying to calm her nerves, she implored, 'Leighton, I need to understand why you wouldn't talk to me back then. I understand you were hurt badly by what John did, but surely you could've told me?'

'I couldn't. Understand that, Alyssa. Not then, and even now it's hard.' Regret filled his face.

Her heart pounded. He was going to walk away again. She'd seen that expression before when he'd refused to tell her what was worrying him, and knew the outcome. She took his hand. 'Come on, walk and talk.' It'd be easier than standing staring at each other. 'Leighton. I love you. We need to do this.' She hadn't said that the last time, too hurt and angry to make him see how she felt about him.

For the first few minutes they walked in silence, then suddenly Leighton began talking fast. 'It was a shock learning I had a brother and that he'd come about through my father having an affair with Mum's best friend, and how everyone covered up the fact that Dad paid Jamie's mother all those years to keep her quiet. Jamie and I missed out on so much. But while that was horrendous, for me the worst was realising I didn't know the man who was my father.'

He paused, breathing heavily, staring along the beach, away from her.

She waited, giving him space, still holding his trembling hand. Given how close they were, it must've been soul-destroying to learn his father's true colours. Her heart ached for him.

He began walking again. 'All my life people joked about how alike we were in all ways.'

She knew that, but didn't agree. Leighton was gentle and kind, cared about other people, something John never had.

Leighton sighed. 'I used to be proud I was like him. Until Jamie turned up, then I became ashamed.' His hand squeezed hers. 'Totally ashamed. I'd come home at night and look at you and know I couldn't tell you. I thought you'd leave me because I was my dad all over again. You'd think I could do the same horrendous things to you he'd done to Mum. I couldn't face that. You were the love of my life but I'd already lost the two other people I loved. I couldn't bear the thought of you walking out on me, or thinking I might betray you, so I pushed you away instead.'

'That's utterly ridiculous,' she snapped through the pain roaring through her. How could he believe that of her? 'I loved you with all my heart. I trusted you, believed in you.' Tugging her hand free, she stopped to stare at this man she'd thought she knew well. 'There's no way in hell you're your father. No way.'

'Easy to say now.'

'Because it's the truth. It was then and still is.' So much for moving forward with Leighton. They really were over because he wasn't giving her the benefit of doubt.

'You have to understand how messed up I became. There was Jamie, a brother I'd known nothing about, wanting to get to know me. As you've seen, we get on great, and did from the get-go, but deep down I still had to accept he was for real. It was hard, given the circumstances with my father. I even went to counselling.' He drew in a lungful of air. 'Throw in Dad demanding I have nothing to do with Jamie and instead support *him*. I fell apart. I was terrified you'd find out and leave me. Then I learned Dad tried to bribe you. I was so proud of you then, but it also increased my fear that you'd never fully trust me again.'

'Thanks a lot, Leighton.'

Calm down. Take this slowly.

A deep breath and she continued. 'I would've trusted you, and supported you.' Her mouth was sour, her head spinning. 'So you didn't trust me.' Without trust there was no relationship. Not for her, anyway. Or Leighton, otherwise they might've made it through the turbulence brought on by John Harrison. She rubbed the goose bumps on her arms. 'I need time on my own.'

'Lyssa, I let you down badly. I'm truly sorry. I just hope that one day you might forgive me and that we can at least be friends.'

Turning around, she headed for her bungalow. Friends? With Leighton? Not likely. With him it had to be all or nothing. Her heart wouldn't have it any other way. Right now she needed to work through all he'd said and figure out where to go from here.

CHAPTER NINE

SINKING ONTO A chair on the deck, Alyssa hugged the robe around her and let the tears flow. No point in trying to stop them. Her heart was broken into so many pieces there wasn't a quick fix. There wasn't anything that would put it back together. Leighton hadn't trusted her. Still didn't if he found it so hard to tell her after four years.

She loved Leighton. As much as, if not more than, she had when she married him. How could she have ever thought she'd got over him? It was so untrue. Within such a little amount of time she'd known he was still the only man for her. Trying to deny it had simply been to protect her heart, and now it lay shattered. There'd be no picking up the pieces and carrying on as if nothing were wrong. He'd undermined her love.

How could he not trust her and talk about his parents? Yet what else had they done to hurt him so much? He'd loved and believed in them. *Trusted* them. He'd been nothing but proud of his family and said he'd grown up happy and feeling loved, then to be treated so callously must've devastated him. No wonder he'd had counselling. Leighton was strong but he'd been dealt a huge blow. It made sense why he'd left the medical centre to work as a locum up and down the country. He was staying clear of involvement. Except with Jamie, which also made sense because that was where this all began and their father had betrayed them both.

If only she'd known, he'd never have been on his own.

More tears spurted down her cheeks. 'Leighton, why couldn't you trust me? I love you. I'd never deliberately hurt you.'

Cuddling further into the robe, she tucked her feet underneath her backside and stared unseeing at the edge of the deck. 'He's gone.' Her stomach ached as it squeezed in on itself. Her head was full of fog. Her hands clenched together. And inside her chest was a solid wall of pain pressing on her lungs and her heart. 'He's gone.'

The sun was lightening the sky when she finally dragged herself inside and onto the bed. Wrapping the pillows around her neck and tucking the sheet tight, she closed her eyes and pretended to sleep. There was nothing else to do.

She woke to the sound of knocking. 'Leighton?' Leaping out of bed, she rushed to open the door, and sagged. 'Karin.'

'Hi. You look wiped out. Big night?'

One way to describe it. 'Sort of. How are you feeling today?'

'Very sore. But never mind. I came to say thank you for all your help yesterday. It meant a lot to both of us.'

Yesterday was another world. Working alongside Leighton, receiving his smiles, looking forward to dinner. Not any more.

'Alyssa? Are you all right?'

Shaking away any thought of Leighton, she said, 'I'm good. As for yesterday, I'm glad I was there to help.'

'I'd better go. We're about to head to the airport. Keep in touch. We might visit you in Nelson in the summer.' Karin laughed.

'See you around.' Back inside she headed for the shower and a long soak while she mulled over what to do next.

Go home was the best she could come up with in answer to that and, once dressed, she went online to see if there was a seat available on any flight before Saturday.

The first available one was for the flight she was already booked on. So she was stuck here, like it or not. Why waste her holiday thinking about Leighton and what she'd lost? Because it was impossible not to think about him. She had to move on. He hadn't trusted her, and still didn't. That hurt bad. But if she left without a word he'd be right. She'd be deserting him and fuelling his distrust right when he'd finally told her everything.

Picking up her phone, she found Leighton's number. She'd talk to him, try to get him to understand she would've stayed. Her finger hovered over the icon. Press and hear his voice. Don't press and get on with filling in her day, wondering if he'd have talked to her or not.

Dropping the phone back on the table, she headed outside. She'd said it all last night. 'Leighton. I love you.' There was nothing to add to that. Not until she'd thought everything through again and was one hundred per cent certain they could make it work. Failing again would be horrific.

For a distraction she went to the resort café where other guests were lazing by the pool soaking up the sun. The coffee went down easily, the croissant not so much, forming a lump in her belly.

Next she drove to Wigmore's Waterfall and walked a little way into the bush up the side of the main hill. When it got too steep, she returned to her car and drove to town to wander through the shops, buying T-shirts she didn't need. In the afternoon she took a board and paddled up and down the lagoon, though her heart wasn't really in it. Back in her room she ordered an early dinner with a glass of wine and sat on her deck reading. Except she read the same five pages numerous times.

Tossing the book aside, she gave in to the question continuously knocking at her. Was there another way to rebuild their trust and get back together?

'Your mammogram's normal,' Leighton told the woman. 'So is your blood pressure. Next we'll take some blood to check your haemoglobin, liver and kidneys, and you can go home.'

Unfortunately she was his last patient for the day.

He'd go home too. To do what? The lawns had been mowed to within an inch of the dirt, the house was spotless, and he'd even cleaned the car. He really needed to get a life, not this lonely facsimile of what he'd once believed in.

You could have one with Lyssa.

If she hadn't already run a mile when she heard the truth behind him getting into such a mess after his father's true self came to light. She'd never liked his dad, and he didn't think that was only because of the offer of money he'd made. He presumed she'd sensed that his father wasn't all he portrayed himself to be. 'I'm a good bloke who looks out for others,' was his constant saying. So untrue.

'Why didn't I see through him?' Leighton asked himself for the thousandth time. He knew there were no answers other than he'd loved his parents and believed in them. There'd been no reason to have gone looking for problems.

Alyssa had got to know his real father when he'd tried to bribe her to leave him, before they married. She hadn't rejected him over that. His heart lifted briefly. How did he make her see how much he loved her? Last night she'd said she had trusted him, loved him. Could she still? He had to convince her he trusted her with his heart and soul, that never again would he let her go to protect himself. He was better than that now. He had to ask for another chance so they could work through everything together. There could be a pot of love at the other end of this. Surely it was worth the risk?

Worst case—he'd be back where he was a week ago, except Alyssa now knew everything.

Best case? His heart would be full of love and he'd be so happy.

Suddenly it seemed so easy. He might have blinkers on but his heart was ready to face anything. Hope of winning back Lyssa was winning over his negativity. Hopefully she'd say again she loved him. If not, he'd set about wooing her. Because he wasn't giving up this time. They belonged together.

His change of heart had happened in a blink but only because the hope and love had been there all along, hidden beneath his pain and fear. If only he'd been able to admit it long ago. But maybe it had taken so long because he'd needed time to reconcile everything for himself. He'd acknowledged his love for Lyssa to himself over the past days, but there'd always been the handbrake in place. That was gone. He was free to love again. He was not going to live under a shadow a minute longer.

Hands in pockets, Alyssa kicked the sand as she strolled up the beach towards her room. Her last night in Rarotonga. It wasn't what she'd hoped for. Dinner in the resort restaurant and early to bed with the book she'd finally managed to get more than halfway through wasn't exactly exciting.

Reaching her deck, she stopped. 'Leighton?'

He turned from where he was leaning on the railing and came towards her. 'Lyssa, I'm sorry. For everything.'

She ignored the tightening in her belly and the sudden thumping in her head. 'I owe you an apology too. I should've stayed with you despite the tension and my bewilderment over what was going on. I'm truly sorry I let you down.'

'Thank you.' His smile was full of love as he pulled a chair out from the outdoor table. 'Are you ready to put it all in the past? To let it go and move forward with me?'

'It is the only way to go if we're going to be seeing each other back home.' Sinking onto the chair, she crossed her legs and placed her elbows on the table. And waited for him to continue. She wasn't trying to make it any more difficult for him, but she was afraid to say anything that might turn him away again.

'I handled everything badly. Sure, what happened was a shock.'

'How did you manage not to say anything to me when I got home?' They had been married, in love. They had shared everything, or so she'd believed.

'With difficulty. I wanted to pour it out and hear you say it couldn't be true and that everything was a lie. Except I knew it wasn't. That's when I started sinking into despair, unable to grasp the fact my life hadn't been what I'd believed. It took the ground out from under me. I struggled with knowing who I was. Everything seemed wrong, even us. I was so afraid you'd leave me when I needed you the most that I put up the barriers that drove you away.'

Guilt hit her. 'I should've stayed.'

'We'll never know if that would've helped or driven a bigger wedge between us.'

'You're right. We can't undo what's happened.' What lay ahead was far more important.

'When did you learn John had offered me money to not marry you?'

'After you'd left. I'd gone to see Mum, naively hoping she'd answer some of my questions. Dad turned up and said you'd be regretting not taking the money because obviously you wouldn't want to stay with me after that.'

'Because I hadn't told you about his offer I inadvertently added to your pain.' It must've seemed she was hiding secrets too. 'I did hide it from you. I was disgusted with John and I also didn't want you choosing between family and me. I figured if you didn't know we could still get married and be happy.'

'It's all right, Lyssa. You told me that last week and I understand. It can't have been easy, especially now I know how manipulative Dad can be. I don't hold it against you, I promise.'

Her stance softened a little. 'Thanks.'

She took his hands in hers, holding tight. 'You are nothing like John. Nothing at all. You are kind and caring, loving and genuine. You don't put yourself first all the time. You never have. You were never anything but loving to me.' Until the end, but they were both off track by then. 'You're more than good enough. Way more.'

'Your words are a balm. After all this time I'm struggling to believe them.'

'I wasn't perfect either, Leighton. I did want to have some fun and you weren't available. I didn't play around, just partied with the girls from work, but it still wasn't the right thing to do. I realise I should've dug deeper into what was upsetting you, not put myself first all the time.' She had grown up since then. 'I'd never do that again.'

'Honestly I was just glad you were out and not demanding my attention.'

'I understand completely, but I mightn't have back then. I was too engrossed in what was going on in my life to think about what you were feeling.'

A silence fell between them.

Alyssa felt a new tenderness for Leighton growing inside. He was the love of her life, and now she could let go the past and move forward. With him. Or not, if he didn't love her back. She'd hurt, but there'd be no point arguing about it. That'd only increase the pain between them.

A scraping sound interrupted her thoughts.

Leighton was standing up. Going? Her heart plummeted. No, please not that.

Then he was in front of her and taking her hands in his, and getting down on one knee. 'I love you, Lyssa. Always have and always will. Will you stay married to me, live with me for ever, have our children?'

Her throat clogged with tears so she couldn't speak and had to nod. Bending forward, she brushed her mouth over those wonderful lips. 'Yes,' she squeaked. 'Yes.'

Before she knew what he was doing, she was being swung up into his arms and carried inside, where he kissed her so intensely she had to pinch herself to make sure it wasn't a dream.

When he stopped, so did her heart.

'Lyssa, let's renew our vows. Here in a month's time before I come home. We could have a honeymoon on Aitutaki too.'

Last time they'd spent a weekend in a high-end hotel in Auckland, then gone home and back to work. 'Sounds perfect.'

As perfect as the lovemaking that ensued.

EPILOGUE

Four weeks later

THE MARRIAGE CELEBRANT stood on the beach in front of Alyssa and Leighton. Beside them were Jamie and Collette, who'd flown over with Alyssa especially for this moment.

'Ready?' asked Clara.

'More than,' Leighton replied.

Clara cleared her throat. 'Alyssa Harrison, do you agree to continue your marriage to Leighton Harrison from this day forward and to stand by his side through everything life throws at you?'

'Try stopping me. Yes, I absolutely do.'

Leighton's eyes appeared bluer than ever as they twinkled at her with love.

'Leighton, I will do everything possible to be a great wife. There will be times I'll annoy you to pieces but always remember I love you with all I am, and I have since the day I first met you.'

A solitary tear escaped to run down his cheek. 'I believe you.'

'Leighton Harrison, will you remain married to Alyssa for ever, and support her through every twist and turn life throws at you?'

'I most certainly will. I love you to the moon and back, Lyssa. Always have, always will. There'll be no more avoiding the tough stuff, and lots more making the most of the good times. You are my for ever woman.'

Clara looked to Jamie. 'You wanted to say something.'

Surprised, Alyssa glanced at Collette and got back a wide smile.

Leighton looked surprised too. 'Hope you know what you're doing, brother.'

'Who? Me? Not a clue.' Jamie cleared his throat. 'Alyssa, I've known you for a while now as a competent nurse and a good friend to Collette, and thought you were an amazing person. What I didn't know until our wedding is that you were my sister-in-law. Welcome back to the family. From the moment you walked into the resort that first night I've known Leighton loved you, even if he didn't. No one could be more glad that you two have found each other again.'

'Apart from me,' Collette added.

Alyssa smiled and smiled. This was perfect.

Her marriage was back intact, and her friends were now her family. 'Thank you, guys.'

Leighton spoke up. 'I haven't finished.' He dug into his pocket and pulled out a tiny box. 'Lyssa, I know we agreed you'd wear the wedding band I gave you on our wedding day, and here it is.' He slipped it onto her finger, all polished and looking beautiful.

She stretched up to brush a kiss on his lips. 'Thank you.'

'I also want you to wear this. It's an eternity ring, which seems appropriate.' He revealed a gold ring with a large sky-blue sapphire in the centre.

'Oh, my. That's beautiful. Which finger?'

'How about with your wedding ring? It's the same size.'

She held her hand out and as he slid it on love filled her for this very special man who did so much for her. 'I love you, Leighton. I always have and always will.' It never hurt to say that again and again.

'Here's to the future, to Mr and Mrs Harrison,' said Jamie as he handed glasses of champagne to everyone. 'Cheers to all of us.'

'Cheers and love,' Alyssa said before sipping her drink.

This was the best day of her life—better than

the first time she'd swapped vows with Leighton. Now they were older and wiser…and happier than ever.

* * * * *

Single Mum's Alaskan Adventure
Louisa Heaton

MILLS & BOON

Louisa Heaton lives on Hayling Island, Hampshire, with her husband, four children and a small zoo. She has worked in various roles in the health industry—most recently four years as a community first responder, answering emergency calls. When not writing, Louisa enjoys other creative pursuits, including reading, quilting and patchwork—usually instead of the things she *ought* to be doing!

Visit the Author Profile page
at millsandboon.com.au for more titles.

Dear Reader,

I'd recently read a book about a family having to settle in the wilds of Alaska and adapting to this new way of life and knew I wanted to set a book there of my own.

But who to place there? What if it was a woman seeking refuge? Someone who thought her anonymity would be guaranteed in such an isolated place, not realising that the isolation in those places brings the people that are there together?

And then I thought, what if the hero was someone whom she thought she'd never see again? Someone from her past? Someone who knew her? Someone who could get close, when that was the last thing she needed?

And so, Charlie and Eli arrived on the page in the fictional town of Vasquez, which I populated with what I hope are memorable characters, who become patients and newfound family.

I had such fun creating their story. I hope you have as much fun reading it.

Louisa x

DEDICATION

For Lorna and Bonny x

CHAPTER ONE

CHARLIE GRIFFIN HAD been told she would need to make two flights to get to the remote town of Vasquez, Alaska, and had assumed, as anyone would, that this would mean two proper aeroplanes.

How wrong could I be?

The first flight had been easy enough, and her daughter, Alice, had sat and watched a cartoon movie for most of it, holding her teddy, and Charlie knew that they would be met and escorted to their second plane, which would bring them into Vasquez. She figured it would be a kind of meet-and-greet service that would whisk her through all the security checks and baggage reclaim and, to a point, it was. But the guy in cargo shorts and a sign that had her name on it led her away from the airport and out towards a car.

Charlie stopped, holding her daughter's hand. 'There's meant to be a second flight that takes us to Vasquez. Have you got the right Griffin?'

The guy, who'd introduced himself as Chuck,

grinned, chewing gum, and nodded. 'That's right. Your next plane is in the bay.'

'The *bay*?'

'It's a seaplane. Ain't no airport in Vasquez… you come in and land on the water.'

'Oh.' Suddenly she wasn't sure. But wasn't this what she wanted? Somewhere remote? Vasquez, Alaska, fitted that bill perfectly. The perfect hideaway for her and Alice. To go someplace where nobody would know her. She preferred to hide. To keep mobile and have no one know her shame and, most importantly of all, *never* become the next hot topic of conversation.

'I get it. I'm a strange guy. Look…' Chuck pulled a piece of paper from his pocket and handed it to her. 'That's the number of the clinic you'll be working at. Why don't you give them a ring and they'll confirm what I'm saying? So you know you're not just getting in a vehicle with someone you shouldn't.' Chuck went and sat in the car.

She had to be cautious. She'd learned that a lot lately. There was paperwork in her purse with the clinic's number on, too. She pulled it out and checked the number against the one Chuck had given her. It was the same. But she wouldn't take any chances. So she phoned the number, told them who she was and the receptionist confirmed that Chuck was who he said he was and that she was perfectly safe to get into his car.

The engine was idling by the time she opened the back door and got in with Alice. 'Buckle up, baby,' she said, reaching over Alice to strap her in. 'How far to the bay?'

'Twenty minutes, if traffic's okay.'

'Thank you.'

'No problem.' Chuck smiled at her in the rear-view mirror and drove them away from the airport. As the journey continued she pulled her instructions and second ticket from her purse and now understood why it looked different from the first. The instructions had said she'd be met after her first flight and escorted to the second, but they could at least have mentioned it was a car ride away.

When they pulled up alongside a big stretch of water, Alice gaped out of the window. 'Is that our plane?'

Charlie hoped not. It didn't look fit to fly! It had to be at least thirty or more years old. It looked battered. Ancient. And was that *rust* she could see? Dirt? She hoped it was dirt. 'I don't know. Chuck, is that…?'

'Sure is! Best seaplane on the Alaskan coast.'

The best? 'What does the worst look like?' she muttered under her breath, trying to put a brave face on things as she dragged her cases out of the trunk of the car.

Alice was excited. She'd never even flown be-fore today. Now she'd experienced a jet and a raggedy old seaplane… This was all an adventure to her and Charlie wished she had the same optimism as her daughter.

Adjusting her sunglasses onto the top of her head to hold back her long hair, she dragged the cases along the pier. The wheels bumped and jolted the cases all over the place and, once or twice, Charlie thought she might lose them in the bay, which looked dark and forbidding. Her heels kept slipping into the gaps too, tripping her, and she must have looked quite ungainly.

Chuck opened the doors and loaded the cases into the back and then helped Alice, then Charlie up into the plane. 'Seat belts on, ladies.' And then he climbed through to the cockpit.

'Wait, you're our pilot, too?'

'You bet!' Chuck grinned, gave them a thumbs up and then reached for a large set of headphones, which he placed on his head, and then began flicking switches and starting up the engine.

It choked a couple of times before the engine started and Charlie began to wish that she had some sort of faith she could cling to. In the meantime, she simply smiled at her daughter, who seemed to be incredibly excited at this new adventure, and hoped that this old rust bucket would get them to Vasquez safely.

'How long?' she called to Chuck.

'Little over an hour,' he called back as the plane began to move away from the short pier.

An hour. She could do an hour, right?

Lift-off was bumpier than she expected, but Alice loved it. 'Yee-haw!' she cried out as they hit another small wave before the seaplane made it into the air.

Just get us there in one piece, Chuck.

Charlie gripped the edge of her seat and wished she'd had the foresight to include travel sickness tablets in her hand luggage. She'd never needed them before, but this small seaplane seemed to feel and experience every piece of turbulence that existed in the air and it dipped and bumped and rattled loudly with every disturbance.

'What made ya want to come to Vasquez? It's a little out of the way for city folks like you,' asked Chuck, looking over his shoulder.

'Oh, you know…needed a change of pace,' she said, teeth chattering.

Chuck laughed. 'You'll get that! It's a different way of life out there, you know? Probably nothing like you're used to.'

'Great.'

That's just what I need.

'You got the Internet out there in Vasquez?'

'Oh, yeah. All the mod cons. It ain't reliable, though. Thing goes on the fritz more often than not, so most folks have a CB radio on hand, just in case they need to call for help.'

Citizens Band radios. Wow. Charlie had thought those things were obsolete. But it made sense if you lived in the middle of nowhere, which was exactly where Vasquez was. And an unreliable Internet sounded perfect.

'What do you do in Vasquez, Chuck?'

'I mush.'

Charlie blinked. She must have heard wrong. 'I'm sorry, what?'

'I mush dogs. Train them for racing. You know, for dog sledding? I raise huskies, breed them, work them when the tourists come a calling.'

'You have dogs?' asked Alice, suddenly enraptured. Alice loved animals more than anything and had been persuaded that Vasquez would be an amazing place for her to indulge her fascination with wildlife.

'Forty-two of them and counting.'

'Mom! He's got forty-two dogs!'

'I heard, honey. Do you need that many, Chuck? I mean…how many tourists do you get?'

Chuck laughed. 'Most of those are pups. I'm just waiting for them to be old enough to go to their new homes. Racers and the like. I got champions in my line and they fetch a pretty price. But when they're gone, I'll only have like sixteen.'

Only sixteen dogs.

Charlie smiled, unable to imagine it. 'What can you tell me about the people?'

'Oh, they're a friendly bunch. Most people live in town, but there are a few homesteads that are isolated, so you don't get to see those folks as often.'

'And Dr Clark? What's he like?' Dr Clark was going to be her boss. He'd emailed her once or twice to let her know her responsibilities during her temporary contract covering for some doctor that had gone on maternity leave. His emails had been short. Sweet.

'Eli? Oh, he's great. Best doctor we've ever had.'

Eli. She'd known an Eli once and it hadn't been the greatest of experiences. But that was a long time ago, in a different life. She didn't have to worry about that any more. It was in the past and she'd moved on. Just as he had, most probably.

'I've had to fly him out to patients in the past, if we couldn't get there by car or dog sled.'

'You don't have ambulances?'

'I am the ambulance.' He laughed and turned back around.

Charlie raised her eyebrows.

I wanted remote. I'm getting remote.

Alice was open-mouthed as she gazed out of the windows of the small seaplane. They flew over some gorgeous country—snow-capped mountains, glaciers, lakes, hills of green, the occasional small town. But mostly Charlie could feel the immensity of the space they were in. The city and all its hectic complications, its computers and endless streams of invasive social media were far behind her and with every mile that passed she felt some of her stress ebbing away with it. There was something soothing about looking out at all that country. At the peace of it. The anonymity of it. Its vastness made all her worries seem insignificant. And the sky... The sky was never-ending. An eternity of blue and space. She dared hope that she could lose herself beneath it and somehow be reborn into the woman she used to be. The Charlie she'd been before meeting Glen.

'Mom, I think I can see a bear!' Alice pointed down at a brown speck that seemed to be making its way alongside a river.

Maybe it was a bear. Maybe it was a moose? Or an elk? It was hard to say. 'I can see it, baby.'

'You like bears?' asked Chuck.

'I do! They're my favourite animal in the whole wide world!' enthused Alice, squeezing her own teddy tightly.

'Well, plenty of grizzlies near Vasquez. You keep your distance. Especially from the mama bears, you hear? They're not as sweet and nice as the one you've got there.'

'I will.'

Charlie felt slightly alarmed by this piece of news, but also protective. She was her own mama bear and would do anything to protect her child from danger. 'How much further?' she asked Chuck.

'You see that lake down there to your right?
With the settlement alongside it?'

'I do.'

'That's Vasquez. That's home.'

They both gazed down upon it. Vasquez seemed
to have been built on a headland that jutted out
from the eastern side of the lake. To the west
were snow-capped mountains, but Vasquez and
the land around it were verdant and green. There
was a forest and within it a river that seemed to
feed into the lake and, beyond the river, hills and
rocks and the occasional homestead.

'Better be ready. Landings can be bumpy.'

Charlie checked Alice's belt first, then redid
her own lap belt, fussing with it until it felt right
and having one last moment where she hoped she
was doing the right thing for both of them.

The plane banked as Chuck turned it to approach Vasquez from the south and then he slowly
began to descend. The green became more de-
fined as plants and trees and grass, the buildings
along the waterfront became more apparent—a
B & B, a diner, a groceries store. And they all
seemed to belong to the Clarks—Clark's Diner.
Clark's B & B. Clark's General Store. And before
she could think about that some more, the plane
hit the water, bouncing slightly until it aqua-
planed smoothly for a while, the engine dying
down as the battered old bucket of a vehicle delivered them safely to another wooden pier.

Chuck got out first, mooring the plane with ropes, and then helped Alice out first, offering a steadying hand to Charlie as she disembarked. 'Boss is here,' he said, grinning and indicating behind her, with a brief nod of his head and a salute to the unseen man behind them.

Dr Clark had said he'd meet them so he could drive them straight to their residence—a two-bedroomed property owned by Dr Clark's own mother. From what Charlie understood, the Clarks owned a lot of property and businesses in Vasquez.

She wanted to make a great first impression, even though she was here only temporarily to cover a maternity contract, and so she adjusted her sunglasses onto the top of her head again, straightened and turned around, with a smile upon her face. A smile that began to fade as the large, massively muscled Dr Eli Clark came closer.

He'd filled out since she'd last seen him.

He'd never been scrawny or short before, but he'd never been this...well...*developed*. But the grin was the same. The eyes, the same.

The boy she'd known as Eli Johns, the boy who'd teased her and played jokes on her endlessly at the orphanage they'd lived in.

That boy who had somehow struck lucky and found a family.

Was now Dr Eli Clark.

Her boss.

Waiting for her with that same cheeky grin across his face, as if his next prank was already waiting...

CHAPTER TWO

'Eli?'

There was so much he wanted to say. So much he could say, but, rather than answer her straight away, he knelt so he could be on the same level as her daughter. 'Hey there. What's your name?'

The daughter was the spitting image of her mother. Long, dark brown hair, same dark brown eyes. Like melted chocolate. The same bone structure.

'Alice.'

She seemed shy, but she was smiling and she had a beautiful smile, too. 'Hey, Alice. Who's that?' he asked, pointing to the teddy bear that she carried with her.

'Mr Cuddles.'

'Mr Cuddles?' He glanced up at Charlie and registered the shock that was still painted large across her face. 'Well, he sounds like a very friendly bear. Can I shake his paw?'

Alice giggled slightly and held out the bear.

Eli gently took a paw and shook it. 'Nice to

meet you, Mr Cuddles. I'm Eli. Is it okay if I talk to your mom for a little while now?'

Alice nodded.

He stood, towering over Charlie and her little girl. He'd always been slightly taller than Charlie, but he'd clearly not finished growing before he got adopted and now he was a good head and a half taller than she. 'I hoped it was you, when I saw your name.'

'Really? You *hoped*? I've emailed you six times since accepting this posting—you didn't think to tell me who you really were?'

He grinned. 'I thought it could be a surprise.'

'Oh, it's definitely that,' she replied, not sounding the least bit happy about it and looking at anything that wasn't his face.

He got it. When they'd been kids, she'd often told him that she could have quite happily punched him in the nose every time he had grinned at her, and he couldn't help but grin now. He liked that they were being reunited. Here was someone who understood his past better than anyone else in Vasquez. And she was only here a short time. It was why he'd agreed to hire her.

'You don't seem thrilled.'

'Why would I be?' Now she looked at him. Intently so and he realised as he stared back that she'd changed too. As a young teen, she'd been scrawny and much too thin. But now, as a grown woman, she'd developed. He noted the hint of delicious curves beneath her blouse and skirt and those heels she was wearing? Well, he couldn't remember the last time he saw a woman wearing heels in Vasquez. Most people wore boots of some kind.

The heels drew his eye to parts of her anatomy that he really ought not to stare at. Little Charlie Griffin had grown from a gauche, skinny teen with angry acne into a beautiful, elegant young woman. A mother herself! And though he wondered what the story was there and why she was alone and hadn't brought a partner, he knew he would not ask. Not yet, anyway. Time would reveal all. It always did. But he envied her the fact that she had real family. That blood connection. The Clarks might have taken him in, made him one of their own, given him their name and their love, but they weren't blood. Eli had always hoped that one day he would have a family of his own. Get married, have loads of kids, but even that had been taken away from him.

So yeah. He envied her having achieved something he never would.

'Aren't reunions meant to be happy occasions?' He grinned, holding out his arms as if suggesting she ought to step into them and give him a hug.

She smiled back. A fake smile. One that didn't touch her eyes. 'You'd think so.' And she sidestepped him, pulling her cases behind her, not realising that the pier was not as wide as she hoped.

The case rumbled over the edge and, before she knew it, the weight of it caused it to slip from her fingers as it caught on the slats and tumbled with a big splash into the water.

'No!' she yelled, collapsing to her knees to try and grab for it as it floated near her, her arms not long enough to grasp it.

Eli tried his hardest not to smile, but he couldn't help it. It was kind of funny. If she'd not been in such a snoot with him, it wouldn't have happened at all. 'Want some help?'

'I don't need any help from you, thank you very much!' she snarled.

'Okay.' He stood there, arms crossed, watching her as she tried to reach her case to no avail. She stretched and grunted and even, at one point, got up to grab a thin stick from the shore to try and prod the case back towards her. Unfortunately she only succeeded in pushing her case further away from her and it began to float away into the bay.

'Damn it!'

'Mom, you swore.'

Charlie turned to look at her daughter. 'Sorry, baby.' But then she glanced up at him. Those chocolate eyes of hers angry and furious.

He knew she would not ask him again, but he also knew he couldn't leave her stranded like this, with the majority of her possessions that she'd brought with her floating away into the bay. Eli began to undo his boots.

'What are you doing?' she asked.

'Helping out.' He pulled off the boots and then his socks. He knew the water would be cold. It always was here in Vasquez, even when they had warmer days and the sun shone, as it did today. The water could be deceptive. Eli didn't bother rolling up his jeans. They were going to get wet no matter what he did and so he splashed down into the water and by the time he reached her case? It was up to his waist.

Charlie could not believe her eyes.

Eli was wading through the water to retrieve her case and by the time he got it the water was creeping up his shirt.

She couldn't think about how kind a gesture it was. She was too busy trying to stop thinking about how hot he looked doing so.

Eli was a huge man. Muscled. And…oh, yes… she could see the dark shapes of some sort of tribal tattoo on his arms and back. And with his shaggy locks and beard, the scar through his eyebrow and all of the things that made Eli *Eli*, he looked like a barbarian. The kind of barbarian that you wouldn't mind invading your village and throwing you over his shoulder.

He hefted her heavy case easily, lifting it out of the water, and began the slow wade back to shore.

His jeans were now moulded to his muscled thighs as he emerged from the water like a demigod and set her case down on the ground. He was breathing steadily and she noticed a necklace around his neck, tied with a leather loop. It looked to be a piece of turquoise and it rested on his slightly hairy chest, drawing her eye. Lust smacked into her like a tsunami.

'Thank you,' she managed.

'No problem.' He smiled at her, as if knowing the effect he was having on her, and for that she didn't like him even more. Felt her anger grow again as she watched him pull his socks onto his wet feet, and then his boots.

'I know you said you'd take us to where we're staying, but if you just give me the address, I'm sure we can find it on our own. You're soaked…' Her gaze drifted over his body once again. His broad chest. His flat, narrow waist. His toned and shapely thigh muscles. She felt heat surge into her cheeks. 'And you probably want to get changed.'

She did not want to feel this way about Eli! She'd been glad when he'd been adopted. It had meant she didn't have to put up with him any more! But this? This was too much.

'It's just water. My truck's seen worse. Come on.' He stepped ahead of her, leading her towards a flatbed truck that was parked on the side of the road near Clark's Diner.

Not knowing how else she could get out of being in his truck with him, she managed a smile at her daughter and took her hand, following him up the slight incline towards the vehicle.

If it were her, she would have wanted to be out of those wet jeans as soon as possible. She hated the feeling of wet material against her legs. She'd been caught in a sudden downpour once and been soaked. She'd not been able to get into work quick enough to put on some nice dry scrubs and feel comfortable again.

Yet he was still happy to show her around? To sit in those wet jeans? Drive in them? The man was crazy, but then she knew that. He always had been the type to look out for odd things. Strange things. To experience life. Perhaps this meant nothing to him?

Eli hefted her case into the back of his truck and then opened the passenger-side door for her and Alice. 'My ladies.'

Alice giggled and clambered in, so that she would be sitting between them, which suited Charlie just fine. She didn't need to be squashed up against him, feeling his body and his heat against her own.

'Let's get you strapped in.' Eli leaned over her daughter, reaching for her seat belt, his face coming alarmingly close to Charlie's, so that she had to turn away for her own seat belt and stare out of the window, while she blindly tried to click it into position, her hands trembling.

Why were they trembling? Was this just shock

at seeing Eli again? Or was it more to do with her body's alarming response to him? If someone had sat her down and told her that whenever the day occurred that she would meet up with Eli Johns again, she would be sexually attracted to him immediately, Charlie would have laughed with obscene amounts of hilarity in their face. Because nothing of the sort could ever be possible.

And yet here she was.

The engine rumbled into life. 'We all ready?'

She managed a smile and tried not to focus on his large, square hands on the steering wheel. He had lots of thin leather bracelets on his wrists. They were old and worn, but contrasted beautifully with his darker skin tone. Her gaze travelled up his arms, hidden by the flowing shirt he wore, and she couldn't help but wonder what his forearms would look like. She liked forearms. Found them sexy. She didn't know why.

'My mom's been in and spruced up the cottage for you. Fresh bed sheets, some flowers. She's even put some things in your fridge.'

My mom.

Eli had received the most amazing present any kid in an orphanage could receive—adoption. They'd both given up on the idea. Teenagers didn't often get picked by families looking to foster or adopt. They'd been told that they were the hardest to place and it was something that you just learned to accept, and yet Eli had got the best gift in the world. Charlie remembered them coming to the orphanage. Had been aware of them sitting at the back of the room, talking quietly with some of the staff. Then they'd been mucking around with an indoor archery kit and Eli had hit the gold every single time he took a shot. She'd thought he was showing off and he'd gone over to talk to Jason, one of the care workers, who'd been standing with the Clarks, and they'd all begun to laugh and joke with one another and after that day Eli had kept getting invited out for day trips, or weekends with this family and then suddenly Eli was gone. For ever.

Charlie had never wanted to be jealous of Eli ever! But she had been back then. And she'd hated herself for it. She'd tried to make herself feel better by telling herself that at least Eli was gone now and she wouldn't have to put up with his teasing any more, or his practical jokes or the way he'd keep looking at her across the room, as if he was planning his next trick. She'd spent most of her childhood being aware of where he was, just so she could keep an eye out and, with him gone, she didn't have to worry about that any more.

What she hadn't expected to feel after he'd left was how much she'd actually *missed* him. It had hit her, unexpectedly, left her feeling emotionally winded. She'd not realised just how much he'd been a part of her life. The two of them, the oldest ones, watching the younger kids arrive and then going, never to be seen again. Losing Eli had been incredibly difficult to accept. That had been quite the shocker. But time had passed. More kids had arrived. Some others had left. And then Charlie had been accepted into medical school and she'd moved out. Moved away. Begun to live on her own and make her own way in life. And Eli had been mostly forgotten.

Until now.

She had a brief, blurry memory of Mrs Clark. Back then, she'd been a tall woman, dark-haired. Quite pretty. And she'd thought nothing of squatting down to talk to and enjoy the company of some of the younger kids. Charlie had never spoken to her, though. She'd always held back to protect herself. If you didn't have hope, then you couldn't be disappointed.

'You must thank her for me.'

'No doubt you'll run into her at some point. Alice? Are you going to go to the school here in Vasquez?'

Alice looked up at her, uncertainly.

So Charlie answered for her. 'Yes. The one on Pelican Point, I think it's called.'

'Yep. That's the one Mom teaches at. She's probably going to be Alice's teacher.'

'Oh. Right.'

There was a brief uncomfortable silence where she determinedly looked out of the truck window, rather than at him, to observe the passing scenery. Vasquez was a small town. Neat, clean streets. Well-tended, older properties with great gardens. Often, people would notice the truck and give them a wave, smiling broadly, and she realised that Eli was liked here. Loved. Clearly he'd settled well into this place and she was surprised. When she'd known him as a young boy, he'd been into rap music and video games and technology. He'd loved living in the city and she would never have guessed that he would settle so well into a place that was a little more remote. Briefly, she wondered where he'd trained to become a doctor.

Beyond the streets she saw mountains, lush and green at the moment, but the tops of them were obscured by the white clouds that drifted high above. Birds soared high above in the sky, but she didn't know what kind. They looked quite large. Seabirds? Or hunting birds like ospreys or kites?

Maybe she'd learn all of that after being here a few months, and thank goodness there was an end date to her contract and she'd not moved here permanently! Because she really didn't think she'd be able to deal with working with Eli for much longer than she had to.

'Here we go.' Eli hit a left and pulled up at a small log-cabin-style cottage that had some hanging baskets full of flowers either side of the front door. It had a wrap-around porch, with a bench and what looked like a hammock and some potted plants too. 'Home, sweet home.'

'For a little while, anyway.' She felt the need to say it. To remind him that she wasn't here very long. It was what she was used to. Always moving. Never quite settling anywhere. It was why she'd never bought a house. Why she'd never bought a car. Why she always worked as a locum, or covered temporary contracts. It made her feel better to keep on moving. To get to know people for a little while and then move on. Because the past could creep up on you unexpectedly and the internet had a long memory. Something you thought was gone could return in a nanosecond, if people wanted it to.

Eli was already hefting her case out of the back of the truck and pulling it towards the front porch and squatting to the welcome mat, lifting it and retrieving a key.

Quaint.

But she didn't want him in their home. She didn't want to see him in there, all damp and muscly and devastatingly handsome. She wanted him gone, so that she and Alice could look around themselves. Get settled in. She'd have to see Eli at work and that would be enough as it was.

He was already unlocking the door and swinging it open, stepping back so they could pass him.

Alice ran in excitedly, but Charlie paused and took the key from his fingers, trying not to register what it felt like when her fingers brushed his. Like electricity. 'We can get settled in, thanks. I'll see you at the clinic on Monday morning?'

He got the message. Well, she hoped so, when he grinned and folded his arms, leaning against the doorjamb.

'Yes, you will. Eight o'clock sharp. You ready for a taste of Alaskan medicine? It might not be what you're used to.'

She had no idea what he meant. Surely all medicine was the same? 'Of course.'

'Great. Okay. I'll be seeing you,' he said, staring at her and smiling in that ridiculous way he'd had when they were kids. As if he'd got something up his sleeve that she simply wasn't prepared for.

'You will.'

'Mom! Come see the back yard!'

'Excuse me.' And she closed the door on him with some satisfaction.

Eli could wait.

Eli could go home.

And she was going to get settled in and hope that the next few months would fly by.

CHAPTER THREE

THE VASQUEZ MEDICAL CLINIC AND HOSPITAL appeared to be the largest building she'd seen here yet. It was long and low, all on the same storey, but stretched out, abutting the lush green mountain that sat behind it.

Charlie was very nervous of going in. She knew she needn't be. She was a very capable doctor and she was so used to having first days at work. Getting to know everyone, finding out where everything was. One of her strongest skills was adaptation and she prided herself on settling somewhere quickly and easily, to make her working life run smoothly. All she had to do was be friends with these people. They didn't have to have any heart-to-hearts. They never needed to know her past. They just needed her to fit in and do her job and that worked for her.

But here? That was going to be a different story.

Earlier this morning, she'd dropped Alice off at the school. It was her first year in kindergarten, but Charlie had no worries about her daughter fitting in either. Alice was a confident and independent young lady, just as Charlie had taught her to be.

Who is the only person you can rely on?
Me!
Who is the only person who can make you happy?
Me!

Sentences she'd drilled into her from an early age. It was important that Alice understand that the world was a harsh place. Because it was. In the early years, of course, Alice hadn't really known they were moving so much. Last year, in pre-kindergarten, she'd kind of got a little upset at leaving her friends behind, but Charlie knew she would make new ones! And everyone always wanted to be friends with the new kid and Mrs Clark, Eli's adopted mother and Alice's new teacher, had seemed wonderful.

'Charlie! Alice! It's a pleasure to meet you, at last!' Mrs Clark had crouched to smile at Charlie's daughter and shake her hand. 'Eli's told me so much about you, already!'

Had he? What was there to tell? What did *he* even know about her?

'Are you excited, Alice? First day!'

Alice was excited. Of course she was. Charlie had raised a confident daughter, there would be no tears, no clinging to her mother's leg.

'We're going to do lots of fun things today, so I hope you're ready?'

'I'm ready!' Alice took Mrs Clark's hand.

Eli's mother stood again and looked at Charlie. 'Settled in all right? Is everything okay with the cottage?'

'It's great, thank you. And thanks again for putting some foodstuffs in the fridge for us. You didn't have to do that. You must let me know what I owe you.'

'You don't owe me anything! It's an absolute pleasure.'

'No, I insist.'

'Look, I tell you what…you can pay me back by coming over tonight and I'll cook you both a nice hot meal. I'd love for us to sit and chat and get to know one another. Six o clock be okay? My grandkids will be there, so people for Alice to play with.'

Charlie couldn't think of how to get out of it. What to say, so as not to offend this woman? 'It won't seem right you feeding us again, when we're the ones that owe you.'

'Then let's call it a potluck! You make something and bring it over—how does that sound?'

'Er…great. Sure. Thanks.' Charlie smiled, figuring she'd do this the once and then gently extract herself and Alice from Mrs Clark's home, claiming a school night. That she'd need to get

Alice in the bath and then bed before school the next day.

It wasn't that she didn't like Mrs Clark. Far from it. She seemed a lovely, warm and welcoming woman. Her hair a little greyer than before, but still the same genuine smile. But this much attention made Charlie feel uncomfortable. Generally she was introverted and liked her own company. Being with someone so…open and full of life was a little…disturbing. It made her want to retreat and hide so she could breathe again.

She'd glanced at her watch and said goodbye and now she was standing outside the clinic, wondering just what awaited her inside. Had Eli told everyone in there who she was and where she was from? She hoped not, because that wasn't something she told anyone, ever. Her private life was her own and no one needed to know it. Exposure, she'd learned, came at a cost.

Mrs Clark had already superimposed herself into Charlie's life with her expectations, what would Eli do?

She pushed open the glass door and headed inside, her gaze instantly taking in all the information. A reception desk straight ahead. An empty waiting area to her right. This looked like the primary care area of the clinic. There was a corridor in the middle signposting X-Ray, Ultrasound, Day Surgery and Inpatient Care. It was bright. Welcoming. A nurse walked up the corridor in pale green scrubs, before turning into a doorway and disappearing.

Charlie walked up to Reception. Behind it sat a lady who looked to be in her fifties. She was working on a sudoku puzzle. 'Hello. I'm Dr Charlotte Griffin. Dr Clark is expecting me?'

The woman looked up in surprise. 'Oh! Are you the new doctor taking over for Nance? My name's Dorothea. Welcome, we spoke on the phone the other day!'

Charlie smiled. 'Thanks. I can't help but notice that you don't have anyone waiting…is that normal? Or haven't you opened yet?'

'Oh, this is normal! The folks around here are quite hardy. We have to be. We don't go running to our doctor with every little twinge or headache like they do in the big city. It has to be gushing blood or about to fall off before anyone will walk in here!' Dorothea laughed. 'Except for Stewie. You'll meet him soon, no doubt.' She leaned in. 'Bit of health anxiety and keeps us on our toes with all his imagined diagnoses, which we have to check out, just in case.'

'I'll look forward to meeting him.' Charlie was used to frequent fliers. 'And where would I find Dr Clark?'

Dorothea checked her watch. 'He'll be in his office. See that corridor? Down to the end, last door on the right.'

'Thanks. Very nice to meet you, Dorothea.'

'Call me Dot.'

Dot. Okay. Charlie smiled her thanks and began to walk down the corridor, feeling the butterflies in her stomach begin their dance. Sweat began to bloom in her armpits and the small of her back, despite the antiperspirant she'd sprayed on this morning, anticipating such a thing.

It really was ridiculous. She shouldn't be feeling this way.

What I need to do is pretend that I don't know him at all. It's just a normal first day and I want to get stuck into treating patients. Just do the job I'm here to do. Easy, right?

She squared her shoulders and sucked in a breath as she reached his office. His door was open and as she turned the corner to enter, hand raised to rap her knuckles on the door, she expected she'd see him behind his desk, either on the phone, or at his computer completing a report or something.

What she *did not* expect was to see him doing press-ups, bare-chested, down on the ground.

She'd never goggled in her life, but she did in that moment.

He was a thing of beauty. As if he'd been carved. Each muscle apparent across his back and shoulders, his long hair loose, the waves touching the carpet each time he lowered himself down. He had a tattoo in the centre of his upper back, just beneath his neck, of the caduceus. The staff, entwined with two snakes, used to symbolise medics.

She had to lick her lips before she could speak. 'Good morning.'

He grunted one last time as he pushed himself to his feet and turned to face her, his cheeks red with effort, his smile broad. 'Good morning, Dr Griffin! Sorry about this, I usually like to start my day with some cardio exercises.'

Charlie could think of other cardio exercises that might be more fun, but she quickly pushed those thoughts to one side.

Be professional. First day, remember. Pretend you don't know him.

'So do I. It's called getting Alice up and ready for school.'

He smiled that charming and effortlessly cheeky smile of his that made her heart go thumpety-thump, raising her blood pressure by a few points. Which made her feel angry and raised it a little more.

Eli grabbed a towel off his chair and began to wipe himself down with it, before grabbing a loose shirt and shrugging that on, once he'd sprayed himself with some cologne he didn't need. It was unfair enough that he looked as fine as he did, did he really need to smell nice, too?

She turned away as he buttoned his shirt. She wasn't sure why. She'd just seen him half naked, why should she turn away as he put clothes *on*?

But then she figured that getting dressed and un-
dressed was something a person normally did in
private and perhaps she didn't want to witness
him doing private things? Or maybe it was because she would focus too much on the disappearing sight of his chest and stomach? Either way it
was because of lust or etiquette.

Quite frankly Charlie was amazed that his
primary care clinic wasn't filled every day with
every young woman in town with drooling issues,
just so they could spend time with him, being
dazzled by his eyes and attention. Imagine what
it would feel like to be besotted with Eli and have
him sitting close to you as he listened to your
chest with his stethoscope... Where would you
look exactly? At those eyes? His luscious hair?
The shape of his fine arms? Or would you just be
so busy trying to slow and calm your breathing?

'Take a seat. Can I get you anything? Coffee?
Tea? Juice?' Eli walked to the other side of his
desk and got settled in.

'I'm fine, thanks.'

'Okay. Well, I thought for this first week you
could shadow me in both the clinic and the hospital and, that way, you'll get to know where everything is and how we work here. I took the
courtesy of making your ID card. Here you go.'
He pulled a lanyard from his top desk drawer.
'This will log you into the system each time you
need it. Just swipe it in the card reader.'

'Great.' She hung it around her neck.

'You'll be expected to take care of patients in the primary care setting, as well as out in the field. We occasionally do house visits. We often get called to accidents themselves.'

'Chuck told me.'

'Yeah. Great guy. He ever tell you about the time we almost had to amputate his leg?'

'No. He didn't.'

'He'll probably save that story for when you're eating. Right! Shall I show you around the place?'

She stood and nodded. 'Sounds perfect.'

She had her walls up. He sensed that immediately. Charlie was trying to show him that she was there to be professional and do the work, but he wished that she'd chill out a little. It was hard trying to be friendly when all the other person would do was give you a tight smile, or a nod.

She'd loosen up, no doubt. She'd have no choice living out here in Vasquez. This wasn't the city. She wasn't living in a place where everyone was strangers. Everyone knew each other here. The same families had lived here for decades. You couldn't walk down the street without stopping to say hello a lot, or passing the time over a garden fence, or waving at someone across the street walking their dog. Everyone relied upon each other here. There was no other way to be when you lived in such an isolated spot.

If you didn't have each other's back, then you wouldn't survive. Alaska could kill you. Easily. There were creatures here that would happily rip you to shreds. The weather could turn in an instant and give you hypothermia, or block off roads, and if you tried to stay within your own bubble here? You wouldn't survive.

She'd begin to understand this at some point, he had no doubt, and he was looking forward to watching her learn. He could tell her outright, but where would the fun in that be? He'd keep an eye on her. Make sure that she and Alice remained safe. He just wouldn't tell her, because he figured that she wouldn't be too happy about that if he got all knight in shining armour on her. But he'd keep an eye out. Help when he was needed. It was always the same with these city folks that came to town. They thought they could continue to live their lives the way they did in the urban jungle, but you just couldn't do that out here. It was a culture shock, that was for sure. Things might be fine right now, but that was because the weather was okay right now, but when it turned?

'I'll show you the primary care clinic first. That's where you'll do the majority of your work.'

'Where do you do the majority of yours?'

'The clinic, but I also do surgeries in the theatre.'

'Impressive.'

'You have to be able to multitask out here.

Some patients wouldn't last if they had to wait for a medical evacuation flight out to a big hospital, so I do what I can here to keep them alive before the big guns arrive.'

'Like a first responder?'

'Pretty much, but you'd be surprised at how much more we do.'

'What was your last big case that got transported out?'

He thought for a moment. 'Cindy Kramer. Pregnant with triplets, naturally. We were all set up, knew how we'd handle it if she made it to term, but she went into labour prematurely at twenty-eight weeks and we simply didn't have the capacity to care for three premature babies of that gestation. Thirty weeks onwards, maybe, but her babies were guesstimated at less than a pound each, it would have been arrogant of us to assume we could help them the best, so we arranged for transport. Before that, it was Ken Palmer. Creutzfeldt-Jakob disease. Cruel way to go. We thought stroke initially. Something neuro definitely, maybe encephalitis or meningitis, and he was deteriorating fast. He got flown to Anchorage and they diagnosed the CJD. He died within the week.'

'It attacks fast.'

Eli nodded. 'Just two weeks prior he'd been telling me about how he'd booked flights to go and visit his grandbabies. He'd been so excited.

Hadn't seen them for three months, not since they were born.' He shook his head. Even now, knowing what he knew about CJD, he still could not quite believe how fast that disease had progressed. Ken had seemed fine. Until he wasn't. And his family had felt as though they'd missed out on saying goodbye, because Ken hadn't been conscious enough to realise.

But Eli believed Ken knew. That he'd heard. Because he did believe that the hearing was one of the last senses to go and that, even though Ken couldn't respond, he heard his family say 'I love you'.

'This will be your room.' Eli stepped back, so Charlie could go in and take a look around. He watched her carefully. Observing her facial expression. The way she moved. The way she now looked. She was a couple of years younger than him, but he'd known, even back then, that she would grow up to be beautiful. He'd just not anticipated *how* beautiful. The acne had gone and now her skin was smooth and soft. Long, thick chestnut-coloured hair. Wide brown eyes, beautiful high cheekbones and full, soft lips. She was elegant. Maybe a little too thin still? But she'd always been highly strung. An anxious mess of nerves as a kid. Maybe she was still the same and living off nervous energy all the time?

Charlie trailed fingertips across her desk, then

stopped and frowned, reaching to pick up the large plastic frog he'd left on top of her computer. 'Really, Eli?'

He couldn't help but chuckle. Glad she'd noticed it. Happy that she'd remembered the reference. 'Just a reminder of happy times past.'

'Happy times past? You should give me the dictionary you're using because I don't think happy times past means what you think it means.'

'Oh, come on, the frog thing was funny.'

She stared at him, no hint of humour on her face. 'For you, maybe.' She threw the plastic frog into the trash can underneath the desk.

Okay, so maybe leaving a live frog in her bed as a parting gift before he left with the Clarks wasn't the greatest thing to do, but he'd been scared! As an orphan, you always hoped the day would come in which you'd finally get a family, but then when you did, it was terrifying, because what if those people weren't what you hoped they'd be? The Clarks had seemed great and he'd got along fantastic with them, but what if it was all for show? What if they weren't who they seemed to be? Other kids kept coming back because it hadn't worked out. Some kids came back because the police had got involved. Eli was having to say goodbye to the one family he did know and he wanted everyone, including Charlie, to remember him. And as he'd joked around and pranked her before, he figured another prank was the way to go!

It was his way of saying *I'm gonna miss you, kid*.

There was a pond near to the orphanage and on the day he knew he was going to go away with the Clarks, he sneaked out quickly after breakfast with everyone and caught the frog. It might even have been a toad. Ugly little thing it was, brown and lumpy, and he tucked it into her bed, down near the foot end, knowing she made her bed every day after breakfast. He could have put that frog in anyone's bed, but he put it in hers, because…well, he didn't know why.

He hoped to be around to see her find it. To give her a hug and say goodbye, but the Clarks made good time in the traffic and they arrived early and so he never got to see her reaction…

I guess she didn't enjoy it.

'Is this how it's going to be every day, while I'm here?' she asked.

'Maybe not *every* day.' He tried to say it as a joke, but it landed on deaf ears. She didn't find it funny and it left him feeling a little frustrated, but he chose not to show it.

'I'm here to do a job, Eli. Not have a replay of our childhood years, which for you might have been great fun, but for me they're not something I choose to recall with fondness. I'd appreciate it if you'd just let me do my job and not tell other people about how you know me.'

Well, it might be a little late for that. Because his family knew. He'd told them already when he'd recognised her name on the information sent over by the agency. 'All right.'

She nodded. 'Good.'

A buzzer sounded. A short, sharp sound.

She looked up. 'What's that?'

Eli smiled. Saved by the bell. 'It means we have a patient in the clinic.'

'Great.'

'Follow me.' He led the way back to his consulting room, a room he loved and adored.

His walls were covered in photographs that he'd taken. The beauty of Vasquez. The landscape. The wild animals. A grizzly catching salmon. A moose scratching its head on a tree. An osprey that had just caught a large trout. But then there were all the other photos. Eli on a parachute jump in mid-air. Eli paddle-boarding on Vasquez Lake. Another of him hand-feeding a wolf cub. Then there were the trophies that lined his cabinets. First place in that chainsaw competition he'd participated in. Second place for most fish caught in an ice-fishing competition. Fastest ascent on Rainier's Peak. Third place in the 2022 Vasquez Ironman Race. A medal for coming tenth in an extreme one hundred K race.

'Are these all yours?' she asked in surprise.

'Just a few that I keep on display.'

'There's *more*?'

'You should see my house.' He grinned, thinking of his trophy room. It was silly really, but it was something his new mom had started when they'd adopted him. Every achievement he ever had, she either made him a certificate or got him a gift. If he got a high score on an essay. When he got into college. When he learned to drive. When he got accepted into medical school. He'd thought she was just being cute, but then he'd realised he really began to value the recognition that he'd achieved something, that he was good at something, and it drove him to join clubs and societies.

At med school, everyone thought that he might fail because so much of his spare time was taken up doing sports or something. But he not only passed, he was top of his year. He had so many friends, so many dudes he knew he could rely on. So much female attention it was almost embarrassing. But he'd never been so admired or loved before and it was heady. Being active, engaging in extreme sports and testing himself became a way for him to feel good about himself. Especially after the cancer. These things, these trophies, they became proof that he was still who he wanted to be. Loved. *Able*. In every way except the one way he craved.

Eli swiped his ID card through the reader and

tapped some details into the computer to bring up the patient who had arrived in clinic.

'Camille Henriksen. Injury to hand' was what it said on the screen. Could be anything.

'First patient is Camille. Fine ol' gal. Must be ninety, if she's a day. Came here with her husband over fifty years ago.'

Charlie nodded.

Eli went to call his patient and stood in the doorway waiting for her. When she came shuffling into view, he noticed that she had a dish towel wrapped around her left hand that looked bloody. 'Camille, what have you done to yourself this time?'

'Oh, I was just cleaning some fish that Marv brought back and the knife slipped. I'm sure it's just a small nick, but Marv insisted I come because I ain't had my tetanus in a while.'

'All right, well, you come on in and take a seat and we'll have a look. I got our new temporary doctor in here with me observing, Dr Charlie Griffin, is that okay with you?'

Camille looked in at Charlie and smiled and tried to wave with her bloodied towel. 'Hello, Charlie. Always nice to see a new face around here.'

'Pleasure to meet you, Mrs Henriksen.'

'Oh, call me, Camille. Everyone does.' Camille shuffled over to the patient's seating area and sat down with a heavy breath. 'Whoo! That's quite the walk. I'm getting my steps in today.'

Eli grabbed some gloves, passed a pair to Charlie and then sat opposite Camille after he'd assembled some gauze pads, a saline wash and some proper bandaging on a small trolley. 'Let's see what we've got here. You okay for me to unwrap this?'

'You do what you have to, Eli, I'm a tough ol' bird.'

'You're a sprightly young thing, Camille. Less of the old,' he said with a smile, playing the game they always played when Camille mentioned her age.

She smiled back at him, wincing slightly as he got closer to the injury.

The dish towel was soaked with blood. And he knew his patient was always dramatically reducing the description of her illnesses and injuries. Once she'd mentioned she was a little hot and she'd been running a fever of a hundred and two. Another time she'd complained about *a bit of a rash* she had and it had turned out she'd had the worst case of shingles he'd ever seen! Considering the amount of blood, he knew he wasn't about to see *a small nick*. Whatever she'd done, he expected to be putting in stitches. The question was, how many?

He unwrapped the final part of the towel and kept his face neutral, but he heard Charlie suck in a small gasp. The *small nick* was her missing the top half of her left index finger!

'Camille…'

'It ain't that bad. You just stitch me up and give me my shot and I'll be on my way.'

'Where's the fingertip, Cam?' he asked.

She grimaced slightly. 'Well, that's a bit of a story in itself.'

'Tell me.'

'It rolled off the chopping board and onto the floor and you know Sookie, you know what she's like when I'm in the kitchen preparing food, she's always there. Watching. Waiting.'

'Who's Sookie?' Charlie asked.

'My Labrador. Been with me eight years.' Camille smiled with fondness. 'Anyway, she might have run off into the garden with it and by the time I'd wrapped my hand and got out there to take it off her, it was all mangled and chewed and so I had to throw it away.'

'It's in the garbage?' asked Eli.

''Fraid so. There'd have been no point in bringing it along here anyways, so just you stitch me up and send me on my way. I've still got that mess to clean in the kitchen and my Marv don't like to wait for his dinner.'

'Marv can make his own dinner just this once. I can't just stitch you up, Camille. I've got to clean this out and somehow join up the edges. I might need to do a small skin graft or create a skin flap.'

'Sounds expensive.'

'Sounds *necessary*,' he replied in a sterner voice, knowing he needed to let her know that they couldn't just rush this or put a sticking plaster on it.

Camille sighed. 'I'm gonna be here a while?'

'You're gonna be here a while,' he answered, this time with understanding and sympathy. He glanced at Charlie. She was listening and watching intently. 'Listen, I'll give Marv a ring, explain the situation and, if he's really put out, I'll get someone to go to your place with a sandwich or something. What do you say?'

Camille smiled and patted Eli's cheek with her good hand. 'You're a good boy to me.'

He cradled her hand with his own. 'You make it easy. Now then. Let me clean this and bandage it up so a nurse can get you to X-Ray. Afterwards you can sit in the TV room for a while, all right?'

'All right.'

He made quick work of cleaning and dressing her wound then got up and went over to his desk. Lifted the phone and punched in a number. 'Hi, yeah, can you send Diana through to take Camille to X-Ray? Cheers.' He put down the phone. 'The nurse is going to take you to X-Ray, just to make sure you haven't chipped the bone.'

Camille nodded and then shuffled away with the nurse after she arrived.

He turned back to Charlie with a smile. 'Yes, before you ask. They're all like that here.'

'She just seemed fine with the idea that she'd lost the top of her finger.' Charlie was helping him clear away the debris left behind by him redressing Camille's wound. 'What do you think she'll prefer?'

He thought for a minute. 'Knowing Camille? Local anaesthetic and a skin flap, so she can get home quicker. If the bone isn't damaged, we can just clean it back a little, remove the rest of the nail and stitch the skin into position. Want to assist?'

'Yes, of course.'

'Ever done one of these before?'

'Yes, but it was a full finger amputation, though.'

'Great.' He went to write up his notes on Camille, his fingers racing over the keyboard. A new file popped up in the corner of his screen and when he accessed it, he saw it was Camille's X-ray. 'Tell me what you see.' He knew she was qualified. More than qualified. Charlie had had experience in many different centres, primary care clinics and emergency rooms, but he still wanted to assess her skill.

Charlie came behind him and leaned forward to look at the screen, her long brown hair brushed over his shoulder and he couldn't help but inhale her scent. It was something soft. Feminine.

Meadow-like? It did delicious things to his insides and he had to silently inhale a long, slow breath.

'Looks clean to me. The bone hasn't been damaged. The distal phalanx looks complete. Some signs of arthritis, but that's to be expected in a woman her age.'

'I agree. Okay. Let's go offer Camille an upgrade.'

Eli looked different in scrubs and, with his hair tied back and a face mask on, all she could see were his eyes smiling at her from across their patient.

It was an unsettling thing being smiled at by Eli. The shared knowledge of their history beamed out from every glance, every twinkle, every crease of his eyes when he laughed or joked and tried to include her. His smile said *I Know You* and all she could feel was fear, because of it. She didn't like people knowing her. She didn't like people getting close. She preferred to be an unknown entity.

Camille was more than happy with the treatment plan and had clutched Charlie's hand intensely as Eli had injected the ring block to numb Camille's finger completely.

Ring blocks were painful, because the needle had to be inserted in sensitive areas at the base of the finger where it met the palm and also had to be inserted a couple of times, on both sides to ensure that the correct nerves were anaesthetised, so that the procedure could be completed painlessly.

'All done,' Charlie said, smiling, dabbing away at the spots of blood that had appeared.

'I think that hurt more than chopping the tip off,' said Camille.

'You just lie back now and think of something nice,' said Eli. 'Think of lying on a nice warm beach, cocktail in one hand and a damn fine book in the other.'

'Hah!' said Camille. 'I'd rather think of a handsome young man wafting me with an ostrich-feather fan. Is that okay, or am I being sexist?'

'You think of whatever you want,' said Charlie, smiling. She liked Camille. The lady was feisty and funny and brave, with a kick-ass attitude to life that Charlie wished she could have. 'You don't want to think of Marv wafting you with a fan?'

'Oh, honey, where's the fun in that? I've seen my husband without a shirt and, though I love him dearly, I'd much rather think of a strongly muscled torso, if you don't mind?'

Charlie couldn't help but remember the sight of Eli half naked doing press-ups in his office and how the sight of *him* had affected *her*.

Eli chuckled. 'Whatever works.'

Thinking of Eli's muscles certainly worked to help fire Charlie's imagination! He'd changed from a tall, lanky teen to a hunk of edible proportions who'd look more at home doing a calendar shoot.

Physically, he'd changed, that was for sure. But mentally? Emotionally? He still seemed like a prankster. A joker. Someone who always saw the lighter side of life, who was always on the lookout for laughs. And that made him dangerous, because she'd had enough of humiliation. Was too sensitive to it.

Maybe he ought to have pursued a life as a stand-up comedian? Because he'd never mentioned wanting to be a doctor. She'd have remembered that conversation. Becoming a doctor was all Charlie had ever wanted to do and she'd adored watching the medical dramas on the TV as a young kid, imagining herself doing the same kind of work. Saving lives. Making a difference.

The human body was amazing. It had a vast amount of different systems within, it had millions of different things that could go wrong with it. Diseases, conditions, bacteria, viruses, genetics, accidents. Sometimes it was a mystery, but, mostly, problems could be resolved and people walked away better. Healthier. Happier. Her entire childhood, she'd felt insignificant. As if she wasn't important and becoming a doctor would make her feel as though she did have a purpose. That what she did mattered. That she *was* important.

She'd never expected to become a mother so quickly, but it had happened, and when she'd given birth to Alice and held her in her arms? She'd known that she mattered now, more than anything. Her daughter needed her. Relied on her. Loved her. Unconditionally. And that love was such an overwhelming force! She no longer felt like a nobody.

That fascination with the human body had then terrified her, because she knew of all the horrible things that could possibly assail her daughter and there might be something that she wouldn't be able to save Alice from. That was what kept her up at night and staring at the ceiling and occasionally creeping into her daughter's room to check on her and stare at her and feel love for her ooze from every pore. And then, when Glen had done what he did…she'd realised all the other dangers that Alice might face in her future, too.

Eli worked quickly. Deftly. Chatting with Camille to keep her calm, making her laugh, making her smile. Doing the thing that Eli did best.

'You hear about Abe being knocked into the bay by a laker?' He chuckled.

'Laker?' Charlie frowned, not sure of the term.

'It's a fish. A lake trout.' Camille smiled. 'And no, I hadn't. What happened?'

'He was out fishing and got a bite. Stood up to reel it in, not realising he'd got a whopper on the other end. Damn thing fought him tooth and nail, he said, and, with all the lunging and fighting, knocked Abe off balance and he fell into the bay. Said it was a forty-pounder, at least.'

Camille laughed. 'Hah! Typical of Abe. I bet it was tiny, but he fell into the bay because of how many beers he'd been drinking.'

'Couldn't say for sure. He didn't come in here afterwards for a check-up, but his wife told me he came home soaking wet with a tall tale to tell.'

'Sounds like Abe!'

Charlie smiled, listening. Everyone seemed to know everyone here and maybe that was a good thing in such an isolated spot? Maybe it wasn't. What about having some privacy? 'Did he bring home the fish?' she asked.

Eli met her gaze and she was hit by the impact of it. It made her feel warm and gooey inside and that disturbed her greatly, so she looked away, breaking eye contact to reach for another gauze pad. 'No. Said we all needed to take his word for it. Now he's obsessed with going out there every day to catch his giant laker. Says it might be a record-breaker.'

'Maybe he's telling the truth,' she suggested.

Camille smiled at her in that way that told Charlie she was being naive. 'Once you've met Abe, then maybe you'll reassess your position on that one.'

'I do like to make my own mind up on people. Not just listen to what others say. Who's to know their reason for telling a story a certain way?'

They both looked at her.

'Fair enough,' said Eli. 'You're absolutely right.'

She smiled, glad to have made her point.

'But we're right, too.' He grinned at her and continued tying off the last stitch, snipping the stitch free with his scissors. 'All done! Gonna get this bandaged up now, then give you your tetanus shot, okay?'

'Okay.'

'We're gonna need you to keep this dry as much as you can and come back in ten days to have the stitches removed. I'll book you in an appointment now. But if you have any pain, or develop any fever or feel unwell, I want you to call immediately, okay?'

'I know, I know. This ain't my first time at a rodeo.'

When Camille had gone home, they returned to the clinic to discover there were two more people waiting patiently. One was sitting with a laptop, furiously writing away with what looked like a large sticking plaster, leaking blood, stuck to the side of her face, and the other was a guy sitting with one gloriously swollen ankle propped up on a chair.

Charlie looked at Eli and whispered, 'Is everyone accident-prone, here in Vasquez? Does anyone turn up with, say, a sore throat?'

Eli smiled at her. 'What do you think?'

CHAPTER FOUR

WHEN CHARLIE COLLECTED her daughter from kindergarten, Alice came running out, happily clutching a painting she'd done of two figures in purples, reds and greens. 'Look what I did!' she said, showing her mom the art.

'That's amazing! Is that me and you?' Charlie asked.

'No, that's me and Mrs Clark, my teacher!'

'Oh. Lovely.' She tried not to act surprised. They'd been here in Vasquez five minutes and by all accounts the Clark family owned most things round here and already Mrs Clark, Eli's mother, had usurped Charlie's position in Alice's drawings. Was this teacher superwoman? She had to be bloody amazing to have inspired this.

Trying not to let it bother her, she walked Alice home, her daughter chatting all the way about what her first day had been like. Apparently kindergarten was *the best*.

She was happy for her. Truly. But this was the first time Charlie had spent so much time away from her daughter and she was already beginning to feel a little displaced. A part of her had hoped that Alice would have missed her and they'd spend this time walking home and making something for the potluck together, so that they could soak up being with each other again, but Alice seemed like a new child.

I mean, it's great. I love that she's so independent. I raised her to be that way, of course.

But was it backfiring?

Who is the only person you can rely on?

Me!

Who is the only person who can make you happy?

Me!

Had Charlie inadvertently ingrained into her daughter that she couldn't even rely on her own mother? Because that was not what she'd intended the mantras to mean. She'd meant that Alice couldn't rely on anyone else *except* her. That *she* could still make her daughter happy.

Charlie bit her lip as she unlocked the door to the cottage and let them in. 'We're going to a potluck tonight at Mrs Clark's house.'

'We are?' Alice looked thrilled and began bouncing around the house. 'That's amazing! She's so great, Mom!'

'So I keep hearing.' She gave a bit of a rictus grin and then turned to open the fridge and examine the contents. 'What do you think we should make?'

'PB and J sandwiches.'

Charlie smiled. 'You don't take sandwiches to a potluck, honey. You cook something. Take something hot.'

'Oh.'

'I could do chicken enchiladas? You fancy those?'

'Great! Can I go outside and play until then?'

'Sure, honey.' The cottage came with a small but pretty enclosed garden, with a six-foot wooden fence at the back that offered some protection from the forest and mountains that rose up behind it. Charlie felt sure that she'd be safe out there. There was no pond to worry about, no rockery for her to fall on and crack her head open—which was what the woman with the laptop had done, needing two stitches for her trouble. The cottage had simple flower beds and a lawn. That was it.

Charlie began chopping onions, peppers and chillies, while a pan gently warmed on the hob, then she set them to frying, while she cut the chicken breasts into small chunks.

She tried not to think of Eli. She tried even harder not to think of Alice's painting stuck to the fridge by magnets, of her daughter and her kindergarten teacher. One day at school and already the effusively warm Mrs Clark had taken Charlie's place in her daughter's affections.

It seemed unfair. It seemed wrong and, Charlie had to admit, she felt a little jealous about it. An ugly emotion she didn't like feeling.

Stirring the refried beans into the passata and sweetcorn, she mused on the day and what it had been like to work with Eli. Apart from the half-naked workout and the frog reminder, it hadn't gone too badly. Clearly Eli was liked by his patients, who all seemed on first-name terms with him, which seemed odd. Charlie was used to being addressed as Dr Griffin. She liked that. It helped establish a professional distance from the patient and she'd worked hard to get the Dr part before her name. Hearing patients calling her Charlie had seemed weird.

'Eli' was a talented doctor, who stitched neatly despite the size of his large hands, who was adept with a scalpel and listened to his patients and involved them with their medical choices and options. He was still as ebullient as ever. Always looking for the joke, always grinning that cheeky grin of his, which she had to admit was actually kind of hot, and so the only two issues she had to face with him were the facts that he knew too much about her and that he was insanely attractive.

But she could never get involved with someone like Eli. Absolutely no way! She had a daughter to think about for one, and her daughter's father had humiliated her to such a level that she could never think of being with anyone else, never mind Eli, who thought that looking for laughs was the way to live life. She didn't need someone like that in her and Alice's life. Men were off-limits big-time. She had no time for them any more. It was just going to be herself and Alice from now on.

Unless Alice runs off with the amazing Mrs Clark.

On the walkover to the Clarks' house, Charlie was giving Alice the rules. 'We're not going to stay long, okay? It's a school night for one and I don't want you out too late. And remember, this is your teacher's house, so you call her Mrs Clark at all times. Once we've been there an hour, we're going to leave, okay?'

'Only an hour, Mom?'

'Alice, please…'

'Okay.' Alice didn't sound thrilled, but agreed. Clearly she had wonderful ideas about learning all about Mrs Clark by exploring her house and holding her teacher's hand all night, without letting go, because she was her *'new, most favouritest teacher ever!'*

The Clark house was the biggest in Vasquez. Of timber construction and painted white, it looked to be only a few years old. A new build? Maybe. The lawns were neatly trimmed and the front porch had a swing seat, lanterns and pots of beautiful flowers that Charlie couldn't name.

A chocolate Labrador watched them approach up the front pathway, thumping its wagging tail against the floorboards.

'Mom, look! A doggy!' Alice let go of her hand and tried to dash forward, forgetting everything Charlie had ever told her about the dangers of unknown dogs. She managed to grab Alice before she could get to it.

Of course the Clarks would have a dog. Of course it would be the cutest, friendliest-looking dog Charlie had ever met. Because for the last year, Alice had been begging her for a dog. She'd bought Alice dog plushies and always answered with *'One day, baby, not yet...'* and Alice would pout and frown and whine.

So, of course the perfect Clarks would have a dog. Why wouldn't they?

'It might not be friendly.' She tried to warn her daughter, as she always did when they were out and about in the world. Strange dogs could never be trusted, Alice should know that.

The front door that was hung with a handmade sign, adorned with ribbons and dried flowers that said *Welcome!* on it, opened and out stepped Mrs Clark with a beaming face. 'Hey, Alice! That's okay, you can give Mitch a cuddle! He loves cuddles.'

Charlie let go and her daughter ran the last few steps to the dog, knelt and threw her arms around it as Mitch proceeded to lick her face as if she were a lamb chop.

'Alice, don't let it—'

But it was too late. Alice was giggling and chuckling as Mitch slobbered all over her.

Mrs Clark smiled. 'Hello, Charlie. Mitch's tail is kind of like an early warning system here. As soon as we hear it thumping on wood, we know someone's coming. How are you, my dear?' Mrs Clark leaned forward and dropped a surprising kiss of welcome on Charlie's cheek. She stood back and waited for a response.

'I'm good, thanks. Alice had a great first day, by all accounts.'

'And did you?' Mrs Clark slipped her arm through Charlie's. 'You must come in and tell me all about it. Eli's told me his version, but I want to hear all about it from you.'

'Eli's here?' She stopped abruptly, surprised as to why she didn't consider that Eli might be at his mother's potluck.

'Of course! Now come on in and tell me all about it. Alice, sweetheart? Why don't you bring Mitch in and I'll find you some treats to feed him?'

And before Charlie could protest or say she'd changed her mind about coming, Mrs Clark was sweeping her into the house, saying, 'And you must call me Gayle.'

The Clark house had that warm and inviting

cottage look. Lots of floral prints and soft, pale stripes on cushions and rugs. Cream-coloured lamps lit pastel-painted bookcases, filled with leather-bound books. Huge, soft sofas adorned the living space, and next to one sat a wicker basket, filled with hand-wound balls of wool and what looked like a hat mid-make on a set of circular needles. Charlie knew they were called that, because a few years back she'd decided to try to knit Alice a jumper and the lady in the shop had told her that circular needles and using the magic loop method was the best way to do so, because then the jumper wouldn't have side seams. Well, Charlie had got hopelessly lost and the jumper, or what there was of it, had ended up being stuffed in a bag and donated to a craft library. A huge waste of money, but at least she had tried, hoping it would give her something to do after Alice was in bed and she had to sit alone in an apartment, pondering her life.

There were lots of people standing around that Charlie didn't know and Gayle lost no time in introducing her to everyone. A sea of names was given—mostly Clark relations—and she had no hope of remembering who was who, or who was a cousin, or an aunt or a nephew, but she saw Alice brush past her, being taken to the back garden to play with a bunch of other kids and Mitch. She wanted to tell her to be careful, but her voice got stuck in her throat, because suddenly Eli was there, holding a bottle of beer and looking ravishing in a soft off-white linen shirt and jeans.

'Hey.'

She awkwardly felt her cheeks colour. 'Hi.'

'It must be lovely to be reunited after all these years,' said Gayle. 'You two must have *so much* to talk about! Let me get you a drink, Charlie. What would you like?'

'Just an orange juice, if you have one, thanks.'

'You don't want anything stronger? We have wine?'

'I don't drink.'

'All right, orange juice it is. Let me take that, it looks wonderful!' and Gayle disappeared with her chicken enchilada dish, through the throng of people.

Charlie looked at the assembled guests, feeling awful. 'Is this a party? A birthday or an anniversary? Am I missing something? Should I have brought a gift?'

'Nope. Just a little get-together.'

'*Little?* You and I have different dictionaries.'

He laughed. 'This is just what it's like here. This is what having a family is like.'

'Is it?' She crossed her arms in front of her, feeling uncomfortable. She wasn't used to this! She'd never been part of anything this large. Even when she was married! Her husband hadn't had any close family. Even when they'd married it had just been a couple of witnesses at City Hall.

'Look, I know you're still feral and all, but try to relax. Enjoy it!'

She looked straight at him. 'I'm not feral!'

'Aren't you? I've seen more confident looks in cats backed into a corner.'

'I'm not feral. I know how to be around people.'

'But you don't know how to be comfortable around people who want to know more about you. I saw it today. You were taken aback when a patient called you Charlie, instead of Doctor. When people close the distance, your hackles go up. I can tell just by looking at you. Standing there with your arms crossed and looking for the exits with that frightened look upon your face. Relax a little. No one's going to bite you.' He took a swig from his bottle of beer.

She hated that he could tell! So she uncrossed her arms, but then she didn't know how to stand all of a sudden, without something to do with her hands, so she crossed her arms again.

Eli chuckled.

'Shut up!'

He laughed some more and she wanted to turn tail in that moment, find Alice and get the hell out of there!

But wouldn't that be proving his point?

So she wasn't great at people being close, so what? Eli had led a different life from hers. Their paths had diverted when he'd got adopted into the Clark family. Hers had continued to be hard, lonely and painful.

'I'm trying my best,' she said quietly.

And he looked at her in that moment, in this strange, intense way, so that she imagined he could somehow see all that had happened to her, every moment of hardship and humiliation, and she felt naked beneath his gaze.

'Here you go! One orange juice. Now then, Eli, don't monopolise Charlie! I want to introduce her to Gran.' Suddenly Gayle was pulling her away from the heat of Eli's gaze and through the crowds once again, into the kitchen this time to be introduced to a tiny silver-haired lady, who wore an apron and seemed to be deeply involved in the mass production of chocolate-chip cookies.

'Gran? This is Charlie, Eli's friend and new colleague at the clinic.'

Charlie extended a hand, but Gran looked at her oddly and stepped forward for a hug, instead.

'Hello, Charlie. Short for Charlotte, is it?'

Surprised by the sudden hug, she squeezed back and, when she was released, nodded, with a smile. 'Yes, that's right.'

'I always wanted to call Gayle Charlotte, but my husband—*may he rest in peace*—didn't like it and so Gayle it was. Eli never told us you were a pretty little thing.'

She wasn't sure how to respond to that. To be pleased that Gran thought she was pretty, or upset that Eli hadn't mentioned it? Not that she needed him to notice, but she worked hard to try and look good. She worked out at home often. Yoga. Pilates. Cardio twice a week. She ensured she always had her hair done every ten weeks and tried to eat healthily. But she wasn't doing it for any man. She did it for herself, for her own strive to perfection. Sometimes, she overdid it. Punishing herself with harsh exercise and high-intensity interval workouts. The last time had been after Glen had...

No. She didn't want to think about that again. It had already occupied too much of her life and decisions.

'Do you bake, Charlie?'

'Er, sometimes.'

'What's your favourite dessert? There's only one right answer, now!'

Panicked under the sudden pressure, she squeaked out an answer. 'Apple pie?'

Gran stared at her for a moment, then chuckled, slapping Charlie on the arm. 'Perfect! You're a keeper, for sure! Now, why don't you help me with the next batch?'

The next hour or so whizzed by in a whirlwind of flour, eggs and chocolate chips. Gran shared all her secrets—a pinch of cinnamon and nutmeg—and talked non-stop while they were in the kitchen.

At first, Charlie felt a little uncomfortable, but

after a while she relaxed into it and laughed and chuckled at Gran's stories of her early years romancing her soon-to-be husband, George, and how he'd sneak up the trellis at nights to knock on her bedroom window and sneak a kiss, and all the romance of their midnight escapes to take a walk beneath the moon and stars, hand in hand. Sometimes, Charlie just stood there and listened, not realising that she had been whisked away into a world of old-fashioned romance and wooing and how much she yearned for the world to be as simple as it was many decades ago. If you made a mistake relationship-wise back then, hardly anyone knew about it. Today? In this modern world? With social media being so prolific? You could be plastered across anyone's page in seconds, for the whole world to see. Until the end of days.

She didn't realise that Eli had been standing in the kitchen doorway watching her, until he spoke. 'Time to eat.'

Charlie turned, blushing, pulled back into the present, and she washed her hands, drying them on a towel. 'How can I help?' she asked.

'You've helped plenty. You're a guest. Gran? You shouldn't have worked her so hard…she's already had a long day.'

'Nonsense, Eli! This girl's got spirit. Now, Charlie, why don't you help me take these cookies through?'

She was happy to help. In fact, she liked helping and feeling a part of them. She wasn't sure how it had happened. One minute she'd been feeling trapped, the next she was revelling in the warmth of them all. This family group. And though, technically, she was an outsider, she'd been made to feel welcome. To feel an honorary member of this family. Even if it was just for this night. Gran had made her feel secure, as if she'd known that Charlie didn't want to answer personal questions, and so Gran had kept her questions light. What sports team did she follow? What was her favourite music? Had she seen last night's episode of some soap that Gran liked to watch?

At the rear of the house was a large porch that had a few long picnic tables set up, which was slowly beginning to groan with food, and, around the tables, all the gathered Clark family, her and Alice. Her daughter was at the far end, chuckling with kids her own age, and Charlie smiled to see her look so happy as she slid into a seat between Gayle and Eli. There didn't seem to be any standing on ceremony, everyone just dived into whatever food they fancied, and she couldn't help but notice that Eli loaded up his plate with her chicken enchiladas, a huge forkful of a green salad and a couple of dinner rolls. Charlie helped herself to some pasta that looked to be mixed with a spicy sausage of some kind and peppers, along with a different salad that was decorated with bacon bits and herby croutons.

'This is delicious,' she said to Gayle. 'How often do you guys get together like this?' She expected her to say that they didn't do it very often.

'All the time! Birthdays, anniversaries, graduations, days that end in the letter Y!' Gayle laughed and took a sip of her drink.

'Really? Isn't it a lot of hard work?'

'No! It's fun! Family is the most important thing in the world and, when you have it, you need to celebrate it as often as you can. Show people that you love them and want them around. That you're there as a supportive network for anything.' Gayle leaned in. 'Life is hard, you know? We know that more than most. But no one has to walk their path in life alone. With family? You can be strong and no matter what the world throws at you, it can't bring you down.'

Charlie smiled, slightly awestruck by the difference in their lifestyles. The Clarks clearly believed that together they were a force to be reckoned with, whereas Charlie had raised Alice to believe in the fact that they stood alone in this world and they could rely only on themselves. Who was right and who was wrong?

'Having family and having love is something you want to share. It's useless on its own when we all have so much love to give. That's why we decided we'd adopt. There are so many kids in this world that just need a chance, you know?'

Charlie nodded.

'Our lives have been so enriched since we brought Eli into our fold. Even through all his trials and tribulations, we wouldn't have had it any other way.'

His trials and tribulations? Surely his life had been perfect?

'We were pulled into his orbit. I mean…how could we not be? Have you seen him? He's gorgeous! But no, seriously, when you know, you know. Eli's vitality for life is infectious. He's always smiling, or laughing, and when we spoke to him, we just gelled, you know? You must know, you knew him back then!'

Yes, she'd known him. And Gayle was right. He did have and still had a vitality for life and seeking joy, but she hadn't known how to deal with him back then and she wasn't sure she knew how to deal with him now. Sitting this close, being part of his family, being welcomed, made her feel confused. It made her question her own life and what she might have been missing in it. It made her feel sad.

'I did.'

Gayle leaned in, conspiratorially. 'He told us about the frog.' She laughed.

Charlie nodded, smiling. 'He did?'

'Took him till last week to tell us, when he knew you were coming.'

'Did he tell you he put a frog in my office today, too?'

'A real one?'

'Plastic.'

'Eli!' Gayle scolded him and he chuckled beside her. Clearly happy to have surprised his mom and made her smile.

His *mom*.

He truly had been accepted as a member of this family. He was one of them, that was clear, the adoption was just paperwork. Eli was a Clark, through and through.

Charlie had always been sceptical of what it might feel like to be adopted. Whether you would truly feel a part of someone else's family. Whether they would accept you and treat you the same as their actual blood relatives.

But it had happened here, or so it seemed. Maybe Eli was just so laid-back and chill about everything, he didn't stress about it the way she once had?

Did she need to take a leaf out of Eli's book?

She couldn't believe she was even having to consider it.

CHAPTER FIVE

He'd been for his usual ten-kilometre run and was just arriving at the clinic in his running gear of sleeveless grey vest and red shorts when he noticed Charlie arriving with Frank Schwarz.

Charlie appeared to be trying to escort Frank into the building, but Frank was having none of it, slapping away Charlie's efforts to get him inside.

'Now, hold your horses there, missy!'

'Sir? You need to come inside, so I can treat you!'

'Hold up! Hold up, Charlie. This is Frank, he doesn't like going into hospitals or clinics.'

'But he's hurt!' she insisted, indicating the large fishing hook piercing his neck.

Eli had noticed the hook already. It had quite the barb poking out of Frank's skin, blood trickling down past his collar and staining his usual blue-checked flannel. 'I know that, but Frank doesn't come inside.'

'Whyever not?'

'Because everyone he's ever loved has gone

into this building behind us and not come out again, plus Frank has quite the phobia about needles.'

Charlie looked at him. 'Oh. I see, but he can't go around with that thing in his neck—it has to come out!'

'*Really?* I was thinking of leaving it in.' He smiled at her and Frank and steered him over towards the bench that was situated out front. 'How'd this happen, Frank?'

'I was prepping *Molly*, moving some fishing gear about, and I slipped on some oil or what have you and when I got up again, realised there was something catching on my collar. I wouldn't have come here at all. Was gonna clip off the barb and yank it out myself. Except this…' Frank gestured at Charlie '…this *lady* insisted. She was very forceful.'

Eli smiled. 'She can be and she was right to do so, Frank, this can't stay in and it's near to some pretty important structures in the neck.'

'You mean my jugular?'

'Or your carotid. Plus that hook's probably not the cleanest thing in the world either, so we're going to need to get you on some antibiotics.'

Frank frowned. 'I don't like taking tablets.'

'Well, you're going to have to, just this once, okay?'

'You can't just snip this thing and yank it out?'

'I'm sure we can, but I'd really like to get a

scan done, first. It does look superficial, but we need to be sure. You hit your head when you fell?'

I don't think so.'

'You lose consciousness?'

'No. I don't want to go inside there, Eli. I lost my Jane in there.'

Jane had been Frank's wife. They'd been married over forty years, until she had a sudden splitting headache, that had turned out to be a burst aneurysm. She died within minutes, before the medical evacuation could be arranged.

'It'll take five minutes, I promise you. Charlie and I will know what we're dealing with and we can get that sorted and have you back to *Molly* before you know it.'

'Who's Molly?' asked Charlie.

'My boat,' answered Frank.

'Oh.'

Eli smiled at Charlie. She looked beautiful today. Mornings agreed with her. Her hair was soft and floaty as she'd not yet tied it back for work and it cascaded over her shoulders like silk. She had a small divot that formed between her eyebrows, like now, when she was concerned, and her eyes looked darker, somehow.

'What do you say, Frank? You'll come in for the scan? Get treated. I'll give you antibiotics that you must take every day for a week and I'll come round to check on the wound in a couple of days. What do you say? I'll throw in a six-pack of beers, too.'

'He shouldn't drink on antibiotics,' Charlie said.

'I'll bring them when his course is over.' Eli smiled at her and winked at Frank, conspiratorially.

Frank gazed at the building behind them, as if considering it. 'On one condition.'

'What's that?'

'That I can sit outside, while I'm waiting. I don't want to feel trapped inside.'

'I'll open up the quad. There's a small garden. A bench. Some ducks have built a nest there next to the pond. You'll have nature.'

Frank considered it and as he did so, Eli's gaze drifted to Charlie.

She looked disbelieving. As if she couldn't quite believe that he was making all of these concessions for a patient. But she had to know that they performed medicine differently up here. It was hard enough getting patients to come in, in the first place. He would make whatever adaptations necessary to ensure they still received first-class treatment.

'Okay.'

Eli grinned. 'Great. Let's get you in, then.'

They got a hesitant Frank to X-Ray and while the radiologist did her thing, Charlie pulled him to one side. 'That man needs a scan, a tetanus shot, antibiotics and surgery that may or may not be minor! You can't let him sit outside in a garden and promise him a beer!'

'Relax! He's going to get the best treatment he will allow me to give him.'

'That *he* will allow *you*?' she scoffed. 'As doctors, it is up to us to give patients the options for treatment that will keep them safe and healthy for as long as possible. I'm sorry that he's scared of hospitals and needles, but I have never heard of a doctor promising to share a six-pack of beer with a patient, as some sort of bribe!'

'No? Maybe you haven't been working in the right kind of hospitals, then?' Eli was not going to be put off by her sterile, big-city ways. It was different out here in Vasquez. Keeping his patients healthy was a journey and it often felt like bargaining, when a lot of them were stubborn as mules and didn't like to admit to weaknesses. It was a tough crowd out here and he'd learned that quickly. Especially when he'd got sick himself. The people out here braved it out. They lifted their chins, squared their shoulders and faced death head-on. Whether that was from the isolation, the extreme winter weather or the wildlife. Or, in his case? Cancer.

Death was everywhere, a constant friend. The people here acknowledged that and they fought that quietly every time they set foot outside their homes. It wasn't so bad right now, what with it being springtime, but as fall approached and winter threatened, the people here hunkered down and looked out for one another. That was what he was doing for Frank. Supporting him. Acknowledging his fear and offering him a trade. That was all. Something for something. The Vasquez way.

'The right kind of hospitals? People need to understand the risks to their health and Frank needs a proper assessment. He had a fall. What caused that? And are you going to take his word that he didn't pass out? He could be lying to get out of here quicker.'

'He could be, but I'll keep an eye on him.'

'What? He needs to be admitted for tests, as well as the procedure to remove that hook from his neck.'

'I get it, I do, and I can pass Frank's boat every day on my morning run and check in on him. It's the best we're going to get with him and you need to understand that.'

'You're too laid-back about this, Eli.'

He smiled. 'And you're too wound up. City life has got you acting all…shrill and brittle.'

'Shrill and brittle?' Her hands went to her hips and he saw an anger flare in her dark chocolate eyes that he liked and was waiting to hear what she said next when the radiologist opened the door and allowed Frank to exit.

'Where's that quad?'

Eli turned to Charlie. 'My esteemed colleague

from Anchorage will show you, Frank. Charlie, why don't you stay with Frank? Sit with him in the garden for a while. Might be nice for both of you to just sit back and relax?'

He saw the frustration in her eyes, but he kept smiling, knowing she wouldn't disagree with him in front of a colleague, and watched her force a polite smile at their patient instead.

'I'll show you. Follow me.'

Eli watched her go. Felt his gaze drop to her shapely behind as she walked away from him towards the quad. She was still the fiery Charlie he remembered from many years ago, but there was something else there, too. Something he didn't remember. Something he didn't recognise. She was scared. And he wondered what of.

And whether he'd be able to protect her from it.

Or whether he was the one causing it?

CHAPTER SIX

IT SEEMED HERE, in Vasquez, that Charlie couldn't walk more than five yards down the street without some local stopping her to say hello or wanting to chat.

It was midweek. Wednesday lunchtime and she'd been given a whole hour for lunch, which quite frankly was something she'd never experienced in the city hospitals. Mostly food was eaten on the run, or sometimes missed completely and she'd try to grab a bite of something if she passed the staff room, gulping it down as she hurried along to her next patient or emergency.

A whole hour felt like luxury and so she'd decided to go out for a walk and get some fresh air. She was greeted by a mailman who seemed to know her name, even though she didn't know him, an older lady waved hello as she wiped the outdoor tables of her diner, and a guy who looked as old as the hills surrounding Vasquez ambled towards her with his walking stick, doffed his cap and said, 'Hello, Charlie. How's everything going?'

'Oh, it's going very well, thank you.' She smiled, felt awkward. 'How are you?'

'Ooh, not bad. Carrying on, as you do.' He winced slightly.

'Are you okay?'

'Bit of heartburn. Just on my way to get some of those antacids.'

Her instincts kicked in and now she noticed other things about this old man. He looked clammy and his colour was off. Of course, he could look like that normally, but she had noticed in the short time that she was here that Vasquez natives all seemed to look quite weathered and healthy, no matter their age. This gent looked somewhat paler.

'How long have you had the heartburn?'

'Came on about an hour ago and the damn thing won't go away.' He winced again and, with his spare hand not holding the stick, he rubbed at his chest. 'Think it's something bad?'

Was he having a heart attack? 'Let's get you in one of these seats for a moment.' She guided him over to one of the diner chairs and sat him down, then placed her fingers on his wrist to check his pulse.

'Everything okay?' The lady who had waved to her earlier came out looking concerned. 'Stewie? You all right?'

So this was Stewie. The frequent flyer. The hypochondriac she'd been warned about. But this didn't seem like anxiety.

Charlie turned around to her. 'Could you call the clinic and let them know that I need them to send someone out to assist me with this gentleman, please? Query MI.'

The woman nodded hurriedly and bustled back inside.

'Okay, Stewie, is it? I need you to look at me and I need you to take nice, steady breaths and remain calm, okay?'

'What's going on?'

'I think you're having a heart attack.'

Stewie raised his eyebrows at her and gulped. 'R-r-really?'

'Do you feel sick? Have you any pain in your jaw, neck or left arm?'

'I guess a little, but it's not bad at all. If I'm having a heart attack, why aren't I on the floor gasping, clutching at my chest?'

'They don't all present the way you see them on TV. Sometimes they're a little like this. Quieter. Less dramatic.'

'Not like me then. Oh.' He rubbed at his chest again and laid his walking stick up against the table. 'I thought it was because I'd eaten too much breakfast this morning. My wife makes excellent biscuits and gravy.'

She smiled at him.

'Guess I was lucky running into you, huh? I promise I wasn't stalking you as a doctor.'

Charlie smiled sympathetically.

'Eli told me you were coming. He's been really excited about it.'

'Yeah?' She was surprised, but also kind of pleased. 'That's nice.'

'He's a good boy. He's looked after me and my wife for years now. It was a shame that he had to go through what he did. It was a nasty business, him just a young man an' all.'

Charlie assumed he meant the orphanage. Having to live in a children's home and not find a family until he was fifteen years old and adopted by the Clarks. 'But he's landed on his feet here,' she said.

'Yeah. The Clarks...they're good people.' Stewie looked at her. 'You seem nice, too.'

'Thank you. So do you.'

At that moment a vehicle arrived and Eli jumped out, with Diana, one of the nurses from the clinic. 'Stewie? When I send my doctors out for lunch break, I expect them to rest, not find patients on the fly.' Eli was already placing an oxygen mask on Stewie's face as the old man chuckled, then he placed his stethoscope in his ears to listen to Stewie's chest.

She caught his quick nod of acknowledgement that Stewie was most definitely having a heart attack. 'Let's get you in the back of the truck and over to the hospital.'

'Will someone call my Joan?'

'I'll do it,' Charlie offered, clambering into the back of the truck with him to hold his hand as Diana got IV access and Eli placed a BP cuff around the old man's arm. He was a sweet old man and, granted, she barely knew him, but he exuded the warmth and friendship that everyone had seemed to give her since arriving here. Even now, in this moment, where his life was hanging in the balance, Stewie was being warm and charming.

'You're a good 'un,' he said, patting her hand with his. 'Don't scare her, will you?'

'I won't, I promise.'

'Your Joan is made of stern stuff. She doesn't scare easily,' Eli said.

Stewie smiled behind the oxygen mask. 'Nigh on fifty years we've been married, you know, and never a cross word between us.'

Charlie smiled at him. That was the dream, wasn't it? To find someone who suited you perfectly. To find someone who loved you deeply every day. Who enjoyed your company. Who was there for you and supported you and adored you. Someone with whom you could live out every day, happily. She'd hoped to have that with Glen, but it had all gone so horribly wrong.

It was the sort of relationship that she'd never

got close to. Her own romantic history being somewhat more…fraught.

'You make sure to tell her I love her.'

'You can tell her that yourself,' Eli said.

But Stewie met her gaze and looked deeply into her eyes and wordlessly begged her to tell his wife what he wanted her to hear. And she saw it in his eyes—he knew. The end was coming.

Charlie knew they would do everything to make sure he got through this, but if Stewie thought he was going to die, then she should also respect his last request, so she nodded and squeezed his hand and mouthed *I will*.

He smiled and then closed his eyes and the ECG monitor suddenly went crazy, beeping out an alarm.

'He's arresting!' Eli said, stepping out of his seat to stand by Stewie and begin compressions. 'How much further, Diana?'

'Less than a minute!'

'Get us there!'

They leapt into action around their patient. Now was no longer the time to hold Stewie's hand. Charlie needed to help and she'd seen enough MIs to know that even when you were right there, with all the equipment, it didn't mean success was guaranteed. Ninety per cent of cardiac arrests in the United States were fatal, which meant you had a one in ten chance of surviving. Those weren't great odds. But Charlie was not one who bet on the odds. At the end of the day they were just numbers and no one could say whether it was pointless or not.

You helped. If someone was dying, you tried to stop it. If someone was flailing, you tried to save them.

She took over compressions as the truck stopped and Eli thrust the doors open and helped manoeuvre the gurney outside, so they could rush it into the clinic. They'd shocked Stewie twice, but he still wasn't responding and as they rushed into the clinic, alarms blaring from the machines, his rhythm changed from ventricular fibrillation to asystole.

Flatline.

You couldn't shock a flatline.

She kept pushing.

Chest compressions, chest compressions, chest compressions.

One, two, three, four...

Eli pushed epinephrine, but nothing was happening and Stewie's walking stick that had been laid on the gurney next to him fell to the floor with a clatter. It was like a sign that it was no longer needed. Final.

Charlie checked the clock. He'd been asystole for far too long. She caught Eli's eye as Eli stepped back and went over the history of the case, rounds completed, drugs given and how

long Stewie had been down for in an unshock-
able rhythm, with no change. 'I think we should
stop. Does everyone agree?'

Charlie continued to do CPR. She would not
stop unless everyone agreed and she quickly met
everyone's gaze as they all agreed. Stewie would
not be coming back.

She stopped. Stood back. Breathless. 'Agreed.'

Eli looked up at the clock. 'Time of death, one
twenty-two p.m.' He looked at her. 'Want me to
call Joan?'

'No. I said I'd do it.' She was grateful to him
for offering but she wanted to be the one. She and
Eli left Stewie in the capable hands of the nurses.

'Are you okay?' Eli asked.

'Of course. I've lost patients before. I'll lose
them again. This isn't my first time.'

'I know, it's just that here in Vasquez everyone is so close that, when we do lose a patient,
we look out for one another. It's not something
that just gets forced under the rug, so that you can
deal with the next patient and save your tears for
when you get home.'

'I didn't know him. Not like you.' She turned to
face him. 'Do *you* need to take some time away?
I can cover for you, if you like?'

'I'd like to be with you when you tell Joan. I'd
like to be there for her. Familiar face and all of
that.'

She nodded. 'Okay. If that's what you want.' It was strange to see him so serious, but expected under the circumstances. She was used to the jovial, cheeky Eli. The one with a constant twinkle in his eye, not this.

When Joan arrived, she was taken to a family room and Eli and Charlie followed her in.

'I'm too late, aren't I? I can see it in your faces.' Joan stood staring at them.

Charlie indicated she should take a seat and when she'd sat down, she began to explain. 'I'm so sorry. Your husband suffered a cardiac arrest and despite our best efforts to revive him, I'm afraid he passed away.'

Joan paused, taking it in. 'He just went out for antacids. Said the walk might help his digestion. He had heartburn. It wasn't heartburn?'

Charlie shook her head. 'I'm afraid not.'

'Did he collapse in the street?'

'No. I met him outside the diner and we began to talk. He described his symptoms, which worried me, and I called for an ambulance. We worked hard to revive him, but we were not successful.'

Tears began to well in Joan's eyes.

This was the difficult moment. The moment where Charlie had to be strong and distance herself. Watching other people lose it and become emotional was always a difficult thing for her.

'We almost didn't get together,' Joan said.

Charlie said nothing. If Joan needed to talk to get through this, then she'd let the older woman talk.

'I didn't like him when we first met. He was so full of himself. Good-looking.' She smiled ruefully. 'But he knew it, too. I thought he was playing with me. That he'd asked me out on a dare from his friends, so I said no at first.'

'When did you say yes?' Eli asked.

Joan looked at him, eyes shining with tears. 'Almost five years later. He'd been away, in the army, seeing the world, and when he came back under a medical discharge he came straight to see me. He'd been writing me letters while he was away, telling me that the thought of me was what kept him going, and my feelings for him changed. So I said yes. I wished I'd said yes before, because then I could have had those five extra years with him. We were good together. Never a cross word.'

Charlie smiled. 'He told me that. He also told me that I had to tell you that he loved you. It was the last thing he said. His last thought was of you.' And she envied Stewie and Joan in that moment. To have had such a strong, enduring and powerful love that had spanned decades. They'd been lucky to find such a rare thing.

Joan nodded and sniffed, dabbing at her eyes with a handkerchief. 'I don't know how to live without him. We've never been apart since he came back. How do I do this now?'

'Everyone will help you, Joan. You know that,' Eli said. 'Vasquez won't let you be alone.'

She smiled sadly at him. 'They'll try, but at the end of the day, I'll be alone in our bedroom and one side of the bed will be empty—' Her voice broke on the word 'empty' and she began to sob.

Charlie broke all her rules and draped an arm around Joan's shoulder and Eli mirrored her on the opposite side, their arms touching as they comforted the older woman. She felt his hand graze hers. It was like a lightning strike and she shifted her hand away, her cheeks flaming. She tried to concentrate hard on Joan, but then Eli met her gaze and Charlie couldn't deal with it and stood up abruptly. Not knowing what to say. What to do. What did most people do in this situation?

'I'll get you a strong cup of tea.' She gave a smile to Joan and left the room, glad to be out of such an oppressive, emotional atmosphere. She'd wanted to comfort Joan and she had, but when Eli had mirrored her and his hand had brushed hers, she'd panicked, feeling that they were somehow more and that had scared the living daylights out of her! She was here to work and keep her distance and finish this contract, so she could move on, but Eli had somehow made her feel that she was being pulled further into his orbit and if she got too close, then what? She'd never leave Vasquez? That was an impossibility! That could never happen!

Here in this town, it was as if the Clarks, and Eli, especially, were the sun, And she were Icarus. She could not get too close, or she would get burned. It was just something that she felt implicitly. And she did not want to crash and burn because of him.

In the small kitchenette, she struggled to find tea. There was coffee, but *where was the goddamned tea*? Charlie rummaged through the cupboards, finally finding a box and adding a teabag to a mug. She had no idea if Joan had milk or sugar and so she prepped a small tray. Doing this helped. Being busy helped. Being away from that small room helped. Eli was a big man and his presence in that small room had felt suffocating to her, especially as she'd listened to Joan's story and empathised with her pain over not being with the man she loved for those lost five years.

Why had that story hit Charlie so hard?

She wasn't sure she wanted to examine that too much, if she was being honest with herself. Maybe it was because of the lost chances? Joan's lost five years with Stewie. Charlie's lost chance at being with her own family. Her biological parents, whoever they might be. Her lost chance at a successful marriage. Her lost chance at a successful relationship. Her lost ability to trust anyone. Her lost chance at giving Alice the father she so desperately deserved.

Joan's life was so different from hers. She'd

been with one man and lived in the same place for years and it had been all that she needed.

Charlie had never had that and, though she told herself she didn't need it, maybe she did yearn for the simplicity of that kind of life? Could that ever be hers? Or were she and Alice doomed to be nomads for ever?

She took a slow walk back to the family room and she inhaled a long, deep breath before she knocked lightly and entered.

Eli and Joan were still sitting close together, Eli listening as Joan told a story about her husband.

Charlie laid the tray down on the low coffee table and sat and listened from a chair, away from the sofa that Eli and Joan sat upon. It was strategic. Protection. By distancing herself, maybe she'd get some clarity?

'Is there anyone I can call for you, Joan? Someone who can come and sit with you? Or take you home?'

Joan thought for a moment. 'I guess you could call my neighbour, Connie.'

'I'll get Diana to come and sit with you, until Connie arrives,' said Eli.

He and Charlie left the room together and Eli looked down at her. 'You sure you're okay?'

His concern for her was touching, but it was heady and dangerous, too. 'Absolutely!' She smiled as sweetly as she could, to imply confidence. 'I'll go fetch Diana.' And she turned and walked away from him, her breathing getting easier the further she went.

Eli was out chopping wood for his woodpile when his phone rang. He answered it and heard his mom on the other end of the line.

'Oh, Eli, I'm so glad you answered! I've got a little problem and wondered if you could fix it for me.'

'Sure. What's up?'

'Well, Charlie rang and apparently there's a leaking tap in her kitchen that won't shut off. She's tried to ring Pete, but he's gone to Fairbanks this week to visit his sister.' Pete was the local plumber. 'Could you pop on over to take a look?'

Go to Charlie's? Sure, he could do that. 'No problem. Let her know I'll be over there in about ten minutes.'

'You're a star.'

He laughed. 'I try.' Eli ended the call and put away his axe, after cleaning the blade. He quickly stacked the blocks of wood he'd chopped over on his winter woodpile and then grabbed his flannel shirt and shrugged it on. It was covered in little bits of wood and he brushed them off, grabbing his car keys.

It would be good to see Charlie and Alice again. He'd not seen Charlie's daughter since his mother's potluck, but he had heard about her. His mother had sung the little girl's praises, telling him how clever she was, how good at English and arithmetic she was. How she had a wonderful imagination and was a very neat painter. The little girl excelled, but the one thing his mom had noticed was that Alice pretty much kept to herself at school, the way she had at the potluck. Yes, she'd been with the other children, but she hadn't interacted much, as if she preferred to be by herself. 'I wondered if it's because they move around a lot. Alice told me there's no point in making friends properly, because they always leave,' she'd suggested.

That was odd. 'Maybe. She'll be okay,' he'd said, because Alice's mom was Charlie and Charlie was the most self-sufficient person he'd ever known. She was a strong, capable woman and no doubt she was raising her daughter to be the same way.

He arrived outside her cottage and switched off the engine, getting out of the vehicle and raising a hand in hello at Charlie's next-door neighbour, Angus, who was up a ladder fixing some guttering by the looks of it.

'Leaves?' he called out, trying to guess the blockage.

'Bird nest.'

Eli raised an eyebrow. 'Any eggs?'

'Not yet. Think I should leave it? Or evict them?'

Eli smiled. 'Your call, my friend.' At Charlie's front door, he set down his bag of tools and knocked.

From inside the cottage he could hear music. And then the door was being opened and there stood Charlie. She looked down at the bag as he reached for it.

'You're my plumber, too?'

'Your lucky day, huh?' He liked what she was wearing. She wore a tight-fitting black tee underneath a pair of loose-fitting khaki dungarees and around her hair she had a bright red headscarf. Some of her hair had escaped, loose brown tendrils that hung in gentle waves, and he felt a pang of something that could have been lust, but was most definitely attraction.

'You can fix taps as well as people?'

'Taps are easy.'

'Then you'd better come in.' She stepped back, her cheeks flushing, averting her eyes as he passed and he smiled, glad to know that he was having just as much of an effect on her. It felt good to know he had an effect, because that meant she was just as uncomfortable with the situation as he was.

'Where's Alice?'

'In her room.'

'Has she been bad?'

'No. She just likes to spend time in her room. I think she's drawing, if you want to go say hi.' Clearly she did not expect him to want to say hi.

But he did.

'That'd be great.' He walked down the small corridor that led to the bedrooms, heading to the smaller one of the two and noting Alice's name plaque on the door. He rapped his knuckles against it.

'Come in!'

He pushed open the door. 'Hey, squirt. How are you doing?'

'Eli!' She put down her pencil and ran over to him and he scooped her up and hefted her onto his hip.

'I think you've grown.'

Alice chuckled. 'Want to see my drawing? I'm making a comic.'

'Sure.' He put her down again and she ran over to her table.

Behind him, Charlie leaned on the doorjamb. 'Since when did you two become best friends?'

'Eli showed me some of his funny drawings at that potluck, Mom.'

'Did he, now? What kind of drawings?'

Eli looked up at her. 'Just dogs and chickens and how to sketch in some basic shapes when she wants to create things, so instead of, say, trying to draw a dog's outline from scratch, you think about the shapes first. A rectangle for the body, rectangles for the legs and tail, circles for the neck and head and then how she can construct her drawing on top of those.'

'She's five, Eli.'

He turned to her. 'Your daughter has a gift. Have you seen her drawings?'

'Of course I have!'

He smiled. 'Good. Then you should know that her skill level is way above that of any other five-year-old. You should nurture this.'

He could see in her eyes that she didn't like being told about her daughter in this way. As if he were criticising her for not noticing or something. 'I'm just trying to help, is all.'

'Then come help me in the kitchen. That is what you're here for.' She disappeared from view.

Eli smiled at Alice. 'While I'm fixing that tap, what are you going to draw for me?'

Alice beamed. 'What would you like?'

'How about a dragon?'

'With flames coming out of its mouth?'

'Sounds perfect. See you in a bit.' And he left Alice in her room and made his way to the kitchen, where Charlie was bustling about with mugs.

'Want a coffee?'

'If you're having one.'

He placed his bag of tools down on the floor and examined the kitchen tap. It was indeed dripping quite a lot. 'Probably just needs a new washer fitted. I should have it fixed in no time.'

'Great.'

Eli got busy opening up the cupboard beneath

the sink to find the stopcock that would turn off the water supply while he worked. Then he stood and put the plug in the sink. 'Got a spare towel?'

'What for?'

'To place in the sink so I don't scratch it with anything.'

'Oh, okay.' She passed him a red-and-white-checked cloth.

Next he began to unscrew the tap.

'Who taught you all of this?' she asked, pouring hot water into two mugs and watching him closely.

'My dad.'

She nodded. 'Is he a handy guy?'

'Oh, yeah. A man with his fingers in many pies, but also a guy that likes to be hands on. When they did up the hotel he could have got in some tradesmen to do all the work, but he liked to save some jobs for himself. Plumbing, carpentry, electrics. He's a jack of all trades and master at every one.'

'He seemed a nice guy at the potluck.'

Eli looked at her and smiled. 'He is.'

There was a pause and then she said, 'You really got lucky, huh?'

He unscrewed the valve to access the washer and nodded, thoughtfully. 'I really did. Did you miss me when I'd gone?' He meant it as a joke.

But she looked at him oddly. 'Are you kidding me? It was lovely and quiet without you there. I could sleep easily without worrying if you'd put itching powder in my socks. I could go sit in the garden and not have you drop a water balloon on me from your room.'

He smiled ruefully at the memories, having forgotten half of the stuff he used to do. It seemed like a lifetime ago and maybe it was. The kids' home belonged to a previous life, almost as if it weren't his at all. But he remembered that day with the water balloon. He'd been messing about with the guys in their dorm and he'd been half soaked himself, then Cam, his bestie, had noticed Charlie sitting outside and dared him to drop one as close to her as possible, without actually hitting her.

He'd tried to back out of it. Said it wasn't right, that she'd hate it. Get mad. But then they'd started winding him up. Saying he must fancy her or something, and he hadn't needed that rumour starting, so he'd done it. He'd forced a laugh, as if he really hadn't cared, but he had. He'd not wanted to upset her and, as he'd suspected, she'd been furious. Storming inside, soaking wet, the yellow dress she'd been wearing stuck to her, and she'd screamed at him. Called him a whole load of names he wouldn't be comfortable saying in front of Alice.

Inside, he'd felt guilty, but because of Cam and the others he'd toughed it out. Acted as if he weren't bothered.

'I'm really sorry about that. Honestly. I never wanted to make you mad.'

'Well, you did.'

He nodded. 'Want to get even?'

She laughed. 'Strangely enough, I don't have any water balloons handy.'

'You have a garden hose.'

Charlie looked at him, incredulous. 'Don't be ridiculous.'

'I'm not.' He replaced the washer. It had worn through. He quickly reassembled the tap, turned the water back on and ran the tap. It worked perfectly. The water shutting off without a singular drip. 'I mean it.'

She laughed, not quite believing him.

So he decided to make her believe. He made a *watch this* face, then walked out to the back porch door, opened it and strode through into the back garden. He located the tap by the hose and turned it on, handed it to a bewildered Charlie and then stood in the middle of the lawn. Arms wide open, smiling right at her. Daring her. 'Do your worst.'

He was kidding, right? How had trying to fix a tap turned into this? It had been a simple Saturday morning, she'd been getting things done and then she and Alice were going to go for a walk around Vasquez later, to get better acquainted with the town. Maybe pop into the diner, because a patient during the week had told her that they made the most amazing pistachio ice cream and she knew that was one of Alice's favourites.

But then Gayle had offered to send Eli round to fix the tap and, though she'd not been happy about that fact, she'd accepted it. How long would it take, after all? Not long, right? He could be in and out within the hour and her day could carry on as normal.

But now he wanted her to douse him in water?

At the end of the hose was a nozzle that allowed her to alter the water. Spray. Mist. Soak. High Pressure. Low Pressure. She could use any one and clearly he wanted her to do it. Was offering her the chance to get even, but she stood there, hesitating.

'Come on! Get your revenge!' Eli laughed.

He was fully clothed! He was going to get soaked! But she recalled their arrival on the pier and how he'd waded into the bay to fetch her floating suitcase and the way he'd driven her to her new home in soaking-wet clothes. Clearly he didn't worry about things like that.

And there was a small part of her that wanted to get her own back.

She raised the nozzle and pointed it at him.

He smiled back at her, nodded. *Do it.*

Smiling, she reached forward and twisted the nozzle to high pressure—and then let him have it full blast.

Eli gasped as the cold water hit him squarely in

the chest, but he didn't try to run, or to avoid the water stream, he just started to laugh and blow water droplets away from his face as it sprayed upwards, splashing him, and before Charlie knew it she was laughing, too. Laughing so hard she almost couldn't catch her breath. So that her stomach began to hurt and, once he was thoroughly drenched, she dropped the hose to the floor and put her hands on her knees to try and catch her breath.

She became aware that he had stepped close to her and she stood up and one look at his face had her laughing again, until he ran his hands through his long hair to get the wet strands from his face and she felt a punch of lust to the gut. The water was making his jeans and tee and flannel shirt stick to every delicious, muscled inch of him and suddenly it wasn't funny any more.

'Mom, what are you doing?' Alice asked from the back door.

Her head whipped round so fast. 'Nothing, honey. We had a bit of an accident with the hose.'

Alice giggled at the state of Eli.

'You'd better come in. Dry off. I can put your clothes in the dryer.'

'It's okay.'

'No. I can't let you drive around in wet clothes again. This seems to be a theme and I know how it feels, so…' She led him back into the cottage and pointed at the bathroom. 'There are towels in there. Bring your wet clothes when you come back out.'

He left wet footprints across the dark, hardwood floors and she mopped them over with paper towel, until he came back out, bare-chested, with a pink, fluffy towel wrapped around his waist.

His chest was magnificent. Developed pecs that were glorious to look at. Beneath, a six-pack that was enviable. Tight and bristling with muscle.

Huh. I didn't think this through. Or did I?

She felt an eyebrow raise and she couldn't stop herself from taking in every delicious inch of skin. She licked her lips and swallowed hard, smiling as she took his wet pile of clothes from him. 'Couldn't wear the bathrobe on the back of the door, huh?'

He smiled ruefully. 'It didn't fit.'

'Ah. Won't be a minute.' She took his clothes to the dryer room and popped them into the machine, praying that the thirty-minute economy cycle would be the fastest thirty minutes in the history of time. Perhaps she could hide out in the laundry room? It needed a little tidy and there was a pile of clothes there that needed folding. But she could hear Alice's bright voice showing Eli her dragon picture that she'd drawn, and leaving her daughter out there alone with a guy who had nothing on beneath his towel seemed wrong, even though she knew that Eli was a good guy.

'That's amazing, Ally! That fire looks great!'

He was calling her Ally? No one called her Ally. Her name was Alice. 'Let's see.'

Alice showed her the picture and, Charlie had to admit, it was pretty great. There was detail there that she would never have expected a five-year-old to have added—creases around the eyes, scales along the body. There was depth to the picture, so that it wasn't completely two-dimensional. 'Alice, this is amazing! You're so good!'

Alice beamed. 'Thanks. Will you put it on the fridge?'

'Better. I'll get it framed. Hang it on the wall and when you're a rich and famous artist, I'll be able to show people your early work.'

Her daughter chuckled and headed off back to her bedroom to draw some more.

'She's a good kid.'

'She's the best.'

'You're lucky.'

She glanced at him. A quick look was all she could safely manage. Anything longer meant her gaze lingered on his finer details and she didn't want to be focusing on anything like that, thank you very much. His nipples were exposed. That low V from his hipbones was visible. She swallowed hard. 'I am?'

'To have had Alice. To have started a family.'

'Well, you have one, too.'

He nodded. 'I do. And they're great. The best, actually.'

But he sounded sad about something and she couldn't work out why. If they were the best, then what did he have to be sad about? 'Wish they'd found you sooner?'

He met her gaze. Briefly. Before she felt her cheeks flame and she had to turn away. 'Sure.'

Charlie nodded, smiling, straightening the pile of magazines on the coffee table. 'Do you, er… want another drink? We didn't get to drink the last one.'

He straightened a leg, drawing her eye as it tracked his movement. She saw a thick, darkly haired leg and swallowed hard, imagining what it led up to.

'Coffee would be great, thanks.'

Charlie scurried into the kitchen, glad of the escape. She rinsed out the old mugs, washed them, dried them and began making coffee again. It gave her something to do with her hands. Made her feel purposeful. Calmed her. At least until he spoke and she realised he was leaning against the doorjamb in his towel, watching her. 'What made you come to Vasquez?'

She turned guiltily, spilling the milk on the floor. Damn! Why was she so clumsy around him? He was making her nervous. He had no right to make her nervous! 'Oh, you know. I fancied a change. Wanted to get away from the big city.'

'You always loved the city.'

She mopped the milk with paper towels, nodding. 'I did, yes, but sometimes you have too much of a good thing.' She stood again and dropped the paper towels into the trash.

He frowned. 'Can you?'

She glanced at him. A muscled, handsome god. He was the epitome of a good *thang*.

'Oh, yes.'

'What did you have too much of in Anchorage?'

What was this? The Spanish Inquisition? Her cheeks flamed at the thought of all she'd gone through with Glen. The way he'd put their relationship online. The secret videos he'd taken of the two of them, in their bedroom. The photos he'd taken of her without her consent, sharing them with his friends. The embarrassment. The *humiliation*.

Glen had thought it hilarious. Laughing at her when she'd turned up at his door, humiliated and furious. It was why she was so sensitive to being made fun of. It brought it all back and Eli was the champion of practical jokes. He wouldn't understand and nor would she tell him about it, because what if he tried to look her up online? He'd see it all and it was bad enough that her work friends at the last hospital she'd worked at—a place where she'd considered putting down roots for the first time—had seen them, forcing her to move away again. To resist the urge to settle. To keep on running. To keep on moving. Never giving anyone time enough to witness her shame. To know that she would always have to do this, if she was to keep her anonymity.

But Eli changed all of that, because she didn't have anonymity with him. He knew parts of her. They'd lived in the same building for years together and, whether you were close or not, that still allowed someone to know you.

'I don't really want to go into all of that.' She handed him the coffee mug and stepped away, almost as if he were poison. As if he was dangerous. And in a way, he was. It should be illegal to look the way he looked. She knew he worked at it. She'd seen him on that first day and he'd told her that he liked to start the day with a bit of cardio. But he made it look effortless. Easy. And she knew it was anything but. He'd not really been into fitness as a teenager. What had changed? Had he just seen all those guys on social media with six-packs? Or all those superhero movies where the guys were ripped and wanted to look the same? Was it ego?

'Why not? Did something happen?'

'You ask a lot of questions.'

'You avoid answering them.'

'Yes, well, maybe I don't want to share with you.'

He grinned. 'Oh, come now. I'm a good listener. A problem shared is a problem halved, or so they say.'

'Well, *they* say wrong. No amount of sharing will ever solve that issue. In fact *sharing* is what caused the issue in the first place.' The kitchen felt small with his hulking form in it and so she walked past him, irritated, into the living space and sat down, cradling her mug and hoping he'd change the subject.

Eli slowly followed her in and settled down in a chair opposite her. 'You know what I think you need?'

'What?' She sounded petulant and hated it. She didn't want to be so irritated, or snippy, but Eli was creeping very close to the big open wound that she nursed on a daily basis.

'You need to relax.'

'Is that your official diagnosis, Doctor?'

He smiled. 'It is. You seem tense. Stressed. You need to experience the Vasquez beauty and chill out for a little while.'

'And how would I achieve that, exactly?'

'Next weekend. You, me and Alice, if you want, go for a drive up to Lawton Lake. I'll take the paddle boards, we'll have fun and then afterwards the beauty of the place will bring your blood pressure down a few notches. What do you say?'

It sounded amazing. But a whole day with Eli? Having fun? Spending time together deliberately? In a beautiful, secluded spot? Could be dangerous, too. But with Alice there…nothing would happen. So… 'All right. I've never tried paddle-boarding. I've always wanted to.'

'Then it's a date.' He smiled.

CHAPTER SEVEN

ELI WOULD DESCRIBE himself as a guy who was comfortable in his own skin. He'd got to know his body quite well over the years, especially during his cancer treatment. He'd had so many scans he was amazed he didn't glow in the dark. And afterwards, when he'd pursued health and fitness? He'd got used to focusing on muscle groups, or improving his cardiovascular system, or taking up yoga to stretch and breathe and focus. He made sure his body was a finely tuned machine and he was proud of it. Felt comfortable in it.

Until he had to wear a solitary towel at Charlie's house and knew he would have to control his thoughts.

Alice was about, for one, even if she was mostly in her room, but as he'd chatted with Charlie in the kitchen and stood close to her a couple of times, he'd felt a definite arousal at being around her and had had to cool his jets.

When she'd sat away from him, he'd taken a little sigh of relief, thanking his lucky stars and praying that the dryer would be finished soon, so he could get dressed, because the thought kept repeating in his head that he was nearly naked with Charlie Griffin and Charlie seemed utterly oblivious to the effect she was having on him.

She was most definitely his type. It was something he'd been aware of back in the orphanage, though he'd been able to hide it in the teasing and the jokes, and it was something he was most definitely aware of now. He'd not meant to ask her out like that. To imply a date of any kind. But she seemed so tense all the time and he knew that if she just sat back for a little while and let the beauty of Vasquez in, then she would feel herself unwinding.

She was wound tight right now. Prickly and unforgiving and he was interested in seeing what she'd be like if she let loose. He always had been.

He'd seen a brief image as she'd sprayed him with that water and collapsed with laughter and it had been in that moment, as the water had gushed at him and she'd been laughing, he'd seen a glimpse of the real Charlie.

And he really liked what he'd seen and wanted more.

Her eyes had sparkled, her mouth wide and her laughter? Her real laugh and not the polite one she used at work when she was humouring him? Oh, dear Lord, that laughter was moreish. He wanted to hear it again and again. He wanted to see her face relax, that broad smile, hear that lovely sound, but more than anything he wanted to be the cause of it. Wanted her to collapse with laughter into his arms and gaze up into his eyes and…

It was the same as when they'd been kids. He'd wanted to make her smile. Wanted to make her laugh, but she'd always seemed to react differently to him joking around and hadn't laughed the way the other kids had. He'd thought maybe the practical-joke route and clowning around weren't the way to her heart, and so he'd backed off for a bit, but then the Clarks had come and he'd been about to leave, and the only way he'd known to say goodbye was to play one last trick…

But he was an adult now and though the urge to revert to type was strong every time he looked at her, he also knew he had to approach her differently.

Charlie was skittish. Someone or something had hurt her and he knew how that felt. But Charlie wore her wound out in the open, whereas he hid his, under layers and layers of smiles and confidence so that something like that would never happen again.

Because he wouldn't allow it.

If you didn't put your trust in people, then they couldn't betray you.

Everyone put their trust in him. He was their doctor. He was a Clark now, and that was fine, because he knew he was dependable and he wanted people to trust him. He just couldn't do it in return, because that was harder and so he remained out in the open, armoured by his sense of humour.

From the utility room, there was a ping and then silence.

'Your clothes are dry!' Charlie got up so fast, he felt a wry smile cross his face, glad that she'd been just as uncomfortable with the situation as he'd been.

When she passed him his clothes they were warm and soft. 'Thanks.'

'I'll leave you to get dressed.' She gave him a smile and closed the door to the utility, so he had privacy.

Eli dropped the towel and put on his jersey shorts, then jeans, then tee, then flannel shirt. She must have put a scented dryer sheet in with the clothes because now he smelled like her, which was a little disturbing and not altogether unpleasant.

He scooped up the towel, folded it and placed it on a wooden rail. When he stepped out of the room, the relief on her face made him smile.

'Well, thank you for fixing the tap, Eli, and coming over so promptly. I appreciate that and I'd hate to take up more of your Saturday.'

'It was no problem. I guess I'll see you Monday?'

She nodded. 'You will.'

He grabbed his bag of tools from the kitchen. 'Say goodbye to Alice for me.'

'Of course.' She opened the front door and stood there expectantly, hoping, clearly, that he would just walk straight out and disappear.

But the urge to mess with her mind one last time surged forth in his brain. Having intently watched her deal with his inherent nakedness and the fact that he'd asked her and Alice to go paddle-boarding with him, he knew he couldn't just walk out.

He stopped right beside her, as he went to go. Smiled and then bent forward to kiss her on the cheek.

He hoped to see her cheeks flame with colour. They did.

He hoped she'd look a little awkward and not know where to look. She did.

He thought it would make him smile.

But brushing his lips over her soft, soft skin and inhaling the scent of her did strange things to his own insides, muddling his thoughts and confusing him, and it was almost as if he couldn't get his mouth to form the word goodbye.

All he could manage was a nod and then he was stepping out into the clean Vasquez air and away towards his truck.

As he got behind the wheel, he was still mulling over how it had felt to kiss her.

But more importantly, he was disturbed by the urge he'd had to press his lips to hers and kiss her as she'd never been kissed before.

CHAPTER EIGHT

'I CAN'T TELL you how nice it is to have a lady doc back again,' said Teresa Muller, who sat in front of Charlie in her own consultation room. Her time shadowing Eli was over and she was familiar with the layout of this place and how Eli liked things done. 'I love Eli to bits, but sometimes you just like to talk to another girl, you know?'

Charlie nodded. 'And what can I do for you today?'

Teresa sighed. 'Well, I think I'm at that age in which I might need a little something-something.'

Teresa was fifty-one. 'What exactly do you need me to help you with?'

'Hormones! That replacement stuff.' Teresa leaned in and whispered, 'I think I'm in meno-pause.'

'Okay. What have your symptoms been?'

'Where do I begin? I get those hot-flash things. Feel like someone's turned the heating way up high in the middle of my chest. It creeps up my neck, makes me go bright red, I begin to sweat like I'm in a sauna.' Teresa leaned in again. 'I'm no oil painting to begin with, but when one of those things begins, I look and feel awful! Don't do my marriage no favours, let me tell you, and that's the other thing.' She began to whisper again. 'It's gone funny. *Down there.*'

'You're experiencing dryness?'

'Damn straight! Makes no sense, when I've got so much water pouring out of my head and down my back, that down there is drier than the Sahara. It hurts when we…you know! And my Greg, he's a patient, understanding man, but I've had to tell him to stop so many times, because it hurts, he's started not even trying to initiate… well…you know.'

'Have you tried lubrication?'

'I ordered some online and it does help, but it takes the romance out of it, when you have to stop to use it first, you know? I'm hoping those replacement hormones might give me back some of my go-go juice, if you'll pardon the expression.'

Charlie smiled. 'Any other symptoms?'

'Does a bear poop in the woods? I'm tired. My body aches. Sometimes I can't remember anything anyone's told me. I get headaches. Ratty. That's the other thing. My Greg says I can go from happy and smiley to grizzly bear in an instant!'

'So you've noticed a change in your mood?'

Teresa nodded. 'I have and he's right. I just

want to be *myself* again, Charlie. I can't remember what it's like to just be me. To just live and not worry. It's just… I feel like I'm losing myself and that's a scary thing. Becoming someone you don't recognise.'

Charlie could understand. She'd like to just live and be the woman she was before Glen ruined her life. Since the humiliation of Glen putting all that stuff out there on the Internet and she'd practically gone into hiding, she didn't like who she'd become, either. She'd always been a little bit twitchy, but since the disaster with him, it had got worse.

She did some basic observations on Mrs Muller, checking her blood pressure, her height, her weight. She read up on her patient's history and saw there was no family history of blood clots, breast cancer or strokes. 'You'll need to check your breasts monthly and make sure you attend all your mammogram appointments. HRT is safe, but some cancers respond to the hormones, so you need to be vigilant. Keep using the lubrication, but this should kick in soon and begin to help in that direction. We'll start you on a low dose and see how you go. Come and see me again in three months and we'll reassess. See if we need to raise it, or if it's causing any problems.'

'Thanks, Charlie. You're an absolute doll. What do you think of Vasquez? Beautiful, huh?'

She nodded. 'It most certainly is.'

'You staying long, or…?'

'I'm just covering Nance's maternity leave.'

'Well, I like you. I think you're very nice and you've been very helpful, too. I hope we can make you stay. You never know!' Teresa stood, grinning, and walked to the door.

'You never know,' she agreed. Hiding in Vasquez for the rest of her life. How would that look? How would that feel? Was it even a possibility, with Eli here?' Probably not. Nance would come back eventually, right? And then she wouldn't have a job and this was such a small town, there weren't any other medical facilities she could work at.

The likelihood was she would be moving on from here at the end of her contract. Not back to Anchorage, though. She couldn't face people there. It would just be tricky. So somewhere else, then. But where? It would all depend on what job opportunities there were.

She had no more patients waiting after Teresa Muller. So she typed up her notes, cleaned down her room and decided she'd go make herself a coffee. See if anyone else had any interesting cases.

As she passed Eli's consulting room, she could hear his voice and she stopped when she heard him laugh out loud.

Her tummy was doing strange things as she lingered by his door, remembering yesterday when he'd seemed to linger slightly after dropping that kiss on her cheek when he'd said good-bye. Her tummy had done strange things then, too. She'd not known where to look. She certainly hadn't been able to meet his eyes, but then he'd been striding away from her, down the path, towards his truck and she'd been mesmerised by the way the wind caught his long hair, the way he moved, the way his eyes briefly met hers before he got inside his vehicle.

It had been like a lightning strike.

Had he really just been practically naked in her home for half an hour?

How on earth did I get through that?

Charlie was so lost in her reverie, she didn't notice that the voices inside the room had changed from conversational to ones of people saying goodbye and suddenly the door to Eli's room was opening and, because she'd been leaning against it, listening, lost in her thoughts, she practically stumbled in.

'Oh! Sorry, I was…er…' Her brain scrambled for an excuse as Eli and a silver-haired old gentleman stared at her quizzically and with wry amusement, as if they knew *exactly* what she'd been doing. 'I was just about to knock.'

There. That seems believable, right?

'Oh? You need me for something?' Eli asked.

He came to stand by her as his patient doffed his cap at her and said, 'Good morning, miss.'

After the patient had gone, Charlie quickly

realised that her mouth wasn't going to work properly, especially as her brain seemed to have stopped functioning. 'Yes, um…it's about next weekend. I don't think I'm going to be able to make it.'

'Oh.'

He looked disappointed, which made her feel… what?

'Yeah, it's just what with Alice being in school now and everything, I don't get to see her and spend time with her as often as I'd like and the weekends are usually our special time and…'

She could see that he was smiling again, almost as if he was tolerating her. That he could see she was using Alice as an excuse. Her voice trailed off. 'Why are you smiling?'

'You're freaking out because I said it's a date. I didn't mean it as a *date* date. Like romance and asking you out. I meant it as *Okay, we've agreed to go paddle-boarding*. I swear to you, I'm not going to try to seduce you.'

'Good. I'm glad, because you would have failed,' she said, feeling a little disappointed that he could so easily dismiss the idea of being on a date with her. That maybe she'd been wrong to imagine all the things she'd imagined, but she always had had a very active imagination.

'If I was going to seduce you, I would have done it yesterday, when I wasn't wearing anything but a towel,' he said seductively, moving closer to her, causing her to take a step back as her cheeks flamed.

She smiled nervously. Wanting to back further away, but the doorjamb was in the way and she collided with it awkwardly. Her brain flooded with the images of him from the weekend. Chest bare. Strong arms on show. His powerful legs and that pink, fluffy towel wrapped tightly around his waist. How his mere physical presence had felt, so close to her in her own home.

Had he meant, just now, to remind her of that moment? Knowing that she would remember how he looked, just to make her blush? Had he mentioned seduction to make her imagine how he might do it? Had he stepped closer to her to see if she would step back?

Was all this just another joke to him? A wind-up? Because that wasn't fair!

'That's good to know,' she managed to say, but her voice didn't sound like her own, it sounded strangled, as if her throat were closing up. His proximity doing alarming things to her blood pressure and pulse rate. And had it got hot in here? Had the air conditioning broken down, somehow?

And then he smiled and stepped away again, as if pleased that he'd had the reaction he'd wanted from her, pleased that she'd amused him, and she didn't like feeling as though she was a plaything. 'I'll take Alice paddle-boarding by myself, if you don't mind,' she said, trying to control the rising anger in her.

'All right.'

Oh. She'd expected him to put up more of a fight. When he didn't, she felt a little deflated.

He'd been testing a theory. Needing to know how she'd react, whether she was as affected by him as he was affected by her.

There was something between them and it wasn't just their shared history. There was something more and he could feel it. It was palpable whenever they were close, or in the same room, especially. It had been there for him when they were kids, but it hadn't been as powerful then, it had just been a crush thing that he'd felt he had to deal with and then forget about when he'd moved away to Vasquez, adopted by the Clarks.

He'd never forgotten Charlie. How could he? She'd been the first girl he'd ever wanted. She was always going to be a piece of his history and that was where he'd relegated her memory.

To history.

But now she was here and, though he knew he had nothing to offer her in the future—she'd always mentioned wanting a large family of her own and he couldn't give her that—he was still sorely tempted by her. One moment he'd be telling himself to just leave it alone. Let her work out her contract and go. But then later, another voice would kick in and tell him to pursue something with her. Let her know in no uncertain terms that what he was offering was temporary but that they both could have some fun, until it was time to leave. Sweeten the history between them.

And so when she'd practically fallen into his office, as if she'd been eavesdropping at the door, he'd wondered why she'd been there. Was she intrigued by him, as attracted to him as he was to her? He'd just had to know, and seeing the look of embarrassment and the way her cheeks had flamed and how fast her pulse had been throbbing at her throat had told him that he was onto something for sure.

He'd kept himself restrained at the weekend, because of Alice's presence, but when they were alone…? That was different.

The only question was…would Charlie want something with no strings attached? Was she that type of person? Or was she so tightly strung, as she appeared to be, that she wouldn't be able to cut loose with him for a while?

He didn't want to use her. He wanted her to get as much out of their short time together as he would. He thought they'd be a great fit together and he knew he would treat her with respect and that somehow, at the end, they would go for a drink and clink their glasses together and toast what fun they'd had. Knew how they'd hug each other and say goodbye on the pier before she flew off with Chuck to go back to the big city.

And then he paused, thinking hard.

Saying goodbye…the thought made him still. Could he lose her for a second time? Would he be able to watch her walk away?

He'd be able to do it. Wouldn't he? He could put whatever they had in a box and push it to one side. He'd have to.

'But it was very kind of you to offer.'

He looked up at her and smiled, nodding.

'I have another offer for you.'

She looked wary. 'Oh?'

'Come on in. Take a seat. You might want to close that door,' he said with a grin, feeling his heart race madly, knowing that if he asked and she said no, then this whole thing was going to be mighty embarrassing. But what did he have to lose?

CHAPTER NINE

SHE WATCHED HIM walk behind his desk and sit down, so after she'd apprehensively closed the door, wondering what this was all about, she did the same, sitting opposite.

Eli gave her an appraising look, a broad smile across his face. 'I think we should get married.'

Charlie stared at him and went still. She didn't blink. She didn't breathe. But internally, her heart raced, her blood pressure went up and adrenaline and cortisol flooded her body. *'What?'*

'I think we should get married,' he said again, watching her intently with amusement.

'This is one of your jokes again, isn't it?' She laughed wryly, but without humour. 'Typical Eli. Always out for a laugh. Well, I don't need it.' She got up out of her chair, glad to see that her legs were still working after that initial shock.

'Okay, okay!' He laughed. 'That was a joke. I couldn't help it, you looked so…tense.'

'I wonder why?' she said, heart still thudding.

'I apologise. Do you forgive me?'

He looked at her with such sweet, imploring eyes, she felt her anger begin to fade. Part of her did not want to forgive him at all! But another, more logical part knew that she still had to work with him for a while longer and work would be a whole lot easier if they were getting along. 'Fine. But only if you're going to be serious.'

'Life's too short for serious. You have to have fun sometimes.'

'Do you really have something you want to talk to me about?'

He nodded. 'I do.'

'Well, get on with it, then! The clinic could be filling with patients.'

He tapped a couple of keys on his keyboard, then turned his screen so she could see. Apparently Eli could access the security cameras in the waiting room. And the waiting room itself? Was empty. There was no way she could leave by saying she had a patient waiting.

'What do you want to talk to me about, Eli?'

'I do want to talk about us, that bit is true.'

Us.

What did he want? Was he going to probe into their pasts? Talk some more about what it had been like together as kids? Or was he going to talk about her being here? That there didn't seem to be enough work for two people sometimes and that maybe he'd made a mistake in asking her here? And that last unexpected thought suddenly terrified her. Because, as much as she hated knowing that Eli knew about her past, the idea of leaving Vasquez was scary. Probably because Alice was settling so well into kindergarten and was loving every minute of Mrs Clark's classes. Probably because she had nothing else in the pipeline just yet. Probably it was because, despite the overfamiliarity of the residents of Vasquez, she had never felt so welcomed anywhere. Probably it was because when she lay in bed alone at night, she harboured secret thoughts of what it might be like to actually settle here.

'Us?'

'Yes. I like you, Charlie, and I think you like me, too.' He smiled, waiting for her response.

'You're not too bad, I guess.'

'I don't mean as friends.'

'You mean as...work colleagues?'

'No. I do not. I mean I think I want to talk about the fact that we're both attracted to one another.' He was searching her face, looking for clues that she agreed with him.

He was right. She was attracted to him. But she didn't normally just come straight out and tell a guy that. She usually let them buy her a drink. Take her out on dates. It was something done gradually. Incrementally. Each date either increasing or decreasing that attraction until it reached critical level and they either fell into bed with one another or split up. Or she moved away.

She never just admitted it out loud.

It felt weird.

'Well, that's the elephant in the room,' she said, not sure what else to say.

'I thought it best to acknowledge it. I'm a straightforward guy.'

'Are you saying this because you mean it? Or are you saying this because you can't actually go out with anyone in Vasquez, because, technically, they're all your patients and that would be stepping over a line?'

He got up out of his chair and came to stand by her. Looking down at her. Intensity in his eyes.

His proximity caused her heart to race again.

'Because I mean it and I think we're two responsible adults, who both have a bit of freedom, who could maybe take advantage of that attraction.'

She stood up to face him, not liking how it felt to have him tower over her like that. She wanted to feel stronger. More assured. Even though her mouth had gone dry and her palms had gone sweaty. 'I thought you said you weren't trying to seduce me,' she whispered.

'I'm not. I'm talking about us both using the time we have together to enjoy a bit of…adult fun. No strings attached. No life getting in the way and when it's over, it's over. We part as friends and with some pretty excellent memories of the time we shared together.'

'You're talking about a fling?'

He took another step closer. His gaze drifting down towards her lips as he smiled 'I'm talking about a fling. So, Charlie Griffin. What do you say to my…proposal?'

She should slap him across the face. Maybe accuse him of sexual harassment? And if she did then he would profusely apologise and make sure he scheduled their work so she didn't have to be there at the same time as him, if that would make her day and time here easier.

He was prepared for both.

But she did neither. For a while, she just stared at him and he could tell her mind was racing with possibilities. Possible actions. Possible responses.

She was fighting an internal battle and he wondered which side would win. The side that just wanted to work out her contract and get away from Vasquez as quickly as she'd arrived? Or the side that was attracted to him and wondered what it might be like if she was brave enough to take this further?

'This…fling…it would be private between us?' Her cheeks had reddened.

'It would. Unless you wanted otherwise.'

'You wouldn't worry about people finding out?'

'I have nothing to hide. Would you be worried about people finding out?'

She blinked. 'Alice. I don't want there to be a string of men in her mother's life that she has to call Uncle.'

So she was seriously contemplating this.

'And this isn't a joke?' she asked.

'Maybe I could prove it?'

'How?'

'By kissing you. And then you could tell me afterwards, if I truly meant it. If it felt real. And if you had any doubts about my intent afterwards, you could end it as quickly as it began.'

She blushed and looked away. 'A kiss?'

'One kiss.' He stepped closer, desperate to touch her. Desperate to stroke her cheek with his finger. To run his hands into her hair. To hold her against him. 'A fair test, wouldn't you say?'

'I could say a lot of things.'

'Charlie?'

'What?'

'Say yes. To a single. Solitary. Mind-blowing kiss.' His voice had grown husky as his desire for her increased.

She looked up at him, deeply into his eyes, searching for something. To see if he was still, somehow, joking? To make sure he was serious? But there was something else there.

Desire.

Charlie wanted this—he could tell. She was just trying to work out how to give herself permission.

Her hand suddenly rose and she pressed it upon his chest and he hoped she could feel how fast his heart was beating for her. Her fingers spread slightly and her hand moved over his pectoral muscle and stilled.

Thump-thump.

Thump-thump.

Her touch made him want to do a thousand things to her. To take her in his arms and push her up against the wall. To rip her blouse out of her waistband and allow his hands to explore her soft flesh. To taste her. To hear her groan with pleasure.

But he'd made a promise. Just a kiss.

One kiss.

A smile hesitantly touched her lips. 'All right. One kiss.'

Triumphant, he slowly began to lean in.

The smile broadened. 'Let's see what you can do,' she whispered.

Eli grinned. 'Challenge accepted.'

And he slowly pressed his lips to hers.

CHAPTER TEN

IT WAS ALL just going to be pretty wrapping. Wasn't it? That was what she told herself before the kiss. That all the muscles, the tattoos, the long, dark brown, Viking-esque hair, the smile, the twinkle in the eyes, were all dressing and that maybe, once she kissed him, she would be able to relax and realise that that was all it was. Because there wouldn't be any depth. There wouldn't be any *feelings* and once it was proved, once and for all, she'd be able to put this irritating attraction that she had for Eli to bed.

But she was wrong.

So *incredibly* wrong.

It wasn't just aesthetics. It wasn't that he was just so tall, and so broad and so strong. His lips touched hers, so softly at first. Tenderly. Tentatively. A whisper of his lips against hers. A brush that promised a heat. An awakening of the senses.

And then it all changed.

Everything. Dizzying. All at once. An overwhelming feeling as his tongue passed by her lips and entered her mouth, and the knowledge that he had penetrated her somehow, that she had allowed him access because she wanted it, seemed to stir something within her as the kiss deepened.

Her hands came to rest against his chest, without her realising, as the rest of the world dropped away and all that seemed to matter was the two of them, pressed against one another as she tasted him. Feeling the brush of his light beard against her skin. Inhaling the scent of him, her senses going into overdrive, every nerve ending alive and expectant of more.

And as she sank into him, as she allowed herself to enjoy and experience his kiss, to yearn for more, to yearn to feel his flesh beneath her fingertips, he pulled back and away and stared at her, smiling. Leaving her breathless. Wanting more. Why had he stopped? Was this another joke?

No…it wasn't a joke. His eyes were dark with desire.

The attraction was real and she wanted him.

And he was offering himself to her if she wanted it.

No strings attached, he'd said.

She felt stunned by his kiss. A little wild inside as if she wanted to lock the door behind him, sweep everything off his desk and have wild and crazy sex with him, right there, in that very room.

His offer would allow her to sate her desires

and then leave again, with no complications, because there'd be no way she was going to fall for Eli. This was lust, pure and simple, right? It was all it could be. But she'd allowed herself to trust a guy before and her instincts had been wrong. He'd secretly filmed her. Had hidden cameras. Had put that stuff on the Internet and Alice might grow up and one day see it. She didn't think she had the misfortune of running into two guys exactly the same. She didn't think Eli would have cameras anywhere, but...this was his office and maybe she could have what she wanted, without putting herself at risk?

'That was a good kiss.'

His smile increased. 'I'm glad.'

'But this is our workplace and we can't do anything here.'

'We just did. Look, come paddle-boarding with me. Come up to Lawton Lake. It's quiet up there. Isolated. We could have some time alone.'

'What about Alice?'

'I can behave myself around your daughter. But I'd like to spend time with you, even if I can't touch you.'

She frowned. 'It's that easy?'

'Stopping myself from touching you? No.' He reached up to stroke her face, had another thought and pulled her close once again, more forceful this time, as if knowing his moments with her would have to be brief.

She sank into the kiss once again, amazed once again as to how the world fell away, all her cares disappearing. Moaning softly, her desire rocketing high, she reached to pull up his shirt, needing to feel his flesh beneath her fingertips, when suddenly, there was a knock at his door and someone was opening it and they broke apart so quickly. Guiltily.

Dot, the receptionist, put her head around the door.

Had she seen? Did she know what they'd been doing?

But Dot's face remained normal. 'Eli? Printer's playing up again. Can you come and give it your magic touch?'

Eli nodded. 'Of course!' He passed Charlie by and she pressed her fingertips to her lips, before smiling at Dot.

'Tech problems?'

'Always. But Eli can fix anything.' Dot looked her up and down. 'And anyone.' She smiled.

The rest of the week passed in a blur. Charlie worked hard and saw a wide variety of patients. A young child who had hurt their hand after grabbing an iron that was cooling down. A case of pneumonia. A spider bite that had become infected. She was enjoying herself immensely here in Vasquez—the range of health queries and injuries that came through their doors at the clinic was wide and varied, from the normal and everyday to the crazy, like the guy who came in after he'd actually tried to juggle a chainsaw and the even younger guy who'd climbed a tree, slipped and fallen through the branches, impaling himself on a stick. Her eyes had nearly dropped out of her head when he'd come walking in through the sliding doors, half a branch sticking out of his abdomen, smiling self-consciously. The kid had been lucky. The branch hadn't gone through any of his major organs, but rather than remove the branch themselves, in case it was blocking any major bleeders, they had stabilised him and flown him out to a major hospital.

It was strange working in the same building as Eli, passing him in the corridors, sharing a secret smile with him around the other staff. Occasionally their hands would brush as they passed each other in the corridor and every single time her body lit up like a fourth of July parade. Once, he'd even pulled her into a linen cupboard, just to kiss her, and when they'd both emerged... It was fair to say they'd both looked a little ruffled. The anticipation of their snatched moments was adrenaline-fuelled. Hiding. Trying to act normal around everyone else.

Her dreams at night filled with him and what it might be like to actually *be* with him. Physically. Her dreams had become so erotic at one point, she'd woken up so aroused that she'd had to take a very long and very cold shower before she could drop Alice off at school and then go into work.

Mrs Clark greeted her every morning that she dropped Alice off and Charlie would smile and feel awkward that her daughter's teacher had no idea about all the sinful and naughty thoughts she was having about her adopted son.

But all the stolen glances, all the thoughts, all the yearnings…they were all adding up into something quite exciting and, though Charlie was still scared, she'd not had this much fun in ages. Because she knew it wasn't just aesthetics any more.

He looked good.

He tasted good.

His kisses and his touch were amazing.

She could only hope and imagine that the rest was just as mind-blowing.

The weekend came around quickly and the day that she would be going up to Lawton Lake with him. She woke, her body fizzing with nerves, her hands trembling with so much anticipation she dropped her tube of toothpaste in the sink and she could barely floss her teeth.

But when she went to wake up Alice, her daughter looked pale and ill.

'Mommy, I don't feel well.'

Instantly, her nerves dissipated as a new concern entered her brain and took prime position. 'What's wrong?'

'My tummy hurts.'

Lots of kids got tummy aches. This was probably nothing. But if Alice was ill, they couldn't go out today. It was her first time being in kindergarten and she was being exposed to a whole new plethora of germs and bacteria, it was no wonder she was ill.

I should have expected this.

'Do you feel sick?'

A nod.

'Okay, honey. Well, we won't go out today, then. Don't you worry about that.'

'I wanted to go paddle-boarding with Eli.'

'So did I. But that lake won't disappear and maybe we could do it next weekend? I'll call Eli and let him know, you just rest. Here.' She passed her daughter her tablet. 'Why don't you watch some cartoons? Take your mind off it. I'll go get you a drink and some dry toast, in case you want to try and eat.'

She felt disappointed, yet also somehow relieved. Charlie had wanted Eli, yes, but the last time she'd fallen for a guy, he'd turned out to be wholly unreliable and weird and, though Eli was nothing like the last one, there had still been that fear that she was rushing into something again, just because of an infatuation. And doubt was an insidious drug, too. Maybe starting something with, not only her work colleague, but her boss was a dangerous thing?

Maybe this was life telling her that this thing with Eli shouldn't get off the ground at all? That they'd had their fun. They'd shared spectacular kisses and fumbles in closets and that would have to be enough.

Downstairs, she picked up her phone and rang him.

He answered straight away. 'Hi.'

'Hey, Eli, listen, I'm sorry, but we won't be able to make it today.'

'Oh.' He sounded incredibly disappointed. 'Are you having second thoughts?'

'No.' She smiled, even though it was partly a lie. 'But I do have an ill Alice. She's woken up with a bad tummy and feels sick. I guess I should have expected something like this, what with her having started school, but I need to stay here and look after her.'

'Of course. Do you need anything?'

'No, no. We're fine. I'm sorry we've had to put off our weekend.'

'Well, the lake isn't going anywhere, so maybe another time?'

She smiled. She'd said the exact same thing to her daughter. 'Absolutely, unless…'

'Unless what?'

'Unless this is a sign that maybe we shouldn't be doing it at all?'

'You believe in signs?'

She shrugged. 'I don't know. Maybe?'

'Okay. Well, is it a sign that you want to follow?'

She thought of him. Of his kisses. His lips. His tongue.

Dear God, his tongue...

Of the way he made her feel all excited and that everything had possibilities. That she wanted to feel that way again. 'No.'

There was a silent pause. 'Good. I'm glad. Want me to come round? I could sit with you. Help you take care of her.'

'I don't know if that's a good idea.'

'I can help. And I promise to control myself in front of your daughter.'

She liked that he was offering to help. And this way? She could still see him. 'Okay.' She smiled.

CHAPTER ELEVEN

HE CALLED IN to the shop first. Bought ice lollies, jelly and some plain dry crackers for Alice. Then he picked up some items for himself and Charlie. They might not be able to go to Lawton Lake, but he was still determined that they would have a good day together.

When he arrived at her door, she opened it with a smile and he raised his bag of shopping. 'I've brought supplies.'

'How long do you think you're staying?' she asked with a quiet laugh.

'Long enough for you to be glad I called round.'

She stepped back. 'Come on in.'

He waited for the door to be closed, then he turned to her. 'Where's Alice?'

'In her room. Sleeping.'

'She okay?'

'It's just a virus, or something.'

He smiled and stepped towards her. Bent his head towards her to let her know he was coming in for a kiss, now that he'd clarified the fact that Alice wouldn't see.

The smile on her face was enough for him to know that his kiss was welcome and he pressed his lips to hers. She let out a small groan in her throat that did all kinds of exciting things to his insides, that told him she'd been looking forward to this.

Because so had he. The thoughts of spending this Saturday with her at Lawton Lake had been all he could think about. He'd imagined getting them both on their paddle boards, teaching them how to balance. How to get back on their board when out on the water, if they fell in. The water at the lake was notoriously calm. Flat. It was the perfect place for them to learn and the scenery around it, breathtaking. But he'd known he wouldn't need to look around to have his breath stolen away. Being with Charlie would do that and so he didn't need to be at a lake. He didn't need to be in a secluded place with her. He just needed her to be close by. And now…? With her lips pressed to his and her body sinking against his…?

When the kiss ended, she was smiling, which made him smile, too.

'Want a drink?'

'You do make me thirsty,' he said.

She laughed. 'Come through to the kitchen. You can show me what you've got.'

'I could show you right here.'

'The bag, silly! You've been to the shop?'

He growled. He'd known exactly what she'd meant, but he hadn't been able to resist. Following her through to the kitchen, he laid the bag on the counter and got out all the goodies he'd bought. Alice's supplies, a rosé wine, cheeses and meats for a charcuterie board, baguettes, fruit, chips, ice cream.

A huge teddy bear.

'Wow.'

'I thought we could have a picnic in the back yard.'

'Great idea. Coffee?'

'Sure.'

She set about making them both a drink and he watched her move about the kitchen. Now that they had a new understanding between them, he felt able to openly watch her and concentrate on her. There were no other eyes watching them. No one making assumptions. Their fling, their relationship, whatever you wanted to call it, was theirs alone. And she was beautiful to watch. His. He liked that.

While the coffee machine did its thing, he reached out for her hand, taking her fingers in his and pulling her close, up against his body. She looked up at him, mildly amused, her eyes sparkling with mischief. 'Something I can do for you?'

'Plenty of things.'

'Such as?'

He smirked. 'Don't poke the bear, Charlie. Not with your daughter just in the next room. I've woken from hibernation and I want to feed. I want to feed a lot and you just happen to be the snack I want to feast on.'

'Tell me what you want to do to me, then,' she said, teasingly, smiling, looking up at him through thick, lush lashes, her lips parted, the glimpse of her tongue, wet and slick, giving him all sorts of X-rated ideas.

He groaned softly. 'I want to know we have a space that is just our own. No interruptions. Nothing else to worry about but each other's pleasure.' He stroked her cheek with the back of his finger. 'I want to be able to slowly undress you and marvel at every inch of your skin. Touch every inch. Your beautiful neck. This collarbone.' His finger trailed down the slope of her throat, brushing aside her top to reveal her clavicle. 'I want to reveal every delicious part of you. Slowly. Admire you. Kiss you. Taste you.'

He could see her breathing was increasing. Felt her push herself against him.

'I want to take my time over you. Discover what makes you breathe hard. What makes you gasp. What makes you arch your back. What makes you move against me as you beg for more. As you beg me not to stop.' He dropped a soft kiss on her collarbone, inhaled her dreamy scent and then backed off, remembering his promise. Remembering that they weren't alone. That her daughter was in the next room and that no matter how much he wanted to take this further, he could not. He sucked in a deep breath. It wasn't easy moving away from her. Not when he wanted her so badly. It was taking an enormous amount of control, especially since he'd been waiting for this weekend so badly.

She looked disappointed that he moved away, but understanding too. And he saw that she respected him for controlling himself. Charlie cleared her throat. 'Okay. Well, I look forward to us finding a place that's just our own.'

He nodded and smiled. 'Can I go see her? Say hello?'

'Sure.'

They both needed the distraction. They both needed to remember the priority here. It was Alice. Not what they wanted physically. And he didn't want Charlie to think that he was only with her because he hungered for her body. He liked her. Really liked her. Always had. But Charlie had a daughter now and he liked Alice too. She was a great kid.

He knocked on her bedroom door.

'Come in.'

Grinning broadly and holding the huge teddy

bear he'd bought, he poked his head around the door. 'Hi. How you doing? Your mum tells me you're not feeling too great.'

Alice's eyes landed on the bear and widened as she sat up in bed. 'Is that for me?'

'Sure is. A friend for Mr Cuddles.' He passed the bear over and smiled as she hugged it tight. He remembered being her age. Young and in care already, he'd always had dreams of someone turning up one day, maybe on his birthday, with a big bear and a load of gifts that were just for him, that let him know that there was someone out there who cared. That maybe his life so far had been a terrible mistake and they'd not meant to leave him at a fire station when he was a baby. That someone would come and rescue him and let him know that actually he was a prince from a far-off country.

Of course, it never happened. He never got gifts and so he started making his own fun. It was the only way to brighten his day and try to make him forget how lonely and alone he actually was.

Luckily Alice didn't have to experience any of that. She had a mom. She wasn't in a kids' home and she was loved very much. And looking around her room, he saw she had plenty of stuff. Toys, plushies, games, books. He wondered if Charlie had ever felt the same way, too.

'What's his name?' Alice asked.

'I don't know. I think maybe you ought to name him.'

Alice turned the bear to look at his face properly. 'He looks like a Sprinkles.'

Eli grinned. 'Great name! Sprinkles it is.' He looked around her room. Saw her sketch pad on the table. 'You been drawing?'

She nodded.

'Can I take a look?'

Another nod.

He picked up her pad and began to flick through the pages. There was the usual stuff. Cats. Dogs. A unicorn that had been coloured in with a multitude of bright, rainbow colours. And then he came across a drawing that made him smile even more. 'Is that *me*?'

Alice had drawn a picture that was clearly herself, her mom, and a seaplane floating on water, with a man wading through water to reach a case. She'd drawn him big, as if he was a giant, with masses of long, wild hair, and he had a huge smile on his face. He liked it very much.

'Do you like it? You can keep it, if you want.'

He thanked her. 'All great artists *sell* their work. They don't just give it away. I tell you what—I'll give you five dollars so I can put it on my fridge.' He reached into his pocket and pulled a note from his wallet and placed it on her bedside table.

'Mom! Eli gave me five dollars for my drawing!'

Behind him, Charlie walked across the room from her position in the doorway and ruffled her daughter's hair, before laying a hand on her forehead to test her temperature. 'I heard! That's great! You should put it in your little safe and when you're better you can spend it on something nice.'

'I'm already feeling better.'

'You feel it. No temperature. Why don't you go out in the garden and get some fresh air for a bit?'

'Okay.' Alice swung her legs out of bed and grabbed her bathrobe, slid her feet into slippers shaped like bunnies and headed on out.

Charlie turned to look at him. 'That was very sweet. You didn't have to pay her for her drawing.'

'I believe in nurturing talent and she's got one.'

'She's five.'

'And already drawing like a twelve-year-old. Who knows where she'll be in a few years' time?'

He wouldn't know. Because she and Charlie would be leaving in a few months' time. It was painful to think about. Sad.

'Maybe you can call me one day and tell me? I'd like to know how she's doing.'

The idea that they wouldn't be around…that he wouldn't…was sobering.

'You don't have to do that, you know.'

'Do what?'

'Show an interest in my kid because you're interested in me.'

'I'm not. I like Alice and I can tell she's something special.' He frowned. 'You never drew. Who does she get that creativity from? Her father?'

Instantly, he saw the walls come up as her hackles raised. Clearly the father was a difficult subject.

'Glen would consider himself an artist, sure. But I didn't like what he created. What he chose to share with the world.'

He wasn't sure what she meant. 'Was it like, abstract? Weird stuff?'

'He experimented with film.'

'Okay. Would I have seen any of it, anywhere? Did he exhibit?' He got the feeling she was trying to tell him the truth, but felt unable to give concrete details, so she was skirting around the edges of the confession.

'Unfortunately.' She walked past him, towards the kitchen.

He followed her from the room and went to stand beside her as they watched Alice in the garden. Her daughter was sitting by a flower bed, watching something crawl over the back of her hand. A ladybug?

'Why did you break up with this… Glen?' He was curious. He really wanted to know. The Charlie he'd known had been keen to find and create her own family. She'd wanted loads of kids—had said she wouldn't be happy until she had loads of them and would surround herself with their love. That she would create a happy home, with a white picket fence.

'I don't really want to talk about him, if you don't mind?'

'Sure. Sure.' He gazed out of the window, trying not to look at her, but he'd heard something in her voice, just then. A hurt. A pain. A deep wound that she would prefer to ignore, but Eli knew, from practice, that hiding pain only caused it to get worse and fester.

He'd hid his own. Not wanting to tell anyone. Not wanting to tell his brand-new family that he thought something was wrong with him, in case they realised they'd made a bad choice in choosing him, and when he'd got so scared that he'd finally spoken up, it had been far too late. The cancer had been well established and, though the seminoma and his left testicle had been removed, he'd still had to undergo chemotherapy and radiation, which had left him sterile. Since then, he'd thankfully had no recurrences, but he maintained his body as if it was the most precious possession he had on this earth, which of course it was, because the one thing he'd always wanted— a child—would never be within his reach.

'But I'm here for you, if you ever want to.'

He felt, rather than saw, her look over at him, then glance away, before her fingers gently entwined with his, squeezing his hand briefly, before letting go as Alice stood up and came back towards the house.

'Mom, could I have a drink?'

'Sure, though Eli brought some popsicles—want one of those instead?'

'What flavour?'

'Orange or cherry?'

'Orange, please!'

He was glad Alice was okay, though she still had a strange pallor that told him that, whatever she had, she wasn't over it yet.

Alice sat in the living area, holding Sprinkles and sucking on her popsicle and then the television was put on.

Eli leaned against the kitchen counter as Charlie put away the things he'd brought from the shop. When she'd got nothing left to fiddle with, nothing left to clear up, she looked at him awkwardly. 'I bet this is the sexiest fling you've ever had,' she said quietly, so Alice couldn't hear.

He laughed. 'You have no idea.' The truth was, he'd never had a fling with anybody. He'd only ever had serious relationships and none since Lenore. Her leaving had pained him greatly, resulting in him feeling like the best way forward was to never get involved with anyone ever again. Not seriously, anyway.

'If you want to go, you can. I'd hate for you to waste a precious day off, hanging around with us.'

'Forget it! I love hanging around with you guys. You're refreshing.'

'We're new, so we're fun?'

'You're not new to me. I know you, remember?'

'Not deeply, though. You don't know all my deep, dark secrets. You don't know who I've cried over, who I've laughed with, who my friends are, what my favourite food is. You just think you know me because we shared a childhood.'

He considered her, knowing he couldn't let her push him away. He wanted to stay. Wanted to prove to her that she wasn't just a plaything. She was important. 'I know Alice's father hurt you and that you don't want to talk about it. Probably because you're embarrassed about it or ashamed for some reason. I think you've cried over him. Or maybe, more precisely, you've cried over losing what he represented—the happy family unit you always dreamed of having. All those kids. He hurt you, took something from you and you're still healing and you're trying to decide if you can trust a man ever again.

'I think Alice makes you laugh. Alice makes you happy, because it's just you and her against the world and she is your world, because you take her with you everywhere you go. I'd like to think you have loads of friends and maybe you do, but you never stay around long enough for them to know.' He smiled, but not with triumph. 'And your favourite food is grilled cheese. Or at least it was before.'

Charlie stared at him in shock, her face a mask of surprise and fear.

He continued. 'Today, you're a great doctor and I know what it takes to become a doctor in this world, which means that you're clever and strong and determined and you've learned how to harden your heart from all the tragedy and upset in this world, but that in private you still feel it keenly and you shed tears when you're home alone. You're a professional and you want to show your daughter that working is important and that if you want success, you have to earn it. You yearn for relationships, but fear them at the same time. Am I even close?'

He knew it was a scary thing to say all of that, but he had to let her know that he could see the real her and not the shiny exterior that she revealed to their patients. But he also said it all with a grin on his face, because he needed her to know that he wasn't judging her, just trying to show that he knew her better than she realised.

She paused a long while before she answered. 'Maybe you should be a shrink, with insight like that. But are you able to turn that keen eye upon yourself?'

He didn't get a chance to answer because suddenly, from the living area, they heard a strange sound and then Alice was being ill all over the hard wooden floors.

Charlie rushed to her daughter, whereas Eli grabbed paper towels and cleaning spray from under the sink before hurrying over.

Alice was crying. 'I'm sorry, Mom!'

'It's okay, honey. It's okay.'

They cleared her up and took her back to her bedroom, settling her beneath the covers with Sprinkles and giving her her tablet to watch some shows on, a bucket beside her, just in case.

When the drama was over and they were back in the kitchen alone, Eli stared at her. 'I can turn that eye upon myself. I don't get involved in relationships any more because I got hurt so badly in my last one, which was two years ago. I maintain my happy-go-lucky persona because it makes me happy and I like making other people smile. Everyone in Vasquez is my friend, but they are also my patients, so my friendships with them are strange ones. The last time I cried I was twenty-one years of age and I cried because I felt like my happy life I'd built was spinning out of my control. And my favourite food is cheesecake, which is a total bummer, because to look like this?' He indicated his own body with his hands. 'You don't get to eat cheesecake often enough.'

She smiled at him, shyly, clearly pleased that

he'd shared something with her, after he'd so expertly psychoanalysed her. And then she laughed. 'Okay.' She picked a piece of imaginary fluff off the kitchen surface. 'What made you cry?'

His cancer diagnosis. But he didn't want her to know about that. What was the point? It was over with now. Done. He'd had no recurrences and he was too busy living in the present to keep returning to the past. 'I don't remember,' he lied. Hating himself for lying.

'I think you do. You remembered you were twenty-one when it happened, so I also think you do know what caused it, you just don't want to say.'

He crossed his arms and stepped closer to her, towering over her, smiling. 'I tell you what…if you tell me about what happened with Alice's father, I'll tell you why I cried.'

She considered it. He saw it cross her eyes. But then she looked down and away. Defeated. 'I guess we'll never know then, huh?'

Alice slept for a couple of hours and when she woke, she looked much brighter and asked if she could come out and watch a movie with them.

She and Eli had spent the time chatting in the lounge, discussing some of his weirdest cases and sharing tales of their medical training. They'd trained in different schools, but discovered that they'd both done a placement in the same emergency room, though obviously not at the same time, and had shared stories about an attending that they both knew, who'd made an impression on the pair of them with his crazy uncombed hair and the fact that he always sounded as if he was winging his way through the day. Eli had been most amused to hear that this guy had even asked Charlie out once and she'd given him the benefit of the doubt and enjoyed a drink with him, only to put up with the fact that his mother kept texting him all night long and she discovered he lived in her basement. That had been the end of that!

They put on an animated movie and Alice lay between them on the couch. Eli was at Alice's feet and Charlie let her daughter lay her head upon her lap. As the movie played, Eli stretched out his hand across the back of the couch, as if reaching for her fingers, and, once she'd checked that Alice couldn't see, Charlie reached out too.

Their fingers entwined on the back of the couch and Eli looked at her and smiled, his eyes sparkling, and she realised that, even though she'd been worried about Alice and they'd never made it up to Lawton Lake, Eli had still somehow made the day special. He'd not shown boredom once. Had never been impatient. Had never been rude. Never selfish. He'd helped care for Alice. Been thoughtful. He'd been kind and funny and made her laugh and his presence had been reassuring and comforting. He'd made the day easier and she liked having him around. An hour ago, he'd insisted on preparing their charcuterie lunch and had pretended to be her private waiter, pulling out her chair for her to sit down, draping a serviette across her lap and calling her 'miss'.

As she played with his fingers, she wondered about what kind of a father he would make. He seemed to adore kids, so she had no doubt he would make a wonderful dad. Look at how he kept trying to nurture Alice's drawing! That had been so sweet—buying one of her pictures. She'd never seen Alice smile so broadly.

Holding his hand secretly felt good and she found herself smiling and imagining what a future with Eli in her life might look like. And when she realised that she would like it very much, she froze, feeling her heart beat faster.

What am I even thinking?

She risked a glance at him, to see if he'd noticed the change in her, but he hadn't. He was staring at the screen, laughing at the antics of a pack of hyenas.

He might be good with kids because, at heart, he was a kid himself, and hadn't he told her before that he hadn't been in a relationship for over two years? That he'd got hurt and wouldn't risk it again? This was not a man looking for an instant family and nor was she in the market for making one with him.

This was a *fling*.

Or at least was trying to be.

We've only shared kisses. Heated fumbles. Perhaps I should stop this before it goes even further?

CHAPTER TWELVE

'CHARLIE! GREAT—YOU'RE HERE. We've had a field call. Hikers trapped down a crevasse. Mountain Rescue have also been informed, but they've asked for two doctors to attend.'

'Oh, okay. But who will man the clinic?'

'The nurses are here and our resident, has said he'll stay as long as we need him to cover.'

She got up from behind her desk, downing the last of her coffee. 'How are we getting there?'

'Driving most of the way, then I'm afraid it might be a bit of a hike. It's up in the White Mountains.'

She stepped out from behind her desk, to reveal sandal shoes. 'I don't have hiking boots.'

'I think we may have some spares to loan you. We keep a supply, just in case. What size are you?'

'Size nine.'

'Perfect. Come on—I'll talk you through it.' He turned to go, hearing her steps quickly catching up with him as he began to stride down the corridor towards the field supply room. Here they kept everything they would need for a field call. Go bags, filled with equipment they might need— oxygen, defib, masks, gloves, bandages, splints, needles, syringes, painkilling medications. There were jackets and high-vis vests, helmets, boots, torches, blankets, supplies of water, IV bags, a bit of everything and anything. All clearly labelled, so it could just be grabbed quickly.

Eli searched the boots labelled nines and passed a pair to Charlie. 'Try these on. Mountain Rescue will have sent out a team via helicopter, but they have to come in from Anchorage, so we might get there before them, depending upon how far up into the mountains the incident is. We've been given the coordinates and Chuck is readying the vehicle now.'

'Pilot Chuck?'

'The very same. The guy knows this area like the back of his hand. He'll get us to where we need to go.'

'I guess I should be glad it hasn't been snowing and we're not going by dog sled.'

He smiled. 'It's a shame you'll be gone before any snow hits the ground. A dog-sled ride is something not to be missed.'

He was hauling equipment onto his back, so almost didn't notice the look of uncertainty on Charlie's face. The way it had changed when he'd said she'd be gone. It was almost wistful. Almost sad.

'Here. Take this.' He passed her a second go bag and then began to lead her to the back of the clinic where Chuck was apparently waiting.

'What do we know about the patient's injuries?'

'We don't know, but a fall into a crevasse could be anything. Broken bones, blood loss, loss of consciousness, hypothermia depending upon how long they've been out and exposed to the wild. Maybe dehydration?'

She nodded, hefting the bag higher onto her shoulder.

At the vehicle, he swung open the trunk and hauled in their equipment. 'You ever attend a field call?'

'Only during training. I did a shift with some paramedics.'

'In the wild?'

'No. Inner city.'

He smiled at her. 'Well, this is a little bit different, but don't worry. I'll keep you safe.'

'I'm glad to hear it.'

Chuck started the engine and began to drive them away from Vasquez and up into the mountain range. There was nothing to do but wait until they arrived, so Eli looked over at Charlie to see what she made of the scenery.

Her face was a mask of awe and wonder as the

urban signs began to drop away and they drove further into nature. The grey-purple mountains rose up all around them, thick with vegetation and, after one turn, the vehicle actually scared a group of three or four deer off the tarmac, sending them scattering into the trees.

'How you settling in, Doc?' Chuck asked her.

'Yeah, good, thanks. How are your dogs doing?'

'Good. Got a new litter of pups due soon.'

'Well, don't tell Alice.'

'Too late. I gave a talk at the school last week and she was there listening as I told her all about it. But don't worry, they're not the kind of dogs you'd want as a household pet. My dogs are working animals and they're made for the outside and pulling sleds and racing, not for lying on a couch and getting fat.'

Charlie nodded and glanced at Eli.

Every smile she gave him made him feel good inside. He wanted to reach out and take her hand in his, but Chuck was here and he didn't think she'd want anyone to know about how they felt about one another, or that they were in a relationship. It was crazy, really. They'd agreed to a fling with no strings, but hadn't actually done anything yet, but kiss. That goodbye kiss they'd shared after he'd spent the day with her and Alice... It had been tropical in its heat and seriously tempting him to break his promise to be a gentleman about this. And he wasn't actually sure how many other guys would agree to a fling with a woman and just be happy to spend time with her, without touching, and help her take care of her sick kid.

Because he'd been more than happy to do that. It had felt nice. As if they were a little family together. And he should have run a mile from that, because it was a dangerous road for him to travel down, hoping like that. Allowing his imagination to run away with all those fancy ideas of settling down with someone, maybe getting married, maybe having a family he could call his own. Because he'd never have that.

He couldn't give Charlie all those babies she'd said she wanted. He couldn't give her the big family she'd once dreamed of. If she got involved with him on a serious level? Then there would be no more pregnancies. No more babies. Alice would be her one and only child and he knew he couldn't do that to her.

So, he should have shut down those thoughts.

Should have turned tail and run. But being with Charlie was just so right and so good that she was a drug at this point.

So instead, he'd found himself lingering at her door, as they'd said goodnight.

He'd so wanted to stay. Had so wanted to suggest that he stay the night and he'd leave really early in the morning, but he'd refrained from doing so, because who knew if Alice would come into Charlie's room in the middle of the night with a tummy ache? What would have happened then? And maybe it was best for them if they just took each other in little bite sizes? So it didn't become overwhelming, so they didn't start getting ideas about each other that they shouldn't?

And so, before she'd opened the door to let him out, they'd stood there, together, staring into each other's eyes, their heartbeats feeling as though they were synced, and he'd gently cupped her face and kissed her softly. The longing he'd felt for her all day long contained in a single, gratifying, mind-blowing kiss.

'Goodnight, Eli,' she'd whispered, her voice husky and a little breathy afterwards.

'Goodnight, Charlie.' He'd swept his thumb over her bottom lip, stared at her mouth some more, imagining the wonders of those lips elsewhere, and then he'd torn himself away, every step that he took walking away from her house a torture.

He'd felt so comfortable there. So right. And maybe he was an incredible fool for letting his mind imagine the possibilities with her, but so be it. He couldn't help it. Charlie was different. Charlie was special and always would be.

It took them just under an hour before Chuck pulled over on a dirt road as a chopper circled overhead, looking for a space to land.

'Looks like we've both got here at the same

time. We'll head off on foot. Chuck, you've got the co-ordinates?'

'Sure have. It's this way,' he said, pointing towards a small dirt trail that led higher into the mountains, before he reached into his flatbed truck and opened up a metal case that contained a rifle. He pocketed some ammo and hauled the rifle over his shoulder. 'Let's go.'

'What's the rifle for?' Charlie asked, looking a little shocked.

'It's preventative.'

Chuck led the way, Charlie second, so that Eli could bring up the rear and keep an eye on her and keep her safe. There could be anything out here. Mountain lion. Elk. Wolf. Grizzly. All manner of creatures. That was the reason for the gun. If the patients had shed any blood, any kind of predator would have tracked that scent over many miles and be on their way too and no one would want to fight off a grizzly, or worse, without some kind of backup to scare off the predator before they could be rescued. The rifle was protection. Chuck wouldn't actually shoot an animal unless he absolutely had to. They weren't hunting here.

The steep incline was quite the workout for his calf muscles and he was glad of all the cardio he undertook. Charlie sounded out of breath and Chuck sounded as if he might be the one to need the oxygen, when suddenly the trail evened out and the pace got easier.

Chuck checked his map, looked out across the view and continued on down the path. It was getting quite rocky underfoot and the scrubby trees were becoming sparse as they began climbing over large boulders that seemed to block their way.

'Watch your footing, guys. You don't want to turn an ankle here,' Chuck advised.

They began to make their way along a ledge that had a stony path. Clearly this was a way up for some mountaineers. The path turned in and out of view, and after they'd been ascending for about ten minutes they saw a guy, dressed in red, waving his arms furiously and calling.

'Over here! We're over here! Jackie, Adam, they're here.'

Jackie and Adam must be the patients, Eli thought.

There was the temptation to rush these last few metres, but Chuck stopped them from pressing ahead too fast and made sure that Charlie kept the same pace they'd been walking at, until they reached the guy in red.

'Thank God you're here! Jackie slipped and fell down a crevasse. She was unconscious for a while, so we think she banged her head. Adam went down to rescue her, but was afraid to move her, so he's been trying to keep her awake and warm.'

'Any medical history we should know?'

'Jackie's just got the all-clear from breast cancer. She had a double mastectomy, chemo and radiation treatments over the last year.'

'Is she on any meds right now? Any allergies?'

'I don't think so.'

'Okay. Mountain Rescue are on their way. Is there a way that one of us can abseil down to Jackie?'

'Sure. We can attach one of you to our ropes.' The guy looked them over and kept his gaze on Charlie. 'It's gonna have to be you. The gap in the crevasse isn't big enough for anyone else.'

Charlie looked at him. 'I've never done anything like that before.'

She looked apprehensive.

'Don't worry. We'll talk you through it, every step of the way.'

She nodded and took note as Gerry, the guy in red, attached her to a harness, rope and karabiners. He gave her instructions on how to hold the rope, how to break, how to feed the rope through so that she would descend.

Eli attached a go bag to her harness with an extra karabiner. 'You're all set. You can do this,' he said, smiling at her, hoping that his encouragement would give her the belief that she needed. But he understood her reticence. She was a city girl. She'd never rock climbed or abseiled in her life and now she had to because someone's life depended upon it. He wanted to have the utmost confidence in her, but knew she'd be afraid.

So would he. He wanted to keep her safe and if it could be him to make his way down to the patient, he'd prefer it.

'Okay.'

She kept her gaze on him as she backed out towards the crevasse. Gerry wasn't joking, there was only a small narrow channel through the rock, which opened out into a bigger chamber below.

Eli looked over and down through the crevasse. It was a long drop. Charlie would have to rappel freely for quite a way and even though Adam was there beneath her at the icy, rocky bottom to help her break or slow down, if she lost control, he still felt apprehensive. Having to place his trust in a guy he didn't know.

He met Charlie's gaze. Saw the fear in her eyes. Nodded.

You can do this.

Her hands were trembling and he wanted to reach out and lay his hand on hers so much, to still them. To let her know he believed in her.

Something in his eyes must have given her the confidence, because suddenly she was moving away from him. Backwards and down, over the edge, hesitating slightly as she looked where to place her feet.

'That's it. Slow and steady.'

He watched her disappear from view and felt a lump of dread settle in his stomach. 'You okay?' he called out.

'I'm okay,' came back her voice, echoing around the rock.

He hated not being able to see her. To not view her progress, or lack thereof, and suddenly he wished they'd waited for Mountain Rescue. Surely they wouldn't have been much longer? They'd seen the helicopter hovering, knew they were close! But the fact that Jackie had lost consciousness and suffered a head injury had made them forge ahead to get a doctor down to her.

'How are you doing?' he called again, his stomach in absolute knots. He should never have let her go. She had a child! A daughter! She had someone who depended on her, he didn't. It should have been him. They could have found a way, surely?

There was no response.

'Charlie!'

A pause. Then, 'I'm okay! I'm nearly there! About ten more metres to go.'

Her voice echoed again and he'd never been so relieved to hear it. But then he heard something he didn't like.

A man's voice, calling out. 'Too fast! Watch out!'

There was the sound of a thud. Of a person hitting rock.

'Charlie!'

There was a cry of pain and he instantly felt sick. 'Charlie!' He spun around and faced Gerry. 'Hook me up. I don't care. I'll make it down there somehow.'

'You're too big.' Gerry looked sorry.

'Doc? I think the other doc has broken her leg or something!' called Adam.

Damn it!

He spun around, wanting to be with her. To scoop her up into his protective arms and take her someplace safe. But that was an impossibility. It wasn't just Charlie he had to worry about, but Jackie, too.

'How's Jackie?' he called.

'Conscious. Her head has stopped bleeding, but she can't remember much.'

'And she's breathing okay?'

'Yes, sir!'

'Okay, you need to get the oxygen out of the go bag and place the oxygen mask over Jackie's face,' he continued to yell.

'Already on it! Charlie here is already telling me what to do.'

He smiled with relief. That Charlie was still putting her patient first over herself was remarkable and proved just what kind of a doctor and person she was. Selfless. But then again, she always had been. Even as a kid, she'd helped out the other kids at the home. Especially the littler ones. Helping patch up their cuts and grazes and trying to cheer them up afterwards. She had to be afraid and in a great deal of pain herself, if it was true she'd broken something from her bad landing, but was still determined that Jackie would receive help first.

As he listened to what was going on at the bottom of the crevasse, he heard Chuck behind him. 'Rescue's here.'

He quickly got to his feet and summarised the situation to them.

Two of the rescue guys, small in stature, thankfully, hooked up some more ropes and began to abseil down the crevasse and Eli felt much better knowing that Charlie would also receive help.

The rescue guys had radios and had passed one to Eli before disappearing over the edge and when they got to the bottom, he was very much relieved to hear Charlie's voice. 'Hey.'

'Hey. How are you doing?' His voice softened.

'I'm all right. I got Adam to put a headcollar on Jackie and they're bringing her up now. I think she may have a broken arm or wrist, but it's the head injury that's the major concern.'

'And you? Run it down for me.'

He heard her sigh. 'Possible lower leg or ankle fractures.'

'Plural?'

'Yeah. Both hurt. My left leg has a noticeable

deformity about an inch above the ankle and the right one hurts like you wouldn't believe.'

'You did drop from a height onto rock. We'll get you X-rayed when we get you back to the clinic.'

'Take care of Jackie first.'

'I will take care of you both. Now, have you taken any of the painkillers?'

'No. I wanted to keep a clear head for Adam while I told him what to do.'

'Then do it now.'

'Yes, boss.'

He heard the slight smile in her voice and had to stop himself from cradling the radio. He couldn't hold *her*, but he could hold the item that was bringing him her voice. He hated the idea that she was hurt and lying at the bottom of the crevasse.

The mountain rescue guys ascended with Jackie, wearing a neck collar and with bandages wrapped around her head and one arm in a sling. The bandage on her head was bleeding through at the right temple and he attended to it by adding another pressure bandage to try and stop the bleeding. But they couldn't take any risks and now that Jackie was out of the crevasse, they were able to strap her to a back board. They would have to carry her back down the ravine towards where the truck was parked and then drive her to the helicopter, so she could be airlifted.

'Sending up Adam.'

Eli grabbed the radio. 'You first. You're injured.'

'I'm sending up Adam, Eli,' she replied more firmly, and before he could say anything else Adam's relieved face appeared as he was pulled back up.

'How is she?' he asked the man.

'Bloody amazing! She splinted her own legs, while telling me what to do!'

Eli stood over the crevasse and clicked the button on the radio. 'Tell me when you're ready.'

'I'm ready.'

Eli nodded to Gerry and they began to winch Charlie back up through the small gap in the crevasse. His heart was already pounding fast, but felt as if it went into tachycardia the second he spotted her rising up through the gap. She turned and her legs bumped against the rock on the edge and she winced, but Eli knelt and scooped her up into his arms and moved her away from the ledge.

'I'm fine. See to Jackie.'

'The rescue guys are already seeing to her. She's fine. Just concussed, I think. I couldn't feel any fractures. Let me look at you.'

'I'm fine and put me down!'

'I'm carrying you back to the truck.'

'That's a long way, Eli.'

'I'm a strong guy.'

As they spoke, the helicopter hovered above

them, brought in by the rescue team, who hooked up Jackie's scoop to a cable and she was airlifted up off the mountain. The downward pressure from the helicopter was intense, but thankfully they were sheltered by an overpass.

One of the rescue team turned to Eli. 'We don't have another scoop for her, but we can help you carry her down.'

'What about Jackie?'

'There's a driver and EMT waiting with the truck, so they'll be able to unhook Jackie and get her loaded into the helicopter.'

'Honestly, I'm fine,' Eli said.

'Mate, let us help you.'

Fair enough. There was no point in being proud and help would be appreciated, no matter how much he wanted to wrap his arms around her and protect her. But already his mind was racing. If one of her legs was broken, then that could be a problem, depending on the severity of the break. If both legs were broken? She'd be in a wheelchair for a while. Because even though he'd advise her to rest, he couldn't imagine her accepting that.

I can work from a wheelchair.

He could already imagine her saying it. But it wasn't just work, was it? What about Alice? What about getting her to school and home again?

The rescue guy and Eli joined hands to make a seat beneath Charlie's rear. She draped an arm around each of their shoulders and they began to make their way back down the ravine.

He couldn't stop himself from glancing at her. Checking her colour. Her respiratory rate. Whether she looked to be in pain. She had one break for sure and was putting a brave face on it. High pain threshold?

It took them some time to make it back to Chuck's truck, as they had to move slower, to make sure their steps were steady and they didn't trip over the numerous obstacles on the path— rocks, roots that emerged from the ground and dipped back in again like sea serpents, loose gravel, divots where rabbits, or some other burrowing animal, had decided to dig.

Chuck lowered the back end and they placed her onto the back of the truck.

Eli climbed on with her and settled beside her.

'What are you doing?'

'Riding with you.'

'I'm fine! You'll get bounced around back here. No need for us both to be uncomfortable.'

'This selfless nature of yours is endearing, but could you keep your trap shut for once? I'm riding in back with you, whether you like it or not.'

Her mouth opened as if to say something, but then clamped shut again.

Eli smiled. 'That's right. Jeez, doctors really are the worst patients.' He sat next to her and draped an arm around her shoulders. He felt her freeze initially and then she sank against him.

'Thanks.'

'You're welcome. I figured you might be cold and that's what I'll say if Chuck mentions it, okay?'

'What about when we drive into Vasquez?'

'I'll repeat it.'

Again she opened her mouth and shut it again, without speaking.

Chuck started the engine, backing up and turning around, giving the rescue boys a lift back to the helicopter. He dropped them off and they watched as the helicopter rose into the air, stirring up dust and dirt in whorls, before it inclined slightly and surged forward and away from the mountains.

'Jackie's going to Anchorage?'

'It's the best place for her, especially if she has a closed head injury. I couldn't feel one, but that doesn't mean there isn't one there.'

'She was a nice lady. Confused, but nice.'

'So, tell me, what happened during your descent?'

Charlie shrugged. 'I don't know. I was feeding the rope through like I was told and then Adam panicked because Jackie got sick and I tried to speed up, but the rope just whizzed through my grip, so then I got scared and couldn't remember which hand slowed me down and which one sped me up. Next thing I knew, I went crashing onto the rocks.'

'You didn't bang your head?'

'No. I landed on my feet.'

He leaned forward to examine the splints. 'You did these yourself?'

She nodded.

Eli looked right into her eyes. 'You're amazing, you know that, right?'

She flushed and this time he really saw it, because her skin had been pale to begin with. He liked that she was affected by his compliment.

'When we get to the clinic, we'll get you into X-Ray.'

'What if it's bad? What if I need surgery? I can't go back to Anchorage.'

'I've done my fair share of orthopaedics. In fact, I worked two whole years on an orthopaedic surgery ward and I worked with the best. If you need plates and screws, then I'm your man.'

'I could make a rude comment for that, but I won't.'

'Don't hold back on my account.' He grinned.

She smiled. 'I was going to say I bet you're good for more than just a casual screw.'

He raised an eyebrow and stared right at her, a smile touching his lips. 'You bet I am.'

'Your left tib and fib are fractured at the distal end, with a rotation. We should be able to twist them back into place and get you in a cast for a while. Your right ankle has a hairline fracture, which shouldn't need anything but rest.' Eli stood by her bed in the clinic, delivering the news.

'You're joking?'

'Nope.'

'Damn it.' How was she going to cope with everything if she had to be off her feet? 'I'll get about in a wheelchair for a bit. I can still work, just you watch.'

'And Alice? How will you get her to school? Cook for her? Clean up after her?'

'She's a capable girl. I raised her right. She'll help me.'

'She's five. She shouldn't have to be her mother's nurse and she'll be tired from having been at kindergarten all day. I have another solution.'

'I'm all ears.'

'I'll help you.'

Eli? Help her? 'How?'

'I'll move in for a bit. I can take Alice to school, drive us both to work, where you can be parked behind your desk all day, and then I'll take us home, cook dinner, help you bathe and get you into bed.' He grinned.

It felt as though her brain suddenly stopped working as her jaw practically hit the floor. Eli? Move in? 'No!'

'It's the perfect solution.'

'No, it's not. What would Alice think with you sleeping over?'

'She'll know that I'm there to help you both. I can sleep on the couch, if that's what you're worried about.'

'I'm not worried about you sleeping on the couch.'

'Good, because I could always sneak back to it, before Alice wakes.'

'No. She comes in my room sometimes. Clambers into bed with me in the middle of the night and I don't know about it, until I wake up.'

He shrugged. 'Then I'll just take my sweet time putting you to bed. Tuck you in nice and tight and stroke your brow until you fall fast asleep.'

'Eli—'

'I'm joking! I'm not going to take advantage of a woman who is incapable of standing on her own two feet.'

'Good.'

'Besides, I've heard bed baths are very entertaining these days.' He grinned.

'Eli!'

'Joke.' He looked around to make sure no one was watching, then leaned forward and kissed her on the forehead. 'It's just a joke. Unless…you *do* want me to give you a bed bath?'

'My hands work perfectly well and I will be more than capable of running a wet flannel over my body all by myself.'

His gaze travelled down her body. 'Shame.'

Honestly, he was exhausting! 'I'll let you stay and help out and I thank you for thinking of me and Alice, but in front of my daughter? In our home? My body is mine and you don't get to touch it, understood?'

He saluted her. 'Understood.'

'Good. Now go see if there's any update on Jackie.'

CHAPTER THIRTEEN

JACKIE, LUCKILY, DID not have a closed head injury, apart from concussion and the need for eight stitches to sew up her head laceration. She did, however, have a dislocated shoulder, a fractured wrist and a proximal break on her humerus—her upper arm bone.

The doctors in Anchorage had treated her with fluids and a couple of casts, but she would need surgery in the morning to help realign and plate her humerus. 'The shoulder has been reduced and the doctors have told me that they believe Jackie's lack of memory will improve after the concussion begins to dissipate.'

'That's great news,' Charlie said as he wheeled her into place at her dinner table.

They'd already collected Alice from kindergarten. His mom had been so surprised to see them turn up to collect Alice together, with Charlie in her wheelchair, and had been amazed at their story, smiling at them both and patting Charlie's hand. Alice, on the other hand, far from being scared about seeing her mom in a wheelchair, had thought it was cool and insisted on sitting on her mom's lap, all the way back to the truck.

'Can I have a go in it, Mom?'

'Maybe later.' She'd smiled, glad that her daughter hadn't been upset to hear of her mother's injuries. In fact, most perturbingly, Alice had been thrilled that Eli would be moving in for a while to help out. 'I can sell him another one of my drawings!'

As she sat at the table, she couldn't help but notice that Eli knew where everything was in her kitchen. He picked the right cupboard when he needed a saucepan. A right, yet *different* cupboard when he was looking for the strainer. 'How do you know where everything is?'

He looked over his shoulder at her with a smile as he reached up high for the cheese grater. 'This is my mom's, remember?'

'And?'

'Who do you think does all the maintenance?'

Of course. He'd fixed her drippy tap and everyone in Vasquez seemed to multitask with their jobs. It wasn't just them in their clinic. It was Chuck who drove ambulance trucks and bred and raced working malamute dogs. It was Eli's mom, who owned, not only this lodge, but the town's hotel and the town's diner and God only knew what else, while *also* being the kindergarten teacher!

'And what are you making for dinner?'

'Pasta.'

'Oh.' Well, that was easy. 'I thought you'd be an amazing chef, too, and not just pour something out of a packet.' It was good to know he wasn't an expert on human bodies *and* house repair *and* cooking.

'I'm making my own dough. You haven't tried real pasta until you've tried my goat's cheese and spinach ravioli.'

Huh.

He could cook, too. 'Where did you learn to cook?'

'My mom.'

'I like that you call her Mom.'

He shrugged. 'It's what she is. From the day they drove me home, I was made to feel like one of them. Like I'd always been there and that the missing years didn't matter.'

'Do they matter?'

He seemed to think for a minute. 'They do, but in a different way now. Those early years I was just trying to find my own way, not knowing where I wanted to steer to. Becoming a Clark gave me roots. It gave me guidance. And they've been there for me through every difficulty.'

Difficulty? 'Like medical school?'

He smiled. 'Yeah.'

She felt then in the way that he looked as if maybe he was referring to something else. The

girl that walked away and left him? Who broke
his heart? He'd mentioned her before, but didn't
speak of her much. Lenore. What had happened
there?

Charlie knew she could ask him, but would he
answer? She didn't speak of Glen and what had
happened with him. She just couldn't get the idea
out of her head that once Eli knew the real truth,
he'd go racing over to a computer and look up
those pictures and she couldn't bear the idea of
him seeing her like that. Vulnerable.

It was bad enough he was seeing her like *this*.
In a wheelchair. It was hardly sexy, was it? This
man had wanted a fling with her and she had
wanted one with him, but it seemed that every
time they tried to be together, something stopped
them. Alice getting ill. Charlie abseiling badly.
Broken ankles... And tonight he would be sleeping in her home. Just yards from her bedroom.
How was that going to feel?

She gazed at the slope of his arm over his tri-
ceps. The way the muscles flexed as he kneaded
dough. The way his hands forced the dough this
way, then that. She could imagine his fingers
tracing over her skin and she shivered.

'Cold? I can get you a blanket.'

He had a splash of white flour on his black tee,
near his waist. She wanted to brush it away and
feel those rock-hard abs beneath her fingers. 'No,
not cold. I'm okay, thanks.'

'Shame.' He looked around them both, checked that Alice was absorbed somewhere in her bedroom, the door closed. 'I would have found a fun way to warm you up.' He winked at her and smiled naughtily.

Okay. She'd play along. Maybe this would have to be a fling with words only? 'How exactly?'

He raised an eyebrow at her, wiped his hands on a clean towel and then sauntered over towards her, leaning down low so that his hands rested either side of her on the wheelchair arms. 'First I'd make you close your eyes,' he whispered. 'Then I'd gently kiss you on the neck. Once. Twice. I'd breathe hot air over your goose-pimpling skin and then brush my lips over yours and then, baby? I'd make you forget the rest of the world.'

Her breathing had become heavy as she imagined each and every delicious image. A smile crept back onto her face. 'How?' She chuckled slightly, feeling incredibly naughty.

He grinned and placed one hand on the back of her neck, beneath her hair, and pulled her in close for a long, languorous kiss.

He wasn't lying. Kissing Eli did make her forget everything. The pain in her legs. Everything that had happened that day. All she could think was…*oh, my God!*

His hand slowly traced the line of her neck, one finger trailing down her chest bone and then circling around her breast to find her taut nipple that was thrusting against the material of her top. She ached—*physically ached*—to feel his skin against hers.

Damn this blouse! Damn this bra!

And then, when she felt as though she couldn't contain herself any more, he released her nipple and stopped kissing her and backed away, smiling.

And with perfect timing too!

Alice's bedroom door swung open. 'Mom, when is dinner ready?'

'Not long, Alice. Twenty minutes?' Eli said, looking perfectly innocent as he spoke to her daughter, while Charlie still sat in her chair, breathless and aroused.

'Okay.' Alice disappeared back into her bedroom.

Charlie met Eli's gaze. He looked happy. Smug. Normally she would want to wipe that smile off his confident face, but her brain wasn't really working well enough to come up with a retort. 'Erm…' She cleared her throat. Swallowed. 'Is there going to be a dessert?'

He grinned. 'There just may be.'

What is happening?

She watched him cut his pasta into squares and spoon little hills of goat's cheese and spinach onto them, before sealing them with another thin layer of pasta. Then he began chopping up some tomatoes, which he added to a sauce in a pan, grinding black pepper over the top.

Draping a dish towel over his shoulder, he then went to the fridge and pulled out some chilled moulds.

'What are those for?'

'Chocolate soufflés.'

Soufflés. That was risky. She'd watched enough cooking shows to know that the soufflé was feared. They either came out perfect or wrong. No in between. But she liked his confidence. That was something Eli had never been short of. Something she envied.

He poured some juice into a large jug that he added ice and slices of orange to and placed it on the table with three glasses. Then he placed the pasta into boiling water gently. 'Let's get you washed up,' he said.

'I can get myself to the bathroom sink. Alice! Time to wash your hands, please!'

She was glad of the cool water. It helped diffuse some of the heat she'd felt earlier when Eli had kissed her. When she reversed out of the bathroom, Eli was waiting for her.

'I can wheel myself.'

'You've just washed your hands. Let me push you.'

She let him guide her to the table, then he held out Alice's seat and draped a serviette over her lap, like a waiter in a posh restaurant. Alice giggled.

'Can I pour the young lady a drink?' he asked, bowing low.

Again, Alice laughed. 'Yes, please.'

After he'd done Alice's drink, he held the juice over Charlie's glass. 'Madam?'

'Please.' She smiled at him, feeling a real warmth towards him. He was putting in so much effort for her, but when hadn't he? Ever since she'd arrived here, he'd been there, helping out, always with a smile or a joke. He'd helped out when Alice was poorly. He'd been incredibly concerned when she'd got hurt and now he'd moved in to help them out.

What had she given him in return?

Feeling a little guilty, she watched him go and drain the pasta, before he transferred it into their bowls, with a helping of the tomato sauce. He brought the three plates over to the table, serving Alice first, then Charlie, then himself, before he sat down.

'Bon appetit.'

'Bon appetit.'

And, of course, it tasted absolutely delicious! The rich, succulent goat's cheese, the freshness of the spinach, the soft, thin pasta, all mixed with the spiced heat of the tomatoes that had a kick of chilli when it hit the back of your throat. But not so much that Alice couldn't eat it.

'Mom…there's a sports day happening soon, will you come?'

'Oh, sure, honey! Of course, I will. I wouldn't miss it.'

Alice smiled. 'Mrs Clark said that there's going to be a parents' race for mummies and daddies. Will you still be able to race in your wheelchair?'

'Oh, sorry, honey, but I don't think so. Maybe next time?'

'I could do it,' suggested Eli.

Charlie looked at him as Alice beamed. 'Yes! Please? Can Eli do it, Mom?'

'Well, I don't know…what would people think? He's not your daddy, sweetheart. It might be cheating,' she said, with a sympathetic smile and hoping Alice wouldn't push it, because what would people think? Eli running in a parent's place at the sports day? The rest of Vasquez would be there. Would it start any gossip? Or had that horse already bolted? People would soon know that he'd moved in to help out. They might assume something anyway.

'I don't think it's cheating, Mom.'

'Nor me,' said Eli, grinning at Alice and dabbing at his mouth with his napkin.

His helpful addition did not go unnoticed. She gave him a look. 'It's a *parents'* race and you're *not* her parent. Thank you for the offer, but I don't think we should do it. You should save your strength and speed for when you have children of your own.'

A look crossed his face that she couldn't read, because it came and went so fast and then he was taking his plate back into the kitchen.

She felt somehow that she'd upset him, but didn't understand why.

He was clattering about. Whisking the chocolate, filling the ramekins, and then wiping the rims with a clean finger, before he placed them into the oven and set a timer for ten minutes.

Charlie put her and Alice's plates onto her lap and wheeled herself into the kitchen and placed them down next to the sink, so she could position herself to open up the dishwasher. But she couldn't quite get the angle.

'Let me.'

'No, it's fine, I can do it.'

He sighed and stepped back and she could feel his eyes on her as she lowered the door, put in the plates and then lifted the door back, shoving it closed.

'Are you okay?' she asked.

'I'm fine!' he said with a smile, before checking his watch.

'You don't need to check your watch. You've set a timer.'

'I know I have.'

'I've upset you, haven't I?'

He shook his head with a smile forced onto his face. 'Nope!'

'I have. When I said you should wait to become a parent yourself. I wasn't trying to imply that you were trying to steal my child or adopt her or anything.' She checked to make sure Alice couldn't hear. 'Or imply that our relationship is anything but what it is.'

'I know that.'

'Then why are you upset?'

'I'm not.'

'I don't believe you.'

'Look, it was just a race. I thought I could be Alice's champion. She's a great kid and she's excited about sports day. Or I could be your champion. Whichever way you want to look at it, that's all I wanted to be. To step in and save the day. To let Alice have someone she could cheer for at the race. I didn't want her to feel left out. It should just be a bit of fun, that's all. I don't happen to think that anyone will read anything into it. And if they did? So what?'

'Well, that's easy for you to say,' she said quietly. 'You've not been the centre of gossip before.'

He raised an eyebrow. 'You don't know that.'

She groaned. 'Okay, so everyone probably talked about the Clarks when they adopted you. Big deal. That's positive talk, nothing horrible. And maybe they talked when you and Lenore broke up. Big deal. You don't know what nasty gossip feels like.'

'Actually, I do. But it sounds, right now, like we're not actually talking about me, but talking about you.' He glanced over at Alice, who was absorbed with the television blaring away behind her. 'You've been the subject of malicious gossip?'

She coloured, thinking of Glen and what he'd done. It hadn't been Charlie's fault. She'd thought she was in a loving relationship to begin with, but it had all turned sour.

'It was a while ago and I don't need people talking about me again.'

Eli glanced at his soufflés.

They were rising nicely, of course.

'If you want, we can talk about this later?'

She nodded. Maybe it was time? She didn't have to tell him *all* the details. It might be nice to tell someone how she felt about it all. So far, she'd kept it all hidden deep inside, where it had begun to fester. But she had been thinking about how it might feel to share her problem with him. Share the burden.

He gave her a wink.

Hesitantly she smiled back.

When the soufflés were done, Eli served the biggest to Alice. 'Be careful. That small little dish is hot.'

They were a delight! Rich and chocolatey,

without being too sweet. The perfect accompaniment to his ravioli pasta parcels. Good-looking, sexy, intelligent, kind, considerate, a good cook, an excellent baker, an amazing kisser. Was there anything he was bad at? Or even moderately bad at? There had to be something. A man wasn't wrapped up in such an amazing parcel, like Eli, without there being something! She just figured she hadn't discovered it yet. The only clue she had was that he'd had a relationship sour and his girlfriend had left. Why? Was it because of something he'd done? Or *hadn't* done? Maybe it was because he was always joking around and laughing? Maybe she'd thought he couldn't take anything seriously?

Leaving Alice to watch the television after dinner, Eli wheeled Charlie out into the garden and sat down on a seat next to her. 'So…spill the beans. What happened to you?'

CHAPTER FOURTEEN

'IT'S ALL TO do with Alice's father.'

'Glen? Okay.' He wasn't sure what the man might have done to result in Charlie being the subject of bad gossip.

'He was perfect when we met. A bit like you, actually. Handsome, charming, suave. Great to look at. What people call a real catch. We just hit it off and we married early and I was head over heels in love. Or I thought it was love. Looking back now, I think it was just infatuation that this great guy wanted to be with me.'

'You're a great catch too. He was lucky to be with you.' He meant it.

'Thanks. Things were great to begin with, but I noticed little things that, on their own, weren't too concerning, but added together threw up a few red flags.'

'Such as?'

Charlie turned to make sure the patio door was closed, so that Alice couldn't hear. 'He was a security guy. Dealt with tech and private home security. He worked for a company that installed cameras and alarms in people's property. Mansions, even. They were top notch. Glen always seemed a little on edge about people knowing our business. I felt it was just because of his job, you know? I thought he was just trying to protect me and at first, I thought it was great, you know, that he cared so much.'

'I'm sensing a *but*...'

'But it was low-level control of me. *"Are you really going to wear that dress at work?" "You look better without make-up." "I don't think you should hang around with Suzie any more, she said horrible things about me."'*

'He was isolating you.' Eli could feel ire building. He'd met a couple of controlling men in his time. There were one or two in Vasquez.

'Yes. But I've always been isolated. I have no family. I have no friends. I've never settled anywhere, until I met him, and he made me feel like he could give me everything I ever wanted in life—stability. A future. Start a family. The works. You know how much I've always wanted a big family of my own.'

He nodded, feeling a pang. Because he wanted the same thing too and couldn't have it.

'He wanted us to try for a kid straight after we married and one morning I woke up feeling sick and took a test. I was pregnant with Alice and that's when Glen changed big time.'

'How so?'

'He just seemed… I don't know…upset at the attention I got from people because of my growing bump. He tried to say it was because he didn't want people fawning over me, touching my belly, because how was I to know whether they had a knife or not? Whether they were dangerous or not? He began telling me to stay at home and I pretty much only left the house to go to work, OBGYN appointments and scans.'

'And…people at your work were noticing?'

'They told me I was beginning to look ill. Pale. Withdrawn. And I guess it was because I didn't want to attract attention, because I knew it would just send Glen into a funk. He didn't hit me or call me names or anything. He kept saying it was just concern for my well-being. But his silences were legendary and I couldn't bear the silence and I would find myself doing anything I could to make him happy again.'

'And you didn't like the talk, because people at work were concerned for you?' It didn't seem that this would be enough to have upset her as she'd seemed.

'No, that wasn't the problem. Glen became even more controlling. Wanted me to give up work, stay at home. He monitored my phone, checked all my messages, questioned me over everything. And then one night, I noticed I was spotting. I was about six months pregnant and very scared, but Glen wouldn't let me go to get checked out. He said he didn't want a man looking at me like that, or examining me. I said I'd ask for a woman, but he still wasn't happy. He locked the doors.'

'You're kidding me?'

She shook her head. 'I'd put up with his behaviours for far too long and when we left to see his mother the next day, I escaped through a bathroom window and went straight to a hospital.'

'Was everything okay?'

'Just a breakthrough bleed. But I couldn't believe he'd possibly endangered the life of our child and put me through a sleepless night, just because he was so paranoid. So I left him. I had nowhere to go. Nowhere to live. I got a cheap room at a motel and that's when everything went incredibly bad.'

'It wasn't *already* bad?'

'He shared things that he shouldn't,' she said, not feeling brave enough to say it straight out.

Eli frowned. 'I don't understand.'

'He…um…he'd had secret cameras around the house.' She glanced at him, judging how much to say. Wanting to say it straight out, afraid of his reaction. 'Ones I didn't know about…in the bedroom…and he'd made videos and taken photos of me when I was naked and…' she paused a long time '…posted them online.'

She couldn't look at him then, afraid to see the

shock on his face. Afraid to see the pity. Or what if she saw something worse? Curiosity? Wonderment. A need to see these pictures for himself? They were in a relationship after all. A strange one, maybe, but perhaps he'd feel possessive, too? And she couldn't bear to see that on his face.

But then she heard him shift in his seat and suddenly he was kneeling before her, her hand in his, and he had to reach up to gently guide her face to turn to his. 'That should never have happened to you. This Glen…he should be the one to feel ashamed. Not you. Did you call the police?'

She nodded, tears forming in her eyes, burning them. 'They got him to take the stuff down, but people can make copies. Save it. They are still out there and I have to live with that and raise a daughter to believe that nothing can bring her down, and yet she lives in a world where men can do this to women and justify their actions to themselves. How do I tell her that? How do I teach her to protect herself, when we live in a world where there are cameras watching us always?'

'You teach her to always be on the alert, but that there are good men out there, too. Men who will respect her if she chooses not to consent. If she chooses to say no. You teach her to live a life well-lived and not one that resides in fear.'

'You mean like me? I live in fear, because of what Glen did. I ran away, unable to cope with the influx of harassment I got after those things went public. I moved. I kept on moving, even when I had Alice, afraid to settle anywhere, afraid to let people know me, in case they found out. And now I've told you, I'm afraid that you will look at me differently.'

He smiled at her. 'I will always look at you the same way. That before me is the most beautiful woman I have ever seen in my entire life. A clever, kind, compassionate woman. An excellent mother. A brilliant doctor. An...' he grinned '...incompetent abseiler. But!' He chuckled and stroked her face. 'Never a victim. Because you fight for everything. You may have moved around, but you stand your ground when you are right. You love your daughter and try the best for her every day. You keep her safe and, in my opinion, she has the best role model a young girl could ever have.'

Charlie made a strange noise. Somewhere between a laugh, cry and a hiccup. But then she leaned forward in her chair and kissed him on the cheek. Quickly. Briefly. Glancing back through the patio doors to make sure that Alice hadn't seen. 'You're a good man, Eli.'

He winked at her, smiling. 'I try.'

Her legs ached, from the injuries, but also from the fact that, normally, she was an active person and this forced sitting down that she was having to do was becoming frustrating. As she sat listening to a patient, she made a mental note to herself that when she saw Eli, she'd ask if she could use crutches, somehow, instead.

He'd been amazing last night, listening to what she had to say, and she had to admit to herself that even though telling him had first felt as if it were the last thing she'd ever do, now that she had? It felt amazing. As if a weight had lifted and she knew now, in her heart, that Eli would not go looking for those images of her if they still existed somewhere in some dark recesses of the web. In fact, she actually believed that even if he did come across them, he would report them and track down the owners and forcibly have them removed on her behalf.

He'd been appalled at Glen.

But he had not judged her for trusting him. Because that was what you did in relationships, wasn't it? You trusted the other person. You gave them the benefit of the doubt. And if that relationship was an important one? As hers had been? Then you forgave people for little discrepancies in their behaviour in case they were having a bad day, or were acting a little out of character, because they just might be stressed. Glen's overprotective nature had seemed cute, at first. She'd loved that he wanted to keep her safe.

She just hadn't realised to what extent he'd been monitoring her.

'…and Chuck was out feeding the dogs and so he didn't see anything. It was all over by the time he came back in.'

Her patient was Chuck's wife, Angela. She'd come in that morning, after experiencing something odd at home.

'I don't normally come to the docs. You can see from my chart, I think the last time I was here was, ooh, a good five years ago and I've always been fit and well.'

'And did you experience anything else with the dizzy spell?'

'The room spun. I felt it *and* saw it. It made me feel incredibly sick and I began to panic a bit, to be honest with you.'

'And when this happened…had you bent down, or were you in a strange position? Or just standing normally when it happened?'

'Just standing. I was doing the breakfast dishes at the sink.'

'Looking down?'

'Yes. I was scrubbing the frying pan. We'd just had eggs.'

'And did you fall, or sway? What happened?'

'I squeezed my eyes shut, so I couldn't see it spinning. I could still feel it though, for just a few seconds and then it felt like it might have stopped, so I opened my eyes and the room was still again, but my heart rate was fast, I felt incredibly sick and shaky and so I made my way over to the kitchen chair and sat down.'

'And then Chuck came back in?'

'Yes. He said I was white as a sheet.'

'And did you have a headache at all?'

'Afterwards, yes. For about a half-hour.'

'Do you normally get headaches?'

'Not really. Not unless I haven't slept much.'

'Okay. Well, it could be an inner ear infection, so I'll check your ears first, okay?'

'Okay.'

'Any history of ear problems?'

'No. I've always been as fit as a fiddle.'

Charlie got out the otoscope and looked in Angela's ears, but both were clear. No wax build-up and no sign of infection. The eardrums looked exactly as they should. 'Any colds, recently? Sore throat?'

'No.'

'Ever get Covid?'

'Didn't everybody?'

'And how were you with that?'

'Fine! Just a cough for about a week. A bit of tiredness, but nothing bad.'

'I'd like to do an Epley manoeuvre, if that's okay? Just to see if it's debris in the ear canals moving around causing you to feel dizzy.'

'Okay.'

'But I'll need to call in Eli. I can't do it myself in this chair.'

'Fine. It'll be lovely to see him, I haven't seen him in a while…probably not since he got sick when he was still a student.'

Charlie frowned. Eli was sick? It couldn't be anything serious, surely? He seemed fine right now. She dismissed it and typed an instant screen message that would send to Eli's computer. Seconds later, she got a reply. He'd be right in.

'He's coming.'

'Bless him. He's a good man.'

'He is. The best.'

Angela looked at her, head tilted to one side in question. 'You're enjoying working together?'

'I am.'

'Vasquez is such a strange place. It must have taken some getting used to?'

'It's been great, actually. Eli and the Clarks and everyone here have been most welcoming.'

'And you get on well with Eli?'

'I think everyone does,' she said, laughing.

Angela smiled. 'He makes it easy. Mind you, it certainly helps that he's so easy on the eye, wouldn't you say?'

Charlie blushed.

'I thought so!' Angela preened with her point having been made, just as Eli rapped his knuckles on her door and came in.

'Angela! How are you?' He smiled at her patient.

'Fine. Just this dizzy spell that was worrying.

I think Chuck thought I might have had a TIA, or something, so best to get it checked out.' A TIA was a transient ischaemic attack. Sometimes called a mini stroke, in which effects of a stroke occurred for a short period of time and then dissipated, leaving no sign it had ever happened. Visually, anyway.

'Ears are normal, BP is spot on. I thought we could do an Epley?' Charlie said.

Eli nodded. 'No problem. Angela, would you be a darling and hop up onto the examination bed for me?'

'Of course.'

Once Angela was on the bed, Eli held her head in his hands and then turned it forty-five degrees to her left and then quickly lowered her to a prone position in which her head was lower than her body over the edge of the bed. Then he turned her head ninety degrees to the other side, watching her eyes all the time for signs of nystagmus—an involuntary movement of the eyes—then asked Angela to rotate her body so it was in alignment with her head, before sitting her up again, with her head still turned to the side. 'Feel anything?' he asked.

'No.'

'Let's do the other side.'

He repeated the procedure, but nothing happened. No nystagmus was reproduced.

'I want you to replicate the stance you were in when it happened,' Charlie suggested.

Angela did so, but again, nothing occurred.

'It might be worth doing some bloods, just a general MOT, see if that flags anything and if not, then we can put it down to being idiopathic in nature. But if you get dizzy again, Angela, I want you to call me right away, okay?'

'Okay. What will you check for in the bloods?'

'A full blood count, blood sugars, thyroid, electrolytes are considered standard in these cases.'

'All right.'

Charlie gathered together the things she would need and procured a quick sample from Angela's arm. 'You go home and take it easy for the day.'

'Are you kidding me? With all those dogs, a house and a husband to look after? Not to mention I've got the grandkids coming over. We've promised them a movie night.'

'Well, maybe let Chuck organise the grandkids?' Charlie smiled.

Angela laughed. 'We'll see.'

'Just take it easy, okay?'

Angela nodded and left the room.

Charlie turned to Eli. 'Thank you for helping out. I hope you weren't busy?'

'Not at all. How are you doing?'

'It's frustrating being in the chair. I'm not used to letting people do things for me that usually I'm capable of doing for myself.'

He nodded. 'I get that. I had it too, once.'

'You ever break your ankles?'

'Not quite. I got sick once and they brought me home from medical school. The Clarks looked after me. Fetched my shopping. Cooked my food. Mom practically never left my side for weeks.'

That had to be what Angela had mentioned. 'What were you sick with?'

'I don't really like to talk about it. It's gone now. No need to worry.' He smiled. 'Well, I'd better be off.'

And then he left her room so abruptly, she was left shocked into silence. No secret cuddle? No secret kiss? Something was most definitely off and she didn't like not knowing. The least he could do was open up to her, the way she'd opened up to him. She felt closer to him now. They were in a relationship in which they could confide their secrets. Their fears. Why wouldn't he share?

Wheeling her chair forward, she began to go after him. There were no more patients scheduled and she was due a break anyway. She found him in his office, staring out of the window. 'What's wrong, Eli?'

He turned. Smiled. 'Nothing!'

'No, you're lying to me. Something *is* wrong and I want you to feel that you can talk to me about anything. The way I talked to you. I told you something about me last night that I swore to never tell you, but I did so because I thought that…' she sighed, unsure as to whether to admit this '… I thought that maybe we weren't actually having a fling and that instead we were in some kind of relationship. One that involved feelings, because I don't know how to explain what else we have here. I mean, we haven't even, you know, slept together yet and yet I feel closer to you than I have to anyone in a long, long time.'

He looked down at the ground, then back up at her when she began speaking again.

'Flings don't help their bit on the side care for their sick child. They don't stay with them all day just to keep them company and then say that they've had a really nice time. They don't come round and cook. They don't move in when that fling has a stupid accident at work. They don't buy their daughter's artwork and buy them teddy bears. They don't look at me the way that you look at me.'

'I know. But we share a past, you and I. We're not just strangers.'

'No, we're not. But what are we, Eli? Is this simply a thing that goes one way? Am I the fool for thinking that you might feel more for me? Am I the idiot for confiding in you my deepest, darkest, shameful secret, when you won't tell me yours? Am I *deluded*?'

'Of course not.'

'Then why won't you speak to me and tell me

what's wrong? How can I feel any of the things I feel for you, if you won't let me know you?'

'You do know me.'

She shook her head. 'No, I don't. After you left? This life you've built? I hardly know anything about it. You got taken in by the Clarks, you had a seemingly mysterious illness you won't talk about and you had a relationship fail, but I don't know the ins and outs of your life. You don't share *anything*. You keep me on the edge and that's not how I want to be! If I'm going to be in someone's life, then I want to be in it. Heart and soul. I deserve that and I can't be with a man who wants to keep his secrets. Because I've been there, Eli. You know I have and look how that turned out for me.'

'I don't have cameras, Charlie. I'm not Glen.'

'But you have something you won't talk to me about,' she challenged him. Staring him down. Waiting for him to lower his gaze, but he didn't. He simply stared back at her and she realised that he was admitting that she was correct. Yes. There was something. 'I see. Then this?' She gestured between them. 'Is over. I can't stay here and look at you every day and pretend that we're close, when clearly we are not. I was a fool to stay here when I found out it was you. I should have trusted my instincts.'

'What are you saying?'

'I'm saying I'll find something else. Another

job. Someplace else. The second my contract here is over, I'm gone!'

'But Alice is settled here! Are you really going to keep hauling her around the country every few months because of a few pictures? What kind of life is that?'

'It's better than what we had.'

'Is that what you want for her? Something that's a little bit better than awful? Or do you want her to have a happy life? A future? In a place where she could build it?'

'What do you mean?'

'She has skills. Way beyond those of a normal five-year-old. She can draw. And here in Vasquez there is so much she could capture.'

'So you want me to stay so my daughter can draw some grizzlies, is that it? Way to go, Eli. Way to go in giving me an astounding reason to stay!' Now she felt angry. How could she ever have believed that this man would ever be serious with her? He never had been and all she'd been was fun to him. A plaything. Someone to entertain him for a bit. 'And how dare you imply that our lives were awful before? You know nothing about us!'

He stared at her then and nodded. 'You're right. I know nothing about you. Nothing that matters.' He turned and walked away and she was so shocked by it, she just sat there, staring at the empty space where he had once been.

CHAPTER FIFTEEN

THE DRIVE TO pick up Alice from kindergarten was tense. Charlie had insisted on getting into the truck all by herself and it had been quite the sight to see, seeing as the truck was higher than the wheelchair. But she'd come armed, he'd seen. Bringing with her some crutches to help support her body weight as she transferred from the chair to the truck. He'd itched to help her, but had known that if he'd tried, he would only have been sworn at or shook off and so, instead, he'd stood back, patiently waiting while it took her over two minutes to finally haul herself into the front passenger seat of his truck. She'd held the crutches tightly, so he'd taken the wheelchair, folded it up and placed it in the back of the truck.

Driving over to the school, he could have cut the tension in the vehicle with a chainsaw. But what could he do? Talk about it? What was there to say? Was there even a point to saying anything? What they'd had never even got properly started, it sure as hell was never going to last.

Charlie would leave with Alice. In every iteration of this scenario she would leave and be gone for ever. Maybe he'd get the occasional email? A Christmas card at best. So it was probably best to just let this burn on out. They'd manage somehow, tensions would finally ease. Probably just as she was about to pack up and go anyway.

He was used to people leaving him. He'd hardened his heart to it. It was the only way to survive. He'd left her behind once, now it was only right and fair that she had a turn.

He left Charlie in the truck when he went to collect Alice. Normally they would meet her together in the schoolyard and listen to Alice natter about her day on the way back to the truck, examining paintings or models she'd made, or hearing her chat about something they'd done, or which friends she'd made.

Alice came running out of her class, as usual, with a broad smile upon her face. 'Eli!' She slammed into him and he whisked her up in the air with a broad smile and, laughing, twirled her around, before putting her down again. God, he would miss this kid!

'Good day?'

'The best! Mrs Clark was telling us about a school trip that's coming up!'

'Oh, yeah? Where to?' He knew where to. His mom took the kids up to the reindeer farm on Elk Ridge each year. They had a small visitor and education centre there, next to a much larger animal rescue and convalescence place.

'We're going to see some reindeer! And elk and bears and owls and all kinds of animals, Mrs Clark says!'

He smiled, knowing how much Alice would love the place. 'It's gonna be wild, huh?'

'It's in September. Think Mom will let me go?'

September. Ah. Charlie's contract ended in August. 'I don't know. You'll have to ask her.'

'Is she here? Why didn't she come with you?'

'Her legs were bad. She, er…wanted to wait in the truck to rest for a little while. It's been a long day at work, so…' He *hated* lying to her. He'd never lied to a kid, if he could help it, because he remembered how much it had hurt when adults had lied to him as a child. Mostly with making promises they knew they could never keep. Okay, so the lies weren't big, right now, but it could be a slippery slope.

'Oh. Okay. She must be in a lot of pain, then, because she always comes.'

He thought of the pained look he'd seen in Charlie's eyes when they'd been arguing. The hurt he'd seen, because she felt that their relationship was all one-sided.

She was wrong. But how could he tell her that?

Best to let her think that it was true. Then she could walk away at the end of all of this without guilt. If she walked away hating him, then that was better than walking away knowing he couldn't give her what she'd always wanted.

He held Alice's hand as she skipped back to the car to keep up with his longer strides. He liked this part. This part was nice. Where he could pretend he was her father.

This must be what it feels like.

He felt a huge pang then of longing. So close to what he wanted, but so far away.

He wanted to harden his heart. Letting go of her hand and not allowing himself to have such thoughts would be better for him when they walked out of his life for good. Pretending to be Alice's dad? Only pain waited for him in that iteration of life.

As they got to the truck, he opened up the back passenger door and lifted Alice in.

'Hey, Mom! Are you okay? Do your legs hurt?'

'I'm okay, baby, don't you worry,' Charlie answered.

He buckled her in and closed her door, then he got back behind the driver's wheel. 'Home?'

'Yay!' Alice said as he started the engine. 'Mom…there's a trip to see reindeer and all these other animals in September with Mrs Clark and my class. Can I go? Please?'

'Sounds great, baby, but I don't think we'll still be living in Vasquez when it gets to September. You'll be in a new school.'

'But I *love* my school. I love Mrs Clark. I love living *here*. Can't we stay here?'

Charlie turned around in her seat. 'There won't be a job for me, baby. The one I have now is only temporary, remember?'

Glancing through the rear-view mirror, he could see a sulk settle onto Alice's face. 'Not fair!'

'I'm sorry, honey.'

He wanted to make it better. He wanted to fix it. He didn't like seeing Alice upset and he hated not being able to talk to Charlie about it. But she was right. There wasn't a job for her. Not unless Nance chose to stay at home and not return to her old post. She might, even though she'd always said she would come back. But Ryan was Nance's first baby and who knew how she might feel about returning to work, now that Ryan was born?

Unable to do or say anything that would help, he drove them home in silence, fetching Charlie's wheelchair when they parked outside her place and standing awkwardly, yet again, as she stubbornly alighted from his truck, down to the seat in silence.

Inside, he went straight to the kitchen, while Charlie helped Alice get changed. He knew he needed to keep busy, or he'd go insane, so he gathered all the ingredients to make a chicken pot pie and began making shortcrust pastry.

He knew the secret to a good shortcrust was to make sure the butter was cold as he proceeded to rub it into the sifted flour with his fingers, to make it a breadcrumb texture. Then he added milk, slowly, until it formed a dough. He wrapped it in cling film and placed it in the fridge, pulling out the chicken breasts so he could chop them into bite-size chunks. It helped to keep busy. It helped to form the dough. It allowed him to not think too hard about what he was having to let go of.

'You don't have to cook.'

He turned to face Charlie. 'No offence, but I don't think you'd be able to do this on your own.'

'Well, that's just it, Eli. I can do everything on my own. It's all I've ever done. Occasionally I've let someone into my life and each time it has been an unmitigated disaster. To be honest with you, I'd feel much more comfortable in my home if I didn't have to see you all the time. I'll finish whatever this is and you can go and pack your things.'

He stared at her. 'You want me to go?'

CHAPTER SIXTEEN

'YOU WANT ME to go?'

Yes, she did. Because it hurt to have him around. It hurt that he wouldn't open up and share his innermost feelings with her. Because he thought if he kept his distance, he wouldn't get hurt.

Turns out that maybe neither of us has changed our ways since we were small.

She'd been vulnerable and though, in the moment, it had felt good to share, now it felt truly awful. There was an imbalance in their relationship and she didn't like how it left her feeling weak and exposed. Because she'd been exposed before and wouldn't be so ever again.

'I can make a pie, or whatever this is.'

'It's a pie.' He continued to stare at her, as if weighing her up. As if deciding to say something else. But then she saw the decision in his eyes that he wasn't going to and he turned away and washed his hands to rid them of the flour. 'I'll pack up now.'

'I'll find a way to get Alice to school tomorrow, you don't have to do it.'

'But—'

'And I'll find a way to work, too.'

He sighed and dried his hands on a towel. 'Fine.' He grabbed his holdall from by the front door and began moving around the place, picking up his stuff. His hoodie from the back of the chair. His toothbrush and toiletries from the bathroom. All thrown into the bag. A book he'd been reading that was on the coffee table.

She'd got used to those things. He hadn't been living with her long, but it had become surprisingly nice how much she liked seeing his things about the place. Seeing them gone felt weird. As if the place was emptying somehow, which was ridiculous.

'I'll see you at work, then.' He stood by the door.

'Yes, you will.'

'Can I say goodbye to Alice?'

Honestly? She just wanted him to be gone. So she could get to the end of this unpleasantness. But she knew how much Alice would complain if he left without saying goodbye. 'Sure.'

'Alice?' he called.

Alice came out of her room, smiling. A smile that faltered when she saw him holding his bag and standing by the door. Perhaps she could even sense the tension in the room. 'Are you leaving?'

'Yeah. Come here and give me a hug.'

'But I don't want you to leave! Mom! Tell him to stay!' she pleaded, tears welling up in her eyes.

Charlie felt awful. This was why she never let guys get close. This was why guys never met her daughter. Because of this moment right here. 'He has to go, honey.'

'But, why?' she cried, slamming her little body into Eli's as he hefted her up into his arms and squeezed her tight.

Alice wrapped her little legs around his waist and cried into his shoulder.

'You'll see him again, some time. It's not like he's leaving Vasquez.'

But Charlie wasn't sure she was heard. Alice was crying so loudly. So hard.

The look on Eli's face was pained, his eyes closed as he held her little girl. It looked painful for him too, and she hated to see that. It made the guilt worse. She'd not expected this. For him to get close to her daughter. But he had.

'Come on, baby. Let him go.'

'No!' Alice cried, squeezing ever tighter.

'Alice? Alice, I want you to listen to me. Look at me. Alice?' Eli pulled back, until Alice looked up at him with a red, tear-streaked face. 'I'm just going back to my place. That's all. You'll still see me around.'

Alice shook her head, as if she didn't believe him.

'I promise you, you will see me around. Okay? Because I need to see all those fabulous drawings you do. I want to be able to say to people, *Oh, you like Alice Griffin's art? I knew her since she was a little kid. I bought the very first piece she ever sold!*'

Alice sniffed and managed a short smile.

'Let go, Alice,' Charlie said as Eli lowered her daughter to the ground.

'Can I walk with you to your truck?' Alice asked.

Eli glanced at Charlie and she looked away. Unable to meet his gaze. She felt awful. That Alice was getting hurt because of this? Of her mistake? Of letting Eli get close?

'Sure.'

She watched from the doorway, witnessing another painful hug, whispered promises and then watching her daughter cry as Eli got in his truck and drove away.

Charlie hoped that now that he'd gone, it would be easier.

She was wrong.

Alice stomped up the path and yelled at Charlie as she passed. 'You always spoil things!' And then she slammed her bedroom door, with the ferocity of a teenager.

Charlie sat there, blinking, unsure of how she'd

even got herself into this mess in the first place. But it was clear. Coming here to Vasquez, staying, once she knew Eli was here, had been a tremendous mistake.

Charlie had not arrived at work at her usual time, and he knew because for the last hour he'd stared alternately at the clock and then out of the window of the clinic, trying to work out what he would say to her when she got there.

An apology. That would be first. Clear. Profound. Touching. He'd let her know that he deeply regretted upsetting her. That he was upset that he had hurt her. And that he would understand if she wanted to be angry with him, but that he hoped that they could put it behind them while they worked together.

His cell rang in his back pocket.

Charlie? Ringing to apologise for being late? She was trying to do everything herself from that wheelchair.

But no. It was his mom.

Odd. Isn't she in class?

'Mom? Everything okay?'

'Well, no. I'm confused, honey. Charlie has pulled Alice from the school—she notified the office first thing and I've only just been told. Has something happened?'

She'd pulled Alice out of kindergarten? 'Oh… er…we had a bit of a falling out.'

'What kind of falling out?'

'We were…um…kind of…seeing one another. But…secretly…like a bit of fun.'

'Did she know it was just a bit of fun?'

And that was when he realised that it hadn't been *a bit of fun* for either of them.

Eli groaned. 'I did something stupid.'

There was a pause while his mom digested this. 'Is it something you can fix?'

'She wants kids, Mom. I can't give her that. Why keep her here when I can't give her the one thing she wants?'

'Honey…well, she wouldn't have been in a relationship with you, if she wanted that. Unless, of course, you didn't exactly tell her? I know you, Eli, better than you realise and you need to understand that sometimes you act like you haven't quite grown up properly.'

She always did have a polite way of telling him off. Mild chiding. Like a proper mom. He smiled briefly, glad to have found his mom in life, if he couldn't have anyone else. 'I couldn't tell her.'

'Why? Hasn't she always been special to you?'

'How do you know that?'

'Oh, honey, I heard the way you talked about her, even before she came here. I saw it in your eyes. She's something special and you'd be a fool to let her get away, without telling her everything.'

'I don't know if I'm brave enough.'

'You're the bravest guy I know. All you've been through? But tell me this…how scared are you of the idea of a future without her in it?'

He let out a breath. 'Terrified. There will always be something missing.'

She sighed. 'The piece of your heart you left behind with her, when you left the first time. When we took you from her.'

'You think she'd want me?'

'I think you should give her the option. Tell her the truth and let her decide, because if you don't, then you'll always regret it. If you tell her and she still wants to go, then at least you will know that you tried and she said no, knowing *all* the facts.'

His phone beeped. Another incoming call. This one from Chuck.

'I gotta go.'

'Good luck, honey. I love you.'

'Love you, too, Mom.'

He answered Chuck's call. 'Chuck? Sorry, my friend, but I got to run. Can I call you back later?'

'Er…sure. Just thought I'd let you know that Charlie rang me.'

He stilled. 'She did?'

'Yeah. She wants me to fly her to the airport. Her and Alice. I'm meeting her at the bay in an hour. She leaving already?'

'I hope not. Listen, I've got to rearrange a few things here, as I've got patients in the clinic, but can you do me a favour?'

'Sure.'

'Stall her?'

'Charlie?'

'Yeah. I need to see her before she goes. I mucked up, I need to apologise and I'm hoping to persuade her to stay.'

'Okay. Can do. I must say we all think you'd make a great couple.'

'We *all*? Who's *we all*?'

'Vasquez.'

'What?'

'Talk of the town, mate. You think patients and staff haven't noticed the way you two look at one another? You think you're hiding it, but when you ride through town in the back of a truck cradling her after a fall, people begin to talk.'

'Okay, okay. I get the picture. But you can stall, right?'

'Sure. I can tell her the right rotavator needs cranking.'

'Do planes have rotavators?'

'Does it matter?' He could hear Chuck's smile in his voice.

'No. I guess it doesn't.'

CHAPTER SEVENTEEN

'WHAT'S TAKING SO LONG, Chuck?' Charlie kept glancing at her watch as she sat in her wheelchair on the small wooden pier.

The pilot had opened a flap to expose part of the plane's engine. It all looked terribly complicated inside.

'Just some final checks. You wouldn't want us to fly without me checking it's safe for you and this precious cargo, huh?' he said, ruffling a sulky Alice's hair.

'No. Of course not.' She checked her watch and looked out behind her. She didn't think Eli would come chasing after her. Not after the way they'd parted. Not after the resignation letter she'd left on the clinic desk. Had he seen it yet? He might not have. Especially if he didn't have any clinic patients yet. She'd wanted to leave it in his office, but the door had been locked and, quite frankly? She'd wanted to get out of there, the sooner the better. Especially in this damn chair.

Nothing had gone right for her since coming here and now she was flying back to what? Home? That was a joke. She didn't really have one. The only place she'd ever felt comfortable living in had been here, strangely. Was that personal growth? Or just because Alice had begun to settle in a place? She'd certainly grown attached to Mrs Clark and Eli…

But so had she.

And that was why she had to go. Because how could she allow herself to get attached to someone who wasn't prepared to get attached to her? He'd only wanted a fling anyway, so this was no biggie, right? And she was sick of making mistakes over men.

'Can't we at least get in the plane? It's chilly out here on the pier,' she complained to Chuck.

'Sorry. Aviation rules. Pre-flight checks have to be completed first.'

She had no idea if that was true, but Chuck didn't look sorry. Not one bit. In fact, he looked a little amused, if anything.

Behind her, she heard footsteps clomping towards her on the wooden pier. Then they stopped. She knew whose footsteps they were and felt her heart sink.

'Charlie?'

It was him.

'Eli!' Alice dropped her rucksack and went running towards him and, as before, he scooped her up high into the air.

'Hey, pumpkin.'

She watched as Eli kissed her daughter on the head and gave her a huge squeeze.

Chuck closed the engine flap, wiped his hands on a dirty rag and gave her a smile as he passed. 'Hey, Alice. Come and look at these geese with me. Leave your mom and Eli to talk in private.'

And that was when she realised that Chuck had been stalling intentionally. Long enough for Eli to get here.

She stared at Eli. 'You made him stall us?'

'Guilty as charged, Your Honour.'

'Why are you here, Eli? There's nothing more to be said. You've made that abundantly clear.'

'You're wrong. There's plenty to be said.'

'Like what? Enlighten me, why don't you?'

He took a few more steps towards her. 'Not here. On the pier, it's exposed. Can we go over there and talk?' He pointed at a waterside bench.

He wore jeans, a fitted tee and a loose flannel shirt over the top. Rugged work boots on his feet made him look like a grungy rock star, rather than a doctor who had just come from a clinic. But that was Vasquez for you. It was more relaxed out here. It was why she liked it. As he settled onto the bench, he took a deep breath.

'I was wrong before. To not tell you what you wanted to hear.' He sighed. 'I was being stupid.'

'You won't hear me arguing.'

'Will I hear you be quiet, so I can say what you want me to say?' he asked with a smile.

She opened her mouth to respond, thought better of it and clamped it shut again.

'Thank you. Charlie…of course I want you to stay. You and Alice. And if not for me, then for that little girl, who loves it here and wants to stay.'

'You want me to stay?'

'Of course I do!'

'Why? Tell me why, exactly, you want me here.'

'Because…you have never been out of my mind, Charlie Griffin. I had to leave you once and I hated it and when you walked back into my life again, I couldn't believe my luck. But I didn't think you'd want to stay for me, because I can't give you what I know that you want.'

'And what do I want?' she asked breathlessly.

'You want a family. You want loads of kids. You said so, only recently.'

'And you think I want that with you?'

'Don't you?'

Now it was her turn to look uncomfortable. 'I'd be a liar if I said I hadn't thought about it.'

'I can't give you kids, Charlie. I'm sterile. I had testicular cancer in medical school and we found out then. The Clarks? They got me through the worst time in my life. A time in which I was scared. Surgery. Chemo. They kept me strong. Mom sitting by my bedside every day. Dad getting me out in the fresh air when I had the energy. Like I was their actual, biological child. They wept for my pain. Would have suffered for me in my place if they could. I couldn't have got through it without them and that was when I realised I truly was one of them.'

Cancer? Her heart ached for him! What an awful thing for him to have gone through! And she'd thought his life had been perfect since he was adopted.

I was wrong.

'I thought if we kept it simple between us—a fling—then it would be easy to say goodbye. But it has never been easy to say goodbye to you and I don't want to have to do so again. I may have gained a family here, but I have also lost so much.'

'I can't stay here. There's no job for me.'

'There is. Nance has informed me that she doesn't want to return full-time after her maternity leave is over. She even said she might not return ever. So there is a post for you. A job share, at least.'

'Why should I stay?'

'Because you love it here. Because Alice loves it here. Because the people here love you and I…' He took her hands in his. 'Because *I* love you.'

It was all so much! He'd gone from telling her nothing to telling her everything and it was all so overwhelming!

'I don't know what to say.'

'If you don't love me back, then say goodbye and do it quickly, because I don't think I could do another long, drawn-out goodbye. But if you feel the same way as me…then stay. We could build a life together. A great life. You, me, Alice.'

'We could adopt,' she said, the words surprising her as they came out of her mouth.

'What?'

'We could do what your mom did. Adopt a kid who needs a home. Maybe more than one, if we wanted. We could build a family that way. We're ideally situated to understand what that gift would mean to a child. What do you think?'

He smiled. Broadly. And she felt her heart lift.

'I would do anything to make you happy.'

She smiled back, felt tears of happiness pricking at her eyes. Wanted nothing more than to stand and wrap her arms around him and pull him close, but she couldn't.

'You make me happy,' she said. 'You're enough. You've always been enough.'

'I love you, Charlie Griffin.'

'And I love you, Eli Clark.'

And he reached for her, cradling her face in his hands as he gave her a long, deep kiss.

EPILOGUE

'I'M NERVOUS!'

Eli pulled her close. One to stop her from pacing, but two…he just liked having her close and looking into her eyes. She softened when he did so. The frantic worry would leave her face and she would relax. 'Take a breath. Look at me. We're gonna do great.'

'How can you know for sure? We've never done this.'

He smiled. 'I know what it's like to be chosen and to drive off in a car with a couple you've only met a couple of times.'

'Do I look okay? Do I look like a good mom?' she asked, glancing down at her outfit. A beautiful soft blue summer dress, dotted with white daisies.

'You look perfect.'

'What about me? I'm about to be a big sister,' said Alice.

They both turned to her. She'd been so thrilled about the idea of having a sibling and she'd wanted to choose a gift to give to David. Picking out a dump truck and a football and a colouring book with a pack of felt-tip pens to go along with it.

'You look great,' Eli said. He liked that he could help reassure and calm them down, because honestly...? He was pretty nervous himself. This had been a long time coming. A lengthy process they'd gone through to be able to go to an orphanage and choose a child with the help of the agency they were doing it through. There'd been many sets of paperwork. Lots of background checks. Plenty of visits. And they'd finally settled on David. A little boy, three years of age, who had been abandoned at a fire station when he was six weeks old.

As orphans, both he and Charlie were in the special position of knowing the gift they were giving to a child and to each other in building their family.

He'd never known a proper home, but he and Charlie had fallen for David's cheeky smile and lively character from day one. He had a great chuckle. It was infectious! And at their last visit, he'd fallen asleep on Charlie's lap for over an hour, snuggled into her and she'd looked so beautiful, sitting there, stroking the little boy's golden hair.

How could it possibly have been anyone else?

And here they were today. Ready to take him home to Vasquez.

It had been a kind of whirlwind, the last year and a half. Charlie had gone permanently full-time at the clinic—though she was going on maternity leave once they got home with David—Alice had had a piece of art win a competition on a children's show on TV and they'd moved into a bigger home. One that would be big enough for the family they aspired to build.

He had adopted Alice officially.

The door opened and in walked Karen, the support worker they'd been working with, and standing beside her, holding her hand, was David. He beamed when he saw them and ran forward into Charlie's arms.

She scooped him up and hoisted him onto her waist. 'Hey, you!'

'Hi,' he said.

'I have a question for you.'

'Okay.'

'Do you want to come home with us?'

He nodded, smiling. 'To stay?'

'Yes. For ever and ever.'

'For ever and ever?' he repeated, his eyes lighting up.

'That's right,' Eli said.

'Yay!'

Eli scooped up Alice and moved closer so that Alice and David could hug. They'd both got on so brilliantly with each other from day one. 'Let's go home.'

They waved goodbye to Karen after she'd walked them to the truck with David's case of clothes and a couple of teddy bears he liked.

As they drove away, with their two kids chattering in the back of the truck, Charlie reached for his hand and squeezed it. 'We did it.'

He raised her hand in his and kissed it. 'We did. I love you.'

She smiled at him, quickly glancing at the two kids in the back seat—the start of their big family.

'I love you, too.'

* * * * *

MEDICAL

Life and love in the world of modern medicine.

Available Next Month

All titles available in Larger Print

The Doctor's Billion-Dollar Bride Marion Lennox
Tempting The Off-Limits Nurse Tina Beckett

....

Falling For The Trauma Doc Susan Carlisle
Country Fling With The City Surgeon Annie Claydon

....

Dating His Irresistible Rival Juliette Hyland
Her Secret Baby Confession Juliette Hyland

Keep reading for an excerpt of a new title
from the Intrigue series,
BIG SKY DECEPTION by B.J. Daniels

Chapter One

Clay Wheaton flinched as he heard the heavy tread of foot-falls ascending the fire escape stairs of the old Fortune Creek Hotel. His visitor moved slowly, purposefully, the climb to the fourth and top floor sounding like a death march.

His killer was coming.

He had no idea who he would come face-to-face with when he opened the door in a few minutes. But this had been a long time coming. Though it wasn't something a man looked forward to even at his advanced age.

He glanced over at Rowdy lying lifeless on the bed where he'd left him earlier. The sight of his lifelong companion nearly broke his heart. He rose and went to him, his hand moving almost of its own accord to slip into the back under the Western outfit for the controls.

Instantly, Rowdy came to life. His animated eyes flew open, his head turned, his mouth gaping as he looked around. "We could make a run for it," Rowdy said in the cowboy voice it had taken years to perfect. "It wouldn't be the first time we've had to vamoose. You do the running part. I'll do the singing part."

The dummy broke into an old Western classic and quickly stopped. "Or maybe not," Clay said as the lumbering footfalls ended at the top of the stairs and the exit door creaked open.

"Sorry, my old friend," Clay said in his own voice. "You need to go into your case. You don't want to see this."

"No," Rowdy cried. "We go down together like an old horse who can't quite make it home in a blizzard with his faithful rider. This can't be the end of the trail for us."

The footsteps stopped outside his hotel room door, followed swiftly by a single knock. "Sorry," Clay whispered, his voice breaking as he removed his hand, folded the dummy in half and lowered him gently into the special case with Rowdy's name and brand on it.

Rowdy the Rodeo Cowboy. The two of them had traveled the world, singing and joking, and sharing years and years together. Rowdy had become his best friend, his entire life after leaving too many burning bridges behind them. "Sorry, old friend," he whispered unable to look into Rowdy's carved wooden face, the paint faded, but the eyes still bright and lifelike. He closed the case with trembling fingers.

This knock was much louder. He heard the door handle rattle. He'd been running for years, but now his reckoning was at hand. He pushed the case under the bed, straightened the bed cover over it and went to open the door.

Behind him he would have sworn he heard Rowdy moving in his case as if trying to get out, as if trying to save him. Old hotels and the noises they made? Or just his imagination?

Too late for regrets, he opened the door to his killer.

"MOLLY LOCKHART?" The voice on the phone was male, ringing with authority.

"Yes?" she said distractedly as she pulled her keyboard toward her, unconsciously lining it up with the edge of her desk as she continued to type. She had a report due before the meeting today at Henson and Powers, the financial institution where she worked as an analyst. She wouldn't have taken the call, but her assistant had said the caller was a law-man, the matter urgent, and had put it through.

"My name's Sheriff Brandt Parker from Fortune Creek, Montana. I found your name as the person to call. Do you know Clay Wheaton?"

Her fingers froze over the keys. "I'm sorry, what did you say? Just the last part please." She really didn't have time for this—whatever it was.

"Your name was found in the man's hotel room as the person to call."

"The person to call about what?"

The sheriff cleared his throat. "Do you know Clay Whea-ton?"

"Yes." She said it with just enough vacillation that she heard the lawman cough. "He's my…father."

"Oh, I'm so sorry. I'm afraid I have bad news. Mr. Whea-ton is dead." Another pause, then, "He's been murdered."

"Murdered?" she repeated. She'd known that she'd be get-ting a call one day that he had died. Given her father's age it was inevitable. He was close to sixty-five. But *murdered*? She couldn't imagine why anyone would want to murder him unless they'd seen his act.

"I hate to give you this kind of news over the phone," the sheriff said. "Is there someone there with you?"

"I'm fine, Sheriff," she said, realizing it was true. Her father had made his choice years ago when he'd left her and her mother to travel the world with—quite literally—a dummy. There was only one thing she wanted to know. "Where is Rowdy?"

The lawman sounded taken aback. "I beg your pardon?"

"My father's dummy. You do know Clay Wheaton is… was a ventriloquist, right?"

"Yes, his dummy. It wasn't found in his hotel room. I'm afraid it's missing."

"Missing?" She sighed heavily. "What did you say your name was again?"

"Sheriff Brandt Parker."

"And you are where?"

"Fortune Creek, Montana. I'm going to need to know who else I should notify."

"There is no one else. Just find Rowdy. I'm on my way there."

BRANDT HUNG UP and looked at the dispatcher. The sixty-something Helen Graves was looking at him, one eyebrow tilted at the ceiling in question. "Okay," he said. "That was the strangest reaction I've ever had when telling someone that their father's been murdered."

"Maybe she's in shock."

"I don't think so. She wants me to find the dummy—not the killer—but the *dummy.*"

"Why?"

"I have no idea, but she's on her way here. I'll try the other number Clay Wheaton left." The deceased had left only two names and numbers on hotel stationery atop the bureau next to his bed with a note that said, *In case of emergency.* He put through the call, which turned out to be an insurance agency. "I'm calling for Georgia Eden."

"I'll connect you to the claims department."

"Georgia Eden," a young woman answered cheerfully with a slight southern accent.

Brandt introduced himself. "I'm calling on behalf of Clay Wheaton."

"What does he want now?" she asked impatiently.

"Are you a relative of his?"

"Good heavens, no. He's my client. What is this about? You said you're a sheriff? Is he in some kind of trouble?"

"He was murdered."

"Murdered?" He heard her sit up in her squeaky chair, her tone suddenly worried. "Where's Rowdy?"

What was it with this dummy? "I…don't know."

"Rowdy would have been with him. Clay never let him out of his sight. He took Rowdy everywhere with him. I doubt he went to the toilet without him. Are you telling me Rowdy is missing?"

Brandt ran a hand down over his face. He had to ask. "What is it with this dummy?"

"I beg your pardon?"

"I thought you might be more interested in your client's murder than his…doll."

Her words came out like thrown bricks. "That…*doll* as you call it, is insured for a very large amount of money."

"You're kidding."

"I would not kid about something like that since I'm the one who wrote the policy," Georgia said. "Where are you calling from?" He told her. "This could cost me more than my job if Rowdy isn't found. I'll be on the next plane."

"We don't have an airport," he said quickly.

She groaned. "Where is Fortune Creek, Montana?"

"In the middle of nowhere, actually at the end of a road in the mountains at the most northwest corner of the state," he said. "The closest airport is Kalispell. You'd have to rent a car from there."

"Great."

"If there is anything else I can do—"

"Just find that dummy."

"You mean that doll."

"Yes," she said sarcastically. "Find Rowdy, *please*. Otherwise…I'm dead."

Brandt hung up, shaking his head as he stood and reached for his Stetson. "Helen, if anyone comes looking for me, I'll be over at the hotel looking for a ventriloquist's dummy." She frowned in confusion. "Apparently, that's all anyone cares about. Meanwhile, I have a murder to solve."

As he headed out the door for the walk across the street to the hotel, he couldn't help being disturbed by the reactions he'd gotten to Clay Wheaton's death. He thought about the note the dead man had left and the only two numbers on it.

Had he suspected he might be murdered? Or traveling alone—except for his dummy—had he always left such a note just in case? After all, at sixty-two, he was no spring chicken, his grandmother would have said.

Whatever the victim's thinking, how was it that both women had cared more about the dummy than the man behind it?

Maybe worse, both women were headed this way.